She Lives

in

Daydreams

She Lives

in

Daydreams

NAKIA CRAMER

SENNEBEC
SHORES
PRESS

Published by: Sennebec Shores Press, Appleton, Maine, in the United States of America. SennebecShoresPress@gmail.com

ISBN (Paperback): 979-8-218-09288-7
ISBN (eBook): 979-8-218-09287-0

Cover Art and Imprint Design: Cynthia Pace for Elevate Media

Editors: Kristen Breanne of Your Editing Lounge, Heather LaneMcCants

For the discovery of joy,
and the freedom that comes from chasing your dreams.

Author's Warning

This book is a work of fiction but does contain content that some readers may deem emotionally distressing or triggering.
For a list of potential triggers please refer to the backside of the Acknowledgements page.

1.

It was a Tuesday much like every other Tuesday I'd lived through over the last few months. I awoke in an empty bed, inside an empty house, in an empty marriage, with an empty schedule for the day—aside from the usual mundane household tasks I deal with that I can never avoid. I laid in bed for as long as I could stand the silence and the cold sheets against my skin, wondering if I was the only person living this type of life. What must it be like for women whose husbands were playful and attentive, who fawned over them and couldn't hide the lust they felt for their wives? Does that even exist, or am I just imagining it's possible to live like that? Sure, I'm living in my dream home, in my dream location, and I don't mean to sound ungrateful, but this is certainly not the life I'd dreamed of.

My husband James and I purchased this 1890s New England farmhouse ten years ago. With its white wooden clapboard siding, wrap-around porch, and a massive amount of land, we'd admired this spot for as many years before securing the financing to finally make it ours. It had been sitting vacant for decades when we finally closed on it, and while it needed considerable updates, we made it livable as we picked away at projects. With each passing year we checked renovations off our to-do list, and finally, last year, all the major improvements had been completed.

The home itself is bordered by vibrant and mature century-old perennial flower beds full of every color you can think of. I work hard three seasons of the year to maintain these sprawling colorful gardens, to attract birds and bees and butterflies. They're my excuse to get out of the house and into my head, so it's no wonder they're so well taken care of; I spend most of my free time on my knees in the dirt. Beyond the gardens are acres of lush green grassy lawn with flowering trees and shrubs dotting the perimeter of the grounds, all of it edged by miles and miles of thicket. It's a paradise that cushions the constant blow of loneliness.

One of the last large parcels of land still available back then, these four hundred and eighty acres have allowed me and James plenty of room to enjoy our separate hobbies. For me, I've always loved tending to my gardens and for James, he prefers being out in the woods. He's spent much of his free time over the years creating pathways through the surrounding forest to explore the property either by foot or all-terrain vehicle, making sure the maze of trails all connect, and nearly all of them arrive at the edge of vast golden fields that extend as far as the eye can see. Our closest neighbors are miles away from us, and the way the house is positioned atop a hill allows us to see company coming up the winding dusty driveway long before those visitors can see us. It's idyllic New England living at its finest. The peace, the quiet, and the nature that surround our home have been a constant highlight in an otherwise dull existence.

Frustrated as usual by the predictability of my morning, I got out of bed, found my robe, and decided the day wouldn't ever end unless I got it started. *What a way to live, Alice*, I thought as I went through the motions of clearing the dishes James left in the sink last night and arranging them in the dishwasher. I mindlessly sorted the laundry before starting a load of towels, and then unloaded the dryer of his work clothes.

James has always been a hard worker, and a great provider, but over the years he's become an increasingly absent husband. I never wanted for much, just his attention and some physical intimacy from time to time, but he was more invested in his own happiness than he'd ever been in any collective joy we could have shared. I don't think it was a conscious choice he made; I just think life's circumstances let him get comfortably set in his ways. We don't share any common interests anymore and spend almost no quality time with each other. After twenty-two years together, it happens I guess, but my day-to-day life is tedious monotony, the same thing over and over without deviation, and there seems to be no light at the end of this tunnel. My hope for seeing any kind of positive change has dwindled more and more as the years have passed.

James had been so attentive and loving when we first met over two decades ago. He chose me over everything, doted on me, and made me feel special, and it didn't hurt that our relationship had started out intensely physical. It was one of the things that thrilled me the most about him, and ultimately what tied us to one another, but over time that aspect had been lost. In the beginning we had been a social couple, going out with friends and attending parties together; he made me feel like a prize he wanted to show off. Then it morphed into James' spending time working on the trails around the house and now, he spends most evenings asleep in front of the television or his weekends are spent anywhere but home. Even when he's in the room with me, I feel alone. And for a long time, I've been desperate to have the old James back, but the more time passes, it seems *that* James has become nothing more than a memory and the James that's replaced him is a quiet, solemn man with no interest at all in making me feel loved, appreciated, or attractive.

I met James the summer I graduated high school. Still early June, I was newly eighteen and working the register in our small-town hardware store. I was attracted to him from the moment we first made eye contact. James came in that day looking for specialty screws that we didn't typically keep in stock, and as I took care of his special order, we chatted about how long he'd lived here and about the kind of work he did. I mentioned I'd never seen him around town before, and quickly discovered he was nearly ten years my senior, so of course he didn't run in the same social circles I did. I made friendly small talk while I input his order, asking him what music he listens to and inquired about his hobbies and how he spends his free time. When I asked him for his phone number he smiled bashfully and turned his face away, hoping I wouldn't notice. It was obvious he thought I was flirting with him, but I laughed and explained I needed his number to get in touch with him when his order arrived. His dark brown eyes drew me in, and the way he spoke to me held me smitten. It was written all over my face, from the light in my eyes to my constant smile, there's no way he could miss the way he made me feel, but I never imagined he might be interested in me; after all he was a grown man, and I was only recently of legal age. I was sure he didn't see me the way I was seeing him.

Three days later, when the screws arrived at the hardware store, I nervously called him for the first time. I could hear him smile when he realized it was me on the other end of the line, and in turn, I smiled too. When he came in to pick up his order, he was wearing a fresh white t-shirt and jeans, his hair still damp from a shower, he smelled of cologne, and his face was freshly shaven. In his hand, he carried a single white daisy; he didn't know I'd seen him snap it out of the garden in front of the store before he came in.

This time, as he approached the register, I couldn't help but notice how toned his arms were, and his tan against the crisp white of his t-shirt was now a permanent visual I tucked safely into my mind. James was solidly built, and just the thought of it awakened parts of me I hadn't let a grown man explore yet, and as he told me how much he appreciated my kindness and handed me the dainty blossom, I began to see him in a different light; his age was no longer a deterrent, or a thought in my mind at all.

For four days after, every time the tiny bell over the door would signal an incoming customer, my heart would race excitedly in hopes that it would be James walking toward me. I'd been unable to concentrate on anything other than how his arms might feel wrapped around me, or how it might feel to lose myself in his kiss, but it was never him that walked through the door.

Unable to shake the thoughts from my mind, on the fifth day, I found the courage to call him. As I dialed his number and waited for him to answer, I had no specific plan in mind; I just wanted to be near him, and when I finally heard his voice on the other end of the line, my confidence vanished. Instantly anxious, I blurted out that I was free tonight after work, and if he wasn't busy maybe we could get together. I didn't ask for dinner or a movie, just to hang out. *What a kid move, Alice.* An awkward silence was followed by hesitation in James' voice when he told me I "seemed like a real sweetheart" and he "really would like to get to know me, but…"

In my head, I knew the subject he was trying to skirt around. I questioned what was holding him back and just as I suspected, he asked me if I had any concerns about our age difference. With renewed teenage confidence, I said, "We're both adults, right?"

In my mind, it was just a summer fling. I was headed to college in New York in the fall and I had big plans to become an architect and get out of the small town I'd grown up in once and for all, just like everyone else my age. A little summer fun couldn't hurt, right? This guy was mature and handsome; he had his own place and worked with his hands—not to mention he was a full-grown adult man, not the puny high school boys I was used to. I was young and gorgeous and thought, *hey, you only live once, might as well enjoy the ride.* And that I did.

The physical aspect of our relationship started the very first night, prompted entirely by me. We spent the evening at James' apartment watching a movie and I was the one to initiate the first kiss, standing at his door at what was meant to be the end of the evening. Mine had been the hands that wandered, sliding beneath his t-shirt and roaming over his bare skin, finding the spots on his ribs that left his body covered in goosebumps. James slowed the trajectory a few times before giving in and taking me back to his couch. We made love in his living room not once but twice that night before I managed to find my way back home at three in the morning, my mother none the wiser.

We spent every night together for the next month. James had given me a key to his apartment after our first night together, and every day I'd go to his place straight from work, intentionally timing the end of my showers for the moments just before he walked in the door. The look on his face when he'd come home and find me naked on his couch or topless at the sink washing his dishes is something I'll never forget. I was no stranger to the effect I had on men; even at my relatively young age, I'd been popular with boys in school, and James certainly wasn't my first boyfriend. I happily allowed him full access to me any time he wanted it, and back then, he never squandered a moment.

The summer pushed on and in late August, barely two short months into our steamy summer fling, I found myself unexpectedly pregnant. I'd been exclusive with James, so there was no chance that it could have been anyone else's. Of course I was shocked, but mostly I was scared. We'd always been so careful despite our spontaneity. And I'd never been pregnant before; I had no idea what to do next or how to handle myself now that I was in this predicament. More importantly, my departure to New York was imminent. I had a life planned for myself, and a child was certainly not part of that plan. When I told James the news, I also let him know I had no intention of keeping it. I couldn't have a baby; my commitments were to myself alone. College in New York was my top priority.

But James didn't feel the same way I did. James was a rugged, hard-as-nails kind of guy on the outside, but on the inside, he'd been in love with me from the moment I'd smiled at him when he placed that special order for screws. He was elated we'd created something out of a shared adoration for each other, and excited at the idea of being a dad, so when I said I wasn't going to go through with the pregnancy, he was devastated. He reluctantly supported my decision, knowing it was my body and my choice, and understood that college was my focus. He did all he could to hide his disappointment from me and reassured me that everything was going to be okay. He even offered to cover any costs, assuring me he would be there to take care of me through it all, yet secretly he was already battling his own grief for a child he was desperate to keep.

I accepted his help; I didn't want to go through any of this alone, and I was determined to keep it from my parents. Of course, they knew about James, and even though they both voiced their concerns about our age difference, they knew they couldn't stop me from seeing him; technically I was an adult, free to make my own decisions. I'd reassured each of them multiple times that this was only a summer thing, that it was nothing to worry about and wouldn't interrupt my plans for New York. *Famous last words, Alice.* There was certainly no way I could admit they'd been right.

When the day arrived, James and I made our way to the clinic in silence. Me, terrified of what was about to happen to my body, and James, terrified to lose his first child. We pulled into the lot and James chose the parking spot closest to the clinic's entry. As he slid the gearshift into park, his hand rested there unmoving, his eyes focused straight ahead. Understandably, he couldn't bear to look at me, and when I leaned over the center console to kiss him, he closed his eyes and slowly shook his head, evading my gaze. I kissed him on the cheek, lingering there for a moment, as tears streamed down his face and came to rest against my lips. When he finally opened his eyes, I closed mine to avoid seeing his sadness, to pretend this wasn't reality, and could no longer hold myself back from crying. I wrapped my arms around him and felt his chest tremble, trying to suppress his sobs, and when I couldn't stand it any longer, I broke away, then without looking back, without saying a word, I made my way inside.

I checked in at the front desk and sat quietly fidgeting in the empty waiting area, my mind a tightly bound mass of anxiety, fear, and sadness. I managed to talk myself into the idea that this was the best thing for everyone involved and, finding some semblance of solace in my choice, the tears finally stopped. It felt like an eternity had passed when the nurse finally called me back into the dismal, sterile room and began to explain the procedure. As she went over the details, I was desperate to hold my ground, and not lose myself to the horrifying thoughts that kept scrolling through my imagination, but when I asked for James, they told me he wasn't allowed in the procedure room. Of course, the tears began again as I tried to talk myself into just toughing it out, just getting it over with, but I was too overwhelmed by it all. Before anything had even happened, I stood from my chair and ran from the room, through the waiting area, and back to the car.

"I couldn't do it, James. I'm so sorry." I was nearly hysterical, unable to catch my breath as I fell against the passenger side door. James rushed from the driver's seat over to my side of the car to console me and wrapped his arms around my trembling body. Burying his face in my neck, he held me, crying with me out of silent relief that his child's life had been saved, yet not admitting that was why.

We returned to his apartment and sat for a long time in silence, both of us immersed in our own swirling thoughts, trying to make sense of it all. Afternoon turned to evening, and in the waning light, James got down on the floor in front of me and looked at me with such deep sincerity, I didn't dare to break from his gaze.

"Alice," he took my swollen, tear-stained face in his strong hands. "I need you to know something. I need you to really listen to me." He was making a concerted effort to keep his breathing even despite his obvious urgency.

I stared back at him; the light that had always been in my eyes was now gone. Gone with my dreams of a life of freedom in New York, and gone with my hopes of being a successful architect. Being self-sufficient and proud of myself were also in the rearview. I had failed both my parents and myself, and now had to figure out what life would be like as a teenage mother.

"I want nothing more than to make sure you're okay. I want to be the one who takes care of you and our baby. I want us to be a family, Alice," he begged.

I looked back at him blankly, no expression on my face, eyes swollen from the day I had endured.

"I want to be your husband...if you'll have me. We can make this terrible day into something better than it's been, Alice. Will you marry me?" There was a desperation in his eyes.

I was now fully and painfully aware that my dreams of a life in New York were a thing of the past; college and a career in architecture ruined. My dreams of a life away from this place were the casualties left in the wreckage of this day. I would have no choice but to tell my parents. I'd have to keep working at the hardware store or find a better-paying job to afford this child. My days would be filled with dirty diapers, spit-up and screaming. I saw all of my dreams crash down around me as James knelt on the floor, begging me to be his wife.

In the coming months, we not only told my parents the news of the baby but also got married. I didn't want my wedding photos forever depicting me pregnant at the age of eighteen, so we quickly planned and carried out a diminutive ceremony at a local park and held a very small gathering at my mother's house afterwards. It wasn't the wedding of my dreams, but it was enough to keep everyone else in my family happy.

James was a good husband; he looked out for me and made sure my needs were met. He rubbed my feet while we watched TV in the evenings, and he fell asleep with his hand on my belly every night. He was fully devoted to me and the baby, and it was clear he was happier about this child than he had initially let on. After all, the man was twenty-seven years old; of course he wasn't afraid of having a child. He wasn't afraid of being married. He was mature enough to be ready for it. *Thank God*, I thought, *someone's gotta be.* Things could have been a lot worse, after all I do love him; it wasn't like this was against my will; I wasn't being held hostage. But it sure was hard to be happy about a new marriage, a full-time job, and having a baby on the way at eighteen when all I really wanted was to grieve the dreams I'd spent my life working toward.

It was just after midnight on Thanksgiving morning when I suddenly woke to stomach pain. James was right there beside me; he held me close, rubbed my belly, and tried to make me feel better, and I loved him even more for it, but it wasn't helping. This wasn't just a fleeting pain; this was something more. The pain got stronger and much more intense and I could sense something was really wrong. By the time we arrived at the emergency room, I could feel myself actively bleeding, and not long after that, the doctor let us know that I was miscarrying.

If I'm being honest, there were parts of me that were relieved. Maybe some of my dreams could be reclaimed, reimagined. Yet the parts of me that had gotten used to the idea of having a child, the parts of me that had finally gotten settled into a marriage with a man who loved me unconditionally, a man I could trust, the parts of me that felt safe in this budding family, were devastated. James was absolutely beside himself, and I watched the color drain from his face as his head fell to his hands, tears falling through his fingers and onto the cold linoleum tiles of the emergency room floor.

The following months were difficult, and only got worse as time passed. The loss of our unborn child had changed us both so deeply that we were nearly unrecognizable to each other. James was a shadow of his former self, sullen and depressed every moment of the day and night. He slept facing away from me now; there was no physical contact at all, and I couldn't figure out if it was the grief that made him act this way, or if he was just afraid to touch me after what I'd been through. Maybe he was scared that if we made love, we'd have to go through that loss all over again. Maybe he couldn't touch me without thinking about what our love had once created. I did everything I could to try to calm his fears and reassure him that it was okay for us to be intimate again, to remind him that I was devoted to him and I needed to feel his touch. But while I grieved the loss of a child that I had grown to want, looked forward to the possibilities of my reimagined dreams, and took care of my grieving husband, no one took care of me. Sadness, resentment, and silence became habit for both of us, and the thriving marriage we shared that was once full of laughter and passion became a vague and distant memory.

If I'm honest with myself, I no longer felt like a priority to him; I was never James' first choice anymore. I was an afterthought. I felt like a caretaker to a stranger in my own home and grieved my marriage while I was still very much in it. I had given up or lost everything I ever wanted, and those dreams? Those dreams never came to be. I spent my days working and taking care of a grown man and a household. Run ragged from daily life that held no vacancy for chasing dreams of something more for myself. I was in a marriage I had never planned on being in with a man I loved but that had completely checked out when we lost the baby. Despite short stints of grief counseling and marriage counseling, nothing ever pulled us out of the rut our grief had dug us into.

Two years after our loss, James came home one day and nonchalantly announced he'd gotten a vasectomy before asking me to grab him a bag of frozen peas from the freezer. He said he couldn't put himself through that kind of loss again, and rationalized that it was better this way. That was all the discussion he was willing to have about the choice he had made. Of course, I was shocked. We'd never talked about a vasectomy. He had never asked me if I ever wanted to try again. The more comfortable I had become in our marriage, and the older I got, the more I'd thought about trying again to have children. I'd imagined it would bring me and James back together; it would revitalize the love he used to show me, bring the smile back to his face, the light to his eyes, and in turn bring me back a happiness with him I'd longed for. I was barely twenty years old and James had decided for the both of us that that was another dream that would never be realized. I knew that day, my marriage would never be the same.

"All I am here is the fucking unpaid maid to a roommate," I cursed as I sorted through laundry scattered on the floor, slinging socks and underwear in the direction of one laundry basket and a smelly hooded sweatshirt in another. "No one gives a shit about my happiness, or how I feel about anything." A sock sailed past the basket I was aiming for. "As long as the toilet is clean and the food is cooked...as long as I balance the checkbook and write out the bills, who cares what I want?" I snatched a pair of jeans off the floor and slung them on top of the sweatshirt, then made my way back to the living room. *No one. No one cares.*

I made myself a cup of coffee and sat down at my desk to send a text to my boss, Arlo.

Just making sure everything is moving forward as expected today on the assigned job site?

I hit Send and waited for his response. A few notations for future clients went into my work planner: "I have to remember to invoice Mr. Broyer, but I still need the final details from Arlo, and Mrs. Kerry still owes us from three weeks ago," I said out loud, knowing no one was there to hear me. I kept meticulous spreadsheets for my remote job, along with various notebooks for tracking purposes, and I was finally beginning to feel proud of myself for the work I was doing. I wasn't designing skyscrapers, but this was respectable work.

It had been a fluke that I landed this job last summer. Keeping track of a small business as a fully remote office manager wasn't something I had done before, but it was something I was succeeding at. My work-related stress levels had melted away since taking this position, and it helped that I made enough money to feel like I was really contributing financially, even

14

though James was the real breadwinner. He didn't mind that I worked part-time from home. For him, he had the best of both worlds, a clean house, a hot meal when he walked in the door, and someone to cover the mortgage.

James had always been an intelligent and accomplished man. He could build amazing things out of nothing and still loved to work with his hands. *Those hands*, I thought. I missed the way his hands felt on my body. I often lost myself in memories of the first time he'd touched me twenty-two years earlier. Sometimes it felt like yesterday, but more often it felt like centuries ago. I always ended up disappointed and mad when I let those thoughts in because they made it painfully obvious to me that that was no longer my life.

Finished with today's work until I heard back from Arlo, I wondered what was next for the day. It was sunny and quite warm for Spring in New England. Maybe I'd go for a walk and take stock of the state of my flower beds. After the harsh winter we'd had, I was sure I lost some of my favorites to the early frost and the bitter wind. Gardening was going to be my summer priority this year; I'd worry less about the house and James, and focus more on the joy I got from my gardens. In February, I'd started a list of the perennials I wanted to buy when it got warmer outside, and more recently I mapped out future locations for new gardens around the yard. I also had a few other things from last year that would need to be transplanted elsewhere or given away. I certainly had plenty to do, but after thinking about it and feeling overwhelmed and indifferent to it all, I opted not to start any of those projects.

Against my better judgment, I stretched out on the couch and logged on to Instagram to see what was new. I scrolled for what seemed like minutes but was realistically closer to an hour. My depression could be like that. I'd get sucked into a world where I didn't have to be responsible for anything. Mindlessly scrolling through photographs of other people's lives, videos of someone's cat or how to make some fancy coffee drink, or even someone complaining about whatever rubbed them the wrong way that day. I could completely disregard and escape my life and live in someone else's for a while, and I did it often. I stopped scrolling and paused to watch when a video popped up that featured a young English actor I had recently started to admire; there was no way I could ignore those green eyes and the way his dimples complemented his perfect smile.

Harrison Edwards, a man twelve years my junior at the age of twenty-eight, had quickly become my most recent source of joy. God, he's striking. Perfectly positioned dark curls over eyes that stopped me dead in my tracks. He's got a smile and charisma that can transform my entire day, hell, my whole outlook on life. An advocate and ally for all, with immeasurable charitable affiliations, he presents as an incredibly educated and articulate man and exudes a healthy level of arrogance and a goofiness that is incredibly attractive to me. He showed up on my timeline out of the blue one day and I have to admit, I was instantly hooked. His solid-as-a-rock, six-foot frame is perfectly bronzed with a collection of tattoos scattered from top to bottom. He's got an infectious laugh and the most adorable habit of scrunching his nose when his thoughts lead him into mischief. Harrison is, by my standards, the total package.

As I watched him on my phone screen, I wondered what it must be like just to be in the presence of someone so heart-stoppingly handsome, so world-renowned, and so universally admired. Ever since his career began thirteen years ago, countless articles portray him as a narcissistic womanizer, but I just couldn't believe that was really true. Something in his eyes, the way he's always so kind to others, made me feel like this man was a genuinely good person.

When the video finished, another popped up, and then a third. All of them featured various shots of him from films he'd starred in, a montage of his best performances coupled with still photos from magazines he'd been featured in. Once they finished, I found myself smiling; my entire mood had changed from this morning. James hadn't spoken a word to me yet today, but had managed to thoroughly piss me off simply by leaving dishes in the sink, and this movie star had no idea I even existed, but had taken my anger and shifted it into unbridled joy. *Profound, the effect a stranger can have on your mood*, I thought.

I searched for a full-length version of one of his recent films, a romantic comedy I could easily fall into for a few hours. I had nowhere to be and nothing left to do until dinner time, other than wait on Arlo's text. As the film began, I snuggled into the couch and let the frustrations of my morning fade away while I shared my afternoon with Harrison.

This behavior was pretty typical for me. Make a list, do what has to be done, get it over with, and then immerse myself in something that makes me feel like myself again. Harrison was that escape for me, my daily dose of serotonin. His energy could shift me out of feeling day in and day out like I'd lost my identity and that my marriage had turned me into someone I didn't recognize anymore. I was so easily frustrated and angry all the time; I'd realized I had very few friends I could actually count on, and I'd become something of a homebody. I'd also put on about forty pounds in the last ten years, which made it easy to believe that was the reason my husband no longer found me attractive.

I hadn't deliberately tried to lose the weight once I gained it, but lately and without discernable reason, my appetite had been nonexistent. I used to love to bake, but I'd completely lost interest in cooking unless it was for James at dinner time. Maybe it was a result of the depression, but I was proud of a recent twenty-pound loss, no matter how it happened, and felt a renewed and unexpected confidence in my forty-year-old body. The fact that Harrison's reported love interests were closer to my age than his own didn't hurt either. I'd begun to feel better about the way I looked in my clothes and I was wearing things a bit more form-fitting, hoping James would notice, or at least comment, but he never did. Working from home didn't require dress clothes, so leggings and a comfortable shirt were my daily go-to choices. Yet no matter what I had on, or how I wore it, James never glanced in my direction. Even when I walked around the house topless, it made no impact. What used to fuel his fire didn't prompt any ignition whatsoever anymore. He wasn't checking me out, and definitely wasn't making any sexual advances. He didn't touch me at all unless he wanted to have sex with me, and I'd lost track of how long it had been since that last happened.

The fact that I'm fully in my prime isn't lost on me, and one day I'm sure I'll look back and wish I'd made the most of these days—that James made the most of these days. But instead, I spend the majority of my time annoyed that I'm always lonesome and wonder how James can so carelessly exist in the same house with me, the same marriage, and not only be oblivious to how I feel, but seemingly be so content with how things are.

Don't get me wrong, I still find my husband physically attractive despite the changes he's endured during our marriage, and I often find myself fantasizing about him spontaneously stripping me bare and having his way with me. Various scenarios play out in my head at all hours of the day and night, but over time, I've become apprehensive to initiate sex, especially since 'the loss', and for a long time now, neither does James. On the few occasions that I did initiate sex with my husband, he had ignored my advances, and that was all it took for me to stop trying.

How did we get trapped in this desolate place? And more importantly, how could we get out of it? I'd asked myself these questions for years and was never able to find the answers. I needed to feel wanted. It had been months since James wanted to be anywhere near me, and I had resigned myself to the fact that I just wasn't who or what he wanted anymore. Maybe this was simply how my marriage was going to be; this would be my life going forward until they put me in the ground. Maybe in my next life, I could be the person I imagined myself to be in my daydreams.

See, in my daydreams, I'm a charismatic free spirit, just happy to feel the sunshine on my face each morning. Enjoying the privilege to travel wherever the wind blows me, relinquishing control to my lover—or *lovers* if that's how I see fit—and radiating joy from an untethered life that allows me whatever freedoms I want. In my daydreams, I'm simply...happy. In my daydreams, I see myself as I was before James, back when I was eighteen.

A key slipped into the front door lock and though the house was no longer empty, I still felt alone. I fixed dinner while James showered, we ate together in near silence in front of the television, and then I rinsed and loaded the dishes into the dishwasher as he sat and watched the news. Just as I finished cleaning the kitchen and reached to turn off the light, James appeared behind me and began to empty his lunchbox, taking the dirty dishes and throwing them in the sink haphazardly. I felt the heat rise in my chest, wanting to scream. It took everything in me not to scale those dishes across the room, to find relief in hearing them shatter against the wall. But instead, I walked away, settled myself back onto the couch, and focused on the TV. James joined me in the living room, and within minutes, he was asleep.

Like *Groundhog Day*, this was my life. Dismissed, ignored, brushed aside, housework, cook, clean, rinse, repeat. As soon as I'd finished cleaning something up, a new mess presented itself. It had become normal, even though I knew it wasn't. No one grew up thinking this was what marriage would be. No one looked forward to this. But I knew deep down I had a good man, even if he no longer wanted to spontaneously rip my clothes off or take me out on fun dates to proudly show me off. He wasn't a cheater; he wasn't running our finances into the ground, and thankfully he wasn't sneaking around online or cheating on me like my friends' husbands were. I was lucky in many aspects and decided keeping my mouth shut and going about my daily life, however monotonous it was, was still better than being alone. Or worse, having to start over.

Spring in New England came and went. I tended my gardens and created new ones and I spent more time outside feeling the sunshine warm my cheeks and being mindful of the small joys in life that brought me some happiness. I took daily walks and spent more time cooking meals that would keep my weight loss journey moving forward. I made time for the things I enjoyed, spent more evenings on the porch sipping lemonade and reading good books, and even made new friends online that shared my interests in gardening—and Harrison Edwards. I'd found a welcoming new community of people online that shared in my joy, supported me when I was feeling down, and lifted my spirits on bad days. For me, this was progress.

Summer arrived and James spent more time with his friends, going on short fishing trips, camping or four-wheeling. He was never gone for more than a night or two at a time, and while he was gone, I enjoyed not having to pick up after him and not having to cook if I didn't want to. The feelings of resentment typically vanished and I felt more like myself when he wasn't around. I'd spend time out on the porch at night, my eyes closed, listening to the crickets, getting lost in memories, or letting my imagination run free with whatever crossed my mind.

More often than not I'd lose myself in some imagined scenario that involved slow dancing in the moonlight with Harrison in a faraway land. I was a daydreamer, always had been. In my youth, it had gotten me into trouble during school, and as an adult I found happiness escaping in ideas or scenes that could never happen in reality. In the beginning, James loved my creativity and called me imaginative. Now, he rolled his eyes and shook his head when he caught me in a daydream, calling me *ridiculous* or *crazy*.

Occasionally, when James would go away on these overnight outings with his buddies, I'd reach into the back of the cupboard where I kept a few bottles of liquor for special occasions and make myself a cocktail to sip on while I sat on the porch and watched the sun set. This time, James was gone just for tonight, so I decided, *why not?* It had been a long, hot day and a rough few weeks at home, and I just wanted to relax. I'd never been an avid drinker; maybe only once or twice a year would I actually give in and indulge in a drink or two. My parents had both been alcoholics for as long as I could remember, and a deep family history of the same had left a lasting negative impression on me. I was normally too frugal to spend money on things just to piss them away, but on these warm summer nights, I'd sip tequila on the rocks until I felt the effects of it flush my cheeks and slowly overtake me.

The sun had long since set, and as midnight approached and the world around me fell silent, I decided between the humidity, the warmth in my chest from the tequila, and my big empty bed, tonight I'd sleep naked. There would be no one there to judge me or make me feel self-conscious. I wouldn't have to worry what parts of me were exposed or lie in such a way to try to flatter my curves; there would be no unmet expectations, just peace. I showered as I always did and braided my long dark hair, then settled my bare body against the coolness of the sheets. Thanks to the alcohol, I found sleep easily.

2.

Tonight, my imaginative subconscious took over as soon as I shut my eyes. I found myself in a coastal seaside town; it was a hot cloudless summer day, and I was slowly driving down a narrow one-way dirt road alone, looking at summer homes of people far richer than I would ever be. I admired the architecture of some and the exterior decor of others. One had an extravagant perennial garden, and I slowed to take a mental note of how to arrange some of my future flower beds before moving on.

As I approached the next home on the winding road, I felt the shade from the trees as they canopied over me and realized I knew the owners. The Blakes were an older couple that never had any children, probably in their late seventies. They were friendly enough when I'd met them years prior, but it was obvious they were only pleasant because they felt they had to be while in public. They struck me as overtly fake, and the type of people that would call the authorities on someone at any given moment if a behavior interfered with their enjoyment.

As I paused to admire their landscaping from the car, I noticed an open gate on a fence clearly marked with a visible 'Private Property' sign. Ever curious, I let the car creep forward a bit for a better view, then peered through the fence as my foot pressed heavily on the brake. In complete disbelief, I saw a pile of clothes on the ground and then someone's bare backside as they jumped into the pool. It was immediately apparent to me that what I was witnessing was an intrusion of the Blakes' private property, and I knew how they would react if they found a stranger in their pool.

Hurriedly, I put the car in park and approached the gate. As I cautiously tiptoed into the Blakes' yard, I planned to simply warn the stranger and then leave, but I stopped when I reached the abandoned pile of men's clothes. A well-worn navy-blue t-shirt, tattered blue jeans ripped at the knees, and a dirty pair of green Converse, the backs of which were folded in as if they had been carelessly walked on. No socks were present, but there were stark white briefs inside the jeans, as if removed together in one swift movement. A black hoodie lay in a heap, and I could make out the word "FREEDOM" across the front. White, thick-rimmed sunglasses and a cell phone had been tossed atop the sweatshirt.

I felt compelled to save this naked stranger from the wrath of the Blakes and cautiously approached the edge of the pool. He was fully submerged, but I could see his form moving away from me beneath the sparkling ripples. My eyes followed the dark hair and tanned skin, zeroing in on the muscular build until he broke the surface of the water.

I could see every inch of his body was firm as he stood, then turned to face me while rubbing the water from his closed eyes. His fingers were adorned with chunky gold rings, and a variety of tattoos covered his chest, stomach, and arms. Around his neck, water dripped from a rolled-up dark blue bandana knotted into some sort of necklace, and clinging to it was a dark claw-shaped hair clip. He shook the water from his chestnut hair, then ran his fingers through the longer curls in the front, pulling them back with a twisting motion to hold the hair away from his eyes. His rings glistened in the sun as he released the clip from his bandana and secured his wet hair in place. When he finally noticed me standing above him, I was so stunned by the sight of him that my eyes widened and my mouth fell open, but no sound came out.

"Oh hi, I didn't see you there. I'm Harrison," he said and flashed a smile that brought attention to the dimples in his cheeks. "Is this your pool? It's gorgeous." His voice was deeper than I expected, and his accent dripped from his tongue.

A British accent. I was speechless. *What was happening?* Then the realization hit me like a ton of bricks. *That's...Harrison.* THE Harrison Edwards, and he was inches from me in the Blakes' pool, trespassing no less, and acting like all was right with the world. *And he's naked.*

Suddenly self-conscious, I smoothed my long floral skirt and became fully unaware of what to do with my hands. First, they went to my hips, but I quickly dropped them to my sides, not wanting to seem rude or aggressive. Then they covered my increasingly flushed cheeks; I could feel the heat radiating from them. *Ugh, why did my face always give me away?* Then my hands finally rested, clasped together in front of me, fingers intertwined, trying to seem approachable and trustworthy. I smiled, albeit nervously.

"Hi, no. I'm sorry, no." Flustered, I struggled to find the words, and began tugging at my white v-neck tee, feeling my cheeks turn redder as the warmth spread to my exposed chest. "This isn't my pool, but I do know who the owners are, and they're tyrants. You gotta get out of there."

"Everything's going to be okay. What's your name, love?" he asked calmly with a Cheshire-cat grin that made me even more nervous. *I could swim in those dimples*, I thought, *but it definitely wouldn't cool me off.*

"It's not. It's definitely not going to be okay; I need to get you out of here. How did you even get here? Do you have a car?" I looked around anxiously, wanting to save him from whatever fate the Blakes may hold for him, terrified they'd appear at any moment.

"No, I was just out walking, and the sun became too much, so I thought I would pop in to take a dip. The gate wasn't locked." Harrison made his ascent on the pool's stairs. "Jeans were not my best choice today."

"I think you mean trespassing on private property was not your best choice today. Come on, I can get you out of here, and hopefully, no one will realize you were ever here. I'm Alice, by the way. Sorry I just approached you like that; I didn't mean to be aggressive. Were you seriously just out here walking alone? That doesn't seem safe." I felt so desperate to protect him I was rambling.

The sun glistened and reflected against every droplet of water on his tanned skin as he bent down and reached for his sunglasses. I was mesmerized by two large birds in grayscale, swallows maybe, tattooed on the upper part of each of his well-defined pectoral muscles, facing each other and down lower, a large eagle with outstretched wings spread across the upper part of his abdomen. It was centered above a six-pack of tightly toned abdominal muscles with such fine and delicate line work I imagined it must have taken extreme strength to withstand a tattoo like that. A thin gold chain holding a gold cross that was nestled into his chest hair caught the sun just right and pulled my attention back up toward his face as he stood and looked at me, smiling. Then the bass of his voice interrupted my increasingly impure thoughts.

"Listen, everything is going to be fine. I promise it's going to be okay. Everything will be alright. Once they know who I am, it won't matter." He was so relaxed, so sure of his celebrity, and completely unfazed by the potential repercussions of his carelessness. I was nearly frantic, and the way his accent crafted the word 'matter' made me take a deep breath and correct my posture. *God, he just effortlessly oozes sex appeal.*

"It definitely won't matter who you are, not to these people. They'll put you in jail regardless. Come on, I can give you a ride." I instinctively reached for his hand, observing that Harrison expressed no sense of urgency at all and was still standing in front of me without a stitch of clothing on, seeming completely comfortable with it.

"Oh Jesus, get dressed." I snatched my hand back. "We need to get you at least out of the line of anyone's vision. The Blakes probably already have you on their security cameras."

He pulled on his briefs, and I tried to stifle a giggle. This very famous man was wearing nothing but white thickly rimmed sunglasses, chunky gold rings, and tighty-whities. *What a sight to behold.*

Be serious Alice, come on, I thought. "Grab your clothes; you can get dressed in my car," I said, trying to sound stern.

In one swift movement, he slid his feet into his shoes, snatched up the clothes, and followed me in the direction of my car.

Once we'd settled into my old Camry, I asked where he was staying or where I could take him. Harrison leisurely got dressed beside me in the passenger seat as I tried to stay within the speed limit so as not to look suspicious in this high-end neighborhood. He still hadn't answered me; I was just driving aimlessly. We were safely in my car, so why did I feel the need to speed away? I wasn't entirely sure, but I knew exactly why I felt I needed to hide him. This man, this maker of cinematic masterpieces, this gorgeous, young, brilliant, tattooed man was a hot commodity all over the world. Not once but twice voted People magazine's Sexiest Man of the Year, and rumor has it he's working on his first studio album. Yet, here he was, nonchalantly sitting in my passenger seat, half-dressed and smiling like there was no such thing as consequences for his actions.

I slowed the car as my mind continued to race. A quick glance in his direction gave me a perfect view of his masculine profile. His jaw looked like it had been chiseled from granite and it made my heart race. Half of me wanted to pounce on him and the other half wanted to run screaming from the moving vehicle. The intrusive thoughts in my head were moving much faster than my car, and like the teacher in a Charlie Brown cartoon, I heard sound come from his mouth when he spoke but wasn't sure if I heard what I thought I heard.

"You what now?" I asked surprised, any semblance of decorum gone.

"I was wondering if you might drive me down to New Orleans." He repeated. "I would cover costs and be forever indebted to you for the courtesy." He said it with the same laid-back attitude he might use if he were asking for a ride to the grocery store, and then flashed the smile he knew would get him whatever he wanted.

"New Orleans?! You want me, to drive you, to New Orleans. LOUISIANA?" Both eyebrows raised, I blinked at him, flabbergasted.

"I need to be there four days from today, so it could be sort of a road trip for us. We could get to know each other." The way his accent formed the word 'four' made me take another deep breath.

"Harrison...I—" I was certainly willing to do it, but unsure if he was serious.

"Come on love, it will be fun for us both." He flashed that unbelievable smile again and the excitement in his eyes was enough to convince anyone. He could have said 'fly me to the moon on your magic carpet' and I would have given it my very best effort.

"I mean, I guess I could. I'll just need to stop at home to get some of my things." My mind swirled with thoughts as I imagined a road trip with a movie star.

"No time for that. I can take care of whatever you might need along the way. Consider it my treat. After all, you are taking me halfway across the country. I didn't travel with anything either. No luggage, just what you see here." He moved in such a way that I took notice. The sheer size of his hands alone was incredible, and I could see the definition of muscle in them against the veins that stood at attention. Faint remnants of white and black nail polish lingered on a few fingernails. *He's such a rockstar*, I thought and smiled.

"So, you just want to go, right now?" I was in total disbelief that this was my life. I stared at the road ahead, unable to compute what was happening.

His left hand touching my wrist brought me back to reality, and when I looked down, I saw a small tattoo on his hand, a single treble clef between his thumb and index finger. When I looked back up, his sea-green eyes were already looking back at me, egging me on to participate in this crazy idea of his.

"Sure, it'll be fun." He said.

That accent! I clung to every word he said.

I sighed and smiled at him, shaking my head. "Okay then, New Orleans, here we come!"

And just like that, off we went, heading south through small towns, making our way to the interstate. No toothbrushes, no clean underwear, no plan other than to head south together. Soon I relaxed into the drive, and we chatted about family, hobbies, and asked each other questions about life goals and aspirations. We made a few quick stops for drinks and snacks or to snap photos at landmarks, as long as no one else was around to notice who he was. I loved that he insisted on setting the camera's timer to snap photos of us together at some of these places. He may have been a movie star, but he was weirdly normal. Fun-loving, thoughtful, and surprisingly down to earth.

I truly couldn't believe this was happening. Things like this just don't happen to people like me. When I got up this morning, I had no plans. I just wanted to go for a nice drive and play tourist for a few hours. Now here I was with a celebrity that I deeply admired and moderately lusted after, driving across the country. This man had the money to charter a jet or buy a bus. He could get where he needed to be with a snap of his fingers, but he chose me and my old car. *What kind of matrix was I stuck in?*

The windows down, the sun shining, and nothing but highway ahead of us, I was basking in pure happiness. With each passing song, the radio grew louder as the miles stretched out behind us. I glanced over to find Harrison immersed in the same joy I felt, the curls at his temples dancing in the breeze, his tanned jawline sharp with the movements of his mouth, and the most electric smile I had ever seen creating fine lines around his eyes as he sang without fear of judgement. If the stories I'd heard were true and he really was working on an album, I could say now with firsthand knowledge, it would be incredible.

Somewhere in New Hampshire I pinched myself to make sure I wasn't hallucinating. Nope. There he was, right beside me, singing along to Journey on the radio, belting out *Lovin', Touchin', Squeezin'* in perfect harmony with Steve Perry while his right hand snaked its way through the warm rush of summer air outside the car window. I gripped the steering wheel with both hands as I smiled to myself and thought, *This is everything I have ever wanted.*

"I think we should stop at a rest area and try to find a hotel," I said as we passed a sign indicating Hartford, Connecticut was only sixty-eight miles ahead.

"We can, or should we just keep driving? Maybe just see where the road takes us," Harrison replied. He was such a free spirit, not worried at all about the details, and I was jealous.

"Well, I feel like this *is* where the road has taken us," I laughed. "And I'm ready to call it a day."

"Fair enough, I'll search for a hotel online while you drive. My bum's starting to ache anyhow." With an exaggerated look of anguish on his face, he reached for his phone with one hand while he rubbed his butt with the other.

"Oh we can't have that. I'll hurry." I winked at him as I pressed down on the gas pedal.

His accent ignored the letter 'R' as he threw his head back and yelled out the window, "She's a speed queen! I wanna go fastaa!"

"You're insane!" I burst out laughing at him.

Harrison chose the Goodwin Hotel as our first stop, and I admired him from the driver's seat as he called to make the reservation. The majority of his dark curls were still pulled back in the clip, and his sunglasses rested just in front of it atop his head. He had fidgeted with the bandana throughout the day. Sometimes it held his hair back from his eyes and sometimes it hung loosely around his neck. His accent continued to melt me every time he spoke and as I listened to him request the best room in the hotel, and then for the entire floor to be closed off for us, it all just seemed so crazy to me. I listened to him explain the need for security and wondered who usually handled this stuff for him. *Where were they? Why was he alone? Shouldn't he have his own security or a manager or something with him?* Realizing that having none of those things present had played well to my benefit today, I snapped myself back to reality. Everything was settled; someone would be looking for us to pull in around back, and we should find them at the private entrance as soon as we arrive.

As we got closer to the hotel, I grew more afraid someone would see him. My old car's windows weren't tinted, and I worried someone would rush the vehicle to get to him. Complete chaos could descend around us and I had no way to protect him from a hoard of people. I was lost in my head as Harrison happily sang along to the radio, totally oblivious to the whirlwind of panic in my mind. Then out of the blue he and asked me if I was comfortable sharing a room with him.

My mind exploded into a new spiral of erratic thoughts and I was desperate to hide my excitement at the thought of his suggestion.

"Yeah, I mean, that's fine with me, but don't you want your own space?" I asked calmly. He could have requested I sleep in the tub and I would have done it.

"I'd like to spend more time getting to know you, and contrary to popular belief, the life of someone like me is actually quite lonely. So, it'll be nice to have someone to talk to," he reassured me.

The thought of sharing a hotel room with this man was currently outside my realm of comprehension. I'd be falling asleep in the same room with him, sharing a bathroom with him, hell, we would be showering in the same shower. *Oh, my goodness, clothes!* We had no clothes. No toothbrushes. No pajamas. We had nothing with us aside from the clothes on our backs and the old phone charger that I kept in my car, which would work for my phone but not for his.

"Well, let's just hope you don't snore," I said and laughed. "I'm not gonna put up with that," and winked at him.

"I like you Alice; you make me laugh. You're a good egg."

"You're pretty great yourself, but I'm sorry to hear it's lonely in your world. I would have thought you'd be constantly surrounded by people, all your wildest whims taken care of at the drop of a hat."

"I mean, it *is* like that, but you don't know true loneliness until you *are* surrounded by people, and still feel alone. I wouldn't wish it on anyone. Fame is a greedy and unforgiving beast sometimes. I spend a lot of my free time with my head in a book, to be honest."

"Well, at least for the next few days, that's not something you need to think about. I'll be right here to keep you company," I offered.

"I'll do my best not to snore then, no promises mind you, and you do your best to keep me from being lonesome, and I think we'll be just fine. Not much further now and we'll be at our destination. I hope you like the hotel I picked out." His eyes were so sincere.

"I'm sure it will be wonderful." I said, then returned my focus to the road ahead.

We completed the short drive to the hotel, and as I pulled into the back lot, I could see men there waiting for Harrison, ready to get him into the hotel safely. Feeling overwhelmed, but also elated at the thought of sharing his personal space, I tried to hide my involuntary smile and said, "Do you want to get in and get settled, and I'll try to find us some clothes?" I was anxious to be in my own space for a bit, to let some of my adrenaline settle and try to regroup before I spent the night in the next bed over from Harrison

Edwards. I probably wouldn't sleep at all.

"Sure, here." He reached for his wallet and handed me his black AmEx card. *Holy shit, these things are limitless,* I thought as I reluctantly took the card from him. "Use this for whatever you need. While you're out I'm going to call my connection at Gucci and set up a few things. If you'll let me, I'd like to get you something to wear in New Orleans. I'm scheduled to make an appearance there and I'd like you to attend with me, if you're willing."

"Like a date?" I said, a little too enthusiastically. I didn't mean to sound so eager and tried to play it off like a joke. "You've fallen in love with me already after just one day! It's my car isn't it?" I laughed, afraid of his reaction.

"You can't blame me, darling, not even a little bit; the car sealed the deal for me. I was head over heels the moment I sat in this exquisite piece of machinery." He rubbed the faded dashboard and laughed, making his dimples appear once again. I wasn't sure if it was the way he said 'darling' or the ease I was beginning to feel with him, but internally I was losing control of myself.

"Harrison, thank you, but I'm not sure I can get away with using this card. Obviously, I'm not you." I stretched out my hand, handing it back to him.

"No worries, I called earlier while you were fueling up the car and added you as an authorized user for the next few days. I wanted to be sure all your needs could be met without any trouble." Harrison looked at me in a way that made my pulse quicken, and instead of needing space, now I wanted to hurry up and get whatever personal items we needed so I could get back to him as soon as possible.

I rushed through Target, gathering snacks, toothbrushes, a hairbrush, a phone charger, and various bathroom supplies. I grabbed t-shirts and shorts for us both, as well as underwear and socks, guessing at his sizes. I tried to find the most flattering and provocative undergarments for myself, unsure if Harrison would end up seeing them or not, but I wasn't taking any chances. I laughed out loud as I grabbed a package of Hanes briefs for HARRISON FRIGGIN EDWARDS at TARGET. *This man's behind hasn't seen a pair of Hanes in over a decade*, I thought. He was used to high-end fashion. The irony was too much and yet I didn't care that people stopped to look at me when I continued to giggle to myself. Once I had everything I needed, I checked out quickly and called the hotel on my way back. My intent was to figure out our room number, but Harrison had already given them my name so when I pulled into the back lot, they ushered me inside just as they had done for him.

Back inside the room, I found Harrison showered and draped across the lower corner of the bed. Lying on his back, loosely wrapped in a plush white hotel robe, each leg hung from a separate edge of the bed. The bottom half of what appeared to be a lion tattoo on his left mid-thigh peeked from beneath the hem of his robe. His eyes were closed, and the tips of his big toes barely grazed the floor. His rings lay scattered on the nightstand along with an untouched glass of bourbon, his sunglasses, and his phone. I looked down at the floor and blushed, realizing when he got out of the shower, he'd had nothing to put on under that robe.

"Welcome back. Didn't have any trouble with the card, did you? I ordered us some fruit and champagne; I hope that suits you?" He grabbed at his hair again as he sat up, a habit I thought was adorable.

"Thank you, that's perfect. I got everything you asked for and no, no trouble with the card. No one even looks anymore to see the name on them. They only care that the charge goes through. I do want to grab a quick shower though; it's been a long day. Be right back." I grabbed a few things from the Target bags and made my way into the bathroom. I could hear Harrison in the other room unpackaging the things I'd purchased for him, and I hoped they met his standards.

The bathroom was still steamy from his shower when I reached in to turn on the water. The shower itself was huge, all white marble with luxurious gold fixtures. It felt so lavish compared to the shower I had at home. I stripped off the clothes I'd spent the day in, a day rescuing Harrison Edwards. I still couldn't wrap my head around it; it all felt so surreal. As the day progressed, I was becoming more comfortable around him; after all, he was turning out to be everything I ever hoped he'd be: thoughtful, humble, generous, and he made me feel welcome and appreciated.

I stepped into the shower; the floor still warm from where he stood just moments ago. I watched the water as it found its way toward the drain, as my toes caressed the smooth marble, I thought of his bare feet, his naked body standing in the same space I stood now. I felt the hot water wash over my skin, and imagined him here, the same stream of water hitting his back, trailing down his sculpted body, landing where I stood. Maybe it was the heat of the water on my muscles, or maybe it was the context of my thoughts, but the tension in my shoulders and neck from driving all day seemed to melt away and disappear. I'd made sure to buy the shampoo and conditioner I always get when I'm on vacation; the familiar scent never fails to put me in relaxation mode. As I lathered then rinsed myself, I remembered I'd also grabbed a bottle of perfume while I was out. I couldn't spend days...and nights...with a handsome man and not smell good. I needed to feel good in my own skin.

I toweled off and put on a new matching set of undergarments. Not the fanciest ones I bought, but a nice set. *You don't want to look desperate, Alice. Women throw themselves at him all the time. Be different.* I threw a t-shirt on over a fine mist of perfume then towel-dried my hair and left it loose, before putting on the other white robe that hung in the bathroom, and made my way out to the living area.

"Were you able to get in touch with Gucci?" I asked and my eyebrows inadvertently rose in confused unison before I could stop them. It felt bizarre for that sentence to come from my own mouth.

"I called them while you were out and let them know what we needed. They'll have it ready for us when we arrive in New Orleans. They know my sizes and I told them to have a few options available for you to choose from. I also asked that a seamstress be available to make sure whichever item you choose fits you like a glove. I hope you don't mind." He was so comfortable with the level of power he exuded. As if calling Gucci and having a seamstress on hand was a thing normal people did. "You did so much driving today and I'm so grateful for you, Alice. I've asked that the hotel send up their best masseurs this evening to help us decompress. They should be here in about forty-five minutes, so we have a little time to eat and enjoy this champagne."

I was once again tempted to pinch myself and I wondered, *Is this what it's like for him every day? Champagne, room service, and high-end fashion on speed dial?*

"Thank you, Harrison. You've been so kind to me, and I just want you to know how much I appreciate you."

"Of course. I could have found another way to get where I'm going, but a road trip is much more fun, and I'm excited you're going to come to the event with me. I think you're going to have a wonderful time."

"You're dolling me up in Gucci, babe c'mon, how could anyone have a bad time?" I flipped my hair dramatically, hoping to make him smile, and it worked.

We laughed and sipped champagne and the conversation turned to our favorite childhood memories and who in our families made our favorite holiday dinners as we lay back and snacked on strawberries and pineapple, feeling like we had been friends for years.

The masseurs came and went and by the time our massages ended the champagne was long gone. Tired heads leaned against the same headboard, bare bodies covered only in hotel robes lay propped close to one another, our shoulders touching. Both Harrison and I lay there giggling like children as the effects of the champagne faded our inhibitions, sharing truly bad jokes with one another.

"Hey, how does the moon cut his hair?" Harrison asked, slurring his already slow words.

My cheeks flushed from the alcohol, I smiled and said, "I don't know, how *does* the moon cut his hair?" and blinked repeatedly while I waited for the answer, my raised eyebrows the only thing keeping my tired eyes open.

"E-clipse it!" Harrison's accent made the joke that much funnier, and we both erupted in laughter.

Noticing our glasses were empty, he got up and reached for the champagne bottle. Finding it empty as well, he raised it and asked, "Should we order another?"

I was aware of how tipsy I was, and even more aware that I didn't want to forget a second of this trip. "No, I think I better switch to water." I nodded as I said it.

Harrison poured himself another bourbon from the bottle on the table, then reached into the mini fridge and got a cold bottle of water for me and returned to the bed with it. He was closer to me now than he was before, and I could feel the warmth of his body pressed up against mine.

I opened the water bottle and said, "Cheers, to new friends, and freedom."

Harrison bumped his glass against the bottle, his cup dwarfed in his hand. "Salute," he responded, and we both took a sip of our drinks.

I felt my nerves start to creep in again, but before I could focus on what might happen next, Harrison placed his thumb gently against my jawline. *Oh God.* His fingertips grazed the back of my neck as his hand cradled my head and I felt every tiny hair on my body rise in anticipation. As soon as he touched me, any buzz I had from the alcohol seemed to vanish. *This is actually happening, Alice. Compose yourself.*

"Alice...my entire body wants to kiss you." His face was so close to mine now I could see the flecks of gold and gray in his ocean green eyes.

"Is that the champagne talking?" I asked quietly.

A half smile appeared, along with one of his dimples, and he shook his head but said nothing.

He leaned in closer and I watched him a moment before I rubbed my nose against his slowly, my bottom lip brushing against the warmth of his breath, relishing in the moment I'd spent so much time daydreaming about. I thought of how his dimples appeared every time he smiled at me, and then gave in to the temptation I'd felt all day. He moved his chin slightly, bringing his mouth to mine, and hesitated long enough to look deeply into my eyes before fully kissing me for the first time, long and slow. I could taste the sweetness of the bourbon on his tongue. The patchy stubble on his chin was softer than I would have thought, and with both of my hands cradling his face, I leaned into him as parts of my body began to throb. Harrison knew the right ways to touch me to make me feel like he might devour me at any moment, yet he never did. Neither of us took it any further than kissing and a little innocent groping, despite the hunger I think we both felt for one another. We kissed and cuddled well into the night and fell asleep in each other's arms.

I awoke to the feeling of warm sun on my face, not the sound of an alarm clock. Harrison was still asleep behind me; his slow and steady breathing so rhythmic it could have easily lulled me back to sleep. I could feel every inch of his masculinity rigid and warm against the back of my body, and I was thankful I still had my robe on; I'm not sure I could handle it otherwise. A mischievous smile crept across my face as I reached for his hand and laid it over my waist, pulling him closer to me, and he snuggled his face into my neck and inhaled deeply.

"Good morning. I hope you slept well," he whispered in my ear as he drew himself up and slowly kissed my neck.

I drew in a deep reactionary breath from the feel of his mouth on my skin and exhaled. "I did."

I turned to look at Harrison and felt like a shy schoolgirl unable to maintain eye contact. *He sure is adorable in the morning*, I thought, as I watched him blink hard, trying to adjust his eyes to the sunlight. Tangles of dark curls hung around his face until his right hand mindlessly pulled them away from his forehead, twisting them atop his head as he always did.

"What do you say we grab some food and see where the day takes us?" Harrison reached for the phone and ordered room service.

We ate breakfast together and talked about whatever came to mind. We started with how far we planned to drive today, but that somehow turned into how Harrison started his career making commercials, and then he told me how he wanted to break into the music industry. He certainly had a lot of goals to reach and specific plans to achieve them, and I was impressed. He went on to express his excitement about New Orleans and the future prospects the event could bring. I was taken with his drive and his initiative; there seemed to be nothing about him that wasn't endearing to me.

An hour later we were on the road, singing along together to oldies and enjoying the summer breeze as it blew through the car's open windows once again, both of us feeling so unencumbered and alive, free to talk about whatever, and now I, like Harrison, felt the weight of any potential consequences slipping away.

We made a quick stop in New York for a bathroom break and as we passed through Baltimore decided we'd spend the night in D.C. Harrison said he had something to show me there anyhow, but wouldn't share the details, and of course I was intrigued. I smiled when he called the Four Seasons and again cleared an entire floor just for the two of us. It seemed a little extravagant, and once we arrived, I found myself tugging at my clothes self-consciously as I walked through the hotel lobby in off-brand shorts and a t-shirt. My face must have given my thoughts life, because Harrison reached for my hand and gave it a squeeze, smiling at me adoringly when I glanced up at him.

Inside and settled, each of us took a little time to relax before hitting the shower; it had been another long, humid day in the car and the further south we traveled, the warmer it got. Harrison opted to shower first while I took advantage of the air conditioning. After a while I heard him humming as he rinsed off and I chuckled to myself. *Why is everything he does so attractive?*

When he was finished and it was my turn in the bathroom, I took my time to once again enjoy the water pressure, and while I toweled off I attempted to listen in as Harrison made calls, but couldn't make out anything he was saying. I assumed maybe he had been ordering room service or was checking in with his management. It wasn't until after we were both dressed that Harrison was willing to give up any more detail about his plans for the evening.

"I called for a car service to take us out this evening, and I'm hopeful this plan of mine is something you'll enjoy." He said, looking nervous for the first time since I had met him. "I'm going to love sharing this with you, I know that much." He smiled like a teenager after he said it, not a twenty-eight-year-old man. He was more than a decade my junior, and I was both proud and nervous about that. I'd only ever dated men older than me, and this was intimidating but exhilarating at the same time. *Don't fuss over the details, Alice. He wouldn't be here if he didn't want to be*, I reminded myself.

"I'm excited to see what you have planned," I said, and for the first time since this morning, Harrison leaned in and kissed me gently. It was slow and deliberate, not something he did flippantly, and I loved that about him. I was learning that he did nothing at all if he didn't mean it with his whole being. His facial hair prickled at my chin, but I didn't mind.

"I know you were nervous earlier; I saw the look on your face when we walked into the hotel," He said as he broke from our kiss.

"Well, it's the Four Seasons, and I'm dressed like a commoner. I feel like I'm casting some sort of dark shadow on your reputation going out with you looking like this."

"Love, I look no different than you do and anyone that has an opinion other than how beautiful you are, doesn't matter. It's just you and me tonight. Everything's going to be alright. Okay?"

I nodded and turned my head away, flattered. As my cheeks flushed to a shade of crimson, he reached for my face with his index finger and pulled my gaze back to him.

"Hey, let's go have some fun." He said, a wide smile on his face, immediately calming any reservations I had.

In that moment I decided I would no longer grant any more time to negative thoughts of insignificance. Harrison had shown me how willing he was to make sure I was okay, and let me know on multiple occasions he would take care of anything that needed to be taken care of; I was sure of it, and I was sure of him. From here on out, I would focus on the fun there was to be had with this incredible man, and nothing more.

I gave him another kiss just as the hotel room phone rang.

"This is Harrison." He spoke assertively into the receiver. "Okay, we'll be right there, thank you," he said and hung up. "The car is here. You ready?" His excitement was palpable.

"As ready as I'll ever be." I smiled as Harrison took me by the hand and led me to the car.

The ride wasn't long, but we enjoyed champagne and sat close in the back of the dark SUV. I made guesses about where we were going and what we could be doing but Harrison shrugged away every idea, telling me it was just going to have to be a surprise. When we arrived at our destination, I was awestruck as we entered through the back door and made our way down a dark hallway hand-in-hand before the room opened up into a massive geodesic glass dome. We were met by thousands of twinkling lights suspended above a room filled with vibrant colorful plants and flowers and I'd never seen anything more beautiful. There was a warmth to the air and the familiar smell of the blooms was a comfort. Harrison's hand fell to the small of my back as we walked side by side through the United States Botanic Gardens, surrounded by hundreds of lush floral exhibits.

"I watched your face light up when you talked about your gardens and I wasn't sure if you had ever been here before, but I wanted to make it special for you. I closed the place down just for us and we're free to explore all we want, undisturbed."

I could see he was looking for my reaction and I was glad to give it to him.

"This is absolutely magical, Harrison; thank you for being so sweet to me." I looked around the expansive space, fascinated by the display of lights above me.

He took my hand and we casually strolled through the different exhibits, picking out favorites and breathing in their different scents. The air was humid but comfortable as the ferns and orchids arched themselves outward in various brilliant colors along the winding pathways that ushered us into another ornate glass atrium, this one much larger than the last.

"Oh, Harrison..." I was nearly speechless as we wandered down a path leading to a small cafe table and chairs situated among what had to be a million brightly colored roses. The smell was intoxicating. I love roses but have never been able to keep even the hardiest varieties alive.

"I hope this is a memory you hold forever," he said.

"How could I possibly ever forget this? This is incredible, Harrison; thank you." I was blushing again. No one had ever thought to do anything like this for me. He hugged me close and kissed my forehead.

Two gentlemen in tuxedos brought out our dinner, and as our plates touched the table, a third gentleman started playing a nearby piano. "Somewhere Over the Rainbow" familiar and beautiful poured from his fingertips and filled the room. I'd always loved the romance of a piano, the delicate touch that could bring forth such tremendously moving music, and it brought back so many positive memories of my grandmother who'd played endlessly for me as a child. The melody from the baby grand filled the air, immersing us in hauntingly emotional sounds, and my eyes began to tear up.

"I've upset you..." Harrison said, puzzled. The worry on his face made me feel terrible.

"No, not at all. Nothing like that, I'm just overcome with happiness. This is all so...I've never felt like this before. No one has ever done this kind of thing for me and I'm just a bit overwhelmed." I looked up and met his gaze as I dabbed at the corners of my eyes with a napkin.

He took both of my hands in his and said, "Darling, you're worth every bit of this, and more. I've never known anyone I felt so compelled to treat this way. These two days with you have been magic. They've set my soul free. I can be myself, and you accept me. You didn't care who I was, you only cared about keeping me safe. You haven't asked anything of me, and I rarely find myself around genuine people in my line of work; usually people only want to take from me or use me to their benefit. You're the most beautifully genuine person I've met in such a long time. I appreciate you so much." Now Harrison's eyes were the ones tearing up.

"Look at us, blubbering fools," I laughed and wiped a tear from his cheek then kissed him. He smiled his award-winning smile and grasped a fistful of his dark curls, delicately pulling them from his forehead. We settled into our dinner together, enjoying the ambiance, the conversation and the food, and once our meal was finished, Harrison said, "I have something for you."

He got up and walked confidently toward the piano, then whispered something I couldn't make out to the pianist. The gentleman strode out of sight as Harrison sat down and began to play "To Make You Feel My Love", a song from one of my favorite movies, it always made me emotional. As I watched his fingers manipulate the keys, I was impressed with his dexterity and, truthfully, it turned me on to watch his hands craft such beautiful sounds. I'd seen him casually strum a guitar in one of his movies, but seeing him actually perform live, and in such a romantic setting, just felt so much more intimate.

At first he hummed, and then he began to sing. His voice was deep and gravelly, with a beautiful rasp that hung on his accent. I was overcome with emotion, and touched that he was so openly sharing this gift with me so soon in our...I don't even know what I'd call this, a friendship? A relationship? Who's to say? But when he finished the song, he returned to the table, a nervous but accomplished smile across his face that made my heart lose track of its rhythm.

"What do you think? Can I make it in the singing world?" He asked.

I hugged him tightly. "It's amazing. *You* are amazing. What a gift you have; your voice is so unique."

"Thanks, love. My heart has always been in music. The acting just happened faster for me."

As the sun began to set, Harrison and I strolled out to the open observation deck, stopping along the way to admire a few more exhibits. The air was much cooler in contrast to the humidity inside, and holding hands, we stood and watched the sun give way to darkness; staring up at the sky together, pointing out constellations until we saw a star shoot across the vast blackness above us.

"Make a wish." we said in unison, both recognizing what had just happened.

"Jinx!" we exclaimed together before bursting into laughter.

Harrison embraced me as we stood there with one another laughing, scanning the sky in hopes of seeing another shooting star. I shivered against the chill of the night air and the warmth of his arms was a welcome comfort but not enough to fend off the dropping temperature.

"Wanna head back, get warmed up?" he asked, feeling my body tremble against him.

"This night has been so beautiful, but I think so." I nodded.

He took my hand and we made our way back to the car. The air in the SUV was no warmer, and Harrison once again wrapped his arms around me in an attempt to stop my shivering. We stayed that way until we arrived back at the Four Seasons. Eager to get out of sight, we made it back to our floor and into our room without being spotted. Room service had set up more champagne, dimmed the lights and turned down the bed, leaving tiny mints on each of our pillows. I suddenly began to feel nervous again. *Was tonight going to be the night?*

"I think I'm going to take a hot bath. You don't mind, do you?" I asked.

"Not at all. I've got some calls to make anyhow. See you in a bit?" That smile of his could stop wars; truly, I was smitten.

I nodded and made my way into the bathroom. I filled the large round tub and added a luxurious vanilla bubble bath the hotel provided. The tub was large enough for four people, which I thought a bit odd. *In what scenario would a tub need to be large enough for that many people?* I let my mind wander as I readied my towel then pulled a hair elastic from my wrist and wound my hair up into a messy bun to keep it from getting wet.

I wasn't the kind of woman to wear makeup. I had never needed to. My complexion was what some would call porcelain, my cheeks always some shade of pink all on their own, and my hair was long with natural waves, a deep chestnut with no signs of gray yet. Typically, I keep my hair pulled back and away from my face, but opted tonight to leave it down for Harrison's surprise outing. He seemed to like my long hair and the fact that it was down and loose. I even caught him staring at me tonight, which made my confidence soar, and more than once, I felt him carefully twirling my hair between his fingers while we walked through the exhibits. *Something tells me he's enjoying my company as much as I enjoy his.*

I slipped into the bubbly hot water and felt my entire body relax against its warmth. I don't have a bathtub at home, only a shower, so a nice hot soak was a luxury all its own. Ten minutes later I was fully immersed in my thoughts, eyes closed, replaying the events of the evening while my head rested against a rolled towel near the edge of the tub. Listening to Harrison sing to me was probably my favorite part; his vocal range is incredible, but I never suspected he could actually play the piano. *He's been keeping his musical abilities a secret for too long*, I thought and sighed just thinking about the rasp in his voice. In my head, all I could see was the strength of his hands tenderly caressing the keys of the piano, creating something so fragile and yet so profound.

The soft knock at the bathroom door brought me out of my thoughts. "Darling, do you mind if I come in?" Harrison's muffled voice penetrated the door and echoed into the large bathroom.

"Just a moment." I sunk lower into the bath and made sure the bubbles covered my chest. "Okay, all set."

Harrison opened the door holding two champagne flutes between his fingers in one hand and a bottle of chilled champagne in the other. To my delight, he was only wearing his shorts. His chest was flawlessly defined like a sculpture from a museum and his tattoos only amplified his appeal; his body was indeed a masterpiece covered in artwork. A tangle of writing adorned the muscles above each clavicle, an empty birdcage covered his ribs, and some sort of ship was on his inner forearm. The fronts of each hip showed what looked like the curved edges of some sort of tribal design but were mostly hidden by his shorts, and once again my mind began to wander. There was tiny script above and below both his knees and something I couldn't quite make out across the front of each ankle and one of his toes. *Even his feet are gorgeous*, I thought. I remembered the large tattoo of a lion on his thigh; I'd seen it before in photos, and I must have seen it when he came out of the pool. I think my nerves must have gotten the best of me because I couldn't remember exactly what it looked like. The bottom of it peeked out from beneath his robe last night, but it was hidden now by the length of his shorts.

"Love?" Harrison questioned, trying to get my attention.

Had I missed something he'd said as I intently looked him up and down daydreaming about this goddamned lion? Pay attention, Alice. "Yes? I'm so sorry." I shook my head to try to focus on the present instead of the images my imagination was feeding me.

"I said do you mind if I join you? This tub seems large enough for us and my entire staff." He chuckled as he said it and again, my mind slipped a little further into the gutter...*Stop it, Alice. Focus.*

"Um, sure. C'mon in." My nerves were back, and it showed in the hesitation of my response. I hoped Harrison would think my cheeks were red from the heat of the water and not from my anxiety.

"Do you want me to keep these shorts on; would it make you more comfortable? Alice, I just want to be near you, I'm not trying to—"

"It's fine," I cut him off. "We're all grown people here, and I did see you fully nude yesterday if you recall." I laughed as Harrison's cheeks flushed despite his tan. "Not that I was checking you out or anything, but you were just letting it do what it does...and you were, you know, just out there for the world to see." My rambling stopped short when Harrison's shorts hit the bathroom floor, leaving him standing naked before me once again.

There's the lion tattoo. Me-ow.

My hand reactively shot from the water to cover my mouth in an attempt to mask my surprise. As I drew in a deep breath, trying to avoid inhaling the bubbles that were now covering my chin, I averted my eyes.

"Oh...okay..." I mumbled through my soap covered hand as he climbed into the bathtub. He slid himself down into the heat of the water and faced me, resting his arms outstretched on the edge of the tub like da Vinci's Vitruvian man. *Muscles. So many muscles. Rein it in, Alice.*

My eyes drank in every single drop of him as they scanned from his fingertips to his neck, across his chest and down the other arm, devouring every perfect, tattooed surface that laid against those well-defined rock-solid muscles. My mind was a tangle of impurity and I tried with all my might to keep my thoughts from showing on my face. After a few moments of silence, my eyes finally met his and found him smiling back at me.

"So...how ya doin'?" I asked, trying to be funny. I drew in another deep breath before exhaling slowly, a sure sign of my anxiety.

"I'm doing just fine, just fine." Harrison nodded and smiled his perfect white smile, dimples and all, and I felt as if my chest could explode at any moment. "Do I make you nervous?" He chuckled after he said it.

"No. Nope. Not nervous. Just, well..." I shook my head quickly then hesitated, flustered, and Harrison sat back, watching me as he maintained his grin and I changed my tune. "Yes. Nervous. Yup," I said, closing my eyes, hanging my head in joking defeat.

Harrison reached over and wiped a few lingering bubbles from my chin with his thumb. His hand paused there, his fingertips cupping my jaw, pulling my eyes back up to meet his. We stared at one another without speaking a word as we traded unspoken intentions, the sounds of the water dripping from his elbow echoing against the bathroom tile. Harrison was no longer able to curb his curiosity; he slowly and deliberately positioned his body in front of me.

His hands gripped the edge of the tub behind me and cradled the back of my head between his forearms. I closed my eyes and let my head fall back against his wrists. The feeling of his warm breath on my neck ignited something in me I could no longer control. *Don't think about it, just give in to it Alice. Let him adore every inch of you.*

The world below the water's surface was entirely different than the one above it. The slippery bare skin of his body against mine drove me mad. Unable to keep my hands off him, I pawed at his back, half scratching, half massaging him while his mouth and tongue hungrily pressed against my neck. His left hand remained behind me, steadying himself while his right hand slipped below the surface, slowly gliding along my curves, pausing to give attention to the parts of me he enjoyed most, giving me a preview of the many talents his strong hands possessed and insight into the things he liked.

It was clear to me Harrison was enjoying every moment of this; the telltale flare of his nostrils and his very obvious rigidity gave him away. He was so strong with me and yet incredibly gentle. Ready to give myself to him fully, I wrapped my legs around his waist, but when I did, he pulled away so quickly that only the sounds of our labored breathing and the splashing of the warm water over the edge of the tub onto the cold marble floor could be heard.

Surprised and confused I apologized. "I'm sorry, have I done something wrong?" I asked, my chest still heaving.

"No, no. Not at all. You've done everything right. I'm just so taken with you Alice; I want to relish in this moment. I don't want to move too quickly. It's not who I am, not...who I *want* to be...anymore." He drew a hand to his chest as he tried to slow his breathing.

I looked at him puzzled, my silence prodding him to finish his explanation.

"In my past, I've seen what I want, and out of some feeling of celebrity or just sheer narcissism I've wasted no time taking it, having it, and I suppose, wasting it. Instant gratification isn't something I want anymore. I want to bask in the glow of you. I want to absorb all of you that I can before we jump into something more."

That accent, I thought, *can have anything it wants.*

"I wasn't wrong to come in here with you; I wanted to be close to you, but I feel it's only right to slow down. You're beginning to really mean more to me than I ever anticipated Alice. Please, I'm just asking you to be patient with me." His eyes had such a longing in them, how could I be upset with this man after all he just said? I pulled him into a hug hoping to make him feel safe with me – even though the sensation of his pecs against my own bare wet chest was tantalizing.

"It's okay. We don't have to do anything, and I certainly hope you don't feel like I'm pressuring you. I appreciate your opening up to me and trusting me, but we have no reason to rush." I reassured him, still holding him in my embrace.

He hugged me back a little tighter then, and I understood his quiet signal of appreciation. When we pulled away, I kissed the bridge of his nose, then softly kissed his lips.

"Let's get out of this tub and see what's on TV. Want to?" I grabbed a towel, handed it to him, and then reached for my own. We toweled off in silence, put on our robes, and made our way back to the living area.

Harrison went back to grab the unopened bottle of champagne and the glasses we left in the bathroom and when he came out I had set the television to reruns of *The Office*. Harrison poured two glasses of champagne and we said a cheers to "Beautiful flowers, beautiful evenings, and bubble baths."

Conversation came so easy for us, we talked about so many things in such a short amount of time that Harrison felt like an old friend; like I had known him my entire life. He was easy to be around, and I felt free to be myself without worrying that he would change his mind about me. We decided tomorrow would be a bit of a longer day and we'd get up early to cover more ground. Harrison suggested we take a little detour to Nashville, and I'd never been there before, so I was excited to see what he had up his sleeve. I'd learned in my short time with him that he never made suggestions like that without a plan in mind.

With tomorrow settled, he wrapped his arm around me and I pulled the elastic from my hair, letting it fall against my shoulders then snuggled in closer to his chest. His skin smelled like vanilla bubble bath, and his chest hair tickled my cheek as we lay there in the dark, his thumb brushing across my temple and his fingertips caressing my earlobe and jaw. Back and forth, back and forth, gently coaxing me into complete relaxation. I fell asleep in his arms, with only the quiet murmurs of the television in the background.

The sounds of a piano woke me early the next morning before daylight arrived. Harrison shut off the alarm on his phone and turned back to kiss my forehead.

"I love waking up with you," he said in the dark, the rasp of sleep still in his voice.

Love. That was a strong word in just three days' time. Maybe he said it without thinking, or maybe I was just eager to let my imagination take control. My heart wanted to believe he meant it exactly the way I heard it; deep down I hoped he was falling for me the way I was falling for him.

"Good morning...you aren't so bad yourself." I gave his body a gentle squeeze and said, "Hey, knock knock."

Despite the dark surrounding us, I could hear his smile as he sleepily said, "Who's there?"

"Alpaca." I stifled a giggle.

His abdomen jerked as he laughed. "Alpaca who?"

"Alpaca the car, you pack-a-the suitcase!" I turned to face him with an exaggerated smile on my face.

"Ohhh, ba dum-bum, tss," We both feigned exaggerated laughter. These corny jokes were becoming our 'thing' it seemed.

I was the first one to drag myself out of bed and into the shower; I really didn't want to leave the warmth of his skin or the feel of his touch but today was going to be a long one and we needed to get on the road. The hotel had washed all our clothes and returned them to our room late the night before, so everything was fresh and already packed in see-through bags. I dressed and as I pulled my hair into a high ponytail, I once again heard Harrison on the phone. As hard as I tried to listen, I could still only make out a few phrases. Between him chewing his breakfast and his thick British accent I understood, "Yes, just the two of us," and "I already know which one," and "...at least one hundred." I shook my head confused, trying to imagine what he was up to. This man was the king of sweet surprises.

When he finished on the phone, Harrison hurried into the shower so we could get on the road. There was a lot of ground to cover and no time to waste. I ate a quick breakfast while he was in the bathroom getting ready, and when he was done, we were back in the car headed for Nashville.

The day turned overcast shortly after we left, and it looked like rain would soon arrive. I drove for the first half of the day, which allowed Harrison to choose the radio station. For a while, he couldn't make up his mind, switching between golden oldies—singing to me as exuberantly and as silly as he possibly could to keep me laughing—and then later he switched over to an easy rock station.

We settled into the long stretch of road ahead of us and talked about more of our childhood memories, favorite vacation destinations we'd been to, as well as places on our bucket lists. Harrison had been all over the world for movie shoots and had some of the most amazing stories to share. I, of course, felt envious of the freedom his job allowed him and the benefits of absorbing life all over the world, all while working. It was rare I ever left the town I lived in, and he was canvassing the planet in the name of art.

I enjoyed listening to him talk about his career and his music; his passion for his abilities burst from him like sunlight through trees, and I wondered in those moments if he had any idea how incredible he was. I think I most enjoyed the happiness he emitted when he talked about his childhood. Every time he shared something new about himself, I found myself falling more deeply in adoration of him.

We rolled into the southern half of the United States and stopped for an early lunch at a little hole-in-the-wall diner. We searched the menu online, ordered from the car, and I went in to pick up the food. It was still a bit of a chore trying to keep Harrison hidden from view of the public. *This must be the downside,* I thought. *Having to constantly hide when you're alone or without security. Not having the freedom to just live without the fear of being mobbed by strangers.*

I remembered a few years back there'd been a news article published about how Harrison had been held at gunpoint late at night while he was out walking in Greece. He told me he liked to walk to clear his head after hectic days of filming, but he hadn't mentioned the specifics of the incident with the gun. I'm certain it must have left some residual trauma he kept safely tucked away. The article reported a group of older teenagers stopped him on the street and first asked for a cigarette. Harrison hadn't ever smoked and told them he was sorry, but he didn't have anything to give them. In that short amount of time, one of them recognized who he was and demanded he empty his pockets. When he refused, stating he didn't have his wallet and wouldn't hand over his phone, one of the boys pulled out a gun and began shouting threats that were much more aggressive. The eldest and largest of the group held Harrison's hands behind his back while another rummaged through his pockets, finding only two crumpled twenty-dollar bills. The third boy quickly drew the gun up to Harrison's brow. Although he held the gun, he was later found to be the youngest, and claimed the others had given him the gun that night. Harrison was quoted in the article saying he felt the gun tremble against his face and had felt the boy was too scared to actually act on his threats. No wallet was to be found. Harrison didn't carry one on his walks. He had only the forty American dollars in his pocket, no rings, no watch, no chain. Just his phone, the cash, and his ear pods for listening to music.

Thankfully it happened on a well-lit main road, and as an officer drove by on patrol, he saw what was happening, came to a stop close to where Harrison was and turned his flood lights directly on the boys, announcing a police presence. The teens took off running and the cop escorted Harrison back to his hotel. No one was hurt, and the boys were found with the gun later the next day and charged with the appropriate crimes.

I resigned myself to the fact that it had to have changed Harrison, deep down, affecting his ability to trust, making him more leery of strangers and fans alike. I also think shortly after that is when he started working out more, maybe as a means to clear his mind or as a way to physically avoid a repeat of that situation in the future. Harrison's such a genuinely kindhearted man, always willing to help everyone without hesitation, and it bothered me that he'd been through that. The more I thought about it, the more I almost felt regret for intruding on him the aggressive way I did at the pool, even though he handled it with ease.

Harrison took over driving after lunch and our afternoon stops were limited to bathroom breaks at truck stops and a few fuel refills. I bought him a hat at a random rest stop somewhere on Route 81 outside of Roanoke, Virginia that said 'Virginia is for Lovers', the O in Lovers made into a bright red heart shape against the black cap with white embroidered letters. He put it on immediately, and as his smile widened and his dimples reappeared, his accent rolled off his tongue into a quote I'd heard him say many times. "Be a lover. Choose love. Give love. Love everyone, always." I knew when I picked up the hat it was going to be perfect. Perfect because of his quote, perfect because we were in Virginia on a road trip, and perfect because I imagined that someday soon, we might actually become lovers.

I was in charge of the car radio while Harrison was behind the wheel, and I chose an eighties music station. Harrison's much younger than I; he wasn't even born yet in the eighties, but his knowledge of music was so vast I was confident he'd enjoy the mixture of rock, pop, and old-school rap the station played. We sang along and had the best time, sharing stories that correlated to the songs and when we first heard them, or for me, what I was doing in my life when these songs were popular. We mixed in terrible jokes and poked fun at people we passed on the highway, and I took full advantage of simply watching him drive. The flex of his arms, the tattoos draped over his perfect muscle tone, the sharp edge of his jaw, and the architecture of his hands. *Mesmerizing to think those hands have been on my bare skin.*

Harrison also casually mentioned that he'd booked the Presidential Suite at the Hermitage Hotel in Nashville for tonight's stay. Me being the passenger and not the driver, I had time to do a little research on my phone before we arrived. At first glance it appeared to be a magnificent downtown hotel, laden with luxury and services to cover its patrons' every whim, and it showcased nearby golf, touting it as World Class.

I learned early on that Harrison tended to drive much faster than I did, and with him making up for the time we lost this morning in the rain, we got to Nashville in record time. We checked in, and once again got settled. The room had an entire wall of floor-to-ceiling windows that allowed for stunning views of the city, and the room itself was massive, boasting a comfortable seating area and a giant California king bed. The bathroom was made of white marble with another huge soaking tub. *Maybe later I'll get an extended replay of last night*, I thought.

As late-afternoon arrived, I noticed that Harrison seemed antsy, and I questioned where his head was.

"Everything okay?" I asked him. "You seem to have wandered off into your own head this afternoon; usually that's my move."

"I'm okay and I don't mean to be distant. I'm just going over a few things in my head for tonight and we're getting close to this appearance in New Orleans, so I'm trying to get that all settled in my mind as well."

"I've heard there's a nice golf course nearby. Maybe we could see about a round if we have time before this evening? I'll warn you though, my grown-up golf skills are trash, but my mini-golf skills…ten out of ten." I gestured with a chef's kiss.

"Any other time I'd say golf would be perfect, but there isn't enough time before our car arrives. I don't want us to be late for tonight's main event." He smiled and scrunched up his nose as he reached out for me, both arms welcoming me. I cozied into them as though they were created specifically for my body.

"Is there anything I can do to help you or make this easier for you? I'm glad to do whatever I can."

"I don't think so; just continue being your beautiful, understanding self and everything will be fine. I do fancy a cup of tea though; do you like to drink tea, Alice?"

"I've had iced tea, but I've never really had hot tea before," I admitted, feeling embarrassed. "But if you're going to have some, I'll try it the way you like it."

How inherently English of him: afternoon teatime.

I'd never been a fan of trying new foods or drinks, and even though I was hesitant I wanted to be a good sport, and it was just tea; it couldn't be that bad. In my defense, someone once offered me a portion of a fancy pasta salad and after three seemingly tolerable bites I looked closer and saw the concoction had tiny, whole, cooked octopus throughout. I nearly vomited when I noticed. Had I not been in an upscale restaurant I likely would have.

I called room service who promptly delivered us both a cup of hot tea, with a squeeze of lemon and a pinch of sugar. No milk, which I was glad about. I sipped on it, but decided quickly it was something I'd only drink if I had no other options. I'm a black coffee with sugar kinda girl, and just couldn't find the appeal of hot tea. This might be one of the few things we didn't have in common.

With teatime behind us, we both showered and got ready for the evening. Having nothing more than shorts and t-shirts still made me feel a little strange in these fancy hotels, and seeing Harrison in the same clothing should have put my worries at ease, but it didn't. He was a celebrity. He was loved around the world. He could do, say, or wear anything he wanted and no one would bat an eye. Hell, they'd applaud him for it; he'd be a trendsetter. But me, I'd be the frumpy nobody that he was caught fraternizing with in a hotel lobby.

It was odd to me that all the hotels he'd chosen so far provided vanilla scented bath products. Now, don't get me wrong, muscular Harrison Edwards covered in tattoos, smelling like vanilla just seemed to work for him and I was perfectly okay with it. But I began to wonder what his cologne of choice was in the real world. The 'real world', as if this wasn't real; I'd pinched myself and everything to verify. Then, like clouds at a picnic, a shadow of sadness washed over me as I began to wonder what would happen after we got to New Orleans. I sat with it a moment before I realized I had to shrug it off and try to think of something else.

The car arrived for us at a quarter to five. Another SUV with blackened windows, a roomy leather interior, and a dark glass divider separating us from the driver. We settled in and Harrison asked me if I'd like a bottle of water. *That's strange, normally he'd offer champagne for a night out.* 'Normally.' What a difference a few days made. I don't know what he 'normally' would do. I only had a few days to base that statement on. Regardless, I did notice that he offered me tea this afternoon and water this evening. *I wonder if this has anything to do with tonight's activity; what is he up to now?* I thought.

I accepted the water as the SUV slowly meandered through traffic. We had only been in motion about fifteen minutes when our vehicle pulled into a parking lot off of Roy Acuff Place. A sign on the building read RCA Studio B. I was confused yet again, but Harrison led me through the air-conditioned building and down a long corridor. There had been no one at the front to greet us, or even direct us where to go; there was no one milling around the place at all. On the left was a row of small rooms, and at the end of the hall, two larger rooms, divided by clear glass.

"Harrison, what's going on? What are we doing here?" I was nervous, and surely must have looked like I was ready to run back to the car at any moment.

"I wanted to make you a permanent part of something that means the world to me. I've rented out this studio to record some adlibs for a song I've been working on for my album. This won't take long." He cocked his head to the side and held my gaze, taming my fears.

A nervous grin spread across his face. "Say you'll help me with this, darling." He took my hand and led me into the smaller of the two booths.

Per his direction, I positioned myself on a stool in front of a microphone, but remained too terrified to speak. There were men in the other part of the studio, and even though they were on the other side of the glass, just their presence made me insecure. *Was this a joke? Am I being punked?* No, Harrison wouldn't do that. He was a playful guy, but he wouldn't prank me like that. Then it occurred to me, *this* is why he wanted to keep both of our voices clear, and the two of us to remain totally sober. It all made sense now.

"Do I have to do anything special? Just speak? Will you tell me if I do something wrong?" I was beginning to panic; this would potentially be on his album and be heard all over the world. Harrison handed me a set of headphones, and I nervously put them on and adjusted them to fit my head. Next, he secured a pair on himself and when he and I were both comfortable, Harrison made eye contact with the men running the soundboards and gave them a quick nod.

"Everything is going to be fine, darling. I'm right here with you. Look at me, focus on me. We'll be alright."

His voice was soothing, and I believed what he was saying as soon as our eyes met. He was sincere and I felt safe with him.

"I—I don't know what to say." My embarrassment made my already scarlet cheeks feel like the skin was searing off of them. I shook my head as if to convey my mind was scattered, unaware that they were already recording, and had been since Harrison nodded to the men on the other side of the glass.

He took my face in his hands and looked so deeply into my eyes that I thought I might fall off my stool. *My God, this man is everything that dreams are made of*, I thought as I struggled to maintain eye contact. My head was dizzy purely from the adrenaline surging through me.

"Darling, I adore you. These days with you have absolutely changed my life. You're a part of me now. You've become a part of my soul that I'll never lose, and I'll carry you with me for as long as I live. I've found something in you Alice that I've never found with anyone else." He paused and took my hand. "Just speak from your heart. Tell me something that you never want me to forget." He kissed each of my warm cheeks softly, trying to comfort me. Who would've known such a kind, small gesture, kissing what I felt was my most embarrassing physical flaw, could melt any self-deprecating thoughts completely from my mind?

My thoughts and emotions were a tangled mess, and I was worried to share how I felt about him out loud. It had only been a few days. *Was how I felt about him normal? Would he think I'm some kind of weirdo for the way I feel? How could he? He all but said 'marry me' just now. Can you even imagine being Harrison Edwards' wife*?! I quickly became even more overwhelmed by my own swirling thoughts. *Stop it, Alice.*

I had never felt like this for anyone, certainly not after only a few days. Now I was supposed to just put it all on the line, out loud, in front of strangers, and while being recorded? He had done it, and if he, Harrison Edwards, the gorgeous, British, green-eyed movie star Harrison Edwards could profess his truth to me, then the least I could do in this moment was be honest with him. I could hear the words in my head, and I could feel my emotions rising to match them.

So, I paused, took a deep breath, and on exhale nervously said, "You feel like home to me." I stopped and looked at him wide-eyed, desperate for his acceptance. As I said it, I felt the weight of keeping my thoughts to myself melt off my shoulders. He seemed touched, but I could tell he was looking for a bit more than six words.

He reached out and took my hand in his as I mustered my courage and continued. "In these few days, I've fallen head over heels for you Harrison. From the moment you first spoke to me, I knew you were someone I could trust. I know you'll protect my heart, always. Without even knowing you're doing it; you nourish my soul. You bring me such complete joy, unlike anything I've ever experienced, and I just want to live in that joy forever. Harrison, I adore you."

I'd never spoken like this out loud to anyone in my life; it was exhilarating and exhausting, but my heart certainly felt freer. I wasn't one to share my innermost feelings, that's for sure, but this, this felt like birds of happiness flying out of me, soaring into the sky, each one lifting my hopes and freeing me to fully be myself with him.

Harrison smiled from ear to ear, his dimples deepening as he beamed, and I knew it was because of me; I did that for him. Then I got an idea.

"Hey, Harrison? Where do you learn to make a banana split?" I stifled a laugh and raised my eyebrows at him, egging him on for an answer.

"I don't know, love, where do you learn to make a banana split?" Harrison's accent rolled off the word 'banana' giving me pause as I thought about it.

"Sundae School." I gave an exaggerated wink and made a finger gun motion in his direction before bursting into laughter.

He got off his stool laughing and yelled, "That's all folks! CUT!"

We both took our headphones off and laid them on our stools, then without hesitation fell into each other's embrace. We'd only been in the studio about fifteen minutes, but we certainly covered a lot of ground in that time. We'd both exposed our true emotions to one another and were now fully aware of how the other felt. It was scary but made my heart feel so full.

As he stepped back, Harrison let his fingertips graze the length of my exposed arm until his fingers were entwined with mine.

"What's the plan for the rest of the night?" I asked, certain he must have something else up his sleeve.

"Well, I thought we could order some food from room service, and maybe find a movie on TV?" Harrison had explained to me how much he valued quiet time, time to decompress from the flashing lights and cameras of movie sets and paparazzi. Now, with a newfound knowledge of how he truly felt about me, I was even happier than before to be near him.

The ride back to the hotel was shorter this time; rush hour traffic had subsided and there was less stop-and-go than before. When we arrived back at the hotel and made our way across the sidewalk into the hotel lobby, something seemed off, and I began to feel oddly uneasy. Up until now, we'd been coming and going through private back entrances and never through any main doors. I held onto Harrison's hand a bit more tightly than usual and when I gave it a quick, tight squeeze he turned and looked at me as if he knew I was trying to send him some sort of signal. Just like someone flipped a switch, his face fell into a blank look I hadn't seen on him before. One of suspicion but also a more hardened, determined look. The happy, easy look of freedom was gone as his eyes shot around the lobby and he quickened his pace. I was even more nervous now.

He pulled our room key from his pocket and gripped it tightly, readying it for use as soon as we approached our door, then pushed the elevator button to go up. There wasn't an abundance of people in the hotel lobby, but there were enough that we could easily lose control of our privacy if we weren't quick and careful. In the time it took the elevator to arrive, more people seemed to congregate around us. I could hear some of them whispering, "Is that Harrison Edwards? Who is that woman?" My heart began to race when I thought I heard someone's camera shutter click, but I maintained a straight face, and pretended to be oblivious to it all.

The elevator opened and an older couple walked out, first with a courtesy smile that quickly turned to a questioning look on both of their faces, then realization finally struck them. This was the first time that I'd experienced anything like this. I was never aware of the people around me; I never needed to be. I had no reason to be suspicious of anyone, ever. But Harrison did.

We stepped into the wood-paneled elevator despite there being a younger couple already standing toward the back. Both of us quickly turned our backs to them to avoid recognition and Harrison jabbed repeatedly at the button to close the door, trying to be inconspicuous as he did it. The tenth-floor button was already illuminated, which was two floors below ours. Before I could push the button for the twelfth floor, Harrison pushed the button for the eleventh floor. He lowered his chin as he stood there glancing at me from the corner of his eye, barely moving his head in my direction, but signaling to me to keep my chin down as well. I lowered my face but lifted my hands to my cheeks, trying to gauge how red they must be based on the heat I felt radiating from them. *Ugh, had I been photographed with him for the first time looking like this?*

"I don't mean to bother you, but you look just like Harrison Edwards." The woman's voice cut through the silence and waivered with excitement. Her boyfriend shushed her. "Leave these people alone. Harrison Edwards is in rehab, Emily. I read it in yesterday's paper." His tone of voice made it clear she had embarrassed him, and he was annoyed with her.

"Shuh, I wish, but thanks for the compliment, bro!" Harrison said without turning around, in the thickest Californian-surfer accent he could manage. My eyes grew wide as I stifled a laugh and squeezed Harrison's hand again.

The elevator doors opened to the tenth floor. "Sorry to have bothered you guys," the young man said, elbowing his girlfriend as they moved past us to leave.

"No problem, dude!" Harrison once again reached for the 'Door Close' button and after pressing it, hit the twelfth-floor button repeatedly. Moments later we stepped out into a long, quiet, door-lined hallway. To our left, a lit-up red exit sign glared back at me, and we turned in its direction. The elevator doors closed behind us, and Harrison let out a deep breath. "Sorry you had to deal with that. We've been lucky so far to avoid being noticed. Let's hurry so we don't get trapped by anyone else."

"It's fine. Love the accent by the way. Totally gnarly." I laughed and twisted my hand into a 'hang loose' sign. "Oh, and rehab? Anything you want to tell me?"

"I tend to overcompensate on hiding who I am when things like that happen. Yeah, rehab, right? Give me a break. Filthy rags will publish almost anything they can think of about me. I've been off the radar, so they make up the most outrageous things they can imagine. It's likely someone in the lobby got a photo of us and that will be the headline for tomorrow." Harrison sounded irritated, but I knew it was with the newspapers and overzealous fans, not with me.

"Where exactly does your management think you are?" I questioned. *Why hadn't I thought to ask him this before? Shouldn't someone like Harrison have a bit more of an entourage around him when he's not working?* I thought.

"They know I'm on holiday, and that I started out in one place and have shifted to another. I've been in touch with the people that need to know, basically just Nick, my manager. He knows I'm safe and all that. Although, he does think I'm a bit mad to be driving around the country with someone I've just met. I told him you all but scooped me naked out of a stranger's pool to keep me from being arrested. That's when he offered to send me a security team." He laughed at himself. "Probably to save me from myself more than from the public."

Harrison slipped his key into the slot on our door, and down the hall the bell rang signaling the arrival of the other elevator. We weren't alone on this floor, despite being in the Presidential Suite, and when I glanced back toward the elevators, I saw the backside of a couple walking in the opposite direction. Thankfully, they turned and entered a room on the far end of the long corridor.

Once we were safely inside, Harrison collapsed onto the bed, pulling me down with him. We lay there on our backs, side by side, staring up at the ceiling for a moment before I took a deep breath and exhaled slowly. "That was...a lot," I said. "I'm sorry you have to deal with this all the time."

"Par for the course, darling. I've grown used to it now. I'm just sorry you had to see my serious face." He turned to me and scowled, scrunching his eyebrows together, wrinkling his nose, and poking out his lips.

"See, I can do that too. I'm ready for the spotlight!" I scrunched my entire face up into something between a scowl and a grimace and Harrison burst into laughter.

"Thank you, love. You take it all in stride." He half smirked, half laughed, his eyes never leaving mine, but then the smile left his face, and his expression turned serious, vulnerable. I shifted my position and took his face in my hands. The hair on his chin that only days ago had been a soft stubble, had now grown into a short patchy beard and mustache. I couldn't resist, and nuzzled my nose against his cheek, then gently kissed the tip of his nose, and then his chin. I smiled at him and when my lips met his, the passionate way he kissed me told me everything I needed to know. There was no longer any need to wonder how he felt about me; for the first time since we met, I could feel him falling in love with me and I, him.

I slipped my wrist behind his neck, and my hand cradled the back of his head, a grip of his curly hair between my fingers, my other hand fell to his chest where I could feel his heartbeat start to quicken the more my hands explored his body. Harrison's index finger traced along the high point of my cheek and down along my jawline before his hand wandered to my neck, down the front of my throat, and traced again across my collar bone.

Goosebumps rose all over my body as he turned to his side to face me. The hand that previously explored his chest was now beneath his t-shirt and I caressed his muscular back, alternating between my palm and my fingertips, gently massaging him as I made my way across his ribs and back to his defined chest. I could feel the strength in his hands as he moved them down to my back and further still to my waist, spending just enough time and attention on each to keep my mind racing, my body aching for more.

My fingertips lingered against the warmth of his bare chest before moving down to his sculpted abdomen. I felt his stomach muscles tense as he moved against my touch. He reached over his head and pulled his t-shirt off, his gold cross pendant falling back against his chest, reflecting light in rhythm with his breathing. My eyes met Harrison's as he slipped my shirt off and tossed it to the floor.

"You sure you wanna do this?" I asked, recalling the conversation we had in the tub last night.

As he kissed his way down my neck to my chest he mumbled, "I think we've made significant progress since last night's conversation." He stopped and made eye contact with me. "Don't you?"

"I'm not the one worried about giving in to my desires."

"Oh? Is that right?" He asked, then returned his mouth to the side of my neck.

"Every part of me knows exactly what I want." I said matter-of-factly.

I ran my fingers up into the back of his hair and gently pulled his mouth from my neck. When his eyes met mine, I smiled at him and kissed him with an unrestrained hunger he had yet to experience with me.

I took my time, teasing my fingertips across his body, moving slowly from one tattoo to the next, softly kissing each one attentively before moving on, his skin warm against my lips. He rolled from his side to his back and laid his head back against the bed, allowing me full control of him. The smirk on his face made it obvious he was enjoying everything I was doing but when I had covered his chest, his arms, and his abdomen with kisses, he stopped me.

"Last chance, are you sure you want to do this?" He laughed, making it obvious he was stalling. "We can stop if you—"

I put my index finger over his lips to stop him from speaking before he could finish his thought. I knew all I needed to after being in the studio with him tonight to be perfectly okay with what was about to happen. I kissed him again deeply and made my intentions clear.

"Do you want me to stop?" I asked and kissed him again, teasing him.

"Because I can." Another kiss.

"If you want me to." And another, this time I sucked his bottom lip into my mouth, teasing it with my tongue before slowly pulling my mouth away from his to watch his reaction.

He leaned in and kissed me again, his intensity increased and the way his hands felt all over my body let me know there would be no stopping. I wanted this, and him, and his hunger for me was evident.

Soon we were tangled in sheets, our bodies bare and sweaty. I gave myself to him completely and while I was a bit surprised by what a deliberate and thorough lover he was, I was not surprised by the ways he made me feel. I'd never physically experienced anything like this in my life. Harrison was a rock-solid machine. He knew when and where to be gentle, and he knew exactly when and where to be rough. Multiple times he discovered new ways to make me climax and he wasn't quiet about the effects I had on him either, which excited me and drove me even further into ecstasy. I found liberation in his outbursts, and it fueled me to push him to his limits. I'd bring him to the brink of orgasm then stop, shift my focus to my own pleasure or spend time teasing his body or his imagination with mine and then begin again. Time after time I did this until he lost control of himself deep inside me. A low primal moan escaped him and with veins clearly defined in his neck, the edges of his hair wet from sweat, he was breathless.

This scene played out multiple times throughout the evening, each of us taking our time pleasuring the other until we collapsed a final time in each other's arms, glistening with sweat, chests heaving and bodies trembling, sleep imminent.

When we awoke again at nearly two in the morning, we hadn't had anything to eat, we hadn't discussed travel for the next day, we hadn't done anything other than make love for hours.

"Alice? Love, are you awake?" Harrison kissed my cheek, still blushed pink from earlier.

"No." I smirked, eyes closed, still exhausted.

"Shower with me. Let's order room service." He said.

There was no response, other than my deliberate fake snoring.

"Alice, you are a feminine dream, love. Truly." Harrison jokingly nudged me, and I could hear his gorgeous smile even with my eyes closed.

"Chocolate cake. French toast. Strawberries," I mumbled, my face half covered by a pillow. "Powdered sugar."

Harrison dialed the front desk and made the special request. He asked that they place the cart just outside the door and not to knock. They obliged and Harrison placed the receiver back in its cradle.

He lifted me from the bed, both of us still naked, and hurled my upper body over his muscular shoulder, his arm wrapped tightly around the back of my knees. I shook with laughter. From my vantage point, I could see the little dimples in his back at the bottom of his spine and took the opportunity to pinch one of his perfectly toned butt cheeks. He reactively thrust his hips forward, nearly dropping me.

"You behave!" He shouted.

"Unlikely," I mumbled under my breath, just loud enough for him to hear me.

When he set me down, the marble floor of the bathroom was cold against my feet, and he wrapped his arms around me as I kissed his chest. He leaned his head back, savoring the feeling of my mouth on him and I kissed up the front of his throat to the underside of his chin. He lowered his face to me again and we shared a kiss that made me eager for another round. I was fully awake now and from the way his body was responding, so was Harrison.

He made love to me in the shower but never turned the water on, he said he loved the acoustics, and he once again made my body his playground. By the time we were done, I could barely stand, my legs were so weak. He showered quickly when we were finished, but I stayed a bit longer, immeasurably happy and exhausted all over again, thankful for a few minutes to myself as I stood blissful under the hot water, thinking about all that had transpired over the last eight hours.

This is real life, I thought to myself as I stepped out into the steamy bathroom, toweled off, and covered myself with a plush white hotel robe.

Back in the bedroom, I found Harrison uncovering the food that room service had delivered. He'd skipped the robe and was only wearing one of the hotel's bath towels. As I watched his movements, I thought, *this man's body is incredible*, and bit my bottom lip.

We ate together, sharing the French toast, strawberries, and good conversation. *If this is what life is like with Harrison Edwards, then life is wonderful*, I thought. I learned about his family in England and how he played football as a kid. Well, soccer to Americans, but football to Harrison. I loved to listen to him talk about himself before he became a celebrity, to watch the smiles that his memories would bring to his face as he told his stories. He talked about how he used to work in a candy shop as a teenager and how his weekends were divided between shifts at the shop and spending time with his granddad. Watching him explain the impact his granddad had on him and his beliefs and the trajectory of his life was heartwarming; he was so joyous when he spoke of his family. I was in love with Harrison, and it became clear to me in those moments at three in the morning somewhere in Nashville, Tennessee.

Long after the French toast was gone and the strawberries had been consumed, we discovered we both preferred each other's bodies instead of plates for the chocolate cake. All I had done was offer Harrison a taste of the frosting on my fingertip; he was the one who had taken my entire finger in his mouth, winding his tongue around it, licking and sucking in such a way that prompted me to unfasten the belt of my robe, offering up the rest of me. Harrison had used the frosting like finger paint, drawing hearts across my abdomen and proceeding to masterfully lick and suck it from my skin before he lifted me onto his lap with one swift movement. My mouth met his and as I opened his towel and let my robe fall away from my shoulders, our bodies once again became one.

This time Harrison was the one bringing me to the edge, and he did, many times. I wasn't sure what I liked more; his mouth did extraordinary work but so did the rest of him. He'd pull me back time and time again until finally I met euphoria like a head-on collision. Our last go-round in those early morning hours left us both in a deep, physically exhausted sleep.

When the sun found its way through the curtains and onto my face at seven-thirty that morning, I was still exhausted, but excited for what the day would bring. I moved to reach for Harrison and realized my entire body ached. It bordered somewhere between actual physical pain and the kind of ache that felt good to flex. I didn't have far to go to wrap myself around him though; he was right there beside me, facing the other direction, shielded from the sun, still asleep in the shadows cast by the curtains.

I lay there in the still of the morning and once again listened to him breathe his slow, even breaths. I imagined his tattoos moving with his ribs beneath the sheets when he inhaled, and I reached out, slid my arm across those tattooed ribs and laid my palm down against his belly. He nudged himself back against my body and I kissed him between his shoulder blades, before resting my lips against his warm tanned shoulder.

"Good morning." I whispered in his ear.

"Good morning," he whispered back to me. His hand reached around behind him and landed on my backside. "Good morning indeed," he laughed as he said it.

"Today's the day; we're going to New Orleans. Tomorrow's your event if you have any strength left for it. I hope I haven't exhausted you too much?" I was eager in some ways to get to New Orleans; I'd been there before and it's one of my favorite places, but I was also dreading what it could mean for me and Harrison. What would happen when this was all over? I didn't want to think about it; things were good and I wanted to ride the wave of happiness for now, no matter how hard it was going to hit the shore.

"I don't know where you learned to do all those things, but Goddamn girl, you are something else." The way Harrison said it made me blush.

"I think it's called…edging." I played dumb, but I knew exactly what I was doing to him, and I loved watching him react to me while I did it.

"Whatever it's called, it's fucking incredible," Harrison shook his head in disbelief. "I love every second of it and frankly I hope it never ends."

I turned to face him, and immediately a look of trepidation spread over his face. Worried he'd said too much, he watched my reaction nervously.

"Um, excuse me, sir, but you nearly killed me last night. Thank you very much." I tried to look stern but failed. I held my ground as long as I could with a straight face. "No really, thank you, VERY MUCH!" Now obviously joking, I couldn't hold back my happiness. "You've made me a VERY happy lady in the last few days, and last night was the frosting on the cake, no pun intended."

"Alice, I—" Harrison stopped, sat up on the edge of the bed, and began nervously running his fingers through his hair "I need to…well…I want to tell you something." He was clearly anxious and began fidgeting with his hands.

I sat up in the bed and turned on the light, needing to see him clearly not just in the shadows, nervous at what he might say.

"Is everything okay?" Of course, my mind began to race. *He's married. He's got an STD. He's on the run from the law. The road trip is over early.* What the hell was he going to say? *He's just not that into you, Alice.* No. That's not what I wanted to hear. None of that.

Harrison was still quiet. His head hung down and his curls fell forward from their loosely twisted position. He took a deep breath and said, "Alice, I don't think I've ever felt like this for anyone. Like, ever. I've met a lot of people, and I've spent time with women before, but never like this. I've been in relationships before. I've cared for people before. But…"

"Harrison." I reached out to him, his head still down, and wrapped my arm around his waist, laying my cheek against his shoulder.

He looked up and then turned to face me. His curls fell against his forehead and despite another attempt at moving them, one insisted on staying loose.

"Alice, I am one hundred percent, fully in love with you." Vulnerability took over his face as he spoke, "It's all happened so fast. I never expected this. I couldn't have anticipated this. I've torn you from your home and dragged you across the country...exposed you to random strangers trying to take your photo; my life is a rollercoaster of chaos, and I don't know what will happen after tomorrow or in the coming weeks or years, but I hope you're there with me. I want you there *with me* for all of it. Every day of it. I don't ever want to wake up another day without you beside me."

I began to tear up at his confession and I exhaled, only then realizing that I'd been holding my breath. I embraced him in an attempt to comfort him.

"Harrison," I said, then held his chin to make sure he was looking directly into my eyes, "I love you too. Just as much. And we'll figure it all out." As I tried to reassure him, he kissed me.

I could see the relief wash over him as his smile returned. *That left dimple might just be the death of me*, I thought.

"I love you. It feels so good to tell you that, Alice! I love you! I love you, darling!" He raised his voice each time he repeated himself and hugged me, then stood and lifted me off the ground, spinning us together in circles as we laughed together.

"I don't mean to ruin the moment, but we've got to get rolling if we're going to make it to New Orleans in time for your appearance. And this spinning is making me dizzy as hell!" I giggled as I said it.

Harrison plopped me down on the bed and gave me another quick kiss before turning to pack his things, humming and dancing as he grabbed for his clothes.

Coffee consumed and bags packed into the car, we left the hotel as quietly and inconspicuously as possible. Back on the road with eight hours of driving ahead of us, the sun beat warm against my face as Harrison drove south on Interstate 65 towards Birmingham. There were times throughout the day when I found myself just admiring him from the comfort of the passenger seat. I no longer turned away when he caught me looking at him, just smiled intently, as if by some telepathic transmission he could hear my voice inside his head telling him I love him.

We stopped a few times along the way for gasoline and snacks. Gummy bears were always his first choice, paired with a piece of fresh fruit. "Because, you know, balance," he would say with a sideways grin. I was sure there was nothing I didn't love about him.

We crossed Lake Pontchartrain in the late afternoon and made our way into the bustling city of New Orleans. I love the South, and New Orleans has always been one of my favorite places to visit. It's steeped in history, full of fascinating architecture, and the massive ancient live oak trees draped in Spanish moss are my favorite. Well, those and the alligators. And the music, and the people, and the traditions. And the food! I couldn't wait to eat.

New Orleans, this time of year, was not only hot but incredibly humid. We had been driving for hours with all the windows down and enjoyed the warm breezes blowing through the car, but now, as we were slowly winding through traffic to get to the hotel, things were getting stickier than I could stand. My anxiety was creeping in as well due to the crowds on the sidewalks, which made my body feel hotter than it actually was. I kept thinking about how busy the city is, and with such incredibly slow-moving traffic, Harrison could easily be recognized and bombarded quickly. *What would I do if that happened?* As usual, my thoughts began to carry me away.

Getting to the Four Seasons on world-famous Canal Street was a headache, a situation I was glad I was only a passenger for, so when Harrison pulled the car up to the curb directly in front of the hotel, I let out a sigh of relief. *Thank God that's over,* I thought.

As soon as I stepped out into the heat of the afternoon, somewhere in the distance a second-line brass band was playing, and I could picture the bride and groom jubilantly dancing through the streets to the beat of the music, their guests following close behind with just as much enthusiasm. The sound hitting my ears was enough to set my body in motion, and I grabbed Harrison by the hand to join me, spinning him in a circle, giggling and dancing with abandon.

"Welcome to New Orleans, baby!" I wrapped my arms around him, despite the temperature, and kissed him.

A team of bellhops rushed from the front of the hotel, ready to carry whatever luggage we had with us. Target bags. Our luggage was currently a bunch of reusable Target bags full of shorts, t-shirts, and random toiletries. If I ever felt out of place, it was now; standing there sweaty in my shorts and sneakers with a t-shirt on, and my wind-blown hair thrown into a messy knot in a heap on top of my head. *Tragic.*

Our reception here was much different than it had been at previous hotels. New Orleans is a city of extravagance, excess and flair after all. From behind the bellhops came a man and a woman each dressed in all black with glistening gold embellishments and white gloves, offering us each a glass of chilled champagne in crystal flutes and directing us into the VIP guest entrance. Once inside, things got even fancier. Orbs of light danced and rainbows flashed off the facets of the chandeliers, soft piano music played in the background accompanied by the brassy sounds of a trumpet. *Of course, this is New Orleans, baby! Play those horns!* I could only smile and gaze around in wonderment at my surroundings as we were introduced to our personal hostess, who showed us to the VIP elevator.

On the way up, we were briefed about how the hotel had been expecting us and had outfitted our room with all the comforts of home, and how they would go above and beyond for 'Mr. Edwards'...anything he needed would be promptly taken care of. No matter the time or the complexity of the request, the hotel could handle all that our hearts desired.

When the spa services were explained, Harrison asked for an in-room couples' massage forty-five minutes after dinner was completed, to be followed by private use of the steam room. He explained that he wanted to be able to pamper his vocal cords ahead of tomorrow's event, then requested two humidifiers be brought to our suite. Harrison also informed the hostess that I was his very special guest and that anything I wanted; I shall have. "My Alice," as he called me, "is to receive top-notch attention at all times."

I'm not sure I can explain the way I felt when he spoke like that. My chest felt tight and my heart felt as if it was swelling beyond the confines of my body. My pulse quickened and my smile was no longer under my control. Being loved by Harrison Edwards felt like an out-of-body experience, like a billion tiny flickers of electricity were igniting from every pore on my body and surging all through my physical being. I felt adored and loved and taken care of.

Once inside the top-floor Presidential Suite, finally alone again, I explored the window-filled space while Harrison called his manager to let him know we had arrived. In the time it took for him to relay that message, I not only discovered the incredible black marble bathroom, complete with the fanciest gold tub I had ever seen, but then wandered out to the private balcony. *These spaces just keep getting more and more luxurious,* I thought. Harrison found me looking out over the city and wrapped his strong arms around me from behind.

"Darling! We made it! We've landed!" he exclaimed. "Look at us, on top of the world!" He stretched his arms open wide. His smile could bring sun to the darkest days, and with every minute that passed, I couldn't help but be more in love with him.

"Yes! I see! Can you believe the power of that water?" I pointed down at the Mississippi River below. It looked like black coffee swirling with creamer, powerfully churning past us. I'd seen the river before, but not from this height – we were on the thirty-fourth floor – and despite my fear of heights, I was enjoying this view.

"Wanna go for a swim?" Harrison jokingly nudged me toward the railing.

"Jesus, no! I'm all set with that, thanks." I turned back toward the suite just as there was a knock at the door.

"I'll get it love; you enjoy the view." I said and headed for the door.

85

I checked the peephole, then opened the door, and standing in front of me was a large clothing rack laden with garment bags.

"The Gucci garments for Mr. Edwards," an older man's voice with a thick southern accent drawled in my direction, but I couldn't find a human to connect it to.

"Certainly, please, come in. Can I help you with that?" I offered, but before I could lift a hand, the rack moved swiftly into the center of the large room. Only once it was past me could I see that it was being navigated by an adorable elder gentleman who, despite his small stature, maneuvered the rack with ease.

Harrison thanked the man with a hefty tip and as he left, a new face appeared at the door. Short in stature but large in personality, she announced in an equally heavy southern accent that her name was Miss Josephine and she had been asked to come here to tailor some gowns.

Harrison welcomed her in and introduced her to me. "This is my lady, my Alice, and we aim to find something on this rack that makes her feel stunning, Miss Josephine! Can you see to tailoring it to fit her like a second skin?"

"Certainly, Mr. Edwards. I'm here to help. These sure are some awful pretty dresses. Miss Alice, you are one blessed lady! You got you a good one, girl!"

I smiled at her and bowed my head as I felt the heat of embarrassment once again boil into my cheeks. I felt filthy after the car ride and didn't realize I would be trying these dresses on so quickly after arrival, but it made sense I guess, considering whatever I chose would have to be altered quickly.

Things like that usually took quite a bit of time, but it seemed Harrison had hired the best to help me look the part.

"Thank you, yes, I certainly do feel quite lucky these days." I sheepishly glanced in Harrison's direction.

Harrison flashed that famous grin and started stripping the bags off of the dresses before hanging them back on the rack. There were gowns of satin, tulle and sequins in various shapes and shades. There was even a short cocktail dress that caught my eye.

"What color will you be wearing?" I asked Harrison as I placed a nervous hand on his shoulder.

"Black mostly," he said, smirking. I could tell he sensed how nervous I was when he reached up and placed his hand on top of mine. "Everything is fine, love. We'll be alright," he whispered in my ear, trying to settle my nerves without embarrassing me in front of Miss Josephine.

"Mostly? What does that even mean? What other color will there be? Which one of these do you prefer?" I questioned as I shuffled through the hanging gowns.

Harrison pulled at the hangers, his eyes dissecting the bodice then the length of each of the dresses, examining them one by one. First, he moved a black, off-the-shoulder, fully sequined floor-length gown with a very high slit to one end of the rack, then a vibrant red satin gown with a plunging neckline, and lastly, a gold sequined floor-length gown that just screamed opulence.

"I like them all, but that's just because they'll be on you. My tux has a little more pizzazz than just plain black, there'll be some satin and some sequined embellishments, there may even be a few feathers. This black sequin gown will go nicely with it, I think." He said, smiling as he continued to move the garments around the rack.

"Pizzazz...and feathers? Hmph, okay. You never cease to surprise me Harrison," I said, smiling. "Let's stop looking and start narrowing down then; we'll be here all night if we don't make a move." I pulled a dress from the rack and went to the other room to try it on.

Over the next hour, I tried all of them on, as well as the short cream-colored cocktail dress and a more dramatic-looking strapless, side-cinched deep burgundy number, but it was a little too over-the-top for me. They *all* felt over-the-top but let's face it, I wasn't going to the grocery store; I was going to a star-studded, celebrity-filled event. I loved them all, but noticed Harrison's eyes light up when he saw me in the black one he had initially chosen. It already fit me fairly well, despite my large chest and wide hips, so hopefully Miss Josephine's job wouldn't be too time-consuming or difficult.

I'm fairly curvy, and I worried it might be hard to pull off a sequined look, but Harrison's eyes and hands had traveled all of my curves and seemed to enjoy them just as they were, so I convinced myself black was timeless, and would match his suit no matter what secondary color he wore. Miss Josephine took all the necessary measurements, marked and pinned the gown, and off she went to make the adjustments. She said she'd be back in the morning around nine to do a final fitting and handle the hem once I'd chosen the shoes I'd be wearing. When the door closed behind her, I collapsed in a panic on the bed.

"Harrison. I don't even know what kind of event I'm going to! Where will I find shoes? How do I wear a dress like that and not have any makeup or a way to do my hair? I don't want to embarrass you." I rolled over and plunged my face into the pillows.

"Darling. I will never let you fall; I've got you. I waited until you chose your gown and sent a text to my team to deliver a variety of shoe options to the hotel. I included a photo of the dress. Trust them, they keep me looking dapper, and they're your team now too. I've called for a professional makeup artist to do whatever you want done, and her team will bring a stylist for your hair. Love, you'll be just as fabulous tomorrow evening as you are to me right now. I promise."

I pulled my face from the pillows, my hair wafting in multiple directions like a lion's mane. I certainly wasn't feeling fabulous at the moment.

"Thank you. I'm not used to this, that's for sure." I was exhausted and really just wanted to relax, so I rifled through my bags to find what I needed for a shower.

"Enjoy your shower, love. When you're done, we'll have a drink and relax for a bit. Then dinner. Be thinking of what would taste good, okay?" Harrison tapped me on the butt and winked at me when I walked by him. There was that left dimple again, just begging for attention.

"Some more of that chocolate frosting would be good." I shot Harrison a crooked smile over my shoulder and my eyes invited him to follow me into the bathroom. He immediately shot off the bed and in the same movement pulled his shirt over his head, throwing it to the floor. As soon as he reached me, he started peeling my clothes off.

As one, we touched almost every flat surface, both vertical and horizontal including the heated marble bench in the shower, the bathroom counter, and even the empty bathtub before moving through the hotel room. Surely housekeeping had cleaned sweaty silhouettes off that wall of windows before, right? I couldn't get enough of this man, and he could rise to the occasion every single time without batting an eye. Eventually, we ended up back in the bathroom, this time to actually get clean.

Washed, dried, and dressed for the evening, we sent out our dirty clothes to be laundered and then ordered room service. Harrison had something French I couldn't pronounce; it was a piece of fish, I knew that much, along with a vegetable soup that he raved about, claiming it deserved a ten-star rating, even though he'd promptly burned his tongue on his first sip. So of course, because he kept asking, I tried it, and indeed it was amazing. I ordered a salad with grilled chicken breast because in the back of my mind I was worried about my measurements for tomorrow. I was already bloated from the heat and humidity; I didn't need to add to it. I rationalized the appetizer portion of Shrimp Creole with the theory that I likely just sweat out 1,500 calories in my romp with Harrison, so maybe it would even itself out. It was a delicious dinner, in a beautiful city, inside a magnificent hotel with a charming, handsome, and caring man. With each passing moment I was more taken with him, grateful for every second we shared.

As Harrison sipped on a bourbon afterwards, I opted for a Shirley Temple, mindful that I needed to be fully aware, awake, and ready for whatever may come tomorrow. Being hungover wasn't on my lengthy to-do list. We watched the sun fall lower and lower in the sky as we snuggled together on a chaise lounge out on the balcony until another knock came at our door. It was time for our couples' massage at the spa.

I was thankful for the relaxation the massage provided. The masseurs worked on us for well over an hour, and their skillful hands melted away all the stress and tension that driving across the country had created. I hoped Harrison felt the same; I'd watched him over the last few days when he thought I wasn't looking, noticing in the quiet moments that he was lost somewhere within himself. I'm certain it revolved around his upcoming appearance, but I still hoped that he was able to find some release from it. As for me, between the massage, the newfound love, and the next-level sex we'd been having, I really had nothing to be overly stressed about, and certainly not in comparison to what Harrison was up against. I wondered if we talked about it, maybe he wouldn't feel quite so overwhelmed by it all.

"Tell me about tomorrow. I've agreed to go as your date, but what exactly is happening? Are you just making an appearance? Will anyone else be doing the same or are you the guest of honor? What kind of a scene is this going to be?" I asked.

"It's a wedding. My manager's brother Jack is getting married, and they've asked me to sing a song for them during the reception. It's likely to be fairly glitzy, and there will be a lot of industry people there. And, like most of these kinds of things, some of the candid photos will likely get leaked to the press. I want you to be prepared for that."

"It's okay, I'm confident you've got a good team to get me all snazzy looking. I won't let you down. I won't embarrass you," I tried to make him feel confident in me even when I wasn't feeling very confident in myself.

"Alice, I won't leave your side other than during my performance; I promise you that. I won't let you feel nervous or overlooked, and I'll introduce you to the people you'll be with while I'm on stage so you can get to know them early on." Harrison's eyes were so sincere, and I appreciated how thoughtful he was being, but his words felt different, more like promises than assurances. Like maybe this is where a past relationship may have gone wrong for him, and he was making sure not to make the same mistakes again.

I squeezed his hand in mine as we walked toward the steam room. "Thank you for looking after me," I said. "It means more than you realize."

"Of course, darling. We'll get there, get our table, have drinks if you like—although I'm only going to be drinking water until after my performance. We may do some dancing if you're up for it. Then around six-forty-five, I perform, then we go back to dancing and mingling. Whenever you're ready to leave, just let me know, and we'll go."

We got comfortable in the warmth of the steam room, and Harrison continued. "I'm nervous, Alice. I've never had to sing in front of such a large group of my peers, and this is a huge deal. Friends or not, these people can be vicious, and they'll all have cameras, recording me. Like I said, likely posting it all over the internet. The scrutiny is coming, and I've got an album in the works. If this goes bad, the album will fail." Harrison leaned his head back and closed his eyes.

I felt for him; the stress of it all must be suffocating. And I could understand nerves, sure, but not on this level. He had a ton hanging in the balance of this performance. It was meant to be one song for fun at a friend's wedding, and it was easy to see it that way as an outsider. But to stand in his shoes, this one blip in time would assuredly send a ripple effect through his entire music career no matter how it's received. Harrison had a few roles in films where he did some minor singing parts; I knew because I'd seen them, and they were good. But I'd also heard him sing to me one-on-one. In my eyes he's amazing, and even though I'm a bit biased, I could confidently vouch for him being a truly one-of-a-kind artist.

"I've heard you sing Harrison, and I've seen your performances in films before. You're incredible. I know it, and you know it, and frankly, they all know it too. It's a wedding, it's not like you're singing for the Royal Family, and I know it's easy for me to say that; I'm not the one whose career is potentially on the line, but it's a private event, and yes, people will record it, and people will post it on the internet. But this is how some careers are started. This could be the launch of your next wild adventure. Before you know it, you'll be winning prestigious awards and headlining stadiums. Just you wait and see. You have to trust in yourself and your abilities. They've never steered you wrong." I meant what I said; I just hoped he believed in himself as much as I believed in him.

"Yeah, I know you're right. I just need to get out of my own head a bit. Feels like the walls are closing in on me." He sighed deeply and closed his eyes again.

Over the next hour, I quietly observed him while we sat in comfortable silence. I didn't want to interrupt whatever process he was using to calm his nerves about tomorrow. With his head laid back against the wall, his curls damp against his forehead from the humidity, I admired the length of his eyelashes as they lay against his cheeks. They made me want to lean over and kiss him, but I stopped myself. The calm rise and fall of his chest and the way the steam created tiny droplets of water in his chest hair was soothing and erotic all at the same time, and the way his nostrils would flare when his thoughts veered into a place he didn't want to be was a sure sign he was working through his fears. Through it all, he never let go of my hand, and it was a comfort to know he found solace in me.

When a soft bell chimed, letting us know our session was complete, Harrison opened his eyes and said softly, "You ready?"

I nodded and we made our way to the shower together. In the silence, we took turns lathering each other's bodies, pausing from time to time to get lost in each other's eyes, trading soft kisses under the stream of hot water. We rinsed ourselves and wrapped fresh new robes around our tired frames before heading back to the suite. Tonight had been a purely emotional experience, not a sexual one. I had seen Harrison over the last few days as his playful silly self, and as a voracious, meticulous, and selfless lover. Now, I was watching a delicate, vulnerable side find its way through. He took his work, his play, and his heart seriously; and as each side of him presented itself to me, I found new reasons and new ways to love and appreciate him.

We got back to our suite and found dinner had been cleared from the room and a new bottle of champagne was propped in an ice bath near the bed ready to be opened. The lights were dim and there were chocolates on our pillows. Everything was calm and relaxing against the hum of the humidifiers. Harrison made a few quick phone calls from the balcony and I busied myself by sorting through our recently delivered clean laundry, dividing it into a pile of my things and a stack belonging to him. Once the calls were made and the laundry was put away, we settled into bed together.

"I extended our stay; I hope that's okay? I thought maybe after tomorrow we could spend a day or two here in the city. You said you love it here, and I've only ever been here for work. I'd love for you to show me around the things that make you happy here."

"Oh, I'd love to. Tell me, how do you feel about kayaking with alligators?" I kept as straight a face as I could, waiting for his reaction.

"Um, not sure I'm quite into that, also unsure if management would be too excited about me risking my life." He played it off like he was joking but I could tell some part of him took me seriously.

"We'll take a regular boat then; it's harder for them to bite through aluminum." Still straight-faced I nodded as if I was making a mental note and waited again for Harrison's reaction.

He scrunched up his nose and his eyebrows pulled together. "Umm…" he hesitated.

My God, I love his face. I watched his apprehension argue with his willingness to make me happy before letting him off the hook.

"I'm kidding!" I nudged him. "No way I'm risking anything happening to you, babe. You might actually find what I like boring though. Architecture, history, folklore. Voodoo! Yes. Oh, and the cemeteries. OH! No wait, the food. And I'd love it if we could go to the zoo. The zoo here is awesome. I got a fried turkey leg at the New Orleans Zoo once and it was one of the best things—" I was rambling, but stopped when I realized Harrison was staring at me smiling, enamored.

He cocked his head to the side. "I love you," he said it as if loving me was something he couldn't stop even if he wanted to.

I took his face in my hands and kissed each of his dimples, and then his nose and then his chin which by now was fully disguised in an ever-lengthening patchy beard. I'd never really seen him with facial hair, but I liked the scruff on him. I kissed him, pausing there for a moment, the fullness of his bottom lip cradled between mine, then kissed him again, full on the mouth.

"Well, I love *you*." I lingered in front of him, holding eye contact, my hands still cradling his face. Part of me was in disbelief that he was the man in front of me, loving me out loud, and the other part of me was blissfully happy that it was. Could he tell how much I cared for him? I hoped so.

I leaned in and kissed him gently again. No matter how many times his lips touched mine, it felt like the first time, every time. The rush of adrenaline, the excitement of it surged through my entire body. His lips were perfect, full and soft, and his kisses unapologetically sensual. There was just something about him that felt like magic to me.

He pulled away from me, smirking, and took a long look at me before he spoke again.

"Tomorrow's going to be fun, but it's also going to be a lot to take in. I'll be in and out in the morning, but we'll have our fittings together first. Then I'll run over to the venue, do sound check for about an hour or so. After that, I plan to steer clear while you're getting your hair and makeup done. We'll head over to the venue a little after three, with our arrival closer to four."

I loved to watch him speak. The way his tongue and his lips worked in unison, and the way his accent dripped off the word 'four' was enough to make me want to strip him naked and do all sorts of scandalous things to him, but I held myself back, as clearly tomorrow was still on his mind. Not to mention, after the last twenty-four hours I wasn't sure he had anything left in the tank. I'd likely depleted his resources and figured he could use a little time to refuel.

"I'm sure it will all be fine," I said. "I can roll with the punches, and having someone else do my hair and makeup takes most of the pressure off me anyhow. I'm sure they'll have us looking like perfection as a couple..." I stopped short of finishing my sentence because I wasn't sure we even were an actual couple at this point. *Would this event be our coming out to the public? How would he introduce me to the world?*

"What will you tell people about us?" I asked.

"I'll simply say 'World, this is my lady, Alice. We've been lucky enough to find one another in the absolute insanity of this world, and we're madly in love.'" Harrison beamed as he said it. "Is that okay?"

"Of course! It's fine with me. I just wasn't sure if I was asked what the appropriate response should be. I want to make sure we're on the same page; the last thing I want to do is say the wrong thing."

"Well, we are together, aren't we? That's what I want, for us to be in an actual, real relationship, exclusively together, working toward forever. I want forever with you, Alice."

I couldn't help but smile at his admission. "I want that too. I just don't want to embarrass you. I'm protective of your image, and I certainly don't want to be the one that causes any harm to it."

"You'll do fine, darling. We're on the same page; don't you worry about a thing." He pulled me into him and kissed my forehead to reassure me.

An unexpected knock at the door tore through the darkness and startled us both. It was late, and we hadn't ordered any room service. *Weird. Who could be knocking at this hour?* Harrison told me to sit tight while he checked it out, then got up and padded off to the door. The way he took control of certain situations was a comfort and I loved the feeling of knowing he could keep me safe and take care of me. I couldn't see the door from the bed but could hear Harrison speaking to the same gentleman from earlier. His slow southern accent was quick to give him away. I heard Harrison usher him into the living room area, then thank him and moments later, I heard the door close.

"Just the staff, delivering your shoes and accessories." I could see he was hiding something behind his back when he reached to turn on the bedside light. "And, well…this." He held out an oversized red velvet box in my direction as he sat down on the bed.

"What's this?" I asked. I'd seen a box like this before in the movies, but not in real life.

"Open it." Harrison's expression remained pensive but eager.

I took the box from his hands and was surprised by its weight. My eyes grew big as I looked at him in disbelief. "Harrison."

"Darling…open it."

Reluctantly I lifted the top and couldn't believe my eyes. There laid a showstopper of a diamond necklace, and as if that wasn't enough, there were matching drop earrings settled into the center of the box. I don't know a whole lot about diamond cuts or fancy jewels, but in my mind, this was reminiscent of something royalty would wear. There were seemingly hundreds of various shapes and sizes of perfectly crystal-clear diamonds laid into intricate and elegant white gold settings. The sparkles nearly blinded me as the millions of tiny facets caught the light. Speechless, all I could do was stare and shake my head. I would have covered my open mouth, but I needed both of my hands to hold the weight of the box.

"They're only on loan for tomorrow." Harrison watched my reaction relax before he reached into his robe pocket and pulled out a much smaller box, with a matching red velvet exterior.

"But this, darling, this is yours to keep if you'll have it. If you'll have...me." Harrison slid down from the edge of the bed onto one knee. He inhaled deeply, bit the corner of his bottom lip as his nostrils flared, then exhaled slowly and looked up at me. I felt as if my heart had stopped beating completely.

"Alice, I don't ever want to live another moment of my life in fear that I could lose you. This is sudden, I realize, but these last few days...they've changed my entire life. You've changed my life. Getting to know you, sharing my days and my nights, and my body with you, allowing myself to be vulnerable with you, and learning what it feels like for someone to truly love me for who I am has changed my entire perspective about the future. I never thought I would ever find someone who's so perfect for me. I thought I'd always be alone, and then you found me. We found each other. This life is fleeting, and I feel like I've already spent enough of my life without you. Alice..." Harrison's hands were visibly trembling as he opened the box, revealing a brilliant and massive emerald cut solitaire diamond engagement ring, the delicate band laden with smaller, intricately cut diamonds.

"Alice, will you do me the honor of being my wife?" he asked nervously.

My chin began to tremble and tears fell to my cheeks as I set the heavy necklace box on the bed beside me. I was in complete disbelief at what was happening, and I struggled to catch my breath. *Things like this just don't happen to people like me*, I thought. *His Wife! He wants me to be his wife?!* I was spiraling. *Get it together, Alice.* I shook my head again, snapping myself away from my internal dialogue and back to the life-altering reality in front of me.

"YES! A million times, yes! Yes! Yes! Yes!" The words burst out of me, as I laughed and cried all at the same time.

Harrison began to get up off the floor to hug me, but I met him halfway, both of us ending up on the floor in a giggling, tear-soaked heap.

"I love you, Harrison. I will absolutely be your wife." I was completely overjoyed and covered his face in kisses. We sat up and faced one another and he carefully slipped the ring onto my finger. I couldn't help but stare at it, then at Harrison's smiling face, and back at the ring, in disbelief.

"How did you...when did you have the time to...I just..." I stammered.

"From the moment you told me to grab my clothes at the pool I knew you were someone that would protect me from the craziness of the world I live in. I knew you would be someone that I could invest my trust and love into, someone that would give back to me what I give to them. Getting to know you during all our hours driving in the car and seeing how you handled the people in the lobby and the elevators and just watching you go from being nervous to being so comfortable with me...Alice, I was in love with you from the moment I laid eyes on you."

"I knew I could fall for you the first time you smiled at me, Harrison. The first time you called me 'darling', I was already falling. I can't wait to share the rest of my life with you. I feel like I'm living in a daydream!" I wrapped my arms around him once more.

"In the morning we'll have breakfast, do our respective fittings, and you can choose shoes and all that. But tonight, let's just soak in the glow of it all, shall we, darling? I'm so thankful for you." He kissed my forehead.

I wasn't thinking about planning a wedding or what the future looked like as we climbed back into bed together. In my mind, I just wanted to live in this moment and stay here for as long as I could. I laid my head and my body against my husband-to-be and, wrapped in the warmth of his arms, I caressed his bare chest with my fingertips, the wisps of chest hair moving against my touch. The weight of the ring on my finger reminded me that I was now someone's fiancée. *What a night this has turned out to be*, w*hat a night indeed.* I nuzzled my cheek further against his chest and let myself fall into thoughts of the future as we lay there together, newly engaged, blissfully in love.

The next morning there was a buzz in the air, an electricity that was nearly palpable. Harrison and I shared breakfast on the balcony while the city came to life. We watched the massive cargo ships and tugboats pass below us and listened to the loud rush of the churning river against the sounds of automobiles and streetcars. I threw small bits of my croissant to the tiny birds that landed on the railing and smiled at the cooing pigeons. Everything was right with the world. *This day is going to be spectacular,* I thought. Harrison was understandably in his head again, and I knew it was because of the responsibilities he had coming up this evening. Despite all of that, there was no mistaking how happy he was with me, and I, with him.

When breakfast was finished, Harrison told me he'd have his final fitting here, then be taking his things with him to another room in the hotel to get himself ready because he wanted to 'pick me up as if we were going on a proper date.' I was okay with it; ever the gentleman, he wanted to do something sweet for me. Plus, I certainly had enough to contend with myself and figured his artistic process shouldn't be hindered by a bunch of people in here fussing over me. I kissed him goodbye long and slow, and we exchanged 'I love you's as he went down the hallway to the other bedroom of the suite for his final fitting with his tailor. I wouldn't see him again until around three this afternoon.

When Miss Josephine knocked at the door, I let her in, and it took her no time at all to notice the new accessory on my hand. She threw her arms around me and gave me a tight squeeze as if she and I were long-lost family. I really enjoyed Miss Josephine's company; maybe it was just southern hospitality, but there was something about her presence that made me feel at ease.

I showed her all the shoes I had to choose from, and we began the process of picking out which would be best with my beautiful black sequined gown. Something understated made the most sense, not too flashy and relatively comfortable. A pair of scalloped-edge patent leather Christian Louboutin stilettos caught my eye, and I knew they would be perfect. Harrison was a little over six feet tall, and I a mere five-foot-three. So, this heel would give me some height, lengthen my legs, and still keep me shorter than my fiancé.

FIANCÉ.

Just the thought of the word sent a shiver over my body. I felt like the luckiest woman alive, having finally accepted that if I was to be Mrs. Harrison Edwards there would only be more of this type of treatment in the future. What felt like a random day of pampering would soon become normal. Hair, make-up, racks of clothes and shoes, diamonds on loan…I'd have a team for myself that would do all of these things for me.

I realized then, Harrison has a world of women to choose from and of them all, I was the one he'd chosen. It was an incredibly empowering feeling, one I wasn't used to, but one I was determined to lean into. My tendency to shy away from attention was going to be a thing of the past.

While I showered, Miss Josephine took care of the final details, making sure the hem landed just right for the height of my shoes and that the slit of my gown landed at just the right spot on my thigh. I couldn't wait for Harrison to see me in my dress, hair and makeup, looking like elegance personified. He'd only ever seen me in ratty shorts and a t-shirt, so if he loved me before, this poor man's heart was going to explode tonight.

Soon, a demure young woman arrived to take care of my nails. I chose a barely-there shade of pink while she focused on what may have been the greatest leg massage of my entire life, then she moved on to my pedicure, then my manicure. I'd always kept my fingernails short, but over the last few days, they'd grown to a length just enough for me to feel a bit more fancy than usual. I opted to keep them long, knowing people would be focusing on, and potentially taking photos of my hands, considering the giant chandelier I now had attached to my finger.

Shortly after the nail technician left, a new group of four women appeared almost out of thin air, loaded down with rolling suitcases and multiple shoulder bags containing hair tools, sprays, various shades and lengths of hair extensions, and enough makeup to paint everyone in the hotel from head to toe. They were a very talkative group, the polar opposite from the woman that just left, and I was glad now for the distraction. One woman talked so fast I could barely understand what she was saying, and I simply nodded along with nearly everything that sounded like a question. They decided to add a few dirty-blonde highlights with the use of clip-in extensions to give my long dark hair more dimension, and over the next few hours coiled my length up into a messy bun, the sides formed into a loose braid encircling the crown of my head. Tendrils of dark curls fell at random for a look that was both elegant and relaxed.

I chose soft neutral makeup that accentuated my eyes and the cheekbones I'd been complimented on my entire life, and paired it with a muted, mauve-toned lipstick, and wispy false lashes. When the ladies had finally finished with me, I turned to the mirror to see myself for the first time since this process began and I could've cried; the woman looking back at me was not at all who I expected to see. I didn't know what I expected honestly, but I stood there shocked at my reflection.

For the first time since I could remember, I felt like a sight to behold, and all the nerves and fears I'd carried about tonight suddenly vanished. And I wasn't even dressed yet! I could feel the tingle in my nose as tears started to form in my eyes but reminded myself that it took hours to get to this point and I didn't want to ruin the hard work these women had so finely crafted. The makeup made my skin look flawless, the usual anxiety-driven redness in my cheeks no longer existed; all that remained was the perfect amount of blush swept across them. The eyelashes, just the right length, not too much. The undertones in my lipstick made my teeth look ten shades whiter, and I wondered how Harrison would react to the peek-a-boo blond in my hair.

The frenzy of the day had finally subsided and Harrison was due to pick me up in about an hour, so I relaxed in the comfort of my robe and bare feet, enjoying the silence now that I was alone. I glanced down at my left hand; the weight of the diamond had caused it to shift and rest against my pinky. I straightened the stone back to the top of my finger and smiled while my mind played back the events that transpired over the last few days. Things had changed so much in such a short time; new memories had been made, a new life path had been carved out ahead of me and the icing on the cake – the absolute dream of a man I now have in my life. I couldn't help but smile to myself the more I thought about it.

I walked to the mirror once again and reached for the earrings Harrison had chosen for me. His fashion sense was impeccable, and I was fortunate to be loved by someone so tuned in to the fine details. I carefully affixed each earring, making sure that each back was attached snugly. Just the thought of one of them slipping from my ear, only to be lost in a sea of dancing feet, terrified me. These things were so heavy that surely, I'd notice if one became loose. Ever the worrier, I reached again for the backs to tighten them just a bit more before I slid my hands carefully into the box that held the necklace, gently lifting the diamonds from their resting place. I drew it up to my neck, careful not to leave a single fingerprint behind to dampen the brilliance of these diamonds. It felt like a weighted blanket across my chest, the heft of the stones was immense. When I felt the clasp connect, I carefully pulled my hands away and stepped back to admire myself at full length in the mirror.

I tugged at the neckline of my robe, pulling it loose to expose the necklace against my bare skin, then untied the knot at my waist and dropped my robe to the floor. Standing there nearly naked, I admired myself. With nothing on but a set of sheer black Gucci bra and panties and the hundreds of thousands of dollars' worth of diamonds that draped from my ears, neck, and now my finger, for the first time in my life, I was truly in awe of myself. The gown went on easily and fit like a glove, perfectly accentuating my every curve, and I shimmered from head to toe in diamonds and black sequins. The earrings were the perfect length, and the necklace draped itself across my décolletage as if it were constructed specifically to be worn on my body with this exact gown. I flashed myself one last smile in the mirror and slipped on my shoes. Harrison Edwards was in for the surprise of his life tonight.

Promptly at three came a knock on the door. I took another quick glance at myself in the mirror, pressed my lips together making sure the gloss atop my lipstick looked perfect, then adjusted my chest for maximum cleavage. When everything was in place, I opened the door, and before me stood the man of my dreams.

The look on Harrison's face was a combination of surprise, lust, and pure adoration. His mouth fell open, but no words came out.

"That bad, huh? You think I should just stay here?" I shifted to turn around and let the door start to close. The exaggerated resignation in my voice prompted Harrison to finally speak.

"My God, Alice, you are...transcendent!" He seemed stunned; his eyes wide with wonderment.

"Thank you, sir. You clean up nicely yourself." I took his hand, almost every finger encircled by one of his chunky gold rings. I took a step back as I raised his arm and tried to spin him, "Show me the goods, babe, this suit is..." I made a chef's kiss gesture with my other hand.

His tux was black on black, laid over a classic black shirt, the peaked lapel a glossy black satin, while his bow tie along with his breast and jacket pocket openings were adorned in eye-catching black sequins. They also glimmered along the outside seams of his pants, leading down to glossy black shoes, while flashy diamond cufflinks accentuated his wrists. I noticed Harrison's facial hair was gone, once again exposing his herculean jawline. His hair had been freshly cut and his dark curls had been purposefully arranged in a quiff up and away from his face.

"Gucci loves me." Harrison's accent always slowed his words, but this time so did the laugh that snuck past his smile.

"I love you more than Gucci does, you can count on that." I shook my head as I checked out my future husband.

"Darling, I think Gucci loves you the most." He stared back at me, fully enamored.

"You don't think we'll outshine the bride and groom, do you?" I asked.

"These people know me, they know my persona, they know what to expect from me. And now, the world is going to know you, my love. Are you ready for this?" I nodded as he took my hand. "Truly Alice, you are a vision. I wanna kiss you but I can't, I'm afraid I'd ruin…all of this." He waved his hand in front of my face then lifted my hand to his lips to kiss it instead. And with that, we headed for the car.

The wedding ceremony was beautiful. With nearly five hundred guests in attendance, it was easy for me to blend into the crowd. Even though Harrison's involvement drew a lot of attention, I didn't feel as self-conscious as I thought I would. Most of the guests were celebrities and all of them dressed like they were attending the Oscars, but Harrison never left my side and fielded most of the questions that were asked about us, which was a relief. Repeatedly he introduced me as his 'fiancée', followed by "I can't wait to make her my wife." Too many photos to count were taken of us together, and each time, Harrison made sure my left hand was in the frame. I could feel how proud he was to show me off and let the world know he was no longer on the market, and that made me love him even more.

Dinner was served and cleared away as the late afternoon slipped into evening. The speeches had been given by the best man and the maid of honor, and the first dance had been shared when guests began to crowd onto the dance floor. I sat at our table with Harrison and another couple, chatting about random topics, glancing around observing what people were wearing and barely sipping my champagne, when Harrison leaned in and whispered to me that he needed to get backstage. I kissed his earlobe, and whispered "I love you" in his ear before wiping away the lip gloss I'd left behind. He kissed my lips and paused to look at me, his eyes searching for reassurance.

"You're gonna knock 'em dead," I said. "I'm so proud of you, babe. Oh, make sure you clean this up before you get started." I gestured at the lip gloss I'd left on his lips.

"One for good measure." He kissed me again, flashed his angelic smile, and disappeared into the crowd.

For some reason I felt anxious without him next to me, but wasn't entirely sure why. After all, I wasn't the one singing for the first time in front of five hundred people, thank God. I think part of my anxiety came from having been left alone for the first time all evening, but the rest, well, maybe that was just secondhand nervousness for him to perform well. I had no idea what song he was going to be singing; I hadn't asked any questions and he had kept all the details pretty close to his chest, so this would be a surprise for me too.

I reengaged with the lovely woman at our table who asked how long Harrison and I had been together. I kept it vague. "Not terribly long, but it feels like we've known each other for lifetimes." I fidgeted with the flowers on the table nervously. White peonies mixed with yellow roses and baby pink stock, three of my favorites all nestled among tiny emerald green ferns in elegant etched clear glass vases. The conversation with the woman I now knew as Stephanie quickly moved on to gardening, and I felt my nerves melt away. Gardening, after all, was something I could talk about until I was blue in the face. Twenty minutes passed as if it were only five, and then my conversation with Stephanie was interrupted by the DJ.

"I'd like you all to take a moment and welcome to the stage not only a friend of the family, a household name, and an all-around great guy, but now, for the first time ever as a singer, here to tickle your fancy with an unreleased original song..." A drum roll began. "It's my honor to present to you, the one, the only, Harrison Edwards!"

The crowd of guests erupted with applause, and as he took the stage, Harrison's expression was intentionally jovial, but I could tell he was nervous. His trembling hands gripped the microphone as he said hello to the crowd and thanked them for being his first real audience before congratulating the bride and groom, wishing them a lifetime of happiness then dedicating his song to them. The music began and I watched his nerves dissipate into pure showmanship. Once he got through the first verse he was relaxed, his movements on stage seemed easy and he made eye contact with different parts of the crowd, but his gaze always landed back on me, followed by those dimples I love so much. I wondered if he could tell by looking at me just how incredibly valiant I thought he was.

When he finished, there wasn't a single person sitting in their seat; everyone was either dancing or standing and clapping for Harrison. The crowd's applause wasn't stopping; they wanted more, and Harrison was absolutely beaming. He thanked them again and smiled then placed his right hand over his heart and took a bow. He raked his hand through his hair, a nervous habit I'd come to love; it came out most often when he was feeling bashful, even when his curls weren't falling forward. He thanked the crowd again and took another quick bow, then made his way backstage.

When he returned to the table there was an ease about him, reminiscent of the day I found him in the pool, a contentedness and a calm that had been lost as his performance date had gotten closer. Silliness had now returned, and Harrison was loving the crowd's acceptance of his singing. He picked up his glass and took a long drink of champagne, grabbed my hand, and led me to the dance floor.

The next few hours of the evening were a blur; there was dancing and so much laughter, and the champagne never slowed down. A continuous flow of celebrities congratulated Harrison for his performance and the two of us on our engagement. Beside me, holding my hand through it all; happiness and love beamed from his eyes and his infectious smile the entire evening. He was proud of himself and of me, and it showed.

The night wore on and as soon as I heard Bill Medley's voice come through the speakers, my eyes grew wide, and I grabbed at Harrison excitedly.

"This is my most favorite EVER!" I exclaimed with an excitement and urgency that was new to Harrison. Maybe it was the acceptance from his friends or maybe it was the champagne, but I was fully out of my shell.

He wrapped his arms around me and we playfully and sensually swayed back and forth to the music, acting out some of the same dance moves as in the film *Dirty Dancing*, laughing and kissing as we sang each part back and forth to one another. I was in heaven; I had everything I ever wanted right in front of me, twirling me around the dance floor.

The saxophone wailed its famous solo, and as the song eased its way to completion, Harrison once again locked eyes with me. Sweetly and softly, he acted out the same singing and dancing that they portrayed in the film, even scrunching up his nose the way I love so much – the same nose scrunch that Johnny gives Baby – before he pulled me into him, our bodies moving in rhythm to the music. Everyone else in the room faded into the background; no one else existed but he and I; we were so swept up in one another.

The DJ morphed the song into "I Wanna Dance with Somebody (Who Loves Me)" by Whitney Houston without missing a beat, and I was immersed in my happy place, carefree with Harrison, who was having as much fun as I was. We sang and danced, as the disco ball cast rainbow sparkles across us and all over the room, the flashing lights pulsating with the beat of the music. We danced until we sweat, and when the song finished I kissed my future husband, without concern for who was watching, then let him know that I was ready to go.

He recognized the sultry look I was giving him and was just as eager to get back to the privacy of the hotel as I was. Hand-in-hand, we made our way back to the limo and collapsed onto the cold leather seats, laughing and singing in unison as the car pulled away and meandered through the streets of New Orleans back to the hotel.

Comfortably in our room, I immediately kicked off my shoes. My feet were on fire and I was exhausted. The day had started earlier than usual and involved more adrenaline than I was used to, not to mention the alcohol I'd consumed tonight. Schmoozing with celebrities for as far as the eye could see, I'd had to find the composure to keep myself level through it all. And then there was the part about being photographed and videotaped all night. After all, I was a movie star's fiancée now, and my cheeks physically ached from all the smiling I did. Harrison threw his jacket over the back of a chair, untied his bowtie and threw it toward his jacket then loosened the collar of his tuxedo shirt before he removed the cufflinks and haphazardly rolled up his sleeves. He poured himself a bourbon and went out to the balcony.

"Babe, I have got to get this makeup off and figure out this hair; I don't even know if I have all the pins out." I searched all over my head, poking and rubbing with my fingertips.

"Come here for just a moment; I've something to tell you, darling." Harrison motioned to me with his hands. *God, I love those hands.*

He set his glass down and wrapped his arms around my waist, his hands landing on my lower back, pulling me closer to him.

"Thank you," he said. "You helped me tonight more than you'll ever know."

"The pleasure was mine. The pleasure's been mine for days now," I smiled at him, my eyes full of mischief and invitation.

He reached up and gently pulled a bobby pin from my hair, dropping a section of waves down my back. Harrison pulled me tighter against him and kissed me with a near-drunken hunger that ignited every part of my body. His tongue tasted like the spicy sweetness of the bourbon, and I savored the intensity of his kiss.

"My God, Alice, you *are* beautiful," his voice low as his hands roamed freely down my back, fumbling for the zipper on my gown.

Unable to release me from the sequined sheath as his desire for me grew, he picked me up, one arm around my back and one beneath my knees, he carried me over to the outdoor dining table. He sat me down to face him on the edge of the heavy table and as he kissed my neck and chest, I pulled at the waist of his shirt, untucking it from his trousers, then undoing each of the buttons I exposed his muscular, tanned chest. My palms caressed his shoulders as I pushed his shirt backwards, and it fell to the floor as I unfastened his belt. Harrison looked up at me then returned his mouth to mine, playfully biting my bottom lip before exploring my mouth once again with his tongue.

He stopped to lock eyes with me and softly laid his index finger against my lips. I drew it into my mouth, sucking gently. He watched me intently as he slowly pulled it from my mouth, dragging it slowly down my chin, his palm now against my throat slipping further down toward my chest, he laid me back against the length of the table and lifted the heavy skirt of my dress until it rested around my waist, his hands separating my knees, then grasping behind them he pulled my body toward his, my ass landing at the edge of the table. He maintained eye contact with me as he dropped to his knees. The lights of the balcony illuminated the glistening trail his tongue left along my inner thigh as Harrison pulled my panties to the floor, and kissed the inside of my knee before showing the same attention to the other thigh, then he slowly made his way back to their center.

I pulled my heels up on the edge of the table and let my knees fall apart, giving Harrison full reign over my body. He took control of me, his groping hands lifted my thighs, moving my bare feet from the table to his muscular shoulders while his mouth wandered between my thighs, concentrating on the spots that had me seeing stars. My back arched from the table as I grasped two hands full of his dark hair and held his head where I needed him, begging him not to stop.

Just as I was about to lose control, Harrison pulled away. My back collapsed against the table, and I let out a sigh, breathless. He pulled me up into a sitting position and looked at me with a smirk.

"Alice." He slowly pulled his bottom lip into his mouth, taking his time and savoring the taste of me on his lips before he smiled and said, "My body craves you, every single bit of you."

Before I could respond, in one swift movement, he scooped me up from the table and kissed me as he carried me to the living room. The strength of his biceps bulged against my body as I reached for the zipper on my gown. My feet dropped to the floor and as I stood before him, he paused, taking one last long look at me in my dress. He bit his lip again, his eyes fixed on mine, and shook his head. His nostrils flared and a devious grin slowly spread across his face as I watched him think about what he wanted to do to me.

The gown slipped from my body and puddled around my feet on the floor as I unbuttoned his trousers. Never breaking eye contact with him I exposed the tips of the tattoos that lay just to the front of his hips on his lower abdomen. I kissed my way down his chest and stomach, and ran my fingertips along the ridges of his abdominal muscles, tracing along both sides of the deep cut V that drives me wild. I paused to look up once again and make eye contact with him.

When I unfastened his zipper, his pants fell to the floor and left him completely exposed. I knelt before him, even more excited knowing he'd been commando all night, and teased his thighs with my tongue until goosebumps appeared. I pushed my hand between his muscular thighs, reaching up behind him to cup one of his ass cheeks, while I pulled his waist close to me with the other. I looked up at him, smiled, then took every hardened inch of him in my mouth.

Harrison drew in a sharp breath and only exhaled after he laid his head back, quickly returning his gaze down to me with a look of unbridled pleasure. When I saw him watching me, I knew what I was doing was working. His breathing deepened as his legs started to tremble and his chest heaved, every muscle in his abdomen contracting with each lustful breath. Harrison started to moan and reached for the back of my head, but as he did, I pulled away, a devious smile on my face. Just as he had stopped before I could finish, I brought him right to the edge and let him teeter there, teasing him for as long as he could stand it. He smirked, knowing exactly what I was doing. Seeing the dimples appear on his face, I pulled him down to the floor on top of me. It took both my hands to guide him where I really wanted him; I didn't want to wait one second longer to feel him inside of me.

Tonight, things felt different. Better. Harrison was my fiancé now, and while the sex had definitely been meaningful and amazing before, this was the first time I felt like Harrison was actually *making love* to me. Strong and slow, unbridled, taking his time to show each and every part of my body his utmost devotion, making sure that he looked me in the eyes, telling me over and over how much he loves me. It felt like we were the only two people on earth.

By the time I finally showered and made it to bed, it was just after two in the morning. When I slipped between the covers beside Harrison, he was already asleep, but I laid my naked body against him and when my skin touched his, a deep sigh escaped him. I could tell his mind and body were both contented, as were mine. Mentally and emotionally, I was fully taken care of. Physically, I was well beyond satisfied in every possible way, and sleep came easily.

The next morning, we had a quick breakfast together, got dressed and ready for the day, then headed out to take in some sights around the city. We'd planned to go to Audubon Park for a picnic under the moss-drenched live oaks after we were done at the zoo, but only an hour into our zoo date, and as we approached the giraffes, Harrison announced suddenly that he had to leave. This wasn't like him at all, and I was puzzled.

"Darling, I have to get back to London. I'm so sorry. You stay and enjoy the city, and once I land, I'll send the jet back for you." He seemed frazzled, as if he had been spooked by something. He hadn't gotten a call or a text. No one had approached him to let him know that he needed to get back. *What the hell was happening?* I couldn't make heads or tails of it.

"Wait! What's happening in London? How will they know who I am and that I'm with you? Why can't I go with you now? What do I do when I get to London? How will I get to you?" I was frantic, and tears came quickly. "What is going on, Harrison?!" I exclaimed. I had more questions than answers.

Harrison had already turned and begun to walk away from me. "Just make sure you get on the jet. Everything will be alright, I promise. I can't wait to see you, darling. Just make sure you get on the jet!" he yelled without ever turning around to face me.

"Harrison, I love you!" I shouted, but by then he'd already turned the corner and was gone from sight. I was confused and completely alone. We had closed down the zoo just for the two of us today so we wouldn't be mobbed by people, and now, I was the only one here. I sat down on a bench and, completely bewildered, began openly sobbing. He hadn't kissed me goodbye, hadn't given me any reason as to why he had to leave. He just disappeared. He was just...gone.

Panic set in as the thoughts in my head zipped back and forth beyond my control. *How will I get to the jet? I don't have any money. I don't even have my phone. How will I get back to the hotel? Do I need to pack everything, or will he send for it? Do I need to drive myself to the airport? Should I just leave my car? What time will the jet be there?* My mind was spiraling.

I need to go right now. I can't miss the jet. I desperately searched for signs that would lead me to the zoo's exit, and when I finally found myself outside the gate, I began to look for the streetcar. But I had no idea which way I needed to go. I was so panicked I couldn't even remember the name of our hotel. My mind was blank, I had no room key, nothing that could tell me the name or the address of the hotel or how to get there.

When a streetcar finally arrived, I asked the driver how to get to the fanciest hotel in the city, the one that overlooked the river.

With an empathetic look, the driver said, "This city is full of fancy hotels, and they're all on the river, ma'am."

I decided I'd get off at each hotel on the line until someone on the hotel staff recognized me. I tried to board but found my pockets were empty and the streetcar required exact change. There was no one else on board to loan me any money and no one around on the sidewalk. *Where was everyone?* I stepped off the empty streetcar and back out onto the hot pavement. *Think*

Alice, think. Forget the hotel; let's just get to the airport. Stop wasting time.

I had no money for a taxi, I had no phone, no map, and no idea where I was. I couldn't get back to the hotel to get the keys to my car, and I had to figure out how to get straight to the airport. My breathing became labored and as I gasped, the humidity felt heavy in my lungs, as if I was drowning in the open air. I couldn't catch my breath. I spun myself around, looking left and then right, trying to figure out how to get from wherever I was, all the way to the airport.

Spinning back to my left, a seemingly nice older woman appeared from nowhere, startling me. When the woman asked me if I needed help, all I could do was repeat myself. "I have to get to the airport; I have to get my things and get to the airport." The woman asked me where my belongings were, and I still couldn't find the name of the hotel in my jumbled mind and just repeated, "I have to get to the airport. I can't miss the jet."

Just as suddenly as the woman appeared before me, she vanished, and there was no trace that she'd ever really been there. I was certain I was losing my mind. I still hadn't caught my breath and was still standing in the same place, lost. Alone. Unable to find actual help or a way to get to the airport. It had only been minutes I was sure, so why was the sun going down? It wasn't even lunchtime yet, but in the blink of an eye it was dark out. All the businesses were closed, their lights out. There were no cars, no pedestrians, no sounds. The city of New Orleans was silent and eerily still. I stood in the dark, disoriented and alone. Terrified. There were no stars in the sky as I searched for the jet in the darkness. I was standing still, in the very spot I'd been all afternoon, but now I was screaming.

"HARRISON! WHERE ARE YOU?!" I sobbed as I screamed. "WHY

WON'T ANYONE HELP ME?" My face was wet from crying and my cheeks burned from the saltiness of my tears. I felt like my chest was going to explode and let out a low guttural scream. "SOMEBODY HELP ME..." The sounds of my pain echoed through the abandoned New Orleans streets into the otherwise silent night.

3.

I awoke in a full-blown panic. My heart was racing as the crushing feeling of a thousand concrete blocks laid atop my chest stifled my rapid breaths. Sweat matted my hair to my temples and my neck as I gasped for air, trying to regulate my breathing. I began to realize I was in my own bed, in my own home in New England. The sunlight poured through the windows and saturated everything in the room. Blinded, I blinked hard and struggled to adjust my eyes to the brightness that surrounded me as I sat up and pulled my long hair off my sweaty body and up into a ponytail.

I tried to replay the images in my head. The road trip. The hotel. The proposal. My brow furrowed as I recounted the way I'd felt kissing Harrison Edwards. I glanced down at my left hand, but all that was there was a scratched up thin gold band a half size too large for my finger. Certainly not an oversized emerald-cut diamond. Alone once again in an empty house, I finally realized I had been dreaming.

A long loud sigh of frustration burst forth as I said aloud, "What the fuck?"

I threw myself back against the pillows. My breathing had slowed, and my heart rate was back at baseline, but my irritation continued. I toyed with the idea of going back to sleep to see if I could pick up where I left off in the dream, but when I glanced at the clock I realized it was already after nine and I had to get the house in order before James returned home. Now that included washing the sheets I had sweat through.

Begrudgingly I got up, took a shower, and got ready for the rest of my day, all the while my mind fixated on the details of the road trip. I washed the few dishes I'd dirtied in the time James had been gone and left them to dry on the counter before stripping the bed and starting the sheets washing. My imagination was immersed in the memories of Harrison and me in the bathtub together. I returned to the second floor with fresh linens, intent on getting these chores done, but my mind was stuck on Harrison. I finished making the bed, dusted the house, and then quickly vacuumed and tidied up anything that was out of place, all while daydreaming about chocolate cake and recording studio confessions.

Unable to focus I decided that was enough housework for one day, and grabbed a chilled glass from the freezer, poured a glass of iced tea and made my way to the porch. *Iced tea, not the hot afternoon tea I'd tried with Harrison.* When I opened the screen door, I was met with the humid air of a New England July day, humidity that reminded me of New Orleans. Then I saw the bottle of tequila I'd left on the table the night before.

"It was you that sent my mind into overdrive," I said to the bottle, angrily pushing it aside as I made space on the table for my glass. Frustrated, I closed my eyes and lost myself in memories.

I'd had some vivid dreams in my life, a few that I could never really shake. There was the one from my childhood when I was around six or seven years old, a nightmare that placed me at my grandmother's house in the woods and I somehow got locked out of the house in the middle of the night. Illuminated from above by a humming exterior garage light surrounded by fluttering moths, a red fox crouched behind a group of early summer ferns and stalked me as I tried frantically to get back into the house. But everyone was asleep and no one heard my cries for help. Its yellow eyes got closer and closer, and with each calculated step forward it bared more of its sharp white teeth, snarling, licking its frothing chops, wanting to make a meal of me. I'd awoken safe in my bed just as the fox leapt to the porch to claw me into submission and devour me.

Another of my dreams happened just before my unplanned marriage to James. We had gathered again at my grandmother's house to celebrate our engagement. Ironically, the same house where the dream about the fox had happened, only this time, there were large owls in the trees watching over the party. They would swoop down and try to land on me, but they were simply too large to fit on my shoulders. I was anxious in this dream, mostly for my extended family's approval of James and approval of our upcoming nuptials, and I just wanted to be sure everything was perfect. I had planned out recipes and cooked everyone's favorite foods, and I set up tables in the yard allowing plenty of comfortable seating. There was music, and the drinks were ready to be poured, but the only people that arrived at the party were long since dead. Both my grandparents had passed and no longer owned that home. They hadn't lived there in years. The neighbors had also both passed, yet there they were. All of them perfectly healthy, yet still very obviously dead. Even the great-grandmother who died years ago at the age of 100 was there, in her best wool suit, in the middle of summer, still very dead. They all were glad to give nodding looks of happiness for me and James, but no one spoke. No one sat or ate or drank anything. There was no dancing. They all just stood there, morbidly nodding their approval. I had woken up terrified from that dream. It had been so vivid I never could shake the images from my mind.

In the distance, I could hear a truck approaching and opened my eyes to see the dust clouds billowing into the air as James made his way up our long, winding driveway in his pickup. I blew out an already exasperated sigh before I got up, picked up the bottle of tequila, and went back into the house. I tucked the bottle back into the cabinet where I had taken it from the night before and went back to the porch to welcome my husband home.

James lumbered up the walkway covered in mud, backpack slung over one shoulder, carrying his old beat-up cooler in the other hand.

"Hey," he said, not waiting for my response as he dropped the cooler on the porch and stomped the mud from his boots, walking past me as if I were a stranger.

He swung open the door and I could hear him drop the heavy backpack on the floor. After a brief pause, I heard the shower turn on. Equally not surprised or impressed, I went to the kitchen to start dinner. He would surely be hungry and probably wanted a hot home-cooked meal. When he finished his shower, he went out to the garage to unload his four-wheeler from the bed of the truck and wash the mud from its shimmering black exterior.

Black sparkles. My mind pictured the sequins on my gown as they reflected the lights from the balcony. For a fleeting moment, I felt Harrison's mouth on my thigh.

I stood over the hot stove for what felt like an eternity, preparing a skillet version of lasagna, something that James was always happy to have dished up and set in front of him. I slid the pan carrying the frozen garlic bread into the oven and set the timer, then went back to stirring the concoction on the stovetop. In the nine minutes it took for the bread to be ready, I was already lost in daydreams about the smell of vanilla I had been introduced to in a bathtub in D.C., the way the roses had looked so vibrant and soft against the rasp of Harrison's voice while he played the piano for me that night, and the feeling that washed over me the first time he'd kissed me.

The sound of the oven timer brought me out of my daydream, and I wasn't sure how long it had been going off. I rushed to turn the oven off and frantically pulled a drawer open looking for an oven mitt; the bread was on the verge of being burnt. My cheeks flushed from the heat as I silently plated dinner for James. I was tired, hot, and embarrassed that I'd overcooked the bread all because I'd gotten lost in my own thoughts.

We ate together in front of the TV and when I finally asked how the four-wheeling had been, James only muttered, "Fine. Dusty," before asking me to turn the volume up. He didn't ask me what I'd done while he was away, didn't express if he had missed me or if he'd thought about me at all. It felt like he just assumed I stayed here doing household chores and pining away the hours waiting for him to get back home, like a dog that had been left behind. Then the realization struck that I had done just that, despite the fact that in my mind I'd been on a life-changing road trip with a movie star that ultimately fell in love with me. *How pathetic*, my thoughts snarled at me.

I finished my dinner in silence, half pissed-off and half depressed, though I wasn't sure if my irritation was directed at James or at myself. After all, no one was forcing me to be here. I chose this for myself every day. *Does this man even think about me at all? Where do I fall on his list of priorities?* The voice in my head prodded me further into anger with each passing moment.

I got up to take my plate to the sink, and James held his out to me in silence as I passed by him. Expressionless, he never moved his eyes from the television. His plate in his outstretched hand, shoved at me as if to say, *here, take this.* His natural expectation that it was my job to just take care of it. Irritated, I took his plate and made my way to the kitchen sink, rinsed the dishes without concern for their wellbeing, clanging silverware and banging plates, then loaded the dishwasher. "Déjà vu," I mumbled under my breath.

Returning to the couch, I picked up my phone as a means of escape and logged into a website where I knew I could find solace in the friends I'd made online. I scrolled through videos they shared with me and chatted with them about what was new in their lives since yesterday, then plugged my earphones into my phone to avoid bothering James. When I looked up, ready to toss the TV remote to my husband, he was already asleep in the chair. *Typical.* I sighed, shut the TV off and went back to chatting with friends for a while before deciding I'd search for videos of Harrison.

I typed his name into the browser followed by the word *singer*. No results. Then I typed his name, followed by my own name. Results listed photos of him at the top of the page, followed by links to my own Facebook page and a few other websites where I'd posted reviews on products I had purchased, but that was it, no videos or photos of him singing anywhere, no photos from a wedding. No engagement.

It was a dream, Alice. Let it go.

Resigned to the idea that my dreams in fact were much better than my reality, I typed Harrison's name one more time into the search bar, followed by the word *videos*, then spent the next hour intently watching one of his first TV appearances, quietly absorbing the sound of his voice through my headphones like a shot of serotonin straight into my brain, hanging on every delicately pronounced word I could while James snored in his chair nearby.

Life was back to normal; day in and day out James and I cohabitated but barely spoke. I think if he'd been asked about his marriage, James would have said everything was perfectly fine. No problems at all, happy even. But I felt stuck. Stuck in one spot. Stuck in a routine that doesn't bring me an ounce of joy and stuck in a marriage that feels stale. There's no romance between us and never any surprises. It's mundane and redundant and predictable. And I believe James when he tells me he loves me, but is love enough anymore? He never deviates from the routine. Never looks into my eyes and tells me he craves me. He never wanders amorously into the shower with me, never takes my breath away on the dining room table. The only part of the daily routine that makes me feel any happiness at all is when I can escape into videos of Harrison, and like an addict desperate for a fix, I do so every chance I can.

July moved into August and August into September. The days grew shorter as fall in New England approached. I didn't have any new dreams of Harrison or the road trip, and I never picked up where that dream left off or found the jet I was so desperately in search of, but I always managed to find him while I toiled away the days working in my flower gardens. I'd taken the last few months to rearrange my perennial beds, dividing some of the more mature plants into smaller bunches, and spreading color around as much as I could. The hues of the tender flower petals reminded me of the way I'd felt in my dream and conjured up images of the two of us together in a new city gazing at ancient architecture or eating some fancy meal somewhere I couldn't pronounce, unable to keep our hands off one another. I imagined our wedding, low-key and private off the coast of Italy in some tiny town no one in the States had ever heard of. The gardens had been a good excuse to busy myself outside, and the fresh air and hard work had been a great way to make me too tired to worry about why my husband didn't want to touch me each night.

The nights began to grow cooler, and I knew James would soon be preparing to go for one last camping trip. He did it every year in late September with a bunch of guys he'd known his entire life. On the warm mid-September Thursday afternoon when the news finally came and James told me he'd be gone for ten days this time instead of just a week, I was surprised.

"What prompted the extension?" I inquired, trying to look interested.

"I've got the vacation time. I might as well use it, right?" He looked at me as if he thought I was an idiot.

"Yeah, definitely. Well, hope you have fun. Will you be going to the same campground as last year?" I didn't care where he was going; it was all irrelevant to me. Not to mention he never used his vacation time to spend time with me. We hadn't been on a vacation together in over nineteen years. We hadn't even had a proper honeymoon.

"No, the guys picked some other place this year, further up north and deeper in the woods, I guess. Better fishing. Might see some bear. No cell service though, so you'll get a nice break from me." He laughed as he finished his sentence and picked up his cell phone, never once glancing in my direction.

With a fake chuckle and a nod, I knew that what he really meant was that he would be the one getting a nice break from me.

"When do you leave?" I asked, trying to hide my elation.

"We're going to head out Tuesday, early probably to make good time as far as the driving and setting up." He never looked up from his phone, texting someone as he spoke.

"Oh, yeah, good plan. I'll miss you while you're gone," I said dryly and waited for a reply.

He chuckled at his phone, and when silence was the only thing I got in response to my comment, I turned and went upstairs to the bedroom. Lying on the bed, frustrated, I thought, *If he can go away, why can't I? I don't have to sit in this house alone. What's good for one is good for another.*

I picked up my phone and sent a text to Arlo, my boss, inquiring if I had any accumulated vacation time I could take, and how soon could I use it. While I waited for his reply, I sent a second text to my friend Emma that lives in Oregon. We'd become online friends back in the spring and had grown quite close, texting every day despite having never met one another. My text to Emma read: *What if I went on a vacation alone, is that crazy?* I hit Send then grabbed the key to my fireproof safe from my nightstand. Once opened, I searched for my passport among outdated documents, rifling through paperwork that could surely be thrown out, a few old photos of my grandparents when they were young, and a baby bracelet that had been mine when I was born. At the bottom of the safe, after all that digging, there was my long-neglected, but always renewed passport. I double-checked the expiration date. 2025. Perfect. My next move was a bold one; I picked up my phone again and typed into the search bar *flights to London.*

Arlo's response interrupted my search.

You never take sick days or vacation. Take what you need, we can make it work. When are you thinking?

I responded to him immediately. *Two weeks, starting Tuesday.*

Within seconds my phone buzzed again,

Sounds good. Let me know when you're back. Enjoy!

I couldn't help but smile to myself. Another buzz from the phone; this time it was Emma.

The best vacation I ever had I took alone, 10/10 would recommend.

I sent her back a smiley face and went back to my search for flights.

It wasn't long before I found a flight that left Boston on Tuesday afternoon with a layover at JFK that would land me at Heathrow the following morning. The return flight was a straight shot with no layover and would get me home long before James. I took a deep breath, reminded myself not to overthink it and with one click, my flight was booked. I couldn't help but smile to myself.

I wanted to spend a quiet, self-indulgent week in a place known for good food, artists and poets, writers and maybe a little royalty. Who was I kidding? Definitely royalty. I'd find a hotel somewhere in the area of Hampstead Heath; I'd heard it was posh but also very welcoming and full of beautiful, natural surroundings. I deserved a bit of pampering, and if I was going to experience London, I was going all in.

After doing a little research to see where I could stay and still have lots of leisure options within a walkable distance, I booked myself a deluxe room at the Clayton Crown Hotel in Northwest London. Their website was beautiful and the hotel itself looked charming, but I was most looking forward to the amenities. A restaurant, a pub, and afternoon tea. *Afternoon tea in London.* My mind shot back to the visual of Harrison, pinky up, sipping his hot tea with sugar and lemon. Though highly likely I wouldn't partake in the tea itself, I could still have fancy snacks and people-watch, and if there were a day I didn't want to venture out, I'd be just fine with what was available in-house.

I had to map out my plans in my head to fully grasp what I'd just committed myself to on such short notice. I grabbed my notebook and a pen and began making a list of things I'd need to pack. I had always been a list maker, a note taker, a calendar keeper, and a bit high strung when it came to making sure things were meticulously done to their fullest extent. I rationalized it as a way to make sure I wouldn't forget anything of importance, but how could I possibly forget when the sheer excitement of it all was already taking over my entire thought process?

I set up the empty page of my notebook into three sections: What to pack, what to see, and things to remember. I'd be leaving the house shortly after James on Tuesday, probably mid-morning, and heading to Logan Airport. It took a few hours to get there, and I'd be timing it just right to avoid lunchtime traffic, get the car parked, and check in for my first international flight. I wanted to get up and dance at the thought of myself in London, but I didn't want to draw attention to myself bouncing around upstairs. *Focus, Alice.*

By the time I landed in London after the layover, I'd have an early check-in on Wednesday morning. I jotted down a note in the 'things to remember' section. *Call the hotel and request an early check-in.* I'd depart eight days later on Thursday morning for an eight-hour nonstop flight home. A satisfied look spread across my face. I'll pack Monday while James is at work and be ready to go when he leaves Tuesday morning.

In making the list of things to pack, I decided right then and there that I could be whomever I wanted to be while away in a land where no one knew me. I could take afternoon tea; whether I liked it or not didn't matter. I could wear flowy skirts and sun hats. I could behave any way I wanted when I was on vacation; no one was going to be there to judge me; I wasn't going to feel scrutinized or out of place. I could be the me I pictured in my head; these people would never see me again.

I finished my list of things to pack and moved on to the list of places I wanted to visit in London. The hotel was near the train, the bus, and the tube—*what a funny name for transportation, the tube.* Or I could also use Uber. I'd never done it before, but some people use Uber exclusively and live to tell about it, *I'm sure it will be fine.* I definitely wanted to see the Kew Botanical Gardens, and all of the royal family-related places like Buckingham Palace, Westminster Abbey, and Kensington Gardens. An absolute must was the Zoo...and the London Eye. *The Zoo.* Flashbacks of being left at the zoo rattled me and wiped the smile from my face. This time

I'd be alone, nothing to worry about and no one to rely on but myself. No one could leave me stranded. I refocused on the list in front of me and added Primrose Hill, Madame Tussauds, and Hampton Court Palace. The list was massive, and I planned to stay quite busy.

"Why are you up here alone?" James asked.

His voice startled me; I hadn't even heard him come up the stairs.

"Well, I decided that if you're going to be gone on a trip, I would take a trip too. No sense for me to sit here alone for ten days." I maintained my focus on my notebook, making notes from the information I was reading on my phone.

"Oh? Where you gonna go?" Upon hearing I wasn't just going to sit idle and wait for him while he was gone, James suddenly became interested in my plans.

"I booked a trip to London." I was matter-of-fact with my response and still didn't look up from my phone. *We'll see how he likes it.*

"London." Not a question, a statement. James wasn't impressed and when I finally looked up, it was written all over his face, I could tell he wasn't pleased. "Seems a little extreme," he said.

To prove my point I said politely, "Would you like to go to London with me?" I kept my eyes focused on him, straight faced, both eyebrows raised waiting for his reaction.

"I have no interest in London," James was quick to respond with an answer I already anticipated.

"Ever?" I prodded.

"For what?" James was never the type to want to leave the country, meaning the backwoods we live in *and* the United States.

"Exactly why I'm going. You don't want to go, ever, and I have the opportunity to see things I've always been curious about. Why deprive myself of it if I have the time to go? You'll already be gone, makes sense to me." I nonchalantly returned my attention to my phone and my notes.

"Who's going with you?" James became curt, and increasingly more condescending.

"No one. I'm going alone," I responded.

"I don't think so. That's not happening." James shook his head, dismissing me, adamant.

"It's already booked. I traveled alone all the time before we were married, James. I'm perfectly capable of handling myself. I really don't think you need to worry about it." I wasn't going to be swayed.

"Right. Well, have fun. I don't think it's a very safe idea, but obviously, I can't stop you. You're just going to do whatever you want." James was doing a terrible job of hiding his irritation. His face and his snide tone gave him away.

"Okay." Now my voice was dismissive and flat. I looked back at my notebook, working out which places I was going to visit first and which mode of transportation I would use to get there, how long it would take, and the costs for each attraction.

James left the room and shortly after he descended the stairs to the first floor, I heard the front door slam. I knew he was mad, not so much that I was going to London but that I had made the decision without him. He was already locked into camping and would never admit it to his buddies or to me, but he likely would have gone with me just to make sure I wasn't alone. Under the guise of keeping me safe, but he'd have been miserable the entire time. I shook my head at the thought of it. *Ridiculous.*

Things remained fairly quiet around the house until Monday night. In the four days leading up to my trip, I'd bought a few new outfits to take with me and started to pack my suitcase. I made sure bills were paid, the usual household chores were all caught up, and the gardens were all tended. James had been nearly silent; he didn't want to speak to me, that part was obvious, and only did so when he had to. It wasn't much different than any other day really. But Monday night while I was at the sink rinsing dishes to put into the dishwasher, on the eve of ten days apart, James walked into the kitchen and dropped the four words no one ever wants to hear.

"We need to talk." His face was sullen.

"Okay, what's on your mind?" I dropped the plate back into the hot soapy water and turned around, leaning my back against the counter as I toweled my hands dry. I was worried about what he was going to say but didn't want him to know it, and chewed at my bottom lip as a means to disguise my fears, trying to appear indifferent.

"I don't like that you're going to be gone that long, alone. I won't have any way to get in touch with you," he said.

Here it comes, I thought. *The guilt trip.*

"James, you wouldn't have any way to get in touch with me if I were here in this kitchen for the next ten days either. There's no difference," I said.

"What if something happens to you? I won't know until I get home." He wasn't being sincere; he was trying to make me feel bad.

"Something could happen to me right here and you wouldn't know that until you got home either. The difference is that I'm going to be somewhere having fun and enjoying myself versus sitting in this house alone." My tone was point blank. "You're trying to scare me into not going. Trying to make me feel unsafe, and unsure of myself. I'm going, James. I paid for it, and I'm going."

"You've never been to London, Alice! Who do you know there? No one! What is *so* interesting that you need to go halfway across the world? What if someone tries to kidnap you or mugs you on the street? What if—" James never raised his voice at me, but today was the exception. He had snapped and I saw red. I was so pissed I fought back tears as I cut off his tirade.

"What if they do, James? What if someone breaks in here and robs me while I'm here alone? What if someone decides they can't live another second of their life without having a piece of me and walks in here one day and rapes me? Beats me? Kills me right here in my own house? If I lived my life by the what if's I'd never get out of my own tracks. I'd never experience life. I'd never feel joy. Why do you insist on trying to suck everything happy out of my life?" I regretted the last part as soon as I said it, and the tears that had welled up fell down my cheeks.

"Wow. Okay." He threw both his hands up and pushed past me.

"I'm sorry. I shouldn't have said that. I didn't mean that, James." I stepped toward him to try to quell the anger I knew he was feeling, but it was too late.

His tone calm again, he said, "You know what, Alice? You can stop your crying. Have the time of your life. I don't give a shit what you do." And he stormed upstairs, slamming the bedroom door behind him.

I finished the dishes and replayed our argument in my head. We never argued. Maybe tonight we did because I finally spoke my truth out loud to him, instead of holding back my thoughts like I usually do. Yeah, I'm sure there is a part of him that's truly concerned for my well-being. I'm sure that he wants me to be safe, but he didn't have to try to scare me into submission. He could have just told me he was worried for my safety without causing such an uproar and storming off. I shut off the lights and made sure the doors were locked, then made my way upstairs to find James in bed but still awake.

"James, I—"

"I really don't want to hear it, Alice. You said your piece and I've been lying here thinking about it ever since. Maybe ten days apart is just what we need. Maybe we need to miss each other or something. I don't know. But what I do know is that you apparently don't like me very much anymore or…maybe at all. I'm sorry you find me to be such a disappointment."

You've got to be kidding me with this bullshit, I thought. I wanted to roll my eyes but didn't.

"James, I don't think you're a disappointment." My attempt to reassure him fell flat, much like the tone of my unconvincing voice when I said it. I felt no sympathy for him, and now wasn't going to be the time I chose to fake it. It was all over his face; James wasn't buying what I was selling.

"Right, well, whatever you want to call it, but it sure seems like you're excited to get away from me, from here for a while, and that's not a very good feeling for me at all. You've never just packed up and gone on a vacation alone before. You didn't even mention it to me. You just booked it all, going halfway across the world with no thought of how your husband might feel about it. What the hell has gotten into you?" He rolled over in bed and faced away from me, his theatrics intending to upset me further.

But I wasn't more upset, I was simply more irritated because I knew he was trying to manipulate my emotions. He was trying to get me to soften my response and feel bad for him. He was looking for his ego to be coddled and I was having none of it.

"James, if anyone needs time away from someone, I think it's probably you. You've completely lost sight of how a marriage is supposed to work, how it's supposed to feel. I don't feel like you like me anymore either, if we're being honest. I feel like your maid and your roommate. Like my entire purpose in life is to take care of you. Who takes care of me, James? No one does. So, I guess it's fine if you go off on overnights with the boys and do whatever you want, but when I do it, I need you to sign my permission slip? I don't think so. That's bullshit and you know it. You're mad because I might find some semblance of happiness elsewhere, and it terrifies you. So, if my booking a trip and having some fun, doing something for myself for a change makes you feel inferior, then I guess you're going to have to just deal with it. I'm well overdue for this. And don't talk to me about making decisions without you. If I remember correctly, once upon a time you went and had a vasectomy without my knowledge. You changed the trajectory of our entire lives with that decision; I'm just going on a fucking vacation."

I felt empowered once I got those last two sentences out of my head and into the open. I'd carried that disappointment and held my tongue for too long. I never spoke up or defended myself like this, and certainly never threw that much anger or resentment in his direction. Would he be infuriated? Sad? I had no idea, and I didn't care.

I realized I'd been holding my breath, waiting for him to turn over and unload more of his bullshit manipulations, but James didn't respond. He just lay there with his back to me, silent. *Maybe he's in shock*, I thought. I'd been on the verge of speaking harsher truths and was glad I stopped when I did. There was no benefit to making things worse than they already were.

After a few moments of sitting there waiting for some type of reaction, I let out a long sigh. Exhaling the remaining irritation I felt and resigning myself to the fact that this wasn't going to be resolved tonight, I got up, changed into my pajamas and crawled into bed. I pulled the covers over my bare legs, plugged in my phone to charge for the night, and shut off the bedroom lights, then sat there upright for a few minutes but said nothing. The clock on my dresser was the only illumination in the room, the neon blue digits stared back at me. 8:42 p.m. I sighed once more and slid my body down into the sheets. With our backs to each other, just as I was about to fall asleep, into the dark silence James confessed, "I do love you, Alice."

I didn't open my eyes and without hesitation proclaimed, "I love you too. And I don't need ten days to miss you, James. I've missed you for the last twenty-one years."

Silence again. Silence until the rhythmic sounds of James' snoring filled the room. I lay there sad, pissed off, and more determined than ever to have the time of my life, starting tomorrow. We had never fought like this, never once in the time we'd known each other, but tonight I felt like a load of bricks had dropped off my shoulders.

I awoke the next morning to the feeling of James kissing my temple. I opened my eyes to a still pitch-black bedroom. *What time is it?* I glanced at the clock. 4:12 a.m. The bright blue numbers hurt my eyes. Clumsily I propped myself up, prepared to try to talk to him, but he had already walked away. I heard him say in the distance that he was headed out and that he loves me as he made his way down the stairs to the first floor.

I sprung from the bed, chasing after him, and yelled, "I love you too, wait! Don't—" But the slam of the front door cut me off and the next thing I heard was the rumbling engine of his pickup.

I stood there, barely awake, halfway down the stairs in my pajamas feeling empty. Part of me wanted to cry. One of those loud, snotty, soul-purging cries. The other half of me wanted to grab whatever was closest and hurl it against a wall. I wanted to hear things shatter. But the tears never came, and I didn't want to pick up the mess that came with breaking things. So, I stood there, in the dark on the stairs, and decided to find the joy in every moment of the next ten days, starting now.

4.

My morning shower was humid and relaxing, then I took the time to carefully apply a little makeup and fix my hair into something easy for travel. I double-checked all my luggage to be sure I had everything I needed for the trip, including my phone charger and a phone charging adapter, and a comfortable backup outfit in my carry-on just in case my luggage was lost. My passport, cash, credit cards, and ID were all where they needed to be. I checked in for my flight online, then emptied the fridge of anything perishable and took the trash to the bin behind the garage.

Back in the house, I stood in the kitchen and looked around at the home I loved. Everything was tidy and in its place, nothing was left unfinished. Everything would be fine while I was gone. I'd made sure to set up an international plan on my cell phone in case our neighbors needed to reach me for anything. We trusted them, and I'd asked them to come by a few times while James and I were out of town to make sure the house was okay.

Everything was settled and I was excited to get this travel day started. I pulled the front door closed behind me and loaded my luggage into the back of the car.

From the time I left home the radio played a string of my favorite songs and with each new tune, I turned the music louder and louder, until I felt a rasp in my voice from singing. *This is what happiness feels like*, I thought. *This is freedom.*

Freedom. A vision of Harrison's sweatshirt flashed through my mind, taking center stage, and halfway through New Hampshire, I thought of him sitting beside me, on the same road, singing with the windows down in the sunshine, and I let my mind unfurl into a full replay of that road trip dream.

It had been an easy drive to Boston and I made good time, arriving just over an hour before my scheduled 4 p.m. departure. I had avoided lunchtime traffic, stopping only once before I got into the city to refill my gas tank in preparation for the drive home. I pulled into a long-term parking space at Logan Airport, pushed the car door open, and was relieved to stretch my legs. It was warmer here than it had been at home and the humidity in the city air carried the smell of aged garbage mixed with diesel fuel and putrid clam flats. It hit me like a slap in the face as soon as I opened the car door. Eager to get inside to my gate and away from this awful stench, I collected my luggage and my purse, made sure the car was locked, and headed inside.

I had been a frequent traveler before my marriage. In what felt like another lifetime, I'd saved for two years, working multiple summer jobs, then the August before my senior year I spent three weeks traveling alone within the United States, so airports weren't intimidating to me. I'd been to Logan Airport plenty of times in the past and it seemed nothing had changed since

I was last here. I went directly to baggage check-in before continuing through security. It was a Tuesday afternoon, so thankfully there were fewer people here than on a weekend.

Once seated at my gate, I realized I had forgotten the most important thing for travel. It had been so long since my last flight, it never occurred to me that I'd need a book. I gathered my belongings and found the closest bookshop in search of something that might hold my attention. I quickly found multiple books that interested me, but chose to purchase only three of them, figuring I'd have plenty of time in the evenings to read before bed.

One was a mystery thriller set in the swamps of the deep South, the second was a combination of historical fiction and romance, and the third was, of course, full-blown smut romance. *I've got a book for every situation*, I thought and added a pack of cinnamon gum, two bags of plain M&M's, and a small bag of honey-roasted peanuts to hold me over on the flight. As I passed the magazine stand on my way to the register, a familiar smile stopped me in my tracks. I turned and looked into the green eyes staring back at me and was immediately reminded of the way those same gorgeous eyes had looked at me when I found their owner in the Blakes' pool. Harrison Edwards was on the cover of *Vogue*. I grabbed it from the rack, added it to my armful of books and snacks, and continued on to the cashier.

The first leg of my flight was quick and uneventful, and I spent most of my time looking out the window and taking photos of the clouds. It took no time at all to get to JFK from Boston, and once there I quickly found my next gate. I settled in and pulled out my phone to see if I had any text messages from James. Finding none, I decided to send him one:

Layover at JFK, all is well. Will let you know when I land at Heathrow. I love you.

He was already out of cell phone range and wouldn't get my message until he was out of the woods and on his way home. By then I'd already be back at the house, but I felt a responsibility to keep him informed of my whereabouts and my safety since he'd made such a fuss about it.

My afternoon was mostly spent people watching and glancing at the news on the television that hung in a nearby corner. JFK was much busier than Logan Airport had been, and I was thankful for closed captions and the increased foot traffic. People watching is one of my favorite ways to pass time. It allows my imagination to concoct stories about where that woman was going, or who the mistress must be that that man was sneaking off to see. Just complete nonsense, really, but I was content to spend hours getting lost in my own thoughts.

Two hours into what was supposed to be a six-hour layover, it was announced that my flight was going to be delayed for an extra four hours, citing mechanical issues. I was in no rush; I'd just get to London a bit later than planned tomorrow morning. *So much for that early check-in.* By my calculations, I would now arrive around 2:30 p.m. in London, 9:30 a.m. my normal time, and I'd likely be exhausted from the overnight flight and jetlag. I was thankful my only plans for day one in London were to sleep and get acquainted with the immediate local area.

As time passed, I grew bored and wandered the halls of JFK before going to the airport bar for a light dinner. While there, I met a nice young woman who was traveling alone on her way to Dallas. We struck up an easy conversation and spent an hour chatting about travel and life experiences, but it wasn't long before the woman was strutting off to her gate, leaving me alone once again.

After dinner I wandered back to my gate, focusing once again on the television in the corner. Despite its determination to make me drowsy, I hadn't dared to fall asleep in the airport for fear someone would take my purse, or I might miss boarding my flight. I wanted to lose myself in the mystery novel I'd purchased in Boston but knew any amount of reading at this time of night would also make my eyes too heavy. I couldn't win. So, I paced the hallways, trying to stay alert.

When I was finally boarded and settled on my next flight, the flight that would land me in London for the first time in my life, I tucked my purse firmly under my arm, and had no trouble at all drifting into a deep, dreamless sleep. The next time my eyes opened, it was because I'd shifted in my seat. We were beginning the descent into Heathrow.

It had been much easier to navigate the craziness of Heathrow Airport and my need for transportation than I anticipated. I retrieved my luggage and found my way by taxi to the hotel. The Clayton Crown was originally a pub built in 1900, showcasing gorgeous dark woodwork and an old-world charm punctuated by ornate architectural details. I was immediately in love with the older parts of the building and made a mental note to research its history. The check-in process had been a breeze; the lovely young woman at the desk even offered to upgrade my accommodations to a suite on their highest floor to provide a better view at no extra cost. I gratefully accepted and as I approached a glass atrium, reminiscent of the glass enclosure at the Botanical Gardens from my dream, I smiled as I remembered how wonderful that night had been, then made my way up into the more recently built tower in search of my room.

At first glance, the suite was smaller than I expected, but suitable for what I needed. The main entry opened into a comfortable living space with a small kitchenette tucked around the corner and gave way to a separate bedroom and ensuite bathroom. There were a few sets of large windows in the living room and bedroom, but no balcony. I took my time inspecting the bathroom for cleanliness and making sure the sheets were spotless. I'd always been a stickler for things like that. After finding everything in pristine condition, I enjoyed the view from the living room for a bit before unpacking my things and settling in. It was then that I remembered I ought to text James.

I tapped at the screen of my phone to check for notifications and finding none, I began typing.

Made it to London after a flight delay, all checked in to my hotel. Safe and sound. Thinking of you, wish you were here, love you

I hit Send and from a pocket in my suitcase I pulled out the adapter and charger I'd brought from home. I plugged my phone in, put it on the nightstand and laid my head on the pillow just to rest my eyes, but within minutes I was sound asleep.

By the time I woke up, dinnertime had long passed, and I was famished. I ordered a turkey sandwich and a piece of chocolate cake from room service, then reached for my tote bag. The deep green eyes on the magazine I'd purchased at the airport were peering back at me. Pulling my notebook and the magazine from my bag, I laid them both on the table in front of me. There he was, Harrison Edwards. Just staring at me. I could hear his voice in my head, his accent rolling from his tongue. *That masterful tongue.* I laid back against the pillows and my thoughts took me straight back to the scene on the balcony in New Orleans; I let it play all the way through, almost to the finish, when a knock at the door interrupted me. I was grateful my dinner was being delivered and tipped the bellman before settling back onto the bed.

I decided maybe reliving the end of that dream would be better suited for later, and that London and all it had to offer would be there tomorrow whether or not I planned activities tonight. I bypassed the notebook and opted for the magazine. Ignoring the rest of the publication, I turned immediately to the full-page photo of Harrison. As I munched on my sandwich, I admired his chiseled features and the familiar dimple in his left cheek until my curiosity got the better of me. Turning the page to the article, it focused mostly on his latest contract to star in a new movie, an action film set to shoot in Brazil, and how it required him to train multiple times a day for months, leaving his body perfectly toned and nearly all muscle. *Just the way I remember it.* It outlined his workout routine and how he had altered his diet for the role.

My mind drifted from the pages and once again back into my dream. I fixated on the way the balcony lights cascaded across his abdominal muscles and how they stiffened when I traced my fingertips along the tattoos near his hips. I felt my pulse quicken at the thought of it and took a deep breath, trying to center myself before letting out a sigh of disappointment and refocusing on the magazine in front of me. The article continued on about how he was going to be taking some time to himself before the shooting of the film starts, and then finished by listing the film's potential title and presumed release date. I set the magazine back on the table, and turned the pages back, leaving it open to the full-page photo of Harrison. *Those eyes.* I couldn't hold back my smile as the photo lay there smiling back at me, then I reached for my phone.

I quickly did the math in my head to figure out the time difference, then sent a text to Emma.

Landed and settled in London! :) It's amazing. Will be here just over a week, so many fun things planned. I'll keep you posted.

Within seconds the phone alerted me to a response.

OMG, WHAT?! So proud of you! Send lots of photos! Love you!

Emma had been my biggest supporter lately and always made herself available anytime I sent her a message. Her responses always made me smile, and they made me feel less alone. I grew up an only child and had never been the kind of woman that kept a lot of friends; I guess I'd been a bit of a loner my whole life, so I was deeply thankful to have found Emma and that she and I had become so close, even if we had never met in person or actually spoken on the phone. As I finished my sandwich, I noticed the time. It was getting late.

I knew my brain wouldn't let me rest until my plans for tomorrow were set in stone, so I picked up my notebook and began making a list. It was important for me to map things out for the most efficient timing, but also to be the most cost-effective. I'd significantly depleted my savings just to be here, and I didn't want to do anything too crazy beyond what I had already planned for.

I prioritized the places I wanted to see most and grouped them all by proximity before deciding tomorrow's adventure would start early with an Uber ride to the Kew Royal Botanic Gardens where I would immerse myself in the gardens and the phenomenal architectural details of the Temperate House, the world's largest Victorian glasshouse. While there, I could check out an attraction referred to as the Hive, which I'd admired online and seen wonderful reviews for, followed by a quick lunch at the Orangery.

Unfortunately, the website indicated that the Mansion at Wakehurst was closed indefinitely. Saddened by that development, I decided after lunch I'd travel again by Uber to the London Zoo and spend my afternoon appreciating the animals. Happy with this plan, I put my notebook aside, laid out my outfit for the following day, and took a long hot shower before returning to bed to relish in the most decadent looking piece of chocolate cake.

It only took one taste of that chocolate on my tongue and my mind flooded with memories of the night Harrison and I shared our bodies and a piece of chocolate cake with one another. I daydreamed as I snacked, and a few bites later, I set it aside and closed my eyes, relaxing into the images that played over and over in my head. Soon, I slipped back into the world of hopeful sleep.

It was always a fine line between rest and sleep for me. I could do one or the other but rarely both. Sleep was a given, I always found sleep; insomnia was a rarity, but actual rest was elusive. Only once or twice a month could I fall asleep and manage to have my mind remain quiet enough to wake feeling actually rested. A static of music and words, overlapped and on repeat, was the norm for me. The dreams had always been woven in amongst the noise. But it had been days since I had any kind of dream while sleeping, and I figured it was just a consequence of the stress of this trip and my fight with James.

The next morning, I woke to the sound of my alarm, feeling rested. I'd slept soundly, my mind had stayed silent and free from any dream sequences. I counted that as a win, a welcome and wonderful way to start my first full day in London, sure to be full of physical touristy fun. The sun was out and the day promised warmth, so I wasted no time getting up, quickly getting dressed and grabbing a muffin and juice to take with me on my forty-minute Uber ride.

I arrived just as the gardens opened and was able to photograph so many varieties of flowers I had never seen before. I was most excited to photograph a large display of cleome, one of my favorites. Unfortunately for me, it wasn't the right season for a flower I'd long admired, the hellebore. There was a large attraction devoted to them here, but they're a spring flower. One day I planned to have a dedicated garden strictly for hellebore in various shades of black, wine and ivory, I just hadn't been able to make it happen yet. *Maybe next year I can focus on that*, I thought as I made my way toward the sunflowers.

The grounds of the Botanic Gardens were even more gorgeously maintained than I expected, and I was in awe when I walked inside the Hive and experienced firsthand its grandeur. Situated in a wildflower meadow, the Hive is an intricately woven steel lattice cylindrical structure over fifty-five feet tall; it's meant to be an immersive multi-sensory experience depicting the buzzing of life inside a bee hive, and it does not disappoint. Inside, there are over a thousand LED lights that activate and flash in seemingly random patterns, but are actually based on the pulses and vibrations from the sounds of live worker bees in a linked nearby hive. Composed orchestral music plays along with the lights, and I was fascinated by the splendor of it all. I ended up spending more time here than I had planned, so I took my lunch from the Orangery to go in order to make up the difference and keep to the schedule I'd made the night before. As I traveled nearly an hour to the zoo, it was nice to have a bit of a break from all the walking I'd been doing.

Once inside the zoo, I got a map and schedule of events and realized I was just in time to hear the talk on giraffes. Ironic, because I'd been abandoned at the giraffe exhibit in New Orleans; hopefully this experience would turn out better than that one. I was one of only a few people present, so when they asked me to hand-feed the giant creatures, I jumped at the opportunity. I even swallowed my fear and asked a kind looking stranger to take my picture while I held out a branch of acacia toward the long-necked fellow they called "Jordan." At the exact moment the giraffe's long sticky tongue wrapped around my fingers, I burst into laughter and I heard my phone's camera shutter clicking. I knew my joy had been captured.

I meandered through the exhibits, stopping to say hello to the curious meerkats, before continuing toward the lions. *The lion tattoo.* I shook my head and sighed. *Snap out of it, Alice.*

My afternoon spent with the animals had been amazing, but I knew it was time to get back to the hotel when my feet started to ache. I called for another Uber, and before long I was happily back in the comfort of my suite.

After a long relaxing shower and a dinner of fish and chips, I opened my notebook to start planning for tomorrow. I used my phone to purchase tickets for a tour of Buckingham Palace; my plan was to arrive right when they opened and be there long enough to take the tour and see the Changing of the Guard, then move on to a verger tour of Westminster Abbey, which allows for special access behind the scenes. Having confirmed both of those tours on my phone, I booked a ride on the London Eye just after lunch, and would move along to Madame Tussauds London after. I found a combination ticket available, and I was glad to save a little money; just like that, my second day in London was confirmed. Day two was going to be a full one.

A creature of habit, I laid out my clothes in preparation for morning and set my alarm. The images of Harrison caught my eye as they stared back at me from the still-open magazine. I snatched it up, staring into his captivating green eyes and said aloud, "I can't have you staring at me all the time," and laughed as I threw it back onto the coffee table, making sure it was closed. "I'll never get anything done."

I placed an order for tomorrow's breakfast, then scheduled an Uber for 8:30 a.m. Everything was set, and in the silence of my hotel suite, I reached for the mystery novel I'd purchased at the airport before snuggling down into the warmth of my bed and letting my imagination escape into the pages of the book.

The next morning once again found me quite rested. *Unusual*, I thought, and assumed it was simply because I'd done so much walking the day before. I was ready to take on the day, and the breakfast I ordered showed up at my door right on time. My scrambled eggs were perfectly buttery and fluffy, just the way I like them, and were complemented by a heaping bowl of fresh assorted fruits, a side of breakfast sausage, and rye toast. *I could get used to this*, I thought before realizing, *This must be what it's like for James; instant gratification with virtually no effort.* Instantly annoyed, I drove every thought of him from my mind as I savored my piping hot coffee and watched London bustle with morning activity.

When my Uber arrived, I recognized the man behind the wheel. He was the same nice gentleman that had driven me yesterday morning, though yesterday I'd remained silent and focused on the landscape for the duration of the ride, unless of course, he spoke first. I'd just assumed I'd never see him again. But, today was Friday and traffic was much heavier this morning than yesterday, which allowed me adequate time to get to know him. His name was Nigel, and I was glad to make his acquaintance. Even though London is quite big, the last two days started with a familiar smiling face, one that I felt in my gut I could trust to deliver me safely to any destination.

Once Nigel dropped me off at Buckingham Palace, I moved from tour to tour as planned, took in all the wonderment of the historic buildings, and snapped more photos than I could count while high above the River Thames aboard the Eye. I was in absolute awe of this magnificent city. The last attraction of the day was the wax museum, and I was floored at how lifelike the figures were. The eyes felt like they were following me around the room and that creeped me out a little, but I made sure to take selfies with Beyoncé and of course beloved Queen Elizabeth II. And now that I'd finally made it to London, the staff tells me the One Direction figures had recently been retired. *The nerve of this place*, I thought sarcastically.

The last two days had been full of sunshine and more walking than I was used to and the non-stop tours left me a bit weary and looking for respite, so back at my hotel I washed off the day in a warm bubble bath and indulged in a traditional dinner of pie and mash. My belly full and my body warm, I propped myself up against the pillows of my bed and stared at the mystery novel I'd almost finished on the nightstand, trying to decide if I should finish it or pick up the list of still unvisited places that was glaring back at me from my notebook.

Making the plan now for tomorrow's 'lazy day' would free my mind up to enjoy finishing the book before falling asleep, so I pulled the notebook from under the novel and began checking off the attractions I'd already explored. Tomorrow I'd do things a bit differently, instead of following a timed schedule, I wanted to wander, to take in the sounds and sights of London and shop without wearing through the soles of my shoes. There was a cafe on my list to try for breakfast, but getting there would require an Uber. I thought of Nigel and wondered if he'd be waiting for me when I walked out of the hotel in the morning. I smiled to myself; Nigel already felt like a friend here in London and the comfort that brought me was immense.

There were a few shops that piqued my interest near the cafe as well, all comfortably within walking distance. I'd seen them on Instagram and fell in love with the photos they posted of flowers and figurines, cute kitchen aprons and books. After that, I could Uber again to historic Kenwood House to admire the art collection and photograph some of the architecture. Their website also listed a sweet little secondhand bookshop on site, which was exciting. Maybe I could find some really old, first-edition English gems. *One could never have too many books, right?*

Not far from Kenwood House was the Spaniards Inn. It would be an easy walk there and I could spend the afternoon reading in their garden, then have dinner before making my way back to the hotel. I made a quick check of the weather and seeing no call for rain, it was settled; my lazy day was going to be just perfect. I scheduled my morning Uber and then plugged in my phone before picking up the unfinished mystery novel from my bedside table. Less than an hour later I'd finished the book. Lying there still wide awake and in need of further mental stimulation, I turned on the television.

Mindlessly flipping through the decent selection of channels, nothing really held my attention. I bypassed a few sitcoms and documentaries, a music channel, and when I reached one of the movie channels, a familiar voice stopped me. Harrison had starred in a string of romantic comedies early in his career, and this was by far one of the best. A mess of long dark curls fell just behind his shoulders, his complexion was paler, and he was short a few tattoos. His body appeared much less toned and lankier than it was now, but those captivating green eyes remained the same, and the dimples that hastened my heart rate were ever prominent. I dropped the remote onto the bed beside me and with a sigh, reached up and turned off the lights. I rolled onto my side and snuggled down beneath the covers. Spending the evening falling asleep to the sound of his voice would do just fine.

The next morning my alarm sounded as planned and I showered then decided that if I was going to wander the streets of Hampstead, arguably one of the most posh local neighborhoods, and admire art at Kenwood House, I should look the part. I pulled my hair half up and away from my face and fastened it with a barrette. I applied a little mascara and my tinted strawberry lip balm. No blush was necessary as my cheeks were rosy enough all on their own. Unlike the previous two days where I wore comfy shorts with oversized t-shirts, today I reached for a white fitted v-neck top and paired it with a navy-blue mid-length skirt. Add a comfortable pair of plain white shoes, and some oversized sunglasses that made me feel trendy but would probably give me away as a tourist, and my outfit was complete.

I didn't care, after all, I am a tourist, and I'd never see any of these people again. I checked my reflection in the full-length mirror and, feeling cute, I made sure my tote bag was loaded with my wallet, my phone, a bottle of water and a snack, as well as the romance novel I planned to start reading today, and made my way to the hotel lobby.

Through the glass doors, I stepped out onto the sidewalk and into the sunshine. There I could see a beaming Nigel, leaned up against the side of the car, feet and arms crossed, waiting for me to make my appearance. I couldn't hide my relief that he was there, and smiled back at him.

"Nigel!" I proclaimed, "We have to stop meeting like this. Someone's gonna think we're involved!"

He looked at me amused as he drew the fingertips of his right hand to his chest and replied, "Oh honey no. You're lovely, but no one would suspect *me* of such a thing."

I chuckled as I gave him a quick hug. Stepping out of the embrace, he opened the car door for me and said, "Where are we off to this morning, darling?" the smile never leaving his face.

I settled into the back of the car and when Nigel was in the driver's seat I said, "Off to Ginger and White for breakfast, and then window shopping before finding my way to Kenwood House. Do you have a lot of clients today?"

"Before *finding* your way to Kenwood House? Darling, what if you get lost?" His concern and his reaction were sweet and hilarious all at the same time.

"I'm not going to get lost. Google Maps is my bestie." I laughed.

"If you say so! As of now, I haven't got anything lined up until this afternoon once I deliver you to your destination." He responded.

"Well then, I'd love it if you'd join me for breakfast! And if I'm being honest, the only shop I was truly interested in was Judy Green's, then if you'd be so kind as to take me to Kenwood House, I'd really appreciate it. Breakfast is my treat; I insist."

"My dear, I would be delighted!" In the rearview mirror, the corners of Nigel's eyes creased as he smiled and pulled the car away from the curb and into traffic.

I was thrilled with the idea that I wouldn't be eating alone and would have someone to talk to other than my Google assistant, and I was excited to get to know Nigel better as well.

The conversation flowed easily between us as we enjoyed decadent omelets, bagels with cream cheese, fresh-squeezed orange juice, and rich mocha lattes at one of the smaller tables outside the cafe. The food in London was proving to be far superior to the food back home. It all felt like luxurious comfort food, elegantly prepared and beautifully plated, the tastes and complexity of the individual ingredients standing out against one another yet somehow mingling perfectly. Nigel and I split everything between us, which made me feel much less guilty about my indulgences.

As it turned out, I'd been right about Nigel; he really was the sweetest soul, and a kindred spirit if I'd ever known one. I trusted him, and told him all about James, and what my day-to-day life was like, and how I finally felt free to be myself since being on vacation, as if I'd been released from a life of emotional chains. Nigel told me all about his wild younger days and named off a few of the famous people he's driven around over the course of his career. He swore me to secrecy, then divulged who was sweet, who gave the best tips, and who was the bitchiest. I shared about my home renovations over the years back in New England and Nigel listed off all his favorite spots in London. We bonded over a shared love of gardening and books, and I learned Nigel was an amateur photographer in his younger days. He even offered to snap a few photos of me at landmarks while we shared each other's company.

The morning pressed on, and we continued to share stories as we pored over the delightful goods offered at Judy Green's Garden Store. An absolutely adorable little spot with one-of-a-kind gifts and an abundance of fresh live plants and unique garden items, it was like something you'd see in a film. I felt like I was walking through a whimsical, quintessentially old-fashioned flower shop. Mindful of what I would be able to carry, I chose two small rabbit figurines as mementos of the day. I even had the shopkeeper take a photo of me and Nigel together. We'd had a wonderful morning and when we were done, Nigel drove me to Kenwood House, making sure to exchange cell phone numbers before parting ways. I felt confident that if I needed him at any time while I was here, he'd be there for me in the blink of an eye. *What a comfort to have made such a wonderful friend so easily.*

As I approached the magnificent and sprawling Kenwood House, I found the sheer size of the place quite daunting; the centuries-old massive structure made me feel tiny in comparison. With a dynamic history, full of ornate antique decor and pieces of art by world renowned artists, I was immediately drawn in by the details and found myself fascinated by all the displays. The ceilings were covered in gorgeously painted artwork and the gardens were lush and mature. I couldn't resist snapping photos with my phone the entire time and I spent a considerable amount of time in their secondhand bookstore, but I kept myself in check, choosing only two novels I felt I just couldn't live without to bring back home with me.

Then, as the morning turned to early afternoon, I searched on my phone for walking directions to the Spaniards Inn. My reservation was for 2 p.m., and Google maps showed it was about a ten-minute walk. I waved goodbye to Kenwood House and set off to find some lunch, planning to dive head-first into one of my newly acquired books. I'd read about the history of the Spaniards Inn, the charm and influence of their gardens and the delicious menu they serve, and couldn't wait to see it for myself. Its atmosphere and garden had inspired many over the years, from poets and authors to actors and directors, and I was eager to spend the afternoon among such greatness.

As I walked along the narrow sidewalk, the route provided views of verdant foliage on both sides of the street, and despite the constant whir of traffic, I could hear birdsong among the canopy above me. I passed an opening in the trees bound together by an old iron gate, giving way to a gorgeous view of someone's private garden. I paused a moment and observed a variety of birds enjoying a birdbath, their delicate little wings splashing water over the filigreed edges and onto the grass below.

I smiled and continued walking, letting the rhythmic crunch of gravel beneath my tennis shoes craft my thoughts into daydreams. I imagined myself lying atop a soft blanket in the plush grass, a dreamy look in my eye and a book in my hands with a bouquet of blue and pink bachelor buttons scattered around me, I picked up one of the delicate blooms and placed it in my hair behind my ear and smiled as a grown man in a paperboy outfit approached and delivered an ice cold lemonade to me, telling me I'm the most refreshing thing he'd seen all day...

A change in the height of the sidewalk made me realize I'd nearly walked right past my destination, but once I was through the door of the Spaniards Inn, I was greeted warmly by a young man who took my name and asked if I had a reservation. I nodded and proceeded to apologetically tell him I'd arrived a bit early. I glanced around the inside of the very busy pub; it appeared the lunch rush was still in full swing and there were very few open tables inside. So, I opted to sit outside, asking for a shady table in the garden where the open-air seating would dissipate the chatter from surrounding diners allowing me to read for a while. The gentleman pulled a menu from beneath his podium and ushered me through the dining room and out into the abundant garden.

The afternoon sun shone through the trees and fell like patterned lace against the table as I took a seat in the far corner, making sure to position myself for optimal people-watching. From the top of my head, I lowered my sunglasses to shield my wandering eyes and proceeded to shuffle through the menu, searching for something tasty. Earlier I'd craved a good old-fashioned cheeseburger, so that made my decision fairly easy, and I paired it with a Shirley Temple just to feel fancy. Being alone and planning to be here for the duration of the afternoon, I was apprehensive to order a mixed drink or to have any alcohol in my system this early in the day.

My lunch arrived when I was still in the early chapters of the romance novel, and I picked away at my food between pages until it was gone. Curious as to whether I was taking too much time at my table, I questioned my waiter to be sure I wasn't expected to eat and then rush off. He assured me that lunch was winding down and people often come to sit and enjoy the garden, and I was welcome to take my time and stay as long as I'd like. That's all it took for me to order another Shirley Temple and relax back into my seat as the waiter cleared my dishes.

When a line in the novel made me think of Emma, I laid it down and picked up my phone. I attached a collage of four photos that included my selfie with the wax museum Beyoncé, a photo of my breakfast from that morning, the photo of me and Nigel, and a shot from the top of the London Eye. I sent a short message that read:

Having a blast, making friends, and eating well. What's new with you?

Before I had time to set my phone down, I got a response.

Not having as much fun as you are, but all is well here. Bey looks a little stiff. Who's the guy?

I responded:

My new friend and navigator, Nigel. At the coolest old pub now for lunch, gorgeous atmosphere. Wish you were here.

Emma responded with a simple:

Ditto.

I returned my attention to my book and was once again oblivious to anything happening around me.

It had been a few hours since lunch and I'd sipped on three Shirley Temples over the course of the afternoon. On my way back to the table from the bathroom, I noticed that the early dinner crowd was beginning to filter in, and I was happy to have new faces to admire. I resumed my relaxed position in my comfy corner chair and found an even balance of reading and observing those around me.

My book drew closer to the end and I was glad; it had been a terrible read. Despite the lackluster literature, my afternoon certainly wasn't wasted, as I was quite content spending time in the garden. I had the other two books in my bag from the secondhand shop to dive into and really didn't feel like leaving yet; it was so calming here, and I enjoyed the smells coming from the kitchen and the sounds of the English accents all around me.

The afternoon turned to evening, and I wondered what the rest of my trip would look like. So far it had been everything I'd hoped for. I was enjoying all the sights on my 'must-see' list, indulging in great food and taking lots of photos. I'd barely thought about James at all, and when I did it only soured my mood. *He'd hate being here*, I thought. *He'd have turned this trip into something miserable I'd have no choice but to endure.*

I realized then that I may never be in this position again, alone on vacation, untethered, free to do as I please without having to explain myself to anyone or worry about what anyone else wants to do or how they like to have fun. I was only in London for a few more days before I'd have no choice but to return to my treacherous reality, *so why not indulge a little?* I thought. After all, it was a warm fall Saturday night in a dreamy faraway land. I was feeling good in my skin, just taking it all in, and if I needed to, I could always call Nigel for a ride.

So, I perused the drink menu, unsure of what I had a taste for. There was no need to get crazy, I just wanted to loosen up a bit, so I decided on a mojito, a drink I'd thoroughly enjoyed once in a dream. The waiter delivered it to me in a tall skinny glass, bits of muddled mint drifting through the clear concoction like tiny emeralds floating among the ice cubes. The smell alone made my mouth water.

As the first sip danced on my taste buds, my mind flashed back to the night I dreamed I was on Miami Beach with a beautiful man whose name I never got. We sat in the warm sand under the stars and listened to the waves pound against the shore as the incoming tide chased us further and further toward the dunes. I could still see his face in my mind. He was timelessly gorgeous, his smile electric against his dark complexion, his eyes the deepest brown I had ever seen. His baritone voice was like molasses, slow and deep. I'd laughed all night with him, and under those stars we shared a few incredible kisses and a few too many mojitos until the sun peeked over the horizon. I wasn't sure where he came from or why he'd appeared in my dream, but there were things about him I'd never forgotten.

Before long, one mojito turned to two, and no matter how slowly I sipped them, I could still feel the heat in my chest from the rum. When the waiter appeared again, I ordered a plate of traditional chips, French fries to us Americans, hoping the starch might reverse the dizzying effects of the liquor, and returned my drink of choice to Shirley Temples. *That's enough of the wild side for today*, I thought. Between the cozy welcoming ambiance, this magnificent garden I found myself in, and the people-watching, I wasn't sure which was the highlight of my day. If I were home, I'd be standing in the kitchen cooking or cleaning the house or ignoring myself and my needs to accommodate James. This trip had truly come at just the right time.

Another hour passed, as did another bathroom break, and as I made my way back to my table for the second time, the sun hung noticeably lower in the sky. I realized I'd been here all afternoon, and despite my waiter's charm and welcoming words, I felt awkward sticking around much longer. In my head I debated whether I should head back to the hotel; I didn't really want to. All that was there was silence and solitude, not much different than being at home. *A little longer can't hurt. You may never be back here again. Just enjoy it, Alice. Do what you want. Who cares?* To avoid the blinding glare, I put on my sunglasses and stayed focused on my book until the warmth of the sun had fallen behind a neighboring building.

When I felt the chill of the shadows washing over me, prompting me to put my book and my sunglasses into my tote bag, I noticed the sunny garden I sat down in a few hours ago had transformed into a dizzying array of sparkling golden twinkle lights woven among the canopy of the trees and draped among the ivy-wrapped pergolas. The only people that remained outside congregated in small groups at intimate tables all throughout the garden space, sharing drinks and laughter and stories. One of the waiters was starting a fire in a nearby fire ring that was surrounded by seating, and soft music was wafting through the air from outside speakers. This place was absolutely as magnificent as I'd always heard it was.

I sat and watched the people around me, thinking back to my childhood. My grandparents had been part of the 'it' crowd when I was young and surrounded themselves with groups of friends almost every weekend. Even when I was there visiting, they'd have gatherings or go out to dinner as a group, always happy to bring me along with them. I was always the kid dancing around, reciting jokes, trying to coax smiles from people, and I'd been a people pleaser my entire life simply because I loved the sound of laughter. As I got older, I'd listen to the adults make toasts when they got together at parties, and I grew to enjoy all the ways people would celebrate one another. I missed those carefree days, my grandparents, and the way things were.

I caught myself smiling at the memories scrolling through my mind and thought, *The people around me probably think I'm nuts, sitting alone in the corner, gazing at twinkle lights and smiling at nothing*, but it didn't stop me from laughing at myself once again.

Nakia Cramer

5.

I was so lost in my thoughts I never even saw the man approach me. He reached out with one arm and gently placed his hand on my shoulder, gaining my attention as the other held him propped above the table. I'd been mindlessly staring in a different direction, reminiscing in my head and smiling to myself, and then suddenly there he was, half leaned over my table, staring at me with a smile that could melt glaciers.

"Excuse me, love, is this seat taken?" he said in a slow English accent, his voice low, his hand warm against my shoulder.

My heart nearly stopped right there inside my chest. I knew that voice, but it was deeper than I remembered. Slowly, I turned my head to meet his gaze. As I looked up, our eyes met and I blinked hard twice, trying to make sure that what I was seeing was real. Dropping my eyes to the hand on my shoulder, I felt the warmth of his palm, the weight of his fingertips on my body. Speechless, I swallowed what felt like a balloon down into my throat and, still in disbelief, I let my eyes follow his muscular arm back up to his shoulder, then found myself once again gazing into his beautiful green eyes, utterly mesmerized.

A singular dark curl fell forward and brushed against the bridge of his nose as he stood there smiling at me, waiting for my response. His hand moved from my shoulder to grasp at the messy waves, using his fingers to comb a fistful of hair away from his forehead. My eyes fell back to the arm that held him hovering above me. *Jesus, the muscles.* As my mystified stare climbed from his hand upward, I noticed his left arm, covered in tattoos. As my mind fully pieced together exactly who I was looking at, my mouth fell open and an inadvertent gasp broke through my stunned silence.

I hesitated and swallowed hard before saying, "You, want to sit…with me?" The words were nearly a whisper as they fell from my lips; my chest heavy, I struggled to find oxygen, like all the air had been sucked from my lungs and I could feel my heartbeat in my throat.

"I'd like to if you wouldn't mind the company." He smiled confidently as he waited for me to respond. A black hooded sweatshirt draped over his shoulder began to fall forward and landed on the empty chair his thigh was leaning against. *The thigh with the lion tattoo*…My eyes widened as the visual flashed through my mind.

Trying to regain some of my composure, I attempted to be funny. "I wasn't sure if you just wanted the chair." A loud nervous laugh burst forth before I uttered, "I'd love you…"

I shook my head and stared down at my lap, trying to shake off the embarrassment. "I'd love *TO*…" I put all the emphasis on the corrected word and then stopped speaking completely after a deep flustered sigh.

"Yes. Please. Join me," I finally managed to say then swallowed hard and held out my hand to let him know any of the seats were available before I quickly placed both my hands to my now flaming hot cheeks. Feeling the fire beneath my skin, I took a long sip of my drink to try and settle my nerves.

When he pulled out the chair to my left, I noticed his loose faded blue jeans and his tanned right knee poking out from beneath a worn tear in the denim as he sat down. A tiny tattoo in a foreign language was disguised by the hair on his leg and his black t-shirt was snug, but not in a pretentious way, and the scent of him that wafted through the air as he sat down was more intoxicating than any alcohol the pub had on hand. He smelled of vanilla and hints of tobacco with a warm spice that hung in the air around him, awakening my senses and triggering memories of the vanilla bath products from my road trip dream. I was getting more and more drunk on him with each passing moment.

He held his hand out and with a playful grin said, "Hi, I'm Harrison. What's your name?"

His smile and the dimples I loved so much were sitting right in front of me in actual real life and they sent my mind into a tailspin. I just looked at him, bewildered. My eyes dropped to the navy-blue bandana coiled around itself tied in a loose knot around his neck. It was exactly the same as in my dream. Just below it glimmered a gold chain and my mind flashed back to the image of him coming out of the pool, stark naked, the same chain catching the sunlight.

I was stuck in my own head, unable to wrap my mind around the fact that this was real life and here he was. This wasn't a dream. This wasn't my wild imagination. He had approached me. He wanted to sit at *my* table. *He* was trying to make conversation with *me*. As the gold cross pendant caught the light and sparkled, it was like someone flipped a switch and I snapped back to reality. I blinked again quickly this time and extended my trembling hand to shake his as I began to apologize, hoping it wasn't obvious how rattled I was.

"You caught me off guard, sorry for my…" I nervously laughed again, and made a face, rolling my eyes as if to signal that he caught me in la-la land. "I'm Alice; it's a pleasure." When our hands touched, it sent sparks through my entire nervous system, and I remembered the way his hands felt in my dream. Strong but soft and gentle as they caressed and groped at my bare skin; just the thought of it evoked an unexpected and embarrassing shiver.

Get it together, Alice.

"Oh, the pleasure is mine." He smiled and lowered his eyes to the table before continuing. "I have that effect on people sometimes, sorry about that. You can wear my sweatshirt if you're cold." He held it out to me, and I was relieved he thought I shivered from the chill in the air and not the images scrolling through my mind of his capable hands against my bare body.

"I'm okay; thank you though; that's so kind of you." I blushed as he looked at me endearingly.

His eyes were even more beautiful in person than any photo I'd ever seen of him. An iridescent mixture of celadon green and shades of gray, against a cool steel blue, the twinkle lights reflecting gold bursts like pools reflecting sunlight. I smiled bashfully as my mind reeled. *He's just a normal person, Alice*, I kept thinking. *Normal, just like anyone else.* I inhaled deeply to try to regulate my anxious breathing only to be met with the scent of his cologne pushing me further into my own spiraling head.

Harrison continued, "I noticed you sitting here alone for a bit and couldn't help but think that anyone as enchanting as you appear, must be as interesting as they are beautiful. I hope that's not too forward of me to say?"

I blushed and muttered, "Oh, thank you; you're sweet..." brushing it off like it was no big deal for someone with Harrison's accolades to be complimenting me, but internally, I was full-on screaming.

"I don't mean to embarrass you. I'm sorry. Can I buy you another drink? If you're open to it, I'd love to share your table for a bit, get to know you. But of course, if you'd rather be alone, I understand." He looked at me so genuinely, there was no way in hell I would ever ask him to leave.

"I'd like that, thank you. Nothing fancier than a Shirley Temple." I laughed as I lifted my nearly empty glass as if to cheers, a lone cherry anchored to the bottom by the weight of ice cubes in what was left of the pink concoction. "But I'll take just a ginger ale if you don't mind."

"Sure, sit tight and I'll be right back." Harrison excused himself and headed toward the bar.

As soon as he walked away, I took another deep breath, and tried again to calm my nerves, hoping the ginger ale might settle my now anxious stomach. I looked around feverishly before closing my eyes, drawing in a few more calculated deep breaths, wringing my still shaking hands together and mumbling under my breath, "Get it together." Again, I glanced over at the tables close by to see if anyone was watching me freak out, but thankfully no one was looking my way.

I could hear Harrison's voice at the bar, "Red wine and a ginger ale, please."

My God, his accent. I could lose my mind just listening to him speak. *My hands are sweating. My hands never sweat; what is happening? Deep breaths, Alice.* Trying to appear normal and unfazed by it all, I was failing miserably. The man of my actual dreams was buying me a drink. Emma would die if she knew what was happening, but I had no time to text her. Harrison was already walking back toward me; a wide childlike smile unearthed his famous dimples again as soon as we made eye contact. *I'm not gonna make it outta here alive.*

He settled back into his seat and handed me my glass.

"Let's cheers, shall we?" he said, the already familiar scent of his cologne following him like a shadow.

I raised my glass as Harrison began to speak, desperate to hide the fact that my palms were still sweaty and my glass was trembling in my hand.

"Here's to new friends with old souls. May we be them, and may we find them." He flashed me a quick smile before motioning his glass toward mine.

He expertly swirled the wine in his glass as I fixated on his every move. Lost in what felt like a slow-motion sequence, I watched as he took a heavy inhale then tipped the glass to his perfect lips; I sat there entranced by the way his mouth met the edge of his glass, hoping he didn't notice. I drew my straw to my mouth and our eyes met. We held eye contact just long enough for goosebumps to cover my entire body.

"I'm glad to see you share the tradition of looking someone in the eye when you cheers," I said. I'd always been horrible with holding eye contact, so much so that I'm terribly self-conscious about it. "It could mean seven years of bad sex if you don't." I playfully raised my eyebrows at him with a look of caution.

"Well, no one wants that," Harrison laughed as he said it, seemingly surprised by my remark.

"No, absolutely not." I smiled at him.

Though the idea of bad sex was still better than no sex, and my mind immediately shot to James. I began to fidget with my wedding band in the darkness beneath the table, nervously rolling it in circles around my finger. Awkward silence. My eyes darted around the garden, unsure what to say next as Harrison remained completely calm and relaxed beside me.

"So, tell me about yourself, Alice. Your accent gives you away as an American. Are you here on holiday?" He was trying to make me feel comfortable around him, and I was thankful for it.

"I am. I'm from a little town in New England you've probably never heard of. Pretty typical for the location, I live in an old farmhouse surrounded by acres of woods and fields and flower gardens. It's a pretty quiet existence but," I shrugged, "it's home. All I've ever known, really."

"That sounds amazing, and peaceful. I'm jealous," he remarked.

"Thanks...I decided recently that it was time to end the redundancy of it all and take a trip, literally, but also out of my comfort zone, so here I am. What about you? What brings you here tonight and alone? Doesn't someone of your status usually travel with an entourage?" I wanted him to know that I knew exactly who he was, and that I understood the weight of his celebrity.

"I'm on holiday myself, technically. I've no work scheduled for the next week or so, and this place is actually quite special to me." Harrison gestured toward the main dining room with one hand and rubbed his chin with the other as he spoke. "I have a home just around the bend you could say, and I tend to either come in for dinner or get takeaway delivered whenever I'm in town. I've always loved the atmosphere here, and how kind the staff are to me when I come in. No one ever makes a big deal and whenever I've been here, I've never felt the need to bring security or scads of people with me; it just draws more attention. It's pretty chill; no one acts too crazy. I guess they've all got used to me by now." He shrugged and raked his fingers through his hair again.

"If I'm being honest, I'm a little blown away that you, of all the people in the world, are sitting here with me right now," I smirked as I said it.

I could only assume that everyone always knew who he was, without any introduction, but he had taken the time and formally introduced himself to me. In hindsight, it was something he was known for. Maybe it was out of courtesy, or maybe he held out hope that who he was was still a mystery to some people. Either way, I had started to come to terms with the fact that I was having a drink and sharing a conversation with a full-blown worldwide movie star, and began to wonder what we could possibly have in common.

"Not gonna lie, Alice, as soon as I walked out onto the deck, your smile caught my eye. I don't know what made you laugh like you did, but I was so taken with you, I actually stepped back inside the dining room and admired you as your eyes drifted from person to person. I saw your smile and I knew I needed to say hello to you. I can appreciate a woman that's strong enough to go out and sit alone and enjoy herself. Not to mention, and forgive me if I'm being forward, I'm quite taken with not only your smile but your eyes. You are indeed, a beautiful lady." He held me in his gaze for a moment, showing his sincerity while his index finger and thumb nervously twisted and stroked the stem of his wine glass. Then, almost as if he were self-conscious, he lowered his eyes from mine, and I noticed the apples of his cheeks begin to flush.

I wanted to make him feel at ease with me as well and said, "Well flattery will get you everywhere, sir," and gave him a flirtatious grin while I simultaneously reached out and placed my hand over the top of his, giving it a quick squeeze.

"For what it's worth, I've always considered you quite irresistible. Had a hell of a dream about you once, too," I nodded as the images scrolled through my mind then sighed deeply. "True story."

"Oh? Well, you've piqued my interest now; do tell." Harrison was intrigued. In one swift exaggerated movement, both his elbows were on the table, and with wrists together he rested his chin on his hands, looking at me quizzically with a wide and curious grin.

I raised my eyebrows and said, "It was pretty steamy...one for the record books, that's for sure. Thanks for that." I laughed and turned my face away to hide the heat bubbling back into my cheeks. "That's all I'm gonna say about that."

"Oh, it's like that? Fine. I see how you are." Harrison scrunched half his face up, feigning annoyance, and started to stand as if he was going to leave. Naturally I laughed at him, and when he turned back to face me, our eyes locked on one another again.

The feel of the evening had been casual and somewhat playful, but sitting here together now, we found ourselves paralyzed in a moment of quiet mutual admiration. We held each other's gaze without speaking while the rest of the world fell away and became silent. Our eyes searched beyond our growing physical attraction to one another and somehow solidified a much deeper emotional connection.

I could hardly breathe. I was lost in the moment, staring back at a man that had an apparent yearning for me in his eyes that I had only ever seen in sappy romance movies, or more recently, in my own dreams. *Breathe, Alice.* I drew in a sharp breath through my nose and exhaled slowly, an anxious reaction I had come to expect from myself. I never took my eyes off of him, elated at the thought of Harrison Edwards being so taken with me he couldn't take his eyes off of me either, and I was somehow able to hold eye contact with him without shying away.

Somewhere in the distance, a drink spilled from a table and landed on the deck, shattering more than just the silence we'd been lost in. Harrison grinned as he realized how long we'd been staring at each other, and in an attempt to ease the awkwardness, nonchalantly asked what my plans were for the rest of my trip.

I smiled at him a moment before responding, "Well, I'm here until Thursday, so I have a few more days of sightseeing. Still on my list are Primrose Hill and maybe Hampton Court Palace. One thing I've always wanted to do was take a drive through the Dales, but that's quite a ways from here and I'm not sure an Uber will make that kind of trip." I shrugged and brushed the idea of visiting the English countryside out of my mind.

"The Dales are gorgeous. North of my hometown. I went there as a kid and remember the vibrancy of the greenery and the historic feel of the place. It's quiet there and a great place to enjoy the slowed-down feel of the country. Definitely worth a trip if you get the time, but from here, it would likely be at least one if not two overnights by car, depending on how much you want to see. Unless you're rushing, but you never want to rush through the Dales; they're for relaxing into and enjoying the experience."

"I saw it's about four hours from London, right? So definitely at least one overnight. Maybe next time I'm here I'll work it into my plans. But, other than that, I had planned to find a few lovely quiet spaces to relax and read, maybe treat myself to a spa day, and find some amazing food. Pretty low-key really. That's just the kind of person I am." I noticed his eyelashes as I spoke to him, so long and dark against the deep pools of his blue-green eyes.

I watched him intently as we traded words, the golden twinkle lights dancing in the night air reflected in his eyes, the volume in his coffee-colored curls, ever present despite their continuously being drug back by his masculine but somehow delicate right hand. Chipped and worn black and turquoise nail polish on intermittent fingernails. The fine lines that appeared around his eyes when he smiled, and the day-old stubble that would have looked careless on anyone else looked inviting and humble on Harrison.

I was learning that he was different than in my dream. Just as approachable and kind, his accent just as extraordinary, but he was far more handsome in person than my dreams or even the internet had led me to believe, his voice was deeper than I'd imagined, and he had a nervous habit of touching his chin or his lips while he searched for words. I was also beginning to feel much more at ease than I had been when he first approached me. There was a humility and a realness about Harrison that made him feel familiar.

My long lost self-esteem had been resuscitated just by his presence; the ease I felt with him ran deeper than my attraction to his physical appearance though, and I felt seen as he nodded in agreement with the things I said, and I felt heard as he articulated his thoughts on shared ideas. He laughed at my jokes, and it was easy to see that he appreciated me for who I am. He focused intently on me, and for someone who was always overlooked and dismissed at home, this feeling was something I had been yearning for and missing for decades.

The night progressed, and I was pleasantly surprised to find that the things we talked about weren't just surface level. In the back of my mind I expected Harrison to have some terrible hidden flaw or ooze some form of thinly veiled narcissism, or that he would only talk about himself and ignore the depth of my thoughts, but he genuinely wanted to get to know me and asked me things about myself that were surprisingly thought provoking and a delightful change from the conversations I was used to.

We dove deep into one another's childhoods, sharing our experiences with how we were brought up and the type of environments we both thrived and struggled in, what helped shape us into the adults we had become. Harrison explained the bond he shared with his granddad and how he'd lost him to Alzheimer's a few years earlier, and I recounted all my favorite memories with my grandmother, sharing with Harrison the lengthy battle she fought and ultimately lost to cancer.

After he finished his glass of wine Harrison switched to water, admitting he wanted me to feel like the things I had to say were his priority. The switch also coincided with my explanation of how my parents had both been heavy drinkers and how it had affected me mentally and emotionally for the majority of my life. A sweet unspoken gesture, it was clear he was listening when I spoke, processing how I felt and reacting accordingly, and I appreciated that about him. Most men I knew wouldn't take any of those things into consideration, much less adjust their behavior to accommodate how I felt. Hell, many wouldn't even hear me at all when I spoke.

Our conversation morphed from deep and emotional to lighter topics, and we found that we had a shared love of travel, historic architecture, eighties music, classic rock, and poetry. We compared bucket lists and found we had more similarities than differences when it came to checking future adventures off our lists. We both talked about losing ourselves in books and discovered that each of us had found our love of literature through our grandparents, and that we both have spaces in our homes dedicated to our personal libraries, which include books that have been handed down for generations. Harrison told me he never would have gone into acting if his granddad and mother hadn't supported him wholeheartedly and pushed him toward the dreams he originally thought were too far-fetched, and I divulged that my love of books and literature secretly drive me to one day become an author.

It was abundantly clear to me that Harrison wasn't the person television and magazine articles portrayed him to be. The media would have you believe he's a womanizer, bed-hopping from woman to woman with no true regard for them, a class-A liar and a jerk who thinks of no one but himself, and that he has a flamboyant, snobby side that makes him unapproachable. Sitting with me tonight, he had been a caring and thoughtful man, unafraid to share his emotions and his hopes with me. He was humble and honest, and after my initial shock of him wanting to sit with me wore off, he was someone that I really enjoyed talking with. He had kind eyes, a welcoming smile, and by my calculations, a sincere soul. He was just a normal, regular human being that had worked hard to afford himself a life of unusual circumstance.

Not once over the course of the evening did either of us question one another or bring up anything regarding significant others. It was almost as if we'd silently agreed not to talk about it. Sure, he had paid me a few nice compliments when he initially sat down, but this was just a conversation, in a public place, not some secret tryst. And sure, I was attracted to him. He was an absolute masterpiece of a man; how could I not be? But that was no reason to scream from the rooftops that I'm married. Nothing had transpired between us to provoke it as a response to anything. And what difference would it make? I didn't need or want to know who Harrison was involved with. We had talked about private family things, but private physical relationships were a whole different topic, and I didn't feel compelled to bring up James. This trip was about finding myself and my happiness again, and at least for tonight, that didn't include discussing my husband.

Our conversation never slowed, but the soft sounds of neighboring conversations had crawled to a stop and when we finally looked around us, there was no one left at the Spaniards Inn besides the two of us and the head waiter that stood in the doorway of the dining room, appearing quite anxious to go home.

Harrison checked the time on his phone, "Oh wow, it's late. Well after eleven already. Do you have a car?" he said as he slipped his hooded sweatshirt over his messy curls and straightened it against his frame.

"No, I was going to call an Uber." I reached into my bag for my phone prepared to call Nigel, and thought to myself, *I wish I could have a photo to remember this night, but it would make me just like everyone else if I asked for one. Let the man have some peace, Alice.*

"I'm just thinking out loud here, but I can have my driver take you to your hotel if you like. Where are you staying?" His concern for me was appreciated and didn't go unnoticed.

"You don't have to do that." I waved him off, reluctant to bother him.

"I want to, come on." He held out his hand to me and smiled.

"Are you sure? If you don't mind, that would be so kind of you. I'm staying at the Clayton Crown in Cricklewood. It should be about a fifteen-minute drive, I think?" Secretly I was relieved that he offered; calling Nigel at this hour might make him less friendly than he had been previously.

"Of course, Alice, I've got you. Let me make a quick call and we'll be on our way." He stepped away from me and quietly made a call, while I made sure all my belongings were neatly tucked into my tote bag, readying myself to leave. I pulled my wallet from my bag and motioned for the waiter, who was eager to help.

Harrison was quick to intervene. "No no, love, no need for that." He placed his hand over mine and used it to flip the top of my wallet closed. "Put it on my tab please, Thomas. Thank you." He reached out to shake the man's hand and in doing so, placed two red-hued banknotes in Thomas' palm that I couldn't recognize. Under his breath, Harrison said, "For being so patient with us."

I wasn't going to let him pay for my entire afternoon at this pub; he was already taking me back to the hotel. I didn't expect him to pay for my lunch and drinks *and* drive me across town.

"Thank you but I can—" I started, but before I could finish my sentence, he interrupted.

"It's fine. I'm happy to do it. Let me, please." He smiled at me and cocked his head cutely in an attempt to halt my protest.

I sighed, fully under his spell, and smiled. "Thank you. You're such a sweetheart."

"Ready to go?" Harrison carefully placed his palm against the small of my back and together we walked to the door.

A large black SUV with heavily tinted windows was waiting for us just a few steps from the front door of the Spaniards Inn. A tall muscular man waited outside the car, holding the back door open for us. Harrison helped me into the back of the vehicle before settling himself into the warm leather seat beside me. Once we were both comfortable and Harrison's driver had returned to the driver's seat, I saw the man's eyes in the rearview mirror as he asked, "Where to, boss?"

"Lawrence, this is Alice. Alice, Lawrence," Harrison replied.

I said a polite hello and watched Lawrence's eyes remain steadfast in the mirror as he dipped his head quickly in acknowledgment.

After a brief pause, Harrison continued. "Lawrence, we're going to be returning Alice to her hotel, the Clayton Crown over at Cricklewood, please."

"Yes, sir, glad to." Lawrence plugged the hotel's information into his navigation system as he raised the blackened glass that divided the front and back seats of the vehicle before gently pulling away from the curb.

Once the partition was securely closed, I turned to Harrison. "I just wanna tell you something. Harrison, I've had a wonderful evening with you. Thank you for your kindness and the wonderful conversation. If it wasn't already before tonight, this trip is definitely memorable now." In my head I still couldn't believe I was in the back of Harrison Edwards' car with him on the way back to a hotel in London after spending the entire evening with him. This had easily been the most surreal night of my existence.

"Well, I appreciate that you turned out to be even more enchanting than I first imagined you to be. It's not often I find myself in the presence of someone that can navigate between who I am as a real person, and who I've been painted as to the public, and truly be able to keep the two versions separate. It makes all the difference in the world to me. I feel comfortable with you Alice, and that's rare."

In the darkness of the backseat he gently took my hand in his and I felt his finger pause as it brushed against the gold band on my left ring finger, just long enough for him to realize what it was he'd found, then quickly moved away from it. My hand remained in his, but no words were spoken by either of us. In the flickering of the passing streetlights, I watched him, nervous for his reaction. I could see his wheels turning in the way his eyes narrowed as they looked away from me and toward the window beside him.

After a few quiet moments, I reluctantly asked, "Are you okay?"

I knew the car ride wasn't going to be a long one and we must be fast approaching the hotel by now. I didn't want to end the night on a sour note after everything else had felt so special.

Harrison turned in his seat to face me and said, "I think we have a lot in common Alice, and this has been the most interesting and enjoyable evening I've had in a really long time."

As he spoke, his eyes shifted from me to the window behind me, then down to our now interlaced fingers, before resting sullenly back into my eyes. His voice had grown quieter than it had been before, with a marked sadness and I could feel the muscles in his fingers still taking stock of the fact that I was wearing a wedding band. There was no doubt he knew for sure now that I was married though he never asked me about it directly, and I didn't offer any explanation.

Harrison drew in a deep breath and exhaled slowly before he said, "I'd like to see you again Alice, but I'm not sure that's something you'd be open to."

My mind raced. Every ounce of my being was screaming "YES!" I absolutely wanted to see him again. Flashbacks from my dream shot through my mind like scenes from a favorite movie, each one a tiny explosion fueling me to accept his invitation, but just as I opened my mouth to answer him, a tiny whisper in my head repeated, *What about James, Alice? What about James?* I'd done nothing wrong tonight and didn't feel bad about any of my behavior. I spent time with someone interesting and well traveled, and so what if he was handsome? If I accepted, I could keep my cool, and just share time with Harrison without it being anything inappropriate; I was in full control of myself. At least, that's what I'd convinced my conscience. *Enough with the back and forth, just go with it*, I thought to myself and pushed James from my mind.

"I *would* like to see you again, Harrison." With every bit of confidence I could manage, I locked eyes with him. Seconds felt like hours before I finished my sentence. "I'd like that, *very* much." I said with a smile.

Harrison reached into his pocket and handed me his phone. "Would you be willing to give me your number? That way I can text you and we can set something up?"

"Of course," I said and carefully entered my number before hitting send and handed the phone back to him. I then pulled my phone from my bag and as the screen lit up, I held it up for Harrison to see. "See, it's really me. Make sure you save it."

"I absolutely will." Harrison smiled his adorable comforting smile, and I was glad the mood had lightened a bit.

The car slowed to a stop and I heard Lawrence get out, presumably to open the door for me. I squeezed Harrison's hand and once again my eyes met his.

"Thank you again for tonight, and the ride and the drinks. It's too much, but I appreciate you. I've really enjoyed your company. And I'll understand completely if you decide you don't want to see me again. Really." I was rambling again.

"The pleasure was mine. Thank you, Alice. But I assure you, you'll be hearing from me," he cooed, with a calmness in his voice and a twinkle in his eye. His accent sent shivers through me.

Control yourself, Alice.

Beside me, the door opened and without a word, Lawrence reached in to help me out of the SUV. As I took his hand and stepped out onto the quiet empty sidewalk, Harrison followed. He reached out and wrapped his arms around me, pulling me into his body. For the first time, I noticed how much taller he was than me. While our embrace lasted longer than a normal hug, my heart began to race and I took the opportunity to nestle my cheek against the softness of his sweatshirt, inhaling his cologne in the process. I could feel how toned his chest was beneath the material, and his arms around me felt like a home my heart had yearned for forever. Harrison thanked me again for the lovely evening and as we broke away from one another, he flashed me that famous smile, dimples and all.

"Talk with you soon love," and just like that, he climbed back into the SUV, and was gone from my view.

I wandered through the hotel lobby in a daze, replaying the evening in my head as I walked to my suite. Once inside, I set my bag down on the bed before collapsing seated beside it. Bewildered, I let myself free-fall backwards against the pillows, a smitten grin across my face, and with eyes closed I tried to decipher how my day had started versus what it had turned into. I just spent the entire evening with *the actual* Harrison Edwards. Not the man from the movies, not the man on the cover of the magazine still sitting on the coffee table. Hell, not even the man from my dreams. The real live, living, breathing, actual Harrison Edwards. I shook my head in disbelief.

"Wild," I said aloud to no one, smiling to myself until my cheeks hurt.

A sudden vibration from my phone still in my bag beside me shook me back to the present. I focused my eyes on a text message from a number not yet saved in my phone.

How does tomorrow sound for a picnic and some scenery? It's me, Harrison.

I smiled as I read it. Not wanting to sound too eager, I laid my head back down on the bed, took a deep breath and slowly counted to ten before picking the phone back up, saving his number in my contacts as simply "H." and then replied:

Sounds perfect. What time?

Almost immediately the phone vibrated again.

How's 9am? Bring that beautiful smile; I'll do the rest.

9 a.m.? I was surprised; it seemed early for a picnic. But what did that matter? I'd be spending the day with Harrison Edwards! I replied:

I'll be ready and waiting. :)

His response was quick:

Lawrence and I will see you in the morning. Comfy clothes. xx :)

My last response to him was:

Sleep tight.

A few minutes passed as I lay there, still mystified at what my life had become in just a few short hours. Tomorrow needed no planning on my part; I'd be spending time with Harrison again. I felt embarrassed just thinking about it, and despite the fact there was no one there to hear me, I said aloud, "Wait a minute..." and reached for my phone again.

I looked back at Harrison's last text, noting how he ended it with 'xx'. I tapped the multi-colored G on my phone to open a Google search and typed in 'xx in a text' in the search bar before pressing Enter to see what that translated to. In America x's and o's were kisses and hugs, but surely he wasn't sending me kisses. Was he?

Suddenly I saw: "xx means 'two kisses.' (Sometimes, the kisses are in lowercase, sometimes they're in uppercase, and sometimes a mix of both.) As a general rule, an uppercase X represents a big kiss and a lowercase x is a light kiss (a peck)."

Oh my God! He was sending me kisses! I didn't know quite what to make of it. *Kisses! Two kisses no less! From Harrison. HARRISON EDWARDS!!* My thoughts were once again a rollercoaster of excitement and shock.

Wait! Stop it, Alice! You need to calm down or you'll never get to sleep tonight.

After a deep breath to center myself, I gathered my night clothes and went into the bathroom, dancing freely to a tune stuck in my head from earlier in the evening. I indulged in a long, very hot bath, and no matter how I tried to push it from my mind, I felt compelled to shave everything on my body that may, or may not, need it, because a handsome movie star had asked me on a date for tomorrow, and trying to keep myself in check by not shaving would be an absolute mistake. I had no intention of needing a shaved anything and rationalized the thought by telling myself it just made me feel prettier and more put-together when I maintained smooth surfaces. *Bullshit.* The imaginary angel on my shoulder rolled her eyes and hung her head while the devil on my other shoulder just laughed.

After nearly an hour in the tub, I toweled off and pulled on a nightshirt before climbing into bed. When I plugged my phone in to charge, I was surprised to see an unopened message from Harrison.

Can't stop thinking of you xx

My heart began to beat harder in my chest. It had come in only a few minutes ago. *And those goddamned kisses again.*

I replied, *Ditto,* and hit Send.

As I lay back against the cool pillows, I felt like I was back in high school; I was so giddy with anticipation. He was lying in bed somewhere not that far away, thinking about me, little old forty-something Alice from Podunk Nowhere, U.S.A., and he was man enough to admit it to me; to want to share his thoughts with me and make me smile. I couldn't remember a time when I'd felt like this, it had been so long. I bit my bottom lip and closed my eyes as I thought about the conversations we'd shared, what he might be wearing right now as he thought about me, and what tomorrow might bring. *God, he smelled good.*

I'd let myself be swept up in the whirlwind of the evening; how could I not? He'd waltzed into my life out of nowhere but also straight out of my dreams, and my mind was blown. The way this night turned out was beyond anything my imagination could've ever conjured up, and it felt so good to have someone genuinely want to talk with me, and even more so about the things I enjoyed, to make it about me and not purely about their needs. To share conversation and laughter about shared interests and joke about things that James wouldn't even begin to understand, let alone find humor in. It felt good to be free of the weight of being someone's unhappy, dutiful wife, and just be myself.

The more I thought about Harrison, the more I was losing confidence in my ability to control my emotions with this man. As it was, I felt like I already knew him based on my dream, and I wondered if anything about that dream would end up being true in real life or if it was all just made up by my subconscious. I set my alarm for 7 a.m., snuggled beneath the weight of the covers and closed my eyes. I couldn't stop smiling. Morning would be here before I knew it.

I was awake before my alarm, my anticipation driving me out of bed, eager to start the day. I glanced out the window to find a pale gray fog hanging over everything. Not one to be discouraged by a little weather, I showered, then pulled my hair back into a loose braid and took a little time to put on the same natural-looking make-up I had worn the day before. It'd had the desired effect, so why not continue the streak? I chose a black ankle-length cotton maxi skirt that had slits up each side to my knees, and paired it with a cream v-neck tee, which I tucked a small section of into the waistband near my hip. I put a spritz of my favorite perfume on each wrist and touched them to the sides of my neck before pumping another spray onto my chest, then my skirt. The floral mixture of jasmine and honeysuckle mingled with musk and amber just made me feel feminine and I'd worn this fragrance my entire adult life. I packed a matching cream-colored lightweight cardigan into my tote bag along with the perfume bottle and the book I was currently reading. Remembering that I had no idea what lunch would consist of, I called room service to bring up a bagel with cream cheese and some apple juice to hold me over for a while. I completed my outfit with some comfortable lightweight sneakers to keep things casual, and of course, my touristy sunglasses.

With a few minutes to spare, I rubbed a generous amount of lotion into my legs and arms, then tidied the suite, and pulled the curtains fully open to reveal the fog had dissipated and the sun was beginning to make itself known. I smiled, thankful that London hadn't been the rainy place I'd always heard it was, and wondered what the day ahead would hold for me.

My phone buzzed from the bedside table.

Be there in five, can't wait to see you xx

I felt my cheeks grow warm and replied:

Same, excited to spend the day with you.

I once again felt like a schoolgirl; I couldn't help it. I double-checked my tote. My wallet was there, my phone charger, my book. I dropped my phone into the bag along with a bottle of water and my strawberry lip balm, then proceeded toward the hotel lobby.

As I pushed the doors open, there was Lawrence standing guard against the SUV waiting for me. He was a dapper man, very tall with broad shoulders and a freshly shaven face. He wore a black suit, a black shirt, and dark black rimmed sunglasses. *Very 'Men in Black,'* I thought, hoping he didn't have

191

one of those light zapper things that would erase all my memories.

"Good morning, ma'am; nice to see you again." He nodded as he spoke and opened the door with one hand as he reached for my arm with the other.

"Good morning, Lawrence. Likewise, thank you." I smiled as he helped me into the vehicle, but I was not prepared for what I saw when I entered the backseat of the SUV.

Harrison was relaxed into the backseat smiling at me, welcoming me in, dressed in a white graphic t-shirt, the logo so worn I couldn't make it out, and loose-fitting blue jeans; the knees once again ripped like the ones he wore last night. The partition was already closed and there were tiny sparkling lights in the ceiling that looked like glittery stars against the darkness cast from the tinted windows. I didn't remember seeing them the night before, but my anxiety was likely to blame for that. And to my surprise, all of the cup holders that flanked the oversized back seat were filled with a mixture of bright tangerine-colored sunflowers, white daisies, and vibrant pink roses in clear glass vases. Harrison's smile, brighter than any of the floral arrangements, greeted me as he reached out his hand to help me get settled.

"There she is! You ready for this adventure?" His eyes lit up as he said it.

"Good morning to you too, sir. You're awfully chipper." I laughed at him as I bent to smell the roses beside me, trying to focus on the scent of the flowers and not the twinkle in his eye. "All this, for me?" I asked.

"Well, you're worth it, and I remembered you said you loved flowers, so..." Harrison's cheeks flushed. *This grown man is so wonderfully bashful,* I thought.

"Mission accomplished." I laughed and felt the car pull away from the curb as I pulled a rose from the vase and tucked it behind Harrison's ear. "Oh, this is definitely your color," I said as I carefully moved his loose curls around, making sure the blossom wouldn't fall from its perch. "Brings out your cheeks." I crinkled my nose up quickly and smiled at him.

"I've got something a little more than just a picnic planned for us today. I hope you're okay with it, but I also want to keep some of it a surprise for you." He rubbed his hands together like he had some sort of trick up his sleeve and smiled mischievously.

This man and his surprises, I thought, remembering all of the times he'd surprised me in my dream. The similarities between 'real' Harrison and 'dream' Harrison were exciting, but so far 'real' Harrison was proving to be just as caring and attentive, and yet somehow so much more.

"Oh? Okay, well I'm game for most anything as long as you don't expect me to go bungee jumping or hang gliding." I put my hand up in protest. "Those will not be something I sign up for." I shook my head vehemently.

"Nothing like that, love, but memorable, I hope anyway. Trust me?" Harrison lowered his head and looked up at me again with those puppy dog eyes, batting his long dark eyelashes, the dimples in his cheeks searing further into my memory.

"Sure, but will you give me any hints?" I asked, desperate to appear relaxed as my heart was pounding inside my chest at the combination of Harrison's apparent need for my approval and the mystery of what the day held for us.

"Well, we *will* be having a picnic, as planned. But we'll also be doing a bit of...sightseeing." Harrison's expression transformed into that of an excited little boy, as if he'd just been handed a brand-new bicycle.

I burst out laughing; I couldn't help it. "I don't mean to laugh at you, but you're hilarious…you're so excited," I said.

"It's been a long time since I was able to show someone around, and how could I not be excited to be on a date with a beautiful woman?" His body tensed as soon as it came out of his mouth and he pulled his lips in together, as if recognizing his mistake, hoping to somehow retract his last statement, his eyes giving away his embarrassment.

"Oh, this is a date is it?" I smirked at him; my eyes playful. I wanted to make him laugh, and there was no need for him to feel embarrassed.

"I mean…if I'm being honest, I'd like for it to be. But I get it if it can't be." He glanced down at my ring finger again, long enough for me to notice, then shifted his eyes back to mine, his expression serious.

I'd shaken thoughts of James from my mind until Harrison glanced down at my ring. Now, suddenly I found myself wrapped up in something that had turned from lighthearted to serious, and I could only stare at him, unable to find my voice. My heart that had been pounding so hard previously, now felt like it had ceased to function at all.

I shook my head, "I can't make any promises, Harrison, but I can tell you truthfully there's nowhere I'd rather be right now than here with you. I'm on my own time, I'm doing what makes *me* happy, what *I* want to do, free from worrying about what anyone thinks about my choices." I tried to sound confident but wasn't sure it came across that way.

"I spent a lot of time last night, half the night really, thinking about...things." He hesitated before saying the word as if that was the new way to describe the fact that I had a husband somewhere, and that there was a marriage standing between us.

"I don't pretend to know your situation, the details of it, or why you're here alone, but I assume you've got your reasons. What I do know is that life can get complicated, and we do our best to navigate it as it comes. And if you were my wife, I'd never leave your side. I half decided last night to stifle the emotions I can feel creeping in on me, but as soon as I saw you this morning, I'm not sure I can do that anymore. I'm attracted to your energy, your intelligence, and your smile makes me smile. You're a beautiful woman, Alice, and I don't want to wonder what might have been one day when I'm on my deathbed. If it's nothing, then we'll know. But if it's truly something, I don't want to brush it aside and miss what could be magic."

"Harrison, I—"

"You don't have to say anything, just know that's how I feel. I'm open to the possibilities, Alice, whatever they may be, and if you feel like you may be as well, then it's okay, I'm here. I'm ready for whatever that brings. And if you aren't, that's okay too. I can deal with my own emotions. I just don't want to impose limitations on something that could be, well, limitless."

I was flattered. I lowered my eyes from his as my cheeks once again began to flush. *He thinks I'm beautiful*, I thought. *He's open to the possibilities? He's basically saying, 'I know you're married but I'm willing to overlook it.' Holy shit. Hell of a way to start the day, Harrison.*

A week ago, I had only dreamed of Harrison Edwards, and now he was right in front of me saying he could overlook a marriage almost as old as he was, just to explore his feelings for me? *Am I in some sort of parallel universe right now? Is this how young people behave these days? Just straight out with what they want, no matter the repercussions?* My mind was a balled up, knotted mess. I took a deep breath in and exhaled slowly, letting it all sink in, and nervously avoided Harrison's questioning eyes as he sat there watching me process what he had just said.

I stared down at my lap, nervously rubbing at the knuckles on my left hand, the thin gold band reflecting the lights of the glittering ceiling. *I take my vows seriously*, I thought. Even after all the bullshit I'd been through with him, I had never cheated on James, never even considered it, and to my knowledge neither had he. I shook my head, trying to ignore the intrusive thoughts that were flooding my mind, trying to remind myself that I could never, and *would* never cheat on my husband.

But just as quickly as they'd disbursed, the thoughts crept back in. My marriage had morphed into some sort of tragedy; I was lonesome all the time, I felt constantly overlooked and undervalued. Dismissed and completely undesirable, but those weren't valid reasons to cheat on my husband. *Were they?* Harrison's eyes were locked on me, and he waited in silence as my mind continued to race.

If James was somewhere with an actress that the entire globe lusted after, that was offering to overlook his wife to fulfill her own desires…I would be livid. I'd absolutely be pissed. But hey, no one was saying I had to commit adultery right here and now. Harrison wasn't outright propositioning me for sex this second. I tried again and again to reassure myself that I wasn't doing anything wrong, but it was pointless. I knew I was already in over my head. Sex was just a fleeting physical act with its own set of long-term consequences, but emotions were an entirely different story. Emotions ran deeper and would hold me captive far longer than any sexual experience ever could. Harrison had already made his developing feelings clear to me, and denying that I felt it too would be an outright lie.

First it was texting and now I was traveling to some unknown location with a man I barely knew, who has just fully laid his intentions out in front of me. I could stop this now and James would likely be upset, but not enough to divorce me. Or I could just free myself of the chokehold my marriage has held me in for decades and see what happens. I hadn't felt like this since high school, since before James, and if I'm being honest with myself, I've relished in every second of feeling wanted by someone. The fact that it was Harrison Edwards was just the icing on the cake.

Cake. My mind went back to the night in the hotel with that damn chocolate cake…and this gorgeous man that was somehow sitting beside me, who was looking at me with the most genuine look in his eyes, hopeful that I'd simply be willing to spend more time with him and see where the path might lead.

"Okay," I finally said, nervously. "Let's just let things be what they are." I shrugged and tried again to lighten the mood. "I might be more than you want to deal with anyhow." Then I shot him a quick wink.

"Unlikely, but I'll be the judge of that." He took my hand in his and gave it a little squeeze as he smiled and crinkled up his nose.

God, I thought. *This man is going to be the death of me.*

Our conversation flowed easily over the next hour; it was as if we had known each other in another life; everything just came effortlessly. There was nothing awkward or strained, nothing felt off limits. I learned Harrison had slept with a teddy bear until he was fourteen, that his granddad had been the one to have the 'sex talk' with him, not his own parents, and that he had taken gymnastics classes as a child to quell some of his endless energy. I shared some of my photography with him, flipping through my favorite snapshots in my phone's gallery. I told him about an idea I had for a book, and how in high school I'd been accepted by all the different cliques. We each went on about childhood Christmases and favorite birthdays we'd had, laughing through it all and never letting go of each other's hand in the process.

When the SUV came to a stop and Lawrence opened the door for us to exit, Harrison was smiling from ear to ear. I looked at him and laughed, apprehensive.

"What's with that tricky look?" I asked, confused.

"Ready for leg two?" he looked like a kid in a candy shop, ready to burst at any moment.

"Leg two? Are we on the Amazing Race?" I joked nervously, but trusted him as I looked around to try to see where we were.

He only laughed in response to my question and climbed out of the vehicle as he reached for my hand, pulling me behind him.

"Okay…I guess I'll follow you," I said reluctantly. He was always making me feel looked-after with the little things he'd do. His hand on my back as we walked out of the restaurant last night, helping me into and out of the car. He was a polite, well-mannered man, and I simply wasn't used to it.

We stepped out onto the pavement and Harrison ushered me around to the front of the SUV. This wasn't a parking lot, not even remotely. We were on a tarmac, and there before us was a private plane, its narrow stairs sprawled out in front of me, inviting us into luxury.

My thoughts began to swirl like tissue-paper party streamers caught in a breeze, and I quickly became self-conscious, worried my clothes weren't fancy enough, or that I was undeserving of such lavish travel. Then, my mind came screeching to a halt. *The Jet. Was this THE jet?* I fixated on the image of myself, terrified on an empty sidewalk in New Orleans, desperate to find my way to 'the jet.' I felt that panic just as I had felt it in my dream and my breathing quickened as my chest began to heave. The flashback was so realistic I thought for sure I was right back in the midst of it all.

Yet somehow, here I was, with Harrison, about to board his private plane with him, and that's when the world around me began to spin. I swung myself around and with my free arm fully embraced him. My knees felt weak.

"I'm so sorry." I whispered as I instinctively buried my face into his chest.

"It's okay, love. I'm right here, you're okay." He kissed the top of my head, something I'm certain he didn't think about before doing; his only intent was to comfort me, but that kiss made me spiral even further.

We stood together in silence, embracing one another, and I focused on the sound of his heartbeat in my ear to calm myself as Harrison calmly repeated, "You're okay. I've got you."

A few moments later, I'd regained my composure and felt sturdy enough to stand on my own.

"Thank you. I'm so sorry. I was just overwhelmed. The sight of that plane just triggered a memory; I've never done anything like this before and—"

Harrison stopped me by putting his finger against my lips. "Darling. It's okay. Truly. At the very least I can say I've taken your breath away today and if nothing else, I've made you weak in the knees."

His head tilted, trying to put a smile on my face as he poked fun at the situation. A lock of dark curls fell forward, covering his eye. He grabbed the lot and with a fistful of his hair, pulled backward, twisting it around itself all in one quick movement, holding it there while he pulled a claw clip from the hem of his t-shirt, then fastened it tightly to hold the curls away from his face. Every time I watched him do it, I was transported back to the times he'd done it in my dream.

"Ha. Ha. Ha…" I said sarcastically. "Where are you taking me?"

"It's a secret." Harrison once again snaked his arm through mine and with a satisfied smile on his face, we boarded the aircraft.

Once inside, the luxury of the jet became apparent. To the left, there was a cream-colored leather couch along one wall with a string of windows above it. To the right, two black leather captain's chairs on either side of a small table that all sat in front of a comfortably sized kitchen space. An ice bucket sat atop the counter, holding two bottles of champagne waiting to be opened, and propped against it was a plaque that read, *'Welcome Alice and*

Harrison,' in metallic gold lettering. Further back, behind a small partition sat another larger couch, plush black velvet this time, intersecting the walkway and flanked on either side by matching black velvet recliners facing a large television screen. Even further back was a full-sized bathroom to the right and a queen bed to the left.

"So, this is how the other half lives, huh?" I asked as I ran my fingers across the furniture, making my way toward the back.

"It makes days like today possible, and it's my absolute pleasure to share it with you." He jokingly poked at my waist with his finger, prompting me to giggle.

"It's like a giant luxury RV that flies." My simplicity was showing.

"Would you like something to drink? We have champagne and soft drinks, water..."

"A water would be good, please. What's the in-flight movie? Wait, are we going far enough to watch a movie?" My eyes grew larger as the idea formed in my head.

"No, I mean we could start one if you like, but may have to finish it on the way back."

I sat down on the black velvet couch, appreciating its softness, then reached for the remote while Harrison went back up front to speak with the pilot. A nice young woman brought me a glass of ice water, a neatly folded cream-colored cashmere blanket, and a movie theater style box of popcorn before disappearing from sight.

I faintly heard Harrison check in on Lawrence as he made his way back to me, but I couldn't make out what they were saying. I did hear there would be a car waiting for us when the plane landed and it shouldn't be too long of a drive. I began to wonder once again where we could possibly be headed.

Finally, he sat down beside me on the couch and said, "Ready to go?"

"Harrison, where *are* we going?" This time I was serious. "Is this a hostage situation? Should I call Liam Neeson to save me? He does have a particular set of skills ya know, and they're pretty next-level, not gonna lie." I grabbed for my phone jokingly.

"We're going North a bit, nothing too crazy, just a quick little trip. You'll be back tonight as planned. No need to call Liam Neeson." Harrison's smile was reassuring, and despite trying not to be, I was enamored with it.

"Okay, I'll trust you this time." I narrowed my eyes at him playfully. "What have we got for movie options?"

I handed him the remote and covered both of us with the blanket as we settled in to watch a romantic comedy from the 1980s. I reminisced about how I'd loved it as a child and Harrison laughed at the fact that he hadn't even been born yet back then. The jokes between us came easy and were becoming constant. From fun little jabs about how young he was, to how bizarre it seemed that I was alive before the internet had been invented, all were in the name of fun and somehow brought us closer. We got deeper into the film and picked apart the fashion, the slang, and the hairstyles while we relaxed on the couch, all the while inching closer and closer to each other under the blanket.

Forty-five minutes later when the captain announced we would soon begin our descent, I realized I'd fully melded into Harrison's embrace and was tucked comfortably under his left arm. I don't know how I hadn't noticed it as it happened, but I could feel his hand resting against my upper arm; his thumb had found its way under the hem of my sleeve and was lightly caressing my bare skin beneath the blanket. I didn't want to move. The softness of his t-shirt against my cheek coupled with the warmth of the cashmere blanket and the rhythm of his breathing made me want to forget the idea of a picnic altogether and just stay here for the rest of the day.

It had been a while since either of us had spoken, conversation dwindled as we fell further into the movie and when I lifted my head from his chest to see if he was still awake, Harrison glanced down at me and smiled.

"Hi," he said, his dimples prominent.

"Were you asleep?" I asked.

"Close but not quite. Just enjoying this." His hand slipped from my arm, and settled at my waist, drawing me in closer to him and giving me a gentle squeeze.

I felt weightless as the effects of that squeeze spread a warmth over my entire body. I'd been mindful to keep my hands to myself the entire time, tightly clasped together under the blanket, despite everything in my being urging me to rest my palm against his thigh.

The plane's wheels touched the ground without so much as a wiggle, and I glanced out the window.

"Where are we?" We were in another city, that much was obvious, but I had no idea where.

"Manchester." Harrison explained, "It's close to where I grew up. Some of the best times of my life were spent in this area; I love it here. But this isn't our destination. We have a third and final leg of this journey to embark on; you ready for it?" The happiness in his eyes was enough to vanquish any lingering worries I may have been holding onto.

He wasn't just some guy that was trying to get me to sleep with him. Harrison was proving himself to be a trusted friend, simply trying to share genuine time getting to know one another. I'd shared details of my life with him that no one else had ever even thought to ask me about, and the more time I spent in his presence, the more I felt at ease, the more I trusted him, and the more I could feel myself genuinely falling for him. And not as some celebrity crush as my dreams would have led me believe, but as an actual, real-life, attainable, *normal* man. We shared so many common interests and had so many similar experiences as children and as young adults, it was hard to ignore our compatibility. And just as if he'd never existed, any trace of James in my mind was gone.

"Ready as I'll ever be," I said, excited for what might be next as I slipped my shoes back on.

Harrison waited as I gathered my bag and sunglasses, then took my hand and led me toward the front of the plane, once again placing his hand at the small of my back to reassure me he was right there at my side.

We made our way down the narrow stairs, and there again was Lawrence, waiting patiently with the back door of another black SUV held open, ready for us to climb in. Harrison shook his hand and confirmed Lawrence knew where he was headed before helping me into the backseat. I was shocked to discover yet another large bouquet, this time various shades of pink and white double-layered peonies mixed with tiny white baby's breath, the delicate blossoms emitting their memorable sweet aroma. Lawrence closed the door behind us, then from the driver's seat closed the dark partition glass, and Harrison and I found ourselves alone once again.

"You've outdone yourself. These are amazing." I picked up the blush-petaled bouquet and drew in a breath of their sweetness.

The amount of thought that must have gone into planning this day, I thought. *It had been nearly midnight when he left me last night; when did he have time to arrange all of this?*

"All for you, love. Glad you like them."

I glanced up from the floral arrangement to find him staring at me, a look of adoration on his face.

"What?" I said nervously, a smile spreading across my face.

"Nothing." He smiled back at me and held his gaze to mine.

"No really, what?" I wondered if my makeup was smeared from leaning against him or if he was staring because my hair was out of place.

"Alice, you are..." He shook his head, smiling. "Ethereal. Do you know that? I'm just so taken with you."

I smiled and felt my cheeks start to warm. Unsure what to say to such a sweet sentiment, I said nothing at all. I simply snuggled back into the warmth of his embrace as Lawrence drove us to our next destination.

With this part of our journey underway, Harrison pointed out places he recalled from his youth as we passed them, but then the conversation flowed so easily we lost sight of what was going on outside the windows. We'd been huddled together chatting in the backseat for nearly an hour when the car slowed to a snail's pace, and that's when Harrison put the windows down and asked me to take a peek at my surroundings.

I sat up in the seat and adjusted my eyes to the light outside the car. I couldn't believe what I was looking at. My eyes met miles and miles of lush greenery, open fields of verdant valleys pieced together like a giant patchwork quilt, sewn together by nothing but sunlight and stone walls in every direction. In the distance, faint shadows of tree lines dotted the landscape. It looked like something out of a storybook.

"Welcome to the Dales, darling," he said and waited for my response.

"Oh my God, Harrison…I'm…I don't know what to…" I couldn't find the words to express the wonderment I was feeling.

"No need to say anything. Shall we get out and have a walk?" Harrison opened the door and helped me out onto the dusty country road.

The edges of the avenue were dotted with cheerful white daisies that danced back and forth in the breeze. Nestled among them were fuzzy lavender jewels crowning jade-green clover and sun-kissed buttercups that all swayed in unison. A lonesome butterfly flitted above them, vibrant orange against a cerulean sky.

The one-lane road we had traveled to get here stretched out for miles behind us and was empty, without another soul in sight. Some of the surrounding fields held herds of sheep, while others held cattle, but many were empty save for the grass that happily billowed under the sun-soaked sky. Harrison reached for my hand and we made our way up the gravel road, only stopping to take the large picnic basket Lawrence had pulled from the passenger seat.

Once we crested the hill, the view grew even more spectacular. Looking down into the basin of the Dales, the varying patches of green continued for as far as the eye could see, the ripples of the River Ure cut through the rolling hills and a dairy farm lay sprawled at its edge. Only the faint sounds of rushing water and cows mooing could be heard in the distance. Harrison led me toward the shade of a giant lone oak tree, its canopy of leaves still a welcoming shade of summer despite it being September.

"How's this for a picnic?" he asked, a proud look on his face as a result of the look of amazement on mine.

"This is...unbelievable." I just stood there, looking around me, drinking in the perfection of the day. It wasn't too chilly, but it wasn't hot, barely a cloud in the sky with no rain in sight and a welcome breeze from time to time.

Harrison laid out a blanket that he retrieved from the basket and helped me settle onto a comfortable spot before we continued to unpack lunch together. There were two small sandwiches, individual bags of chips (or crisps as he called them), and a few bottles of chilled water. As well as a small bowl of freshly cut fruit and two individually bagged chocolate chip cookies, tied at the top with a small white ribbon.

"I hope turkey is okay?" Harrison asked as he handed me a sandwich.

"Turkey is perfect. This place is perfect. This entire day has been perfect. I don't know how to thank you, Harrison. I've always wanted to see this, and…I've only ever dreamed of it, yet here we are. This place…exceeds any dream I could have ever conjured up. You've brought me right to the epicenter of extraordinary."

I wanted to focus on him; he deserved it; but the photographer in me was still looking around, anxious to start capturing the light and the textures of my surroundings.

"No need to thank me. As soon as you mentioned the Dales last night I thought, 'I want to share this with her. I want to create this memory with her.' My wheels started turning instantly."

"It's highly unlikely I would've ever made it here on my own, and I just can't express how much this means to me. You're spoiling me, you know."

"That's the goal, love."

We ate our lunch, comfortable in near silence, taking in the day and our surroundings, sharing glances laden with flirtation. When lunch was finished and the remnants packed away, we wandered a bit as I snapped a few photos then returned to the blanket and lay together on our backs as we watched a plane cut its way across the deep blue of the cloudless sky, leaving only a tiny white trail behind it as proof that it had ever existed. We giggled together as we made up stories about who was inside and where they were going.

Conversation with Harrison was effortless, as was lying beside him, basking in the autumn sunshine of the English countryside. I felt happier with him in the last twenty-four hours than I had ever felt with anyone else in my life. I closed my eyes and allowed myself to daydream, slipping back into the images from my dream that had been burned into my memory, my subconscious highlighting his kiss. I remembered the way his hands roamed free over my entire body and the way it felt when he had proposed to me. I let out a sigh, and thought, *God how I wish that dream could come true.*

The sudden warmth of his hand on my hip brought me out of my thoughts and I blinked hard as my eyes adjusted to the light. Harrison had turned to his side and had been watching me. He'd removed the clip holding his hair back and a lock of curls hung near his right temple.

"Hi," I said bashfully.

"Hi." He was smiling back at me, but his eyes were saying something much more intense.

"How ya doin'?" I nervously tried to fill the silence.

"I'm well. You doing okay?" he asked and inched closer to me on the blanket.

"It seems I'm getting better as time passes." I was blushing.

"I can see the truth in that." Again, he inched closer to me, his body now just centimeters away from mine.

"Oh?" I swallowed hard and licked my lips. The tip of his nose was just barely touching mine.

"Mhmm," he nodded slightly, the sound barely a whisper.

He was so close I could feel his breath on my top lip as he said it, and my mind raced at the thought of actually kissing him. I had admired this man's lips for as long as I could remember, and they were right here for the taking. I tried hard to regulate my breathing, but was failing. His gaze fell to my mouth and lingered a moment before he looked back up and into my eyes. His eyelashes were long and dark and unlike any I'd ever seen on a man before, the color of his eyes indefinable, green and gold, blue and gray all at the same time.

He drew the corner of his bottom lip into his mouth and grazed the tip of his nose alongside mine, still teasing me with his intentions. My heart was beating so hard I was certain he could hear it and I tried to hide my smile. My nerves getting the better of me I averted my eyes, unable to maintain eye contact. His gorgeous smile was still visible in my peripheral view.

"Alice..." his voice was nearly a whisper.

I smiled now, unable to stop it, as he used his index finger to direct my chin, aching for me to make eye contact with him. Slowly, softly, he pressed his lips against mine. Lingering there, he drew his palm up and against my jaw, tilted his head a bit, teasing my mouth with his, then kissed me more deeply. His tongue found mine and I drew in a deep breath through my nose, my anxiety now gone, I leaned in and kissed him exactly as I had always imagined I would. His lips were soft and his tongue sweet, and the way he kissed me was more nuanced than even I could have imagined. I lost myself in the moment and indulged in him completely.

When we finally broke apart, my eyes still closed, I took another deep breath and let it out slowly, savoring what was left of his kiss on my lips.

"I hope that was okay," he said nervously, unable to stop himself from smiling.

Cheeks burning and once again unable to maintain eye contact, I responded, "It was...perfect."

"I wasn't out of line, was I? I've been wanting to kiss you since last night." He paused and looked away like a schoolboy with a crush. "If I'm being honest, it's all I've thought about."

"No, not at all." I blushed, embarrassed. "I enjoyed it."

Harrison was the one blushing now.

"Ten out of ten, would recommend," I added in hopes of bringing some comedic relief.

"So, you'd recommend it, but would you do it again?" he asked, a flirtatious look in his eye.

"Would you?" I shot back with a questioning glance.

"Oh, I can't wait to do it again." Trying to hide behind sarcasm, he bit his lip to hide his smile, but his efforts were again wasted.

This time, I was the one that leaned in and kissed him, slow and sensual. I wanted to leave my mark on this man, create a memory he couldn't possibly forget.

"There, now you don't have to wait," I said playfully.

"Oh, you better believe I still can't wait to do it again." He laughed and as he did, I once again fell a little deeper.

"I have more planned for us. You wanna see what's next?"

"There's more? Harrison, really you don't have to go to all this trouble for me."

"It's no trouble at all. This is the best day I've had since...well, since last night." He smiled as he watched my reaction.

"You flatter me," I said bashfully before continuing. "But yes, I'm ready for whatever is next. Lead the way."

We packed the blanket into the basket and walked hand-in-hand back to the car. Once again in the backseat together, Lawrence drove us from the expanse of the velvety green hills and fields to a tree-covered lane flanked on either side by ancient stone houses. The vehicle came to a stop just as we crossed over a narrow stone bridge, and Harrison put the window halfway down for me to see, but this time, I was on the opposite side of the car. In my eagerness to find out what was making such a loud splashing noise just outside the window, I failed to realize I'd crawled over him to get a better view. The front of my knees pressed firmly against the outside of Harrison's thigh, one hand on the top edge of the window and the other on the arm rest of the car door, I peered out, eyes wide.

"Aysgarth Falls," he said.

The falls were dotted with people swimming, splashing, and sunbathing on the rocky shores as the dark water happily churned and swirled over multiple levels of rock and earth, puddling into shallow pools, the spray from the water catching the sunlight, creating rainbows in the air. Families lined the edges with brightly colored umbrellas and beach towels, their conversations and laughter echoing off the water as I took in the view.

"Oh, Harrison. This is magical! Look at all the rainbows!" I pointed excitedly. "What a beautiful spot." I reached for the door, but it was locked.

"We can't get out here love, there are too many people around. It's probably not safe. I'm sorry." His disappointment was evident as he said it.

"Oh...okay. I get it, I guess." I couldn't take my eyes off the prismatic mist billowing up into the sky. "It must be torture for you sometimes, huh? To have something so beautiful right in front of you and have it be so far out of reach, unable to fully experience it."

"Torture indeed." He looked at me longingly.

I hadn't meant for him to take it that way. I wasn't talking about me, but his eyes spoke volumes.

"Oh Harrison, I didn't mean..."

Lawrence's abrupt knock on the partition startled me. Moments later, he lowered it just enough so we could hear him as he asked, "Do you mind fully lowering the back windows, Boss? I have an idea." The partition closed and as Harrison lowered the other backseat window there was Lawrence.

"Miss Alice, may I see your phone for a moment?" he held out his hand.

I handed him my phone and Lawrence asked us to turn around and face him as he lowered himself to our eye level. Focusing on our faces with the falls in the background, he asked us to smile then snapped a series of photos and turned the screen to show us what he'd captured, making sure we were happy with the result before handing the phone back to me.

"Oh Lawrence, thank you!" I was so pleased he'd thought to photograph what we couldn't get out and document ourselves.

"Of course, my pleasure," he said, as he nodded dutifully then returned to the driver's seat.

"Harrison, he's wonderful. How thoughtful. You two make a great team." I was grateful to both of these men for their generosity and care. I'd carefully caught Harrison in some of the shots I took after lunch, but opted to shoot from behind him or capture his profile, trying diligently to protect his privacy while creating a visual reference to this incredible day.

"Lawrence is my right-hand man, always thinking, always helping. He keeps me safe from the craziness but also looks out for those I cherish." He kissed the top of my hand and closed the window. "I'm sorry we can't stay here longer or get out and explore. I wanted to share this place with you though, and I'm so glad you love it."

Harrison tapped the partition and as the car pulled away from the falls, we were on to our next destination.

"I went there often when I was young, to work through some tough times. It's a good thinking spot when it's not so busy and helped me sort through a lot in my life. Especially when my parents got divorced. I was able to work through my emotions and essentially made up my mind that all my sadness could be crumpled into a theoretical ball and tossed into the river. The waves would drag it all away from me."

"What a beautiful way to look at it; I love that. My parents divorced when I was too young to remember really. My earliest memory in life though, is my father sitting down with me as a young child, tearfully telling me he couldn't live with us anymore. I think I was three or four then, but it stuck with me my entire life. I can still see it in my mind. I may have to try your method one day. Throw my sadness into the river and watch it drift away, never to be seen again. Sounds like a good way to strip some weight off my shoulders, weight I've carried for far too long." I squeezed his hand in mine, hopeful he felt validated by my being so open with him.

We continued to share our childhood traumas in all their varying forms, finding comfort in one another as we shared some things that neither of us had spoken out loud before, oblivious to the true depth of the bond we were forming. Harrison was a far more complex man than I expected. You see the glitz and the glamor of celebrity and assume there's a charmed life behind it all, but he was proving to be much more regular at his core. Not that I was glad he'd suffered trauma, but I was thankful we had a shared understanding of loss and hope and the want for unconditional love.

Back on the tarmac, we boarded the plane, snuggled into the couch, and resumed our movie, but I was only half present in the moment. I was more aware of how close we were, how easy it had been to fall back into his embrace under the blanket, and how comfortable I felt with my cheek once again pressed against his chest. The other half of my mind was thinking about how this wonderful man had cleared his day to fly me across half the country just to show me waterfalls and share a picnic with me. All because I flippantly mentioned I wanted to see it. He listened when I spoke, and he paid attention to me even when I didn't realize it. He acted without me having to make a request. And the way I caught him staring at me while I was lost in daydreams? His attention was like a breath of fresh air, and I'd long forgotten a man could behave like this.

Just like in my dream, our physical attraction to one another was immediate and our emotional connection solidified further with every glance, with each topic of conversation covered, and I knew what I was feeling, what I was doing, was wrong on every level for a married woman, but I was no longer worried about the consequences of my actions. Those concerns were in the past. For the first time in my adult life, I was fully living for my own happiness.

I felt Harrison lower his chin to nuzzle against the top of my head. His chest rose against my cheek, and I could feel him breathing me in. When he exhaled, a whisper of satisfaction escaped with his breath. His arm tightened around my shoulder, then his hand fell to caress my arm briefly before shifting down to my waist, his thumb reaching, rubbing back and forth against my t-shirt.

Unable to focus on anything other than his hand against my body, I took a deep breath in an effort to calm myself, then shifted my hand to rest on his leg under the warmth of the blanket. His jeans were worn to a comfortable softness, and I let my fingertips drift back and forth over the material, alternating the weight of my touch. I teased him with each slow swirl, my fingertips tracing my name against the denim. Each letter inched my hand higher and higher on his thigh and with my head still pressed against his chest, I could hear his heart rate increase with each of his quickened breaths.

My reciprocated touch was all it took; Harrison opened his hand fully against my ribcage, the tip of his thumb slowly reaching to graze the underside of my breast but hesitant to overstep his bounds. He held me firmly, the strength of his hands enormous. As his breathing quickened, so did mine; it had been so long since I could feel someone's unspoken hunger for me, it was almost palpable. I allowed my palm to fall still against his inner thigh before my fingertips followed suit. The warm pressure of my grasp caused him to inhale slowly, brace himself against the couch and hold his breath before it eased from his nose with a quick, "Mmm," that made me want him even more.

"Alice..." he whispered.

I pulled away from his chest long enough to look up at him but said nothing. He laid his head back against the top of the couch, the sharp outline of his jaw aching to be touched. His head lay still, and his eyes remained closed as I moved, repositioning myself, pulling my skirt up just enough to straddle him. I could feel how hard he was getting as I carefully lowered myself down onto his lap and he sighed as I rested against him. The warm spice of his cologne was intoxicating and invigorating at the same time as I delicately began kissing his neck, slowly alternating upward from one side to the other, my lips pressed against the pulsing of his jugular vein. The closer to his face I got, the longer my mouth lingered on his skin. I kissed along one side of his jaw while tenderly tracing the other side with my fingertip until my mouth landed on his chin. I paused and watched his nostrils flare, his chest gently heaving, and waited for him to make eye contact with me. When he finally did, I bit the side of my bottom lip and looked at him lustfully, my head lowered just slightly to appear as if I were looking up at him.

"You okay?" I asked with a devilish look on my face.

He exhaled and looked back at me intently, as if every shred of gentleman was losing the war inside of him.

I didn't wait for an answer. I leaned in carefully, slow and deliberate, never breaking eye contact. From where I sat on top of him, I could feel him throbbing between my bare legs, his jeans serving as the only barrier. I nuzzled my nose against his and placed my hands on each of his shoulders before running my fingertips up the back of his neck and into his hair. I kissed his chin before lightly dragging my bottom lip up to meet his. I bit at it playfully, and when his mouth fell open, I kissed him deeply. His hands grasped at my body before settling one palm firmly against the small of my back, pulling me harder down onto him, as the other hand cradled the nape of my neck, keeping my mouth focused on his. The reckless way he kissed me caused my hips to move instinctively against his.

With fists full of his dark hair, I continued to kiss him, my tongue snaked itself around his, and I allowed his hands free reign over my body. Moving from my waist, I felt them glide up to caress my breasts, greedily and animalistic. He broke from my mouth long enough to feel the softness of the cleavage peeking out of my shirt against his cheek, then looked at me as if asking my permission. I gave him a lustful half smile and he pressed his mouth against my chest, taking his time to taste my exposed skin. I drew in a deep breath, the side of my face buried against his curls. His hair smelled as sexy as the rest of him did, like amber mixed with white musk and citrus.

His lips moved up my chest to the front of my throat, kissing and sucking until he reached my mouth again. Reconnected, we kissed one another so passionately I thought for sure I was going to lose my mind. His wandering hands moved around to my back, grasping at the tops of my shoulders from behind before dropping down and tickling my spine, landing feverishly on my calves.

Unable to hinder his growing desire, he moved to explore me further and slid his hands beneath the side slits of my skirt, then inched higher and higher, squeezing at my bare thighs. He paused, and I watched him as he noticed the faint birthmark that lay just above my left knee toward my mid-thigh. His index and middle fingertips rubbed tenderly over its surface.

"You've got a birthmark…" his accent made his sentiment even sexier than the feeling he gave me of truly being seen.

"That's my little lemon wedge, see?" I said, outlining its shape with my finger, then looking up at Harrison, making eye contact again.

"It's part of what makes you beautiful." He brought his two fingertips up to his mouth and kissed them, then laid them back against my skin.

He shot me a quick smile before returning his mouth to mine and gripping both of my hips, then shifting his hands backwards, fitting his palms to my ass cheeks.

The sound of the captain's voice startled us as it crackled through a speaker, announcing we would soon begin our descent into London. I heard increased movement in the cabin from the crew, and before moving myself back down onto the couch, I gently cupped his face with my hands, gave the dimple on his left cheek a soft kiss, then moved to his mouth once more, kissing him with a tenderness I never wanted him to forget.

"My God, Alice," he was breathless as he positioned the blanket to cover the front of his jeans.

I smiled at him.

"You are…something else. Something else indeed." As his grin unfurled he shook his head in disbelief. There was no question I had piqued his curiosity. It was written all over his face. But this was not the place, and now was not the time to explore that curiosity further.

"I told you I might be too much for you. You didn't believe me." I shrugged and chuckled to myself as I proceeded to gather my things, making sure everything was packed neatly into my tote bag.

"Give me a proper opportunity, love, I'll show you how I handle you. You'll see." He oozed confidence and I loved the way he wanted more of me.

"I suppose we will." I shot him a mischievous look over my shoulder, and as I did, Harrison quickly slid up behind me on the couch, his hand gliding up across my ribs and between my breasts, his palm against my throat as he turned my head and greedily kissed me once again, full on the mouth.

All I could do was sigh as he broke away and fell back against the couch smiling. *My God I want this man*, I thought. It had been decades since someone had made me feel this way. Lust hung in the air and the excitement of not knowing what to expect next with a man I had spent months dreaming of was exhilarating. I no longer looked at him like an unattainable movie star, that was for sure. He was just Harrison, and although it was still unclear yet whether he would become someone I 'used to know' or someone that I would forever be close with, I was ready to see where this path would lead.

Shortly after the plane landed, Harrison and I were back in the SUV. The thick scent of the morning's roses filled the air after being left in the unmoving warmth of the backseat for the afternoon. The heat of the September day had caused their petals to open wide, exposing their centers. I wasn't sure where we were going next; I only knew I didn't want to go back to the hotel.

We had just crossed into a territory together that was new and exciting, and I wasn't ready to step away from that. We'd been interrupted by the plane's captain like a couple of high schoolers getting caught by someone's mother after barely sliding into second base. Now, more than ever, I wondered how it would feel to follow through with what we had started. *Would physical intimacy in the real world be like it was in my dream? Or would it be better?* The likelihood of it being worse was incomprehensible. The way he'd kissed me made my heart race, it made my lungs feel full, and it made the parts of me that were neglected in my everyday life throb with anticipation.

Harrison's voice cut through the silence. "Where's your head?" he asked.

I continued my gaze out the darkened window, undeterred, lost in those thoughts with the images replaying in my head of the way his mouth felt against mine, the softness of his lips against my throat, the heat from his hands against my body.

"Alice?" he repeated.

"Sorry, just thinking about all the beauty I've seen today, and all that I've...done." I smirked as I said it. "I can never thank you enough for sharing your thoughts and these places with me, taking time out of your life to show me around. You've been incredibly generous."

"No trouble at all. I've quite enjoyed myself. It's not often I find myself able to indulge in things that bring me joy without some type of work getting in the way. Usually, my life is centered around my work projects and responsibilities. This has been a truly special day with a truly special person." He reached out and ran his thumb along the edge of my jaw, his curled fingertips tickling the underside of my chin with their movement. He fixed his eyes on his hand as it moved against the softness of my skin, then looked up at me, the color of his eyes beautiful against the darkness of his lashes. "You are one of a kind, Alice. I could very easily get used to being near you all the time."

"I feel the same way about you." I said it so quickly it was as if I couldn't control my own mouth, I was so taken with him. I bowed my head and looked away. I wanted to be honest with him but felt conflicted at the same time. I wasn't a single person, so even if I did have feelings for Harrison, they came tangled with obligations and consequences.

"Would you like to have dinner with me tonight? Maybe let me show you one more spot in London?" he asked.

Without hesitation, I responded, "Yes, I would love that." I stopped myself as a means to curb my enthusiasm and smiled at him, then calmly said, "Do I need to change or stop back at my hotel for anything?"

"If you like, we could stop there first. No need to change unless you want to. I think you look beautiful as you are," he said through a bashful smile.

"If we have time, I'd like to wash off the day and change clothes. You don't have to wait; I can meet you somewhere if it's easier?"

"Of course not. I have all the time in the world. I don't mind waiting for you. As long as you don't mind me coming up with you to wait. It draws attention if the car just idles out front, so I'll have Lawrence handle some things while we're at the hotel, then circle back to pick us up. Or I can go with him if you need some space."

The look of frustration on his face when he said 'it draws attention' made me feel sad that his privacy was always compromised. He was a grown man, living a very full life but kept himself guarded from so many things that commoners like me take for granted. People look at him as the epitome of fame and fortune, which in America tends to equal freedom, but I could tell he didn't feel free. On the inside, he was just a person trying to navigate fame, and with fame came loneliness and feeling caged, like a wild animal held captive, groomed purely for performance and profit. I wondered if that was why we understood each other so well, the constant heaviness of being lonesome, and the weight we both carried trying to keep everyone around us happy, outwardly projecting contentment while internally feeling incredibly sad, neglecting our own desires.

"You are certainly welcome to come in with me. I don't mind at all." I put my hand on his thigh and patted it lightly. "It's nothing glamorous though."

"Is it a quick walk to your room or is there a faster way than the front door?" he asked.

"We can go in through the side, near the atrium. It will be quicker."

I remembered the lengths we went to in my dream to keep him hidden. *What a terrible way to live*, I thought, and began to wonder if I could ever live a life like that.

"It's kind of a pain to have to slink around and hide from crowds.

Sometimes I go places and it's no big deal; no one pays attention or bats an eye. Then other times it's complete chaos. I'll follow you, but don't think I'm weird if my head is down and I keep a steady pace. I have to always be aware of my surroundings."

"It's okay, Harrison, I'll make sure it's a quick, straight shot, and if someone acts crazy, I'll create some wild diversion. I've got you; I promise." I squeezed his leg again and smiled to reassure him.

He turned toward me and brushed the loose strands of hair that had escaped my braid away from my face, a glimpse of an appreciative smile finding its way to his lips. His green eyes met mine and held my attention for what felt like days, trading amorous looks as our faces drifted closer, his lips barely grazing mine before his hands reached up to cradle my face.

One last gentle touch of his lips to mine, and then he kissed me deeply. He took his time, indulging in me, showing me what it could feel like to be loved by him. Harrison Edwards certainly knew what he was doing, there was no question about that. His eyes and his mouth worked in unison with his hands to create a space that made me feel open and unafraid of giving myself over to him, and I had no interest in trying to stop him.

When Lawrence brought the car to a stop near the side entrance of the hotel, I left the vehicle first, keycard in hand along with my tote bag, followed closely by Harrison. As Lawrence pulled away and left us, I noted that the sidewalk, as well as the street, were both empty, save for an elderly couple, their backs turned and walking in the opposite direction. Hand-in-hand, we quickly made our way inside. Through the lobby and into the elevator, no one seemed to notice us. The elevator opened and still, there wasn't a soul in sight. Moments later, we were safely in my hotel suite.

I offered Harrison a bottle of water, then turned on a light in the living room before going around the suite and closing all the drapes in an attempt to show him I was thinking of his safety.

"Make yourself at home; I won't be long. I just want to grab a quick shower and change clothes, then we can go." I said as I strode barefoot into the bedroom area, leaving Harrison on the couch with the remote control and his bottled water.

I pulled a soft cotton flowy skirt from the dresser along with another v-neck t-shirt. Practically every shirt I own is the same. I just buy them in various colors, and I had packed for comfort, not for traipsing around with movie stars. From the top drawer, I chose a matching set of sheer black underwear. Nothing fancy by any means, but black was certainly cuter than the usual beige.

I intended for my shower to be quick, but as I began to lather my hair, my mind once again began to wander, through thoughts of our first actual kiss, thoughts of me perched on top of him in a private jet, the way his hands felt against my backside, and his mouth against my breasts. I tried to shake the image from my mind, tried to focus on the task at hand, but I kept slipping back into the way his tongue felt against mine, and thoughts of how it would've played out if we hadn't been interrupted. Thinking about the way he had brushed my hair from my face in the car on the way to the hotel gave me goosebumps, despite the heat of the water against my skin. The physical aspects of Harrison Edwards had an effect on me unlike anything I had ever experienced.

Now with my hair and body both clean and rinsed, I dried off and got dressed before I opened the door to release some of the steam from the room. I was startled to see Harrison sitting on the edge of the bed scrolling on his phone.

"You scared me!" I laughed as a way to mask my surprise; my long dark hair still wrapped in a towel. "I expected you to still be on the couch." I turned my back to him and pulled the towel from my hair, using it to wipe the steam from the mirror. His reflection stared back at me attentively from the bed.

"Didn't mean to scare you, love." He smiled, his eyes saying everything his mouth wasn't. His dimples made me want to crawl back on top of him and pick up where we had left off on the plane.

Trying not to think about it, I quickly ran a comb through the length of my dark curls and applied perfume to my neck and wrists as he continued to watch me. The mixture of jasmine, honeysuckle, and feminine musk enveloped me and wafted through the air as I used my hands to define the waves in my hair.

"You smell divine." Harrison stood and approached me, fixated on my reflection in the mirror.

"Thank you, I—" But before I could finish my statement Harrison was standing directly behind me, pressing his torso against my back. He carefully pulled my hair to one side and slowly kissed my neck, his eyes fixed on mine in the mirror as he did it. He watched me as I tilted my head to the side and his lips worked their way up and behind my ear, landing on my earlobe. I steadied myself with one hand clutching the bathroom vanity and the other reaching back to pull him closer, my fingertips finding the bare skin beneath his t-shirt. His left hand under my shirt, he cupped my breast as he whispered in my ear, "Alice, I want to feel you." His mouth was hot against my neck, and his hands gently but determinedly groped at my body.

I knew what I was doing was wrong as the voice in my head said, *You shouldn't be doing this Alice; you made a commitment*, but I had felt unattractive and undesired for too many years and no longer cared about the commitment I'd made. I no longer wanted to deprive myself of a man's touch and adoration purely because I had promised to love one man for the rest of my life, a man that ultimately made me feel invisible. A man that wasn't holding up his end of the commitment to love me as I deserved, and a man who made me feel like nothing more than a nuisance. I silenced my conscience and let the years of neglect and dismissal fan the flames I felt for Harrison.

I turned to face him and held both sides of his perfect face in my hands; lifting his mouth from my neck, we locked eyes once more. I held him there, my eyes searching his to determine if this was lust or something deeper, and as I watched the flecks of gold in his eyes catch the glimmer from the bathroom light, I asked him point blank.

"Is this real for you Harrison, or is this just fun? Because this is simpler for you than it is for me, and I've got a bit more to lose if this is just some fleeting physical thing."

He seemed surprised that I would imply he might be doing this casually. His brows furrowed and he paused before he answered me.

"Alice, from the moment I saw you at the pub, sitting there so confident, beauty unmatched, I knew you were a once-in-a-lifetime kind of person.

Something about your aura drew me to you and there was no way I could escape the feeling of wanting to know you. It's not easy for someone like me to approach a woman. Most have this predetermined opinion about me based on the trash they read in gossip rags. They believe everything they see online, like I'm some sex-crazed, perverted womanizer. They just want to use me for their fifteen minutes of fame or their own sexual escapades. If we're being honest, Alice, I've slept with maybe four people my entire life. I'm not just out here running through it because it's being thrown at me; that isn't who I am. I never let anyone in to really know me. And it's painfully obvious that people don't see me as a real person with actual feelings. But you, Alice. You are something else. You came out of nowhere and caught me off guard. You took the time to share your world with me, to open yourself up to who I am as a person and accept my flaws and my past, my quirks, and yeah, I tried to impress you with the jet, but that's just for fun. I wanted you to feel safe and taken care of and also to make wonderful lasting memories with me and have a good time. This isn't just a physical one-off for me, Alice. Trust me, this is more than I ever could have bargained for. I haven't stopped thinking about you since the moment I laid eyes on you. Everything about this feels so right to me and I can feel myself falling in love with you, despite all the things that complicate this for us. I fell asleep last night with visions of us decades from now still together, living a beautiful life, maybe with some kids, hell, maybe even a dog in the yard. That's what this is for me and I—"

I had heard enough. I leaned in and kissed him with an unbridled passion, with more emotion than we had yet shared. I took my time, trying to convey the love I was beginning to feel for him too, hoping to make him feel adored and accepted after everything he had just divulged. But Harrison was the first to pull away, and as he did, he nuzzled his head between my neck and my shoulder and tightened his embrace. He seemed to have found comfort in simply holding me close to him. The energy in the room shifted and I could feel that this was about more than physical intimacy.

We were two people with a shared disdain for loneliness, who each had lived our lives disconnected from others for one reason or another. Both of us desperate to feel genuine human touch and unconditional emotion, standing there embracing one another in silence. Me, a housewife from small-town U.S.A., who'd been settling for a life of sadness, frustration, and solitude, just going through the motions. Harrison, a globally recognized and beloved actor with the world at his feet, who could never trust anyone enough to let them in, and had been spending his life in emotional and physical isolation. We had nothing, and yet somehow everything, in common.

What was moments ago hungry and ravenous had now turned into something loving and heartfelt as we absorbed and accepted each other's unspoken needs. It was almost as if we were freeing one another of the burdens we'd been carrying and understanding what the other was going through without having to speak a single word. Minutes passed, and when I stepped back, prepared to share what was on my heart, I was surprised to find Harrison's eyes had welled with tears.

"Talk to me, what's wrong?" As I said it, tears fell from his eyes and I used the backs of my fingers to gently wipe them from his cheeks.

"Is this insane? I've never felt like this for someone so quickly in my life, Alice. Am I losing my mind?" Harrison shook his head and looked away, frustrated.

"Harrison." I reached out and touched his chin, directing his focus back to me. "I feel the same way you do. Is it crazy? Yeah, maybe. But how else does it happen? Should we ignore this for two weeks, or a month that we don't have available to us, and then explore it? Is that an acceptable time frame that would make this less crazy? Does it matter that I don't care if it *is* crazy? There's no rule book for this kind of thing." I shrugged as I attempted to dispel his fears.

He looked at me, searching my eyes before he spoke again.

"I guess I need to know something before I lose myself any deeper into this than I already am. I know it might be uncomfortable, or maybe you can't tell me everything and that's fine, but I think if you're telling me that you feel the same way I do, and you expect me to believe you when you say it, then explain to me how you can say those things to me and still have that ring on your finger." Harrison was stern with his words but the look in his eyes was one of vulnerability.

He was absolutely right to feel the way he did, and I couldn't blame him for asking; I would have done the same thing if I were him. I took him by the hand, sat down on the bed and patted the space beside me, inviting him to sit with me. I drew in a slow deep breath, mentally calculating how I could put this into words before I let forth a deep, anxious sigh then turned to face him.

"Try to understand, Harrison, my situation is this: I had grand plans when I was a senior in high school, plans for a future I was excited about. I was set to go to college to become an architect. I had dreamed of it almost my whole life. Then, a summer fling turned into an unplanned pregnancy I never wanted and a failed attempt at an abortion, and that turned into a very unplanned marriage. I was still a teenager with my entire life ahead of me, and then the future I had planned was gone, just like that." I snapped my fingers. "My head was spinning with all the changes that were happening. It made the most sense to be married so when he asked, I said yes. And when I finally wrapped my head around my new reality and settled into being someone's wife, I lost the baby. The process of grief was extraordinary for him, and for me. But I lost more than just a baby that day. My husband shut himself off to me, emotionally, physically. Everything was just gone. So, there I was in what felt like an empty marriage with a man that became emotionally hollow. I had no support from him at all. And now, decades later, it's not the same as it was in the beginning. We're not who we used to be. Loss like that changes people fundamentally. And we don't talk about it; it's just something we don't do. He and I have been living life in the same house, but fully void of true happiness, void of touch, void of compassion or empathy. We barely speak to each other. We go through the motions every single day, and he makes me feel like I'm some pain in his ass that exists to cook and make sure that the house is clean. He doesn't see me. He doesn't listen to me, and he damn sure doesn't touch me. He has no idea who I am anymore. So, I'm ready to be free of that. I want to feel wanted, heard, desired, and to be understood. You give me those things. In the short amount of time we've been in each other's company, I finally feel alive. After what has felt like decades trapped in the dark, you've thrown open the curtains and let all the sunlight pour in." My nose started to tingle and I tried to keep myself from crying.

I felt like someone had taken the backpack full of rocks I'd carried for far too long off of my shoulders and laid it at my feet. The weight of the sadness I had struggled with for so many years was no longer holding me to the ground. I was free to float however and wherever I needed to bask in my newfound freedom.

Harrison's eyes were empathetic as he watched me struggle to keep my composure. "It sounds to me like you've tried your best with something that no longer serves you. Seems, honestly, like it hasn't served you for some time now, love. I want you to know, I'm here. You've got my devotion, and my arms are open…I do want you. I want all of you, Alice. Days, nights, mornings. I want to make sure you feel that sunshine forever. You deserve it, darling. I'm so sorry that you've had to endure all of those things for so long."

Harrison was right; my marriage no longer served me. It only alienated me from my hopes and my dreams, which ironically were staring me in the face.

I wiped the tears from my cheeks and again, tried to reassure him. "Now you know the short version of the madness. I hope you can see my perspective a bit better, and trust that when I tell you that I'm falling for you, I mean it. It's not easy for me to say. My head keeps reminding me of the commitment I made, but my heart tells me that he gave up on me, and those commitments, long before now. I just want to feel happy."

"I meant what I said before, about wanting you, but I think I was caught up in the heat of the moment. So, I hope you'll forgive me if I was too forward. I don't want our first time together to be out of control against some bathroom countertop in a hotel, Alice. I want to make you feel like a goddess. Like you're the only woman on earth that could ever satisfy me. I want you to feel like I truly, genuinely love you. But, my God woman, for the record, you get me hot as hell." Harrison playfully wiped away nonexistent sweat from his forehead as he said it.

I couldn't help but laugh.

"Good, I'm glad I made you smile. Now, let's get back to the fun stuff, want to? We understand one another a little better now, so let's go have some dinner. I sent a text and told Lawrence to come pick us up just before you opened the bathroom door, so he should be waiting for us." Harrison stood and reached for my hand, and together we grabbed my things and made our way back to the SUV.

As the evening crept on, I learned that Harrison had sent Lawrence away earlier to close down the Spaniards Inn exclusively for our use for the evening. When we arrived, the entire place was quiet aside from the crackling logs burning in the historic fireplace and the sporadic clinking of dishes coming from the kitchen. The scent of the dining room was a cozy combination of the hearty Sunday sirloin roast that had been the daily special and the warm cinnamon of an unknown dessert. The shades had been fully drawn, and faint candlelight from the sconces adorning the walls illuminated the room just enough to allow me and Harrison the privacy we sought. The pub itself emanated old-time charm. From the dark, wood-paneled walls draped in 16th-century ornate details, to the soft creaking of the wood floors, the interior of the Spaniards Inn was reminiscent of something out of a Dickens novel. Of course, Harrison had been here many times, but this was my first time enjoying the inside of the pub. We made our way to the privacy of the back corner of the room and I found my senses delighted by every aspect of the place.

We sat side by side, snuggled together at a small candle-lit table near the fire and shared a variety of elegantly plated entrees and a few fruity cocktails while stories of our pasts and hopes for the future flowed between us with ease. I could feel myself growing more and more attached to Harrison as he shared some of the most intimate details of himself with me. I caught myself numerous times completely enamored as my gaze fixated entirely on him. I was happy to simply listen to the sound of his voice for hours, the way his accent rolled off his tongue, and the happiness that would light up his eyes as he talked about his feelings for me was something I was getting used to.

Dinner had been delicious, and the atmosphere nothing short of perfection, but now, as he placed his hand once again on the small of my back and ushered me toward the SUV, I was no longer surprised when Harrison announced he had something else planned. We rode together quietly, hand-in-hand, in the back of the vehicle, our bellies full, and our hearts contented. Harrison said the ride would be short, only about twenty minutes and as we traveled out of the quiet darkness of Hampstead, I noticed we were headed back toward the city.

Soon, the streetlights lit up the long rows of townhouses that lined the streets, showcasing their intricate iron balconies and their vibrant pastel façades. Like something out of a fairytale, I imagined myself living in one of them, the neighborhood ladies dropping by to sip afternoon tea from delicate floral-patterned china, all while basking in the sunlight that poured through the oversized windows. *I could be happy here*, I smiled at the thought, and snuggled closer to Harrison without a word.

First a right, then a left before Lawrence slowly pulled the car into a parking lot, bringing it to a stop between two other large dark SUVs. There was a knock on the partition, which startled me, and after a brief pause, Lawrence lowered the dark glass. The interior lights remained off, but I could see that he was turned around to face us in the backseat.

"Everyone is here and ready, sir. You should be all set." Lawrence nodded and then closed the glass.

"Everyone?" I asked, confused.

"Security. It's after dark, so there's some safety in that, but also, a different element of danger, as this is a fully public and popular place. But it's okay; we've got it under control. My team are professionals." The confidence in Harrison's voice in the dark had an eroticism to it that made the hair stand up on the back of my neck.

"I trust you." I gripped his hand tighter and started to move toward the door.

"Hold on a second." Harrison gently pulled me back into him and kissed me slowly, flashing me a smile when we broke away from one another.

"Okay, now we can go. I think you're going to love this." He grabbed a dark blue baseball cap from the console, and after securing it to his head, he leaned over and tapped the window beside me. Lawrence opened the door, helped me out of the backseat, then handed Harrison a dark colored blanket as he exited the vehicle.

There were two very large men standing at the back of the SUV, each of them well over six feet tall and incredibly muscular. Wearing black trousers and long-sleeved black shirts, with matching black baseball caps, I assumed it was to blend into the darkness of the night, though if I'm being honest, they weren't terribly inconspicuous. Like giants in a room full of toddlers, they were painfully obvious to me and must have been to anyone else nearby as well. They did, however, make me feel safe, and that was the goal.

Each of them nodded to me and mumbled a quiet, "Miss," as I walked past them. Harrison introduced them as Victor and Hank, noting that if I noticed anything suspicious while we were out tonight to simply speak one of their names and all would be resolved. I nodded my understanding and thanked the gentlemen. Harrison took my hand and we strolled off into the dark, with Victor and Hank a safe but reliable distance behind us.

"Welcome to Primrose Hill, love." He put his arm around my shoulder to both protect me and to bring me closer to him. I slipped my hand into his back pocket, cupping his backside playfully as we walked together down the manicured pathway. Beneath mature oak trees sat sporadically placed benches, lit from behind by pathway lights.

"A park? At nighttime? What goes on here after dark?" I jokingly nudged him. "You cheeky fella!" I laughed.

The park seemed rather quiet to me, especially for a Sunday. We hadn't passed a single person since we arrived and based on Harrison's feeling the need for security, I expected the place to be packed with people. I glanced at my watch to find that it was approaching 8 p.m. *Maybe it was close to closing time*, I thought, *or maybe he's just being extra careful*. Then just as quickly as I thought of it, I shrugged the thought from my mind.

We rounded a corner in the dark and the path spilled into a large open space then Harrison said calmly, "I thought you might like to see this."

I stopped in my tracks, in awe of yet another breathtaking view that spread out below me. As I looked down across a large sprawling valley, hundreds of tiny orbs of light danced among the shadows of trees, directing pedestrians through a maze of pathways and pulling the shades of green beneath them into view. Above, the darkness of the canopy, and higher still, the skyline of London. Sparkling lights of red and white, blue and green drew my eyes across the vast skyline of the city.

"Oh, Harrison. I've never seen anything like this before. All day long, you've taken my breath away and left me speechless." My eyes grew wider trying to take it all in.

As he laid out the blanket for us to sit on, he said, "Sit with me a spell, let me tell you what we're actually looking at." He patted the blanket beside him once he was finally seated, but I was still staring at the view. "Love?" he said.

"Oh, yes. Sorry." I laughed as I settled onto the blanket and found my place beside him. "Give me all the details; I'm ready."

Harrison pointed out the Shard Building, as well as the BT Tower, he rattled off details and endless facts about some of the other buildings that were in view and about how Shakespeare had a tree planted in this park in his honor. I recognized the London Eye from my visit the other day and wished Harrison had been with me to share the experience. I was learning the history of this country was much more interesting and complex than I originally thought, and having a handsome tour guide didn't hurt either.

We spent the better part of an hour talking about the buildings in the distance, about how I was used to the sounds of silence at night but never had a view like this from the farmhouse. Secretly I longed to take him home with me, show him what it was like to live quietly in the country without the stir of the city or the feared frenzy of the crowds. I wondered if he would enjoy small-town life, or if he'd be bored with it.

When the evening air began to feel damp and fog drifted between us and the city skyline, Harrison helped me to my feet, folded the blanket, and hand-in-hand we walked back to the car. There was no one else around, and when we got back to the parking lot it was empty other than the vehicles we arrived in. Victor and Hank waited for us to be secured in the SUV, then loaded into their respective vehicles; their presence as a safety measure had proven unnecessary. Harrison handed Lawrence the blanket and then he helped me settle into the vehicle before easing in beside me.

His chivalry didn't go unnoticed. I could see he had taken the lead, once again making me feel safe and doted on rather than letting Lawrence handle the door and helping me into the vehicle. *Sure, there were people for that*, I thought, *but he wants me to know that he can take care of me on his own.*

"So. It's getting late, are you tired? Back to the hotel? Or...?" Harrison asked.

"Well, in my usual day it's still only around four in the afternoon. So, I'm awake but we can head back if you like. Maybe just hang out, watch a movie?" I didn't want him to leave me yet. Something in me feared I'd never see him again if he left, or that I'd wake up and find this was all just a dream again.

"Wonderful." He lowered the partition and let Lawrence know our intended destination.

The ride was spent snuggled together in the darkness of the backseat, getting swept up in kisses and laughter while recounting the day's shared adventures. In no time we arrived at the hotel and the streets, as well as the hotel lobby, were once again void of people, which made getting back into the suite a breeze.

I dropped my bag into an armchair in the corner and grabbed two cold waters from the fridge.

"Sorry, I don't have anything fancier than this," I said as I handed a bottle to Harrison.

"This is good, love. I don't think I'm nearly as fancy as you think I am." He laughed as he said it.

"I mean, caviar on gold bars for breakfast, and champagne with diamonds for ice cubes in crystal flutes for dinner darling, c'mon." I said it in my most lavish snooty drawl.

Harrison burst out laughing before saying, "You're right, that's exactly me. You've nailed it. Hey, can I use your loo?"

"Of course; you know where it is." I plopped myself down on the couch, grabbed the remote, and turned the TV on. As I quietly flipped through the channels, Harrison's voice called to me from the bedroom.

"Alice, let's watch in here."

I smiled, took a nervous deep breath and shut the TV off in the main living space. My heart rate quickened as I stood, centered myself, then made my way into the bedroom. I found Harrison lying on his side, one arm tucked under a crumpled pillow, looking at me and smiling as I paused in the doorway. His shoes had been kicked off and laid askew on the floor; the glare from the TV was the only light in the room.

"Hi," I said smiling back at him.

"Hi," he chuckled softly again. "Come, lay with me."

I felt the heat rise in my cheeks as I pulled my shoes off and made my way to the bed. My heart was now pounding in my chest, but this time I couldn't stop myself from smiling. I felt like a teenager again, like this was the first time I had a boy over to my house unsupervised.

Harrison handed me the remote as I lay down beside him and watched me intently as I flipped through the channels. I settled on the first movie I recognized: *The Proposal.* We had only missed the first ten minutes.

"How about this one?" I asked, keeping my focus on the television.

He was still watching me; I could feel it. "Mhmm," he mumbled.

I turned quickly to look at him, triggered by how sleepy he sounded. To my surprise, he was still wide awake, staring at me, a flirtatious smirk across his perfect lips.

"Can I help you?" I said jokingly.

"Oh, you definitely can," he replied, his voice low, his smirk turning to a full-blown smile, never breaking eye contact with me.

"And what is it that I can do for you?" I bit my bottom lip.

"You can come closer."

I moved onto my side, positioning myself right in front of him.

"How's this?" I said, staring into his eyes.

"Not close enough." His voice was almost a whisper.

I leaned forward, my face less than an inch from his.

"How about now?" I whispered as he stared back at me.

"Closer." His accent was prominent.

I paused a moment, holding his eyes to mine. Then without a word, I softly kissed his top lip, then his bottom lip, lingering just long enough to feel his chin softly nuzzle against mine before I kissed him again, open-mouthed. He reciprocated with his own tenacity; our tongues hungry to explore one another.

I felt the strength of his left hand slide up my ribcage, his palm cupping my fully clothed breast as his other hand found its way to my neck. His thumb lightly traced my jawline before his fingertips slid into my hair and around to the back of my head, then he grasped a handful of my hair and gently pulled my head backward, exposing my neck. He kissed along the front of my throat and down to my cleavage. My breathing deepened as Harrison released his grip on my hair and held my face as his mouth returned to mine. His intensity slowed, trying to keep himself from moving too fast.

I inched my body closer to his and slipped my hand under his shirt to feel the warmth of his bare skin against my fingers. This man was pure muscle and I felt it as my hand wandered to the top of his well-defined back, and carefully tickled along his spine on the way back down to the waistband of his jeans. I traced along their edge until his abdominal muscles allowed my fingers to slip between the waist of his jeans and the waistband of his boxer briefs. I rolled onto my back and gripped the front of Harrison's jeans at the same time, pulling him on top of me.

He hovered over me, studying me in the faint light cast by the TV. I stared back at him for what felt like an eternity before I reached up and pulled his t-shirt off over his head, exposing not only his incredibly sculpted chest, arms, and abdomen but all of the tattoos that covered them. I watched his deep, even breaths as his ribs and the muscles that surrounded them heaved under my touch. My eyes cascaded over his body, taking stock of the artwork that adorned him.

I put my palms against his lower abs, each of my ring fingers wrapped around the chiseled v-shaped muscles that defined his waist, my thumbs caressing the tattoos that lay across the fronts of his hips. Slowly my hands moved upward to his pecs, my focus on their trajectory as I did it, devouring him with my eyes. I could feel his heart beating as my hands rested there, and I stared into his piercing green eyes. Harrison lifted my left hand from his chest and raised it to his mouth. He gently kissed the back of my hand, like the gentleman he is, smiled at me, and then slipped my ring finger fully into his mouth. With a slow deliberate twist of his tongue, he gently sucked the gold wedding band off the length of my finger and into his mouth before pulling it from between his lips and placing it on the nightstand.

I watched him intently as he did it, his eyes locked on mine with a seriousness about him that somehow relayed the depths of his emotions. And when he returned to his place in front of me, he smiled his slow Cheshire-cat grin, displaying the dimples in his cheeks. I smiled back at him, my body throbbing in anticipation, thinking that was the most erotic thing I had ever been a part of. I reached for the back of his neck, pulling him down toward me, I whispered against his ear, "I adore you," then kissed him once again.

Harrison took his time discovering me, a quality I wasn't used to in the bedroom. His touch was soft, and somehow more masculine than anything I'd ever felt. His hands canvassed my body, stopping frequently to massage and kiss me in places I had never imagined to be erogenous. The tips of my toes, my inner ankle, and the inner sides of my knees. Each stop he made along the way made my body pulsate with anticipation. He ran his hands along my hips as he bypassed my center, opting first to dedicate his time to kissing my neck and shoulders, whispering how wonderful it felt to be close to me and how much he cherished me. As soon as his breath touched my ear my back arched instinctively, and goosebumps covered my skin.

"Any time you want to stop, Alice, you tell me," he said.

"Don't stop. Don't ever stop," I responded, as I stripped my t-shirt off and tossed it away.

Harrison's mouth was magnetic. I never wanted to stop kissing him but loved the way his mouth felt as it explored the rest of my body. His lips moved from shoulder to shoulder. Slipping my bra straps down one by one, his fingertips teasing along the cupped edges of my breasts, his tongue keeping pace right behind them.

I unbuttoned his jeans, then slid down his zipper. "Take these off." As I said it, my bottom lip brushed his earlobe and I took it in my mouth, sucking it gently. His hair smelled like his tobacco cologne and I breathed him in as he reached behind me to release the clasp of my bra. My fingers tangled in his dark curls as his mouth groped at my neck and down to my cleavage.

He pulled away from me and stood at the end of the bed long enough to drop his jeans to the floor. His boxer briefs were black against the contrast of his skin and his tattoos, and I wanted him so badly now my hands that once were confident, were trembling. I pulled my bra off and tossed it in the direction of my t-shirt. Any self-consciousness I had felt in the past was gone.

As Harrison crawled back onto the bed in my direction he stopped at my knees and looked up at me, his expression intense. His eyes against the dim light of the room were electric, and I knew exactly what he wanted. He pulled my skirt from around my waist, exposing my sheer black panties and as the skirt fell from the edge of the bed, his hands caressed the length of my legs and landed on my hips.

"Is this okay?" he asked, once again giving me an opportunity to stop if I wanted to.

"It's incredible," I replied, granting permission, breathless at the thought of what was about to happen.

"I bet it is…" Harrison's mischievous smile brought out his dimples again.

His dark hair disheveled, he bit his bottom lip as his nostrils flared and his hands gripped the sides of my panties. Until now, I'd been watching his every move, but as he slid my panties down and tossed them aside, I closed my eyes and laid my head back against the pillows.

He took his time, using his mouth and his tongue to kiss and bite his way up my thighs and across my abdomen while his hands explored my breasts, finding exactly what pleased them. Just like in my dream, Harrison knew when to fluctuate between soft touch and rough, how much pressure was enough to have my back once again arching, my body aching for more. The warmth and the suction of his mouth on my body, against my breasts was nearly enough to send me over the edge.

Just as I thought I couldn't take any more, I raised my head from the pillows and met his gaze. Harrison liked to watch his effect on me, that much was clear, and in turn I watched as he snaked his tongue down the center of my abdomen, never breaking eye contact with me, he separated my legs, and tasted me for the first time. I tried to stifle a gasp and after a moment let out a restrained sigh. His tongue was his secret weapon. From the skillful way he kissed me, taking his time, engaging my mind and my body and bringing all my senses to full attention, to the way he now used it to bring me to a mind-blowing orgasm, I had never experienced a lover that was so intent on finding my bliss, at least, not since he'd done it in my dream.

"My God Alice, you are...perfect." Harrison wiped his chin against his shoulder as he said it, his accent manipulating the word into something breathy. *Puhr'fect.* It replayed in my head, and I ached to feel his tongue against mine again.

"Come here. Your mouth's been away from mine for too long." I reached for his face and pulled him up to kiss him deeply once again, tasting myself on his tongue.

As Harrison kissed my neck, our bare skin pressed against each other, I basked in the afterglow of a long overdue release, my legs continuing to quiver. *This is better than any dream I could ever have,* I thought, and we had barely scratched the surface.

After a moment I reached down and gently tugged at the band of his boxer briefs.

"These need to go," I whispered and let my hand slowly graze over the now very hard length of him.

Harrison raised himself up and I stripped the briefs from his body. My dreams hadn't given him the credit he deserved; that much was evident. *Every part of this man is magnificent,* I thought, and I traced my fingers over the tattoos that covered his abdomen, imagining all the ways I wanted to please him.

"Wait, Alice. I don't have any...protection. This isn't something I do. I didn't plan on this..." he said. "We can stop; we don't have to go any further."

"I don't want to stop," I said breathlessly. "Do you?"

"Pleasing you is my priority; I'm not worried about me. I want to make sure you're okay." His voice sincere.

"I'm not on anything. So worst case scenario is, you're stuck with me forever," I joked.

"If I'm being honest, that's all I want, Alice. Just you, me, and forever." He locked eyes with me and held my gaze. "You're all I want."

I kissed him again to show him I understood and agreed.

"It's been a really long time..." I said nervously as I looked at him for reassurance. "I don't want to stop. I just need you to know, it's been a while, that's all."

Harrison kissed me, then held my face in his hands and looked into my eyes. "I've got you, okay?" I nodded and he could tell I was apprehensive. "I've got you, love," he repeated.

He kissed my forehead, then each cheek before kissing me again on the mouth. His hands returned to my breasts and he lowered his body to mine, pressing his pelvis against me. He gripped the back of my thigh as he raised my knee to his mouth, kissed it softly, and returned his mouth to my neck. His breath was warm against my ear as he whispered, "Alice, I think I'm falling in love with you."

Moments later as he penetrated me for the first time, I relaxed into a deep exhaled moan. I closed my eyes and clutched at his back, lost in the moment, losing myself to the feeling of him. Slowly, rhythmically, as the night wore on, he repeatedly brought me to climax before we shared a final orgasm together.

At some point, the TV had been shut off, and now we lay tangled with one another in the quiet darkness. Gentle caresses and tender kisses were what remained after a fervent and sweaty night of lovemaking.

"Can I stay here with you tonight?" His voice was soft and his breath warm against my neck.

"I never want to be without you." I said as I twirled a lock of his hair between my fingers and kissed his forehead before snuggling closer into his body. Both of us exhausted and fulfilled, we let sleep overtake us.

6.

The curtains, backlit from the morning sun, cast ribbons of light across the room, spilling over us as we lay wrapped around each other. It had only been a few hours since we'd closed our eyes, but a rumbling from my belly woke me from a dreamless sleep. Nearly this entire trip had passed without me slipping into my dreamworld. Maybe it was because I'd worked myself into pure exhaustion each day sightseeing, or maybe it was because all of my dreams were lying right here beside me.

I kissed Harrison's forehead, trying to wake him. As he lifted his cheek from my bare chest, he sleepily wiped the drool from his face then sprung up in horror.

"Oh my God, I'm so sorry!" He was embarrassed and quickly wiped at my skin then turned away from me, drawing the back of his hand across his face.

I laughed. "It isn't that serious. Guess I'm comfy to sleep on, huh?" I said, still chuckling.

"I'm mortified, truly." The rasp in his voice emphasized his accent. *That familiar morning rasp from my dream.*

"Don't be; are you hungry? I'm—" Before I could finish my statement my belly growled again. "Room service?" I asked, laughing.

"I'd love an omelet and some rye toast, black coffee with four sugars. And a toothbrush."

I called room service and placed our order while Harrison checked his phone.

"What's the plan for today?" I asked. "Are you busy?"

"I've got nothing on my schedule; do you have plans already?" he asked.

"I have no steadfast plans for the rest of the trip, actually. I had a few more places I wanted to see while I was here, but I've already done what mattered most to me. Speaking of which, you, sir, are next level." I blushed as I said it and made eyes at him, then bit at my bottom lip again, something I now knew triggered Harrison's libido.

"I see what you're doing there..." He shook his finger at me and moved his body up against me in the bed. He quickly kissed his way up my arm, then my neck and landed just below my jaw, inhaling me. "Alice, you are intoxicating." He closed his eyes and exhaled against my skin.

Even in the morning he smelled of cologne. His hair was a disheveled mess and he drooled in his sleep, but to me, these were the parts of him that reminded me he was real. This wasn't a dream sequence; this wasn't a movie or some fantasy. I woke up and he's really here with me. This was actually happening. I wondered what this would mean a week from now or next year. *Would it still matter? Would I still matter? What would happen when I went back home? How in the hell had I arrived at this place in my life?* A week ago, I lay in bed falling asleep to the idea of this man, and now I was lying naked in a London hotel room with him.

"In a perfect world, how does this play out for you?" I asked quietly.

"The world I'm in right now is pretty perfect." His lips pressed against my neck as he said it, kissing me softly.

"I'm serious. Write the rest of this story."

"Well," he sighed deeply before continuing. "We spend the next few days together. I'd really love it if you stayed with me the rest of your trip, at my house. We continue to grow closer, see what it's like to be together all the time until you have to go." He kissed my shoulder.

"And then?" My tone grew more serious.

"Honestly?" he questioned.

Oh, this is it, I thought, *this is when he says, 'I don't know, see where it goes?' and leaves me to trudge through my emotions alone.*

"Yes, always honestly, please," I said, bracing myself for the worst.

"And then..." He hesitated, looking over at the ring on the nightstand before turning back to meet my eyes and said, "Then you go back and file for divorce from the man you said doesn't see you, doesn't love you properly, and doesn't spark joy in you anymore. I don't know if that house means enough to you to fight for it or just walk away from it all. Stay and fight for what you want until you get it, or drop it all, but in the end, come back here to me. Be with me. Choose yourself and then choose me." His eyes, his mouth, and his heart were pleading with me in unison.

"And then?" I said.

"And then, spend your life letting me appreciate you, letting me really, truly love you. Let me ignite a fire in you, Alice. Travel the world with me and live a life of happiness, where joy isn't something you seek but something you exude."

"That all sounds incredible, Harrison, but what happens when work takes you away for months, or we argue about something foolish, or my age becomes a factor?"

"What's your age got to do with it? Wherever work takes me, it takes you, and as long as we communicate and we're honest with each other, I think we'll be fine. I'm not saying we won't have our share of hard times or that disagreements won't creep up from time to time, but Alice, I think this can really be something. It's fast, I know. It seems unconventional, but that's because it is. My life's not normal, but I have the means to share a life with you that you deserve. You'll have the freedom to go back to school if you want without worrying about the mortgage. You can lie by a pool or create skyscrapers, you can be creative or you can head a foundation if you want. The world is yours to grab by the bollocks Alice, and make of it whatever you choose."

I stared at him, no expression on my face, searching his eyes for something other than words to make me believe that the picture he painted was actually plausible.

"I want you in my life permanently, Alice. Don't you want that too?" he asked.

"I do want that. I want you. I want all of it. For someone like me, whose life hasn't been anything I envisioned it would be, someone who long ago settled for the hand I was dealt, someone who doesn't ever rock the boat, it's terrifying, Harrison."

"What's terrifying, I imagine, is going back and staying in a life that makes you feel like you've been thrown in the deep end with weights on your feet, drowning while no one offers to pull you to the surface," he said calmly, but adamantly.

"You're right. It is. Staying in it is terrifying. Leaving it, change—change *that* huge—is terrifying." I looked away as I said it, unable to keep eye contact with him.

"Even if you remove me from the entire equation, Alice. Even if you never met me, wouldn't you owe it to yourself to find actual happiness in life? You left the country looking for it. You went off in search of something more for yourself. Somewhere in you, you know the life you've been living is no way to live."

I stared toward the window. *He's right*, I thought. *It isn't any way to live.*

"I've been angry for so long...real happiness just felt like something other people could have, not me. I don't know if I've been mad at him or at myself for being so willing to just live with it instead of change it. I don't know." I shook my head, frustrated.

"Alice, we have what? Three more days together? Let's see how they play out. You might hate me by Thursday. I might drool during the day too." He nudged me, trying to lighten the mood.

"Ugh, God…" I said, jokingly grimacing, then smiled back at him.

When breakfast arrived, we ate and continued to discuss the what ifs. What if the divorce took months? What if he decided three weeks from now that he didn't want me to come back? What if I decided I couldn't uproot myself? What if he met someone else while I was in the middle of a divorce? What if I got home and decided not to get the divorce? Each of us slung different scenarios at one another that ultimately left the other hanging, but each scenario revealed the insecurities we both had. He was afraid to lose me just as much as I was afraid he would replace me.

We agreed that the rest of my time in London would be spent at Harrison's house, living as if we were together, working through those insecurities and embracing each other's habits. Digging deep to get to know one another to see just how compatible we could be long-term. I was excited because I knew this could be the beginning of something incredible for us, but nervous because everything is always perfect in the beginning. Playing house with him could change a lot of things, but in the meantime, I'd be staying at Harrison Edwards' actual house, per his request. I let that sink in while I got dressed and ready for the day, then packed all my things into my luggage, including the narrow gold band that lay on the nightstand. Choosing not to return it to my finger, I tucked it into my purse. I couldn't help but giggle at Harrison as I packed, hearing him humming while he brushed his teeth in the bathroom, I wondered if the rest of my life could really be like this.

When we were ready to go, I called the front desk and asked to pay my bill in full, advising I would be checking out early.

"Yes, ma'am. We also have a message here for you," the gentleman at the front desk responded.

"A message? Who left me a message?" I asked, perplexed.

"A gentleman named James, ma'am. It says, *'Came into town for supplies. You didn't answer my text. Hope you're okay. Miss you. James.'* He called last night asking to be connected to your room, but got no answer. When he rang us again, I assumed you must have been out, that's when he left a message with us at the desk."

I was stunned. He must have called while Harrison and I were at dinner or in the park, and I hadn't looked at my cell phone since yesterday. The last time I had it out was to take a photo; the rest of the night I was...preoccupied.

"Why am I just getting this now? No one called the room last night or this morning to let me know I had a message waiting," I said, annoyed.

"I'm very sorry, ma'am; guests don't typically get written messages as there is a voicemail option on the in-room phones. I do apologize for the lack of communication."

"No, that's okay, no need to apologize. If you could go ahead and charge the card on file for my stay and incidentals, I'll leave my key here in the room and be checking out in about half an hour. Thank you for the message; I have enjoyed my stay here very much." I hung up the phone, still perplexed.

I sat on the edge of the bed puzzled, trying to figure out what would possess James to call the hotel. He could have left that message on my cell phone voicemail, as a text, or on my in-room voicemail. I began to second-guess myself. *Had I even given him the name of the hotel?* The longer I sat there, the more confused I became. I pulled out my cell phone and checked for the missed call. Sure enough, it was there along with a text.

Getting supplies, hope you're ok, all good here.

There was no 'miss you' on this one. No surprise there.

I typed my response:

Sorry, just got this message and the hotel message. Wasn't ignoring you. Sorry I missed you. See you in a few days.

I always finished my texts to James with a habitual 'love you' at the very least, but not today. I wasn't feeling the love, and he probably wouldn't notice anyhow. James wouldn't even get the message until he was on his way home, but I sent it to prove I hadn't been mugged or murdered while away. I tossed my phone back into my tote bag and glanced around, making sure I wasn't forgetting anything as Harrison came out of the bathroom toward me.

"I'm all set, I think," I said to him, then threw my tote bag onto my shoulder. He grabbed my suitcase and we headed for the door.

The hotel lobby was empty except for a couple standing at the desk. No one seemed to notice as we made our way toward the main set of doors, but Harrison paused when he saw the crowd that blanketed the sidewalks flanking the exit. There were cell phones already held in the air, ready to catch a glimpse of the movie star.

 Harrison didn't spend any time wondering how they found him, just whispered to me to head for the side exit and gave me the handle of the suitcase.

"Now wait a minute. Let me act like I'm on my own. I'll cut through the crowd and Lawrence will let me into the car. We'll pick you up around the side. Go quick." I said it with conviction. I wasn't afraid of these people. *They'll be disappointed when all they get is me and not Harrison*, I thought.

"You better turn yourself around," I advised, the New Englander in me came out and I spoke as if I were reprimanding a child.

Before he could respond, I shoved my sunglasses into his hand and self-assuredly pushed my way through the double doors.

Harrison spun around and tried to be as cool as possible as he walked back through the lobby toward the Atrium exit, making sure my sunglasses covered his eyes. Once he was past the front desk, he quickened his pace and burst through the side exit just in time to find Lawrence and I in the SUV turning the corner, making our approach. Harrison reached for the handle just as I unlocked the door; once again safely in the backseat with me, he kissed my cheek.

"You're brave. And brilliant. And fiercely adorable." he said, smiling at me affectionately as he handed me my glasses.

I couldn't help but smile back at him. "Thank you love. Told you I'd create a diversion when needed; now whether or not anyone got a photo before we realized there was a crowd out there is another story." I shrugged and reached for his hand, threading my fingers between his.

"I appreciate you. You might be a bit crazy, but I appreciate that too." He nudged me, as he always did when he was joking around.

"Well, it's nice to be able to say for once that I've got *you*, instead of the other way around." I said and put my arm around him.

"I think you're going to do just fine dealing with the public; you seem fearless when it comes to protecting me, and I've never had that in a partner Alice; thank you."

I kissed him on the cheek and asked, "So, tell me, what kind of bachelor pad am I walking into?"

"It's not far, we'll be home soon enough and you can see for yourself." As soon as he said it, we both smiled. *Home.*

We weaved our way through London, Harrison pointing out his favorite parks, restaurants, and coffee shops as we passed through the city, promising he'd take me to all these places any time I wanted to go. He pointed out the flower shop where he had gotten all the beautiful blooms for yesterday's adventures, and as he talked, I watched the landscape shift from hulking historic stone structures surrounded by people into a quieter, green, tree-filled landscape. The drive was familiar; we'd driven it last night to get to the Spaniards Inn for dinner, and I remembered the night we met he said he lived close by.

The roads narrowed and the traffic thinned, we circled a roundabout and veered to the right, following what felt more like a country road, passing open fields and deepening forests as my anxiety began to creep up as a result of my intrusive thoughts. Harrison's voice faded into the background as the questions in my mind began to swirl.

What must his home be like? Does he have a staff? Is he messy? Does he have a maid? Does he let everyone do everything for him? I hope he's not one of those men. I wonder if he's one of those secretly eccentric weirdos behind closed doors. So far, he seems more normal than I would have thought, but everyone has a side to themselves they don't share with anyone, don't they?

As I spiraled, I began to wonder how I could possibly fit into this life of his. I wondered how, in just a few days' time, I had arrived at the decision to leave the security of my husband of two decades for a movie star I'd spent thirty-six hours with while I was in an entirely different country. Was I behaving purely from a place of lust? Were pheromones in control of my choices, or was this the clearest decision-making I'd done in a while? Was the fight I had with James before I left home the driving force in this? Sure, I love my husband, but was I still *in* love with him? It certainly didn't feel like it, and he didn't treat me like someone he was in love with either, and it had been that way for many years. Was I willing to continue to settle for this treatment the rest of my life?

Maybe it was as simple as the fact that I'd discovered life was short, and it was in fact worth living to its fullest extent in the moment. Maybe I had found something in this man, this beautiful, selfless, caring man, despite who he was to the world and the work that he'd become famous for. Despite our wildly different lifestyles, maybe this was something worth throwing caution to the wind for and letting myself blossom. *Insanity is doing the same thing over and over and expecting a different result.* Maybe it was time to stop doing the same thing and open myself up to the world of possibilities that the universe had laid around me. I was deserving of good things, happiness, and freedom from a life that had been choking the light from my eyes for far too long.

Harrison Edwards was a boost of serotonin in the most beautiful physical form. He was the warm tingle of sunshine after living years in the depths of darkness. He was the dopamine I had been devoid of for twenty-two years. *Harrison Edwards...feels like a once-in-a-lifetime love that I would absolutely regret walking away from for the rest of my life.* And somehow, when I thought of leaving James, it carried no regret at all.

"We're here, love." Harrison's voice brought me back to reality.

Regaining focus, I looked around as we turned onto a well-manicured cobblestone lane edged with large old oak trees. About half a mile in, a tall stone wall clasped together by an iron gate came into view. Its doors swung open as our vehicle approached, allowing us entry up the paved drive. I wasn't sure what to expect; there were trees all around, blocking the view of anything else. When we reached the top, the winding driveway leveled and Harrison's house came into view.

It appeared both new and antique, with the lower half of the exterior made of stone and the upper of an ornate, aged wooden shingle. The entrance wasn't grand, and no maids were rushing out to greet us. In fact, it seemed like quite a humble home compared to what I had imagined a movie star might live in. The grounds were well maintained and remained a lush velvety green despite October's approach.

Harrison took my hand and led me from the car toward the entrance while Lawrence took care of my luggage. The house was engulfed in flower gardens, much to my surprise. I lingered at their edge, taking stock of all they had to offer.

"One of the things I love most about this house are the gardens. I see you approve?" he asked.

"They're gorgeous. You never told me you had all these flower beds," I said, fascinated.

"I can't give away all my secrets at once, darling. You'll fall head over heels for me in an instant!" he joked.

"Too late." I shot him a flirtatious glance.

"Let me show you the inside. Come with me." He ushered me toward the front door.

Once inside, I dropped my tote bag onto the entry mat and slipped off my shoes as I took in my surroundings. The inside of Harrison's home was large and open, a masculine post-and-beam style home with tall ceilings, terra cotta tile floors worn glossy and smooth, chunky wood accents, and lots of windows that showcased the entire surrounding property. The step down from the wide entryway into the open concept room allowed me to see most of the first floor right from where I stood.

"There's a loo right here to your right, a guest room with ensuite off to that side, and a room I've transformed into a library off the other side. Obviously, the kitchen, dining, and living room are here..." He gestured around with one hand as he spoke while the other gently pulled at his cheek unwittingly.

"It's beautiful Harrison. I'm so curious to see your library," I admitted.

"Of course, this way." With his hand carefully at the small of my back, I was reminded again why I had chosen to be here with him.

We passed by the kitchen to reach the library and I knew immediately this was a space I could easily get used to. Gorgeous granite counters, professional appliances, and a large soapstone sink was positioned to overlook the sprawling backyard. There was a heavy wooden table that could easily fit twelve people in the dining room, and the living room was further sunken, an inviting oversized leather sectional sat in front of a behemoth open stone fireplace. The mantle was adorned with photos of family and friends, and the hearth held a wooden tray of half melted cream-colored pillar candles on one side and a large trailing vibrant green pothos plant on the other. His home felt cozy and welcoming and smelled like a mix of warm vanilla and clean eucalyptus. *Vanilla...I should've expected that.*

The library was painted a deep navy blue, and in the center of the room sat a large antique desk, its top vacant except for a closed laptop and vintage desk lamp. The long wall of windows behind it were draped with rich gold velour curtains and flanked by large potted indoor palms. The other three walls housed floor-to-ceiling built-in bookshelves, complete with a rustic rolling library ladder on a solid brass track. In one corner, an oversized leather chair was draped with a cashmere blanket and made for a perfect spot to curl up and get lost in one of the hundreds of books Harrison kept here. A decanter of some dark liquor with a single etched glass sat atop a small side table and above it hovered what appeared to be an antique brass floor lamp.

Harrison seemed to be a very tidy person and everything so far was neatly in its place. The desktop was free of any papers, and the blanket had been folded neatly and positioned on the chair. All the books were lined up perfectly and tucked into the shelves. His kitchen counters were free of clutter and the living room looked as if no one ever lived in it. I moved along the wall of books, pausing as I found familiar, beloved titles. Our taste in literature was similar.

"Harrison this is...elegant. Your collection is gorgeous." I ran my fingers over the spines of his books as I said it, working my way toward the windows for a better view of the yard.

"Thank you. Books, travel, nature...they each allow us to use our imagination, to transport ourselves and our minds, our hearts, somewhere else. We love many of the same things, Alice." His gaze lingered on me long after he stopped speaking.

I felt him watching me and tried to busy myself observing what was beyond the windows to avoid his stare. Moments later, hesitantly I turned to face him.

"What?" I asked bashfully. I felt my cheeks flush as he continued to study me.

"I'm just so happy you're here with me, Alice. This house has felt like, I don't know, too much for just me, for a really long time. You know, like the element of 'home' has never been present. But just having you here now, makes it feel like an actual home instead of just a house." he gushed.

"Well, I'm happy to be here with you too, and I'm glad you feel you've found the missing piece. You really have no idea how much it means to me to hear you say that." I winked at him, hoping to make him smile.

"I never thought I would find someone like you, Alice. I've searched such a long time, and had sort of given up. It's part of why I've moved so quickly with you. I don't want this...us...to slip through my fingers. I don't want to lose everything I think we could be."

"Well, I'm here now, and all yours for the time being." I approached him as I spoke, then kissed him slowly, and as I pulled away gave him a peck on his left dimple.

"These might be my favorite part of your body, these dimples," I said and kissed him again, my fingertip gently grazing over the beloved indentation.

"Is that right?" He chuckled as he said it.

I looked him up and down in an exaggerated way. "Well, top five, for sure."

"Oh, really?" He laughed and raised an eyebrow, intrigued.

"Come on, show me where the magic happens." I took Harrison's hand and nudged him to lead me back to the main living area.

It was obvious the upstairs of Harrison's house was his sanctuary. It was welcoming like the lower level, and just as masculine, but appeared more relaxed, more lived-in than what I had seen downstairs. The landing at the top of the stairs was airy and spacious and flooded by sunlight that poured through the windows. To the right was his home gym, outfitted with all the equipment you would expect, and to the left, a comfortable sitting area with an antique lamp and a scattering of books laid atop a small table nestled between two well-worn, brown leather wingback chairs. A plush cream-colored area rug blanketed the floor, and the walls were bathed in a deep rich chestnut color.

I peered from the closest window down to the yard below. A huge stretch of flat manicured lawn rolled out before me. Large stone steps were tucked into a slope at the back and led to a flagstone patio with a matching post-and-beam pergola erected over a firepit with cushioned chairs surrounding it. Everything was framed by well-maintained flower beds and various fruit trees.

"Do you think you could tolerate being here full-time and calling this ours, not mine?" Harrison asked, wrapping his arms around my waist from behind.

"I mean, it certainly doesn't suck." I joked, then matched his sincerity. "I could easily be happy here; I already am. I think I could be happy anywhere with you."

I laid my head to the side and instinctively Harrison nuzzled into my neck. We stood there a moment in silence, wrapped up in one another, gazing out across the quiet yard. I smiled as I imagined how each day could feel like this if I were here with him all the time. His arms around me felt safe. His rogue curls tickled my cheek as he rested his chin on my shoulder and reminded me that he valued me, he sought out my companionship instead of running from it. I didn't have to wonder if he enjoyed being close to me, touching me. New love, being wanted by someone, it all felt foreign to me until these last few days with Harrison.

"Let me show you the rest." He took me by the hand and led me through two tall, carved wooden doors into his bedroom.

The scent of his cologne was the first thing I noticed as I entered the room. I paused and closed my eyes, slowly drawing in a deep breath, absorbing the smell of him into my lungs. Flashbacks of my dream blasted through my mind. The way he smiled at me when I gave him the hat in Virginia. The glances I stole while driving, hearing him sing along to the radio, watching him play the piano surrounded by flowers. The way he looked at me when he picked me up for our date to the wedding.

"Love?" his voice cut through my daydream.

"Sorry, I was lost there for a second." I shook my head as if to clear my mind.

He laughed at my reaction. "You okay?" he asked.

"Your bedroom smells like your cologne; I was just...enjoying it." I smiled and then my eyes widened as I caught my first glimpse of the ensuite bathroom.

"Harrison!" I exclaimed and rushed toward the second set of open doors.

Straight ahead, glossy black marble floors gleamed against an oversized hammered-copper soaking tub that stood regal below a string of enormous windows. There was a double vanity to my immediate left and beyond that, a massive piece of solid glass stood between the rest of the bathroom and a cavernous state-of-the-art shower. There were multiple copper shower heads and nozzles, an overhead rain feature that spanned the length of the shower, recessed lights, and teak benches along the entire back wall. A large bunch of eucalyptus hung from one of the shower heads, and in the front corner hung a healthy variegated pothos plant, its vines outstretched along the top edge of the glass. To the right of the bathtub was the private water closet, and further still were the entry doors to his and hers closets.

I couldn't help but peek my head into each closet; the first one was entirely vacant. Nothing but wooden hangers adorned the otherwise empty rods, and the shelves were bare.

"This is an awfully big closet to just be vacant. Why don't you use it?" I asked.

Harrison hung his head before looking up at me bashfully. "I called to have it cleaned out while you were on the phone at the hotel; that way it would be available for you when you got here. I wanted you to feel like there was plenty of space here for you and your things."

He's taking the initiative and carving out a place for me in his life. I smiled at the thought of myself living here, really thriving here with this beautiful thoughtful man that truly thinks of everything to make me feel welcome.

Harrison's closet was huge, but also quite sparse. I expected he'd have an abundantly overflowing wardrobe, based on his known affiliations with designers and big-name brands, but the racks in his closet said otherwise. He leaned against the doorway, watching me.

"I really don't keep much as far as clothes go. I'm a pretty simple guy," he offered when I looked back at him puzzled.

"I archive most of my stuff, and I keep a few things here." He pointed toward the dozen Gucci suits that hung against a singular tuxedo. "Other than this, I'm more of a jeans and t-shirt guy."

Gucci. Just the thought of it made me smile.

I let my fingertips trail along the fabrics of his suits, pausing when I reached a floral patterned black and white ensemble.

"This is familiar," I said and gave him a knowing look over my shoulder.

"Yes, the infamous floral suit. I wore it to my first red carpet; I couldn't bear to archive it. It reminds me of where it all started," he smirked, exposing his dimples. "Keeps me hungry."

"Personally, I always thought it was incredible," I said.

"Me too. Some people just can't appreciate good fashion. It's not for everyone, I guess. Neither am I, I suppose." I could tell he was in his thoughts as he said it.

"Makes it easy to find the ones who matter though," I added before continuing to poke around the closet.

I noticed he kept his everyday clothes on the opposite side of his suits. Jeans were folded neatly over hangers and his shirts were grouped by tanks, tees, and long-sleeves while jackets and hoodies hung on the far end of the closet. The wooden hangers all evenly spaced and facing the same direction caught me off guard, but was certainly impressive.

He had designated a space in his closet for a small group of watches that were propped up on their own stands. Beside them sat an elaborately carved wooden tray that held various chunky rings, 2 bottles of the same cologne and a half dozen bottles of nail polish grouped together and pushed into the back corner. A large mirror hung above the long dresser they all sat on. Further over, a beaded necklace dangled from a hook, the opalescent beads grouped together displaying the words 'I Am Loved,' each word separated by a shiny onyx jewel. Beside it on another hook hung a few leather bracelets in varying shades, and above them, a lone navy-blue bandana, rolled into itself like a headband lay draped over the corner of a framed family photo hung on the wall. *Just like in my dream.* I reached out and touched it gently and smiled.

"Everything is so neatly in its place. Do you keep the house clean like this, or do you have someone that helps?" I asked as I walked back toward the bedroom. "It's so organized; I'm impressed."

"I have someone come in daily in the mornings to take care of cleaning and all that. I rarely see her though. Shelby's quick, and quiet, and worth every penny." He laughed as he followed me. "But I don't leave the place in shambles either. I tidy up and do all that a grown man should do in his own home."

"Well, that's refreshing to hear. I can't wait to see what *that* feels like to be around." I said as I peered out onto the yet unexplored balcony.

"Wanna see?" he asked, smiling as he opened the door to the outside space.

The large balcony extending off the bedroom was beautifully designed and decorated, featuring a large two-sided fireplace also visible from inside the bedroom. Cushioned chairs were placed facing it, and behind them, a hot tub perfectly suited for two. There was a dedicated outside dining space and several lounge chairs around as well. All of it overlooked the spacious back lawn.

"You really have everything you need right here in one spot," I said, looking around.

"When the weather is clear, you can see the city from out here," he said. "And yes, I do feel like everything I need is here, especially now." He lifted my chin and kissed me softly.

I smiled and shook my head. "You're more than I ever could have dreamed of, Harrison."

"Speaking of dreams, you said you had a dream about me. I'm still waiting to hear about it."

"Yeah, I don't know about that. Maybe one day I'll tell you, but today is not that day. I can't have you getting all hot and bothered this early in the morning." I spun around laughing and went back inside, heading for the stairs. "What's the plan for the rest of the day?" I asked as I made my way back to the living room.

"Well, that's completely up to you. I can show you around, get you familiar with the immediate area, show you what my days are like normally. Or we could lock the doors and turn off our phones and just melt into one another upstairs for the next three days." His toothy smile and raised eyebrows made me laugh.

"How about a little of both? One then the other. I'm eager to know the lay of the land and really get a feel for what it's going to be like being here with you. This is a foreign concept to me you know, everything that comes along with who you are, and I'm not gonna lie, it's a little overwhelming." I collapsed into the overstuffed couch, laying my head back to face the ceiling. "You're not just some Joe Blow off the side of the road, you're...you. I don't know if I've even fully realized that yet." My cheeks puffed as I exhaled.

Harrison sat down facing me and took my hand. My eyes remained focused on the large wooden beam on the ceiling. "I haven't withheld any part of myself from you, Alice. Yeah, I make a little money pretending to be someone else in front of a camera; people know who I am because of that, but you've had the real me from the beginning. No surprises are waiting around the next corner, I can assure you."

"I don't think there will be. I know that you've been honest and up-front with me. I'm not worried about any of that. But being at home with you will be the easy part of our relationship, I assume. I'm not sure how your *public* will like you being seen with a woman my age, without credentials like yours. I can only imagine how they'll tear me apart. My age, my physical appearance, and I mean, I think I can handle it because I'm secure in us, I'm confident in us. It's just...I just don't want to ruin anything for you." I looked at him forlornly. "We both have to prepare ourselves for however your fans may react, I think. Someone's always got something to say. And this is a real part of what will be our life together. We're gonna have to talk about this stuff."

"You absolutely will not ruin anything. Please, love, don't think like that. If we just look out for one another, take care of each other, and stay honest with each other, we'll be alright. You feel like home to me, Alice, and there is nothing more comforting than that. As long as we stick together, we'll make it. Fans are great, I love them, but they don't govern my life, and I certainly won't give them the leverage to. For the most part, they have always supported me no matter the situation. I honestly think they'll be happy for my happiness."

"Hey...how do we get into these deep conversations so quickly?" I asked, changing the subject.

"I don't know." he said, standing up to face me.

"I guess that's the point of the next few days though, the heavy stuff?" I asked.

"Yes, and the good stuff, and the fun stuff. I'm glad we aren't afraid to talk about heavy things, but I think we've hit our quota for the day. Time for some fun?" Harrison flashed a smile and took my hands, pulling me up from the couch.

Before long, we were back in the car with Lawrence, getting me acquainted with Harrison's neighborhood and talking about his daily routine while he showed me his favorite grocery store, the best places to get wine, his favorite park with his favorite running trails, and his most prized wild-swimming spot in the Heath.

"I'm usually a pretty early riser, typically awake by 5 a.m. and headed for a wild swim before 5:30. The cold water strips the sleep from my mind and leaves me feeling like a blank canvas for the day ahead. And well, it gets in the necessary cardio with a better view than the home gym."

"I'd love to come along from time to time, get in the habit with you. It could be something we share, unless you'd rather keep that time for yourself," I offered. My mind flashed back to finding him in the Blakes' pool, the way his skin glistened from the water and the sunshine, and his infectious smile. "I understand how important it can be to sit with your own thoughts and have an outlet."

"I would love to have you share that with me Alice, but it's not for the faint hearted; this water gets cold in February."

"You swim all year round?" My eyes grew wide with surprise.

"Of course. You've never taken an ice bath I presume?"

"A what? Heck no. I prefer warmth." I laughed as I said it and faked a shiver, all while looking at him like maybe he might be crazy.

"Well, you can stay warm on the bench and keep my time for me while I cut through the ice. How about that?" He waited for my reaction.

"While you what? That's insane. You don't really get in when there's ice, do you?"

Harrison burst into laughter and I pushed his shoulder jokingly.

"What about it makes it 'wild' instead of just regular swimming?" I asked.

"Just the fact that you're doing it in a natural body of water instead of a lido, I guess."

"Okay, I'm sorry, forgive me. What's a lido?" I laughed.

"Oh, just a swimming pool. So, it's 'wild' because it's not a pool." He explained.

"Well, that seems simple enough, makes it seem much more exotic than it actually is, but okay." I shrugged. *The terminology around here is gonna take some getting used to*, I thought.

"When I'm back from swimming I usually spend about an hour in the gym, then shower and get ready for the rest of my day. I make myself breakfast and eat outside when the weather allows. I like to absorb the morning sun as much as possible; it almost feels like it energizes me, I guess, like I'm solar powered." He laughed and continued, "I bring my newspaper, and do the daily crossword then read the comics before I jump into whatever is on my schedule for the day. Sunshine, sustenance, and laughter are the best ways to start any day, if you ask me," he said.

I looked forward to the day I could begin enjoying all those things with him permanently.

"I couldn't agree more; it sounds like a wonderful way to start your day. So, what happens when you're working? You must have much longer, busier days that don't start out with much leisure?"

"Oh, when I'm working it's a much different story. Early call times, and, well usually I'm on location somewhere and a car delivers me to set from a hotel for long days of filming. It's a lot of stop and go on set. Not much fun really; a lot of waiting around."

"That sounds much less inviting, but still exciting. Out there creating cinematic masterpieces and whatnot." I nudged him and smiled.

"Making films isn't as glamorous as most people fantasize it to be, but I hope you'll want to come with me when I have to travel. It's lonesome as hell when I'm gone, and I want you with me all the time, unless you have commitments of your own when the time comes."

"Wherever you are, is where I want to be. Nothing you've said sounds like a life I wouldn't want to be part of. Though life on a movie set is probably something that will take a little getting used to, at least we can be together between takes, or whatever it's called." I had no idea what the proper lingo was.

"I don't ever want to spend a night without you, Alice. Once you settle things back home, and return to me, I'll make sure we always fall asleep together and greet a new day in each other's arms, even if I have to fly you across the world to do it."

"You're just the sweetest soul, Harrison." I said as I laid my head on his shoulder.

"Let me think…" he rubbed his chin with his hand, "As far as the stuff around the house, Shelby comes in and does daily cleaning and laundry like I said earlier, but I do my own cooking mostly. She lives on the property but in her own place. She's single, the last I knew, and she doesn't have any kids. Umm, what else? I keep a list near the fridge to keep track of groceries I want, and usually by the end of the day Shelby's made them appear out of nowhere. She's wonderful, and trustworthy. Things would surely fall apart without her help," he explained.

"Okay, well that's good to know. How do you think she's going to feel with me there, both short-term now and permanently later?" I asked.

"Shelby's cool, she'll probably love having someone she can pal around with, and it will give you someone you can trust and do girl talk with, too, if that's something you fancy. If you're asking me if I expect you to do any of what she does, the answer is no. I don't have any expectations like that. If you want to cook or do the wash or do the gardening, you certainly can do anything you like, love, but if you don't, that's fine too. None of these decisions are permanent rule. It's your home too; I want you to do whatever pleases you."

"Well, I don't want to step on anyone's toes, but I also have never had anyone look after me the way she does for you. So, I'm sure there are some things I'll end up doing out of habit, especially if I'm not working. I can't just hang around the house while she's picking up and doing laundry. It's not the way I'm built."

"I'm sure you and Shelby will work out the details; no need to spend any time worrying about any of that, love." His words of reassurance put me at ease, as always. "And Lawrence is on hand any time you need to go anywhere. Eventually you'll have your own security detail and your own driver too, but until then, Lawrence has you covered."

I immediately thought of Nigel.

"The first few days I was here, I met a delightful man named Nigel; he was my Uber driver a few times when I was out sightseeing, and I would love to have him as my personal driver one day. I don't know what's involved with making that happen, but I can give you his phone number and maybe you can do whatever you do to get him on the shortlist?"

"Of course, that actually makes it much easier. It's not easy to find someone you can trust, but if you like this gent, Nigel, then I'll ring him and set up a meeting of sorts. We'll see what we can do." He nodded as he spoke.

I thought for sure my heart would explode as I listened intently to him open his life to me. He'd divulged the inner workings of his home, his private life, and offered to share it all with me. This man, this young, humble, brilliant man, was so in touch with himself, and so open and free with his emotions. He didn't stifle the way he felt for me; his emotions didn't seem to scare him away from vulnerability. Our conversations weren't strained, and they made me feel like I'd known him forever. His spirit awakened mine. *Maybe it's a generational thing*, I thought, *but it's an incredible feeling to have someone give me love so freely, after such a short time.*

Lawrence had driven us all over town as we talked at length about everything including a few of Harrison's habits and personal quirks, and I willingly highlighted a few of my own. When we circled the familiar roundabout, Harrison phoned in a lunch order and it was waiting for us when we arrived back at the house.

After lunch, we spent the rest of the afternoon wandering the property in the late-day sun. I soon discovered that Harrison owned far more than just that perfect backyard. We followed a manicured path down over the rolling lawn and into the forest that surrounded his home. The same stone wall that had greeted us at the gate, actually encircled the entire property. As a lover of nature, Harrison had created the paths as a means to escape the sounds of the city and find tranquility in what at times could be a hectic life.

We rounded a corner and a small clearing came into view. The ground was blanketed in pea stone and scattered fallen leaves from the canopy above. A stone bench perfect for two people sat against a large old oak tree. There was no view, just a quiet space to sit and be at one with nature. In the distance, a stream babbled somewhere out of sight. I shook my head in disbelief; it felt so tranquil here.

"The further we go, the more surprises I get. This is beautiful, Harrison," I said, approaching the bench.

He rushed ahead of me and brushed the fallen leaves from the seat before I sat down.

"I come here sometimes when my head's a mess. Just to think, sort things through. When I bought this place, I walked the grounds and knew this spot was special. I love this old tree and the sound of the brook. It's not the river Ure, but in my head, I can send those thoughts into the wind to be carried off by the brook; never to be seen or worried about again." His expression softened as he gave me a half smile. "Kind of like I did as a lad at the falls."

"They say you can't go home again, but it seems like life certainly gives us what we need, doesn't it?" I asked.

"Indeed," he nodded. "It does."

Harrison sat down beside me on the bench and took my hand in his.

"It's important to me Alice, that you become familiar with the ins and outs of this place; I want you to feel completely at home here," he said.

"I do feel at home. Once I've met everyone, I think everything will be fine. Just make sure you explain to them who I am to you, so I don't have to. I don't wanna look like I'm some random conceited American that just showed up and started saying 'Oh I'm his—'" I stopped mid-sentence and looked down at my hands nervously. I don't even know what I'd call myself, his *married* girlfriend?

"My what?" he asked me, a new sparkle of hope in his eyes as he glanced at me.

"I—I don't know. What am I?" I asked him.

"I think it would be okay to call you my...girlfriend? That's what I'd like to think of you as." He looked to me for reassurance and found me blushing; my happiness from his admission battling with my modesty.

"Okay then, you tell all of them...that." I nodded and quickly changed the subject.

"This place feels like the idyllic English countryside that all of us Americans read about in magazines," I said. "The lush greenery dotted with the pink climbing roses against the stone structures up near the house. The cheerful sounds of birds drifting through the treetops and the rustling of squirrels foraging among the sporadically fallen leaves. There's a calmness about this place, even though it's tucked against the outskirts of a major city." I looked around, taking in the wilderness around me, nodding in approval. "How do you feel about me putting up some bird feeders?"

He burst out laughing, "Nice transition."

I laughed out loud with him.

"On a serious note, this has been a wonderful day, Harrison. I still feel like I need to pinch myself. I know it's real, but I keep thinking I'm going to wake up from this dream and all of this, you...it will all be gone," I confessed.

"I can assure you; I'm not going anywhere and this is very real, love." He squeezed my hand when he said it.

"Alice, thank you for trusting me and being open with me. Thank you for stepping into this world of mine, being authentic, and...showing me that true happiness is worth waiting for. Darling, *you* are everything I've *ever* wanted." He touched my chin and leaned in and kissed me.

"I could say all the same things to you, you know," I responded.

He shrugged in an exaggerated and bashful way. "Want to head back?" he asked.

I stood, ready to make the trek back up the hill to the house with him, but before we set off, I wrapped my arms around him, my palms feeling the muscles in his back flex as he returned my embrace.

"Harrison," I dropped my hands to his waist, my thumbs locked around the belt loops of his jeans, my fingertips barely grazing his backside. I looked deeply into his eyes and sighed.

"Harrison...I'm just going to say it. I can't *not* say it anymore, and I certainly can't *stop* it. I don't want to stop it. I love you. I'm *in* love with you," I said earnestly, truth and fear battling for the majority.

Moments passed as he stared at me, straight-faced, studying me, vetting my sincerity. When the creases at the corners of his eyes appeared from the softening of his glance and the rising of his cheeks as a result of his smile, he again took my face in his hands and held me there.

"I'm so in love with you, darling. So madly, *madly* in love." He shook his head as he said it, then kissed me again, and again before lingering at my lips. His eyes closed, he pressed his forehead to mine and said, "I love *you* Alice."

"I can't wait to share the rest of my life with you." I said, my voice just more than a whisper.

"I promise you won't regret a moment of it." Smiling happily, he wrapped his arms around my waist, lifted me off the ground and spun me around.

When my feet were finally back on the ground, Harrison kissed me again, then took my hand and we headed back up the hill toward the house, smiling at each other like lovesick fools.

That evening, as music played softly in the background, we cooked dinner together for the first time, each of us demonstrating skills that complemented the other, working flawlessly together. As fettuccine bubbled in the background, we slow-danced, my cheek pressed to Harrison's chest as his six-foot frame twirled me around the kitchen. Then later from behind, he held my swaying hips and softly kissed my neck while I whisked the alfredo sauce, repeatedly whispering, "I love you," into my ear.

A vintage bottle of red wine pulled from his personal collection paired well with our meal and we recounted our last few days together. Harrison expressed how eager he was to take me back to the Dales when there'd be more time to sight-see, and how excited he was for us to do more exploring together. And I confessed to him when he'd approached my table at the Spaniards Inn the first night, how I'd been awe-struck and nearly speechless. Never in my wildest dreams, and I've had plenty of those, did I ever imagine I would run into him, let alone that he'd approach me. He laughed as I explained it from my perspective.

"It seems like it was so long ago," I said. "Two days, and it feels like I've known you my entire life." I shook my head in disbelief.

"We've covered a lot of ground since then, literally, emotionally…physically. I wouldn't change a thing," he said, smiling. "It's all fallen into place perfectly."

"If you had asked me three days ago what I would be doing tonight, I would never have said 'cooking dinner with Harrison Edwards while he tells me he loves me in his kitchen and we make plans for our future together.' That's for damn sure." I laughed and sipped my wine.

"I surely wouldn't have imagined that either. You took me by complete surprise, Alice. I wasn't expecting you or any of this. What I *was* expecting was to sit in the garden and have a leisurely drink, then go about my evening. Certainly, I never thought I would share it with an incredibly beautiful woman who would steal my heart before she even spoke a word to me." His eyes divulged more than the words he spoke. I was still enamored with his accent, especially when he spoke so sweetly to me.

"Thank you, but I think you give me a bit too much credit." I shook my head and felt the heat rising into my cheeks again.

"I feel like I've been waiting for you, Alice, ever since I took my first breath in life, and now, it's like I can't breathe if you're not right here with me. Promise you'll come back to me as quickly as you can. I don't want to miss one more second of life with you."

The look in his eyes, coupled with the evening we'd shared so far, drove me out of my seat. I couldn't help myself, and came around to his side of the table and leaned down to kiss him, my fingertips teasing his neck as I did it. As he kissed me he dropped his silverware against his plate and pushed his chair out, allowing himself better access to me, exposing more of his lap.

Without moving my lips from his, I slowly drew my leg up and across his thighs before I settled myself down on top of him, straddling him in his chair.

My hands slid up his chest and around to the back of his head, my fingers gliding through his curly hair as I kissed him. A slow, sensuous moan escaped him as my body rhythmically writhed against him. The crackling of the fireplace, mingled with the hollow sounds of the record player circling without song, were dampened only by the heightened sounds of our breathing. I could feel him getting hard as I continued kissing him, which only fueled the fire within me.

I let my breath escape against his ear as I asked him in a whisper, "You like that?"

Harrison's head fell back further into my hands, my fingers tugging at his hair from behind, and I moved my mouth from his earlobe down to his throat.

He mumbled a breathy "Mhmm" before I felt him swallow hard, his Adam's apple moving against my tongue.

Harrison's hands slid up under my shirt and landed on my ribcage, my back arched in response to the heat of his touch before he dropped his hands to my hips, gripping them tightly and instinctively lifting his pelvis into mine.

Abruptly he stood up from the table, sending his chair falling backward, the wood cracking against the tile floor and echoing throughout the room. His palms cradled my behind firmly, and he proceeded to carry me across the room and up the stairs. I clung to him, one hand clasped full of his hair and the other gripping at the bulge of his bicep, my tongue continuing to explore his neck and his mouth as we moved closer to the bedroom.

He carried me past the bed and into the bathroom, his hand only leaving my ass long enough to turn on the bedroom light and the multiple shower heads. As water splattered across the shower floor and against the walls from the bevy of rain heads, Harrison sat down on the shower bench, leaning himself back against the wall and settling me back down onto his lap. I broke my mouth away from his just long enough to lean myself backward against the strength of his hands into the warm stream of water behind me, wetting my hair and letting the water flow down over my still clothed chest, matting my shirt to my skin.

Water dripped from my eyelashes before rolling down my neck and into my cleavage, Harrison's fingertips following their lead. I smiled at him in the dim light that poured through the doorway behind me and leaned in as if to kiss him, but teased his bottom lip with my tongue instead. He rubbed his nose against mine and I kissed him, taunting his tongue with mine while his biceps flexed and his fingertips gripped the tops of my shoulders from behind, pulling my body down onto him further.

The shadows danced with our movements as I pulled him toward me and peeled the wet shirt over his head, throwing it against the glass behind me. I pressed him back against the shower wall and in unison with the warm water ran my hands down over his wet chest, my fingers soft against the goosebumps that had appeared on his rippled abdomen. His chestnut curls glimmered against his forehead, catching light in the droplets that clung to their curves.

I rose to my feet and looked down at him, lust dripping from my gaze; both physically and emotionally I'd never felt more free. Tugging at the hem of my t-shirt, I exposed more of my chest before stripping it off and letting it rest with Harrison's on the shower floor. I watched him watching me, his blue-green eyes fixated on mine. He smirked as I reached for my skirt, the dimple in his left cheek catching a water drop as it dripped down his face from his hair.

"Let me," he said as he reached for my hips.

Harrison pulled me a step closer to him so my belly was only inches from his mouth. He slipped his index fingers beneath the waistband of my skirt just below my navel, and pulled it down slightly, gently drawing my exposed skin to his mouth. His tongue was warm against my flesh as he kissed all over my abdomen, his hands stripping my wet skirt down over my legs before he looked up at me, once again locking eyes. This time he wasn't asking permission. His palms pressed firmly against my back, he drug his fingertips down to the band of my panties, slipped them off of me, and let them fall to the floor.

I stood before him, my wet bra the only piece of clothing left on my body, clinging to me like a second skin. I stared wantonly into his eyes and pulled Harrison to his feet by his chin. When he tried to kiss me, I turned my face away and smiled as I unfastened his jeans, then pushed them down over his sculpted backside before crouching to pull the wet denim down his legs. I paused on my way back up to drag my cheek over his rigid bulge before locking eyes with him once again. I bit at my lip, trying not to smile.

He let out a quick breath. "Such a tease..." His abs flexed as he said it.

I kissed my way up to his belly button then pulled his boxer briefs to the floor. My hands canvassed his wet body, as the light gleamed off the copper tub and cast tiny bursts of light across his abdomen like glitter.

"You think I'm a tease?" I asked, then took him fully into my mouth.

His exhale morphed into a moan that echoed through the bathroom. My curious tongue caused Harrison to reach for the wall to brace himself. Moments later, I pulled my mouth off of him, and pushed him back into a seated position on the bench.

"What was I?" I asked, grabbing his chin to focus his eyes upwards, locked again on mine.

Then just as I'd done in the dining room I crawled on top of him, straddling him on the shower's bench. My left hand on the wall behind him, I hovered my nearly naked body above his waist and used my right hand to unhook my bra and throw it into the mounting pile of clothes behind me.

I whispered in his ear, "You think I'm a tease?" then let my tongue caress his earlobe.

But before he could answer I lowered myself down on top of him, letting him slowly penetrate me, and began a rhythmic gyration that caused a long, deep moan to ease from his lips.

"Jesus Christ, Alice." He laid his head back against the shower wall, eyes closed, warm water continuing to roll down his neck and his chest.

"What's wrong? You want me to stop?" I said playfully with a devilish grin and arched my back; drawing my breasts up to his face as I rolled my hips and slowed my pace.

"Don't stop," he said quietly, his chest heaving as his breathing got heavier, his abdominal muscles perfectly defined with each breath.

"No?...You sure?" I asked, cradling my slippery chest in my hands.

"Fuck! No! Don't stop!" His nostrils flared and his deep voice was more urgent this time, echoing hard against the shower glass.

Harrison held me steady against his slick body with one hand, while the other hand moved from my ass to my breasts, his mouth and tongue taking full advantage of their proximity. My hands in his wet hair and my mouth on his, I continued to grind against him before locking eyes once again. I wanted to watch him as he enjoyed me, smiling to myself as his brow furrowed, I worked him closer and closer to orgasm, and I didn't stop until I had accomplished exactly what I'd set out to do.

Maybe it was the wine, or maybe it was the way Harrison made me feel like an absolute goddess, but I felt like I was living outside of my own body. A man cooked dinner with me tonight, ate at the table with me, and engaged in stimulating conversation. He took me upstairs and we made love to each other, he welcomed me taking control of the pace, and was submissive to my desires. We washed one another's bodies before he wrapped a robe around me and led me to his bed where he had pulled the covers down for me. He held eye contact with me, he listened when I spoke, not just so he could respond but to actually hear what I was saying. He was engaging and made me laugh, and most importantly, lit an emotional fire inside of me I hadn't felt in years. The contrast between my past and my present was distinct, and lying there in the midst of that realization, I wondered if my marriage had been doomed to fail because of the way it started, or if all love was meant to fade into despair over time.

"Will it always be like this?" I asked, my hand lovingly rubbing his chest.

"I hope so," he responded.

"You make me feel so special." I sleepily nuzzled my cheek against his shoulder and into his neck, closing my eyes.

"Darling, you *are* special. There isn't one single thing about you that isn't absolutely extraordinary." He let his cheek fall against the top of my head. "I think I'll start a fire, and we can relax a while until we fall asleep."

He slid from the comfort of the bed and I watched as he built us a fire. In the quietude that followed, we lay in bed together, still euphoric from our shower. The softness of his touch along my curves brought goosebumps to my skin, their tiny silhouettes visible in the light of the flames that danced in the fireplace. His accent had the same effect as his fingertips as poetry poured from his lips like warm honey.

"Bring me your pain, love. Spread

it out like fine rugs, silk sashes,

warm eggs, cinnamon

and cloves in burlap sacks. Show me

the detail, the intricate embroidery

on the collar, tiny shell buttons,

the hem stitched the way you were taught,

pricking just a thread, almost invisible.

Unclasp it like jewels, the gold

still hot from your body. Empty

your basket of figs. Spill your wine.

That hard nugget of pain, I would suck it,

cradling it on my tongue like the slick

seed of pomegranate. I would lift it

tenderly, as a great animal might

carry a small one in the private

cave of the mouth."

Drenching my senses, the way his tongue crafted his accent around the words, sticky in their innuendos, the metaphors in the poetry were so erotic to me, much like his lips on my skin between verses. I stared at him, mesmerized.

"'Basket of Figs' by Ellen Bass. It's one of my favorites." He seemed bashful about it. "It came to mind as I was lying here thinking about us. About you."

"It's gorgeous...sensual. You've studied it, dissected it even, if you've been able to memorize it and deliver it like that. What does it mean to you?" I asked.

"To me, I feel like it's a soul opening, inviting another in. Welcoming them with the strength they may not have themselves, and telling them they're safe here. Lay your burdens out, spread them apart, let me shoulder what you can't handle. Let me carry the weight of it all, take care of you, your wounds, your happiness; it's all safe here with me."

"That's beautiful Harrison."

"I want to be all those things and more for you, Alice. I want you never to feel the weight of sadness or loneliness again, and never to feel like you have to hold back your truth or abbreviate who you are to please anyone."

"I wanna be that person for you too, Harrison. I'd carry the weight of a thousand worlds for your happiness."

He kissed my temple.

"It's so interesting to me the different ways people interpret poetry, the way you break it down is so…I don't even know the right word for it. Thank you for sharing that with me."

"I'm just glad you didn't think I was mad rattling it off like that. I should be thanking you for listening to me."

"I could listen to you speak for a hundred lifetimes and it still wouldn't be long enough. You can quote poetry to me fireside every night for eternity if you want; I'll never ask you to stop."

I fell asleep with my body pressed against a man who, in many ways, was still a stranger to me, but felt like more of a partner than the man I'd spent decades with. I was no longer grappling with whether it was right or wrong to be doing what I was doing, sleeping with and loving a man that wasn't my husband. I had come to terms with the fact that for the rest of my life, I felt confident I would be genuinely loved and appreciated by the man lying beside me. I was choosing myself, stepping into a joy I deserved. Even if Harrison hadn't come along when he did, I no longer wanted to live a life of mediocrity and sadness. I didn't want to trudge through life neck-deep in depression just because it was the least scary option. I wanted to live my daydreams out loud; I wanted to bask in happiness.

For the first time since I'd been on vacation, sleep took me back home to New England that night. I stood in my kitchen, bags at my feet, a look of resolve on my face. James leaned against the doorway, blocking me from leaving. I'd told him of my plans to divorce him, that he could have the house and I would be just fine without it. He hadn't been sad, hadn't reacted at all when I'd said it. All he had done was try to intimidate me, scare me into staying. "You'll never make it without me. I provide for you, Alice. I work hard to give you this life, this house, and you think you're just going to leave?" he'd said. His words echoed in my mind as he spoke.

My response had been simply, "This marriage has been broken for a long time, and there's no change in sight. I'm drowning and you're oblivious to it. I can't live like this anymore, and I won't; I'm done." When I'd picked up my bags and attempted to push past him to leave, he'd grabbed me by the shoulders and shoved me back into the kitchen, my back landing hard against the wall. My bags dropped to the floor as he held me there by my throat, his palm firm against my windpipe; intent on delivering his message, demanding I hand over my car keys; that I must be crazy to think I was going anywhere.

Struggling to breathe, I looked at him with fear in my eyes, tears streaming down my face, and said, "The first time you touch me in months, it's this?

You think *this* is going to make me change my mind and stay?"

Anger boiled up behind his narrowing eyes, his furrowed brow scowling back at me, his jaw clenched with rage. He drew his open hand up as if he were going to slap me across the face, but just as his palm approached my face he curled it into a solid fist, and I awoke from my nightmare with a sharp gasp.

It was still dark in Harrison's bedroom as I reached out for him. He lay beside me on his stomach, facing the opposite direction. My shaking hand found his hip first, pulling him onto his back in an attempt to have him face me. I pulled my body against his and wrapped myself around him as he became aware of what was happening.

"Are you okay, love?" his voice raspy with sleep.

"Just a nightmare. I didn't mean to wake you up, I just needed to be close to you." I tried to dismiss it, but I was still trembling.

"I'm right here. You're okay. I've got you." He adjusted his body to embrace me, smoothing my hair before kissing my temple.

I took a few more deep breaths, before I relaxed into his body.

"Does this happen a lot?" he asked.

"No, normally I dream pretty vividly, but this was no dream. This was awful," I said.

"Do you want to tell me what happened?"

"I told James I was leaving, and he didn't seem to care, which is…whatever." I shook my head, trying to rid myself of the images. "But then when I actually tried to leave the house, he choked me against the wall. He raised his hand to hit me in the face, and that's when I woke up." I sighed as the visual replayed in my mind.

Harrison sat up urgently in bed and looked at me, concerned. "Has he been violent with you, Alice? He doesn't hit you, does he?" The sleep was gone from his voice and he sounded ready to fight, depending on what I said next.

"No, nothing like that, he's never laid a hand on me, ever. I don't think he ever would. But this was just so realistic, it just, it scared me is all." I felt bad. I hadn't meant to upset him. "It's just a nightmare. I'll be okay." I pulled Harrison back against me and tried to remind myself that I was fine.

After a quick pause in conversation, his voice broke through the darkness. "Do you want me to send Hank home with you? I will. I refuse to let anything happen to you, Alice."

"No, no. You're sweet, thank you, but no. I'll be fine. Like I said, it was just a nightmare. Let's get some rest, okay? I didn't mean to worry you." I rubbed his chest while I attempted to get back to sleep, but instead I lay there in the quiet, my mind racing.

James is never going to see this coming. He's so comfortable in his life, and with the way things are. How in the hell would I drop this bomb on him? What would I say? My mother had told me long ago that when a man gets married, his life becomes one of comfort, one of ease because a woman will look after her husband without hesitation, make sure that she's doing all she can for him. But when a woman gets married, her life becomes one of constant work, selflessness, and frustration. A man takes on comfort, a woman takes on insurmountable volumes of unending work. My mother had been right, in James' case anyway. Would I feel him out and wait for an opportunity to say something, or just cut right to the point? It wasn't that I didn't care for him, it was just that—

"I love you." Harrison's voice rescued me from the spiral, almost as if he knew where my mind had gone.

"I love *you*," I said, my smile audible.

He tightened his arms around me and kissed my forehead, and within minutes his breathing let me know he was asleep again. Shortly after, I too found sleep, wrapped in the reassurance that Harrison would go to war for my safety just to be sure I made it back to him.

The next morning arrived with gray skies and thick fog. I opened my eyes to Harrison once again on his stomach facing away from me, crisp white sheets wrapped around his waist leaving his back exposed. I carefully slid myself down in the bed and put my lips against the dimples in his lower back, kissing my way up his spine, across his neck, and to his jaw. He inhaled deeply, and I watched as his tattoos moved against his ribs. I brought my hand around to his chest, then down across his rippled abs as he rolled over to face me.

"What a way to wake up," he said, the rasp back in his voice.

"Good morning, gorgeous," I responded.

"What time is it?" he asked, rubbing his eyes.

"I think just before seven. Other than my waking you up in the middle of the night with all my craziness, did you sleep well?"

"I'm not used to having someone in my bed with me, but I slept well knowing you were right there in arm's reach. I hope you were able to get some rest after your nightmare," he said as he stood up and stretched.

I watched every muscle in his body flex as he did it, still fascinated that this incredible man was actually into me.

"Yeah, I did. Took me a little bit to fall back to sleep, but it came after a bit."

"Hold that thought," he said and padded off toward the bathroom. "I need a wee."

A wee? I chuckled to myself at the terminology and watched him walk across the room in his boxer briefs. His entire body was tan and toned; his thighs and his calves flexed with each step. Hell, even his bare feet were beautiful. When I heard the toilet flush, I called out to him.

"Safe to come in?" I asked.

"Sure."

Would I ever get used to how sexy that accent was? I hope not. The surge it gave me every time he spoke was addictive.

I opened the door to find him doing exactly what I intended to. I grabbed my toothbrush from the vanity, wet it, squeezed out some toothpaste, and began brushing my teeth alongside him at the second sink. We traded glances in the mirror and midway through, he tapped me on the shoulder to gain my full attention. I looked up at him to find his eyes crossed, his head cocked to the side, mouth full of toothpaste, and his nose scrunched up in an attempt to make me laugh. Holding back, I shook my head, and finished the task at hand just after he did.

"You're foolish, you know that right?" I asked, shaking my head again and putting my toothbrush back in its place on the vanity.

"But I'm fun," he retorted.

"Indeed, you are that."

"Now I'm not a total dirtbag, c'mere."

He put his hands around my waist and pulled my nearly naked body against his, kissing me as if we'd been apart for years, soft and slow, his hand sliding up into the back of my hair while the other held me firmly against him.

"We won't get anything done today if we keep this up," I whispered against his cheek as his mouth moved to my neck.

"We're on holiday; plans are overrated," he said, his lips on my collarbone.

"True, but..." I let out a deep sigh. *Who am I kidding? I didn't want to stop.*

"But nothing...let me have you, Alice." His hands on my chest, the tip of his tongue moved up my neck until it found my mouth. He looked at me eager with anticipation.

Before I knew what happened I was atop the vanity, my back against the mirror, my panties being pulled to my ankles. He pushed the backs of my thighs upward and outward, my feet resting on the edge of the counter just as they had in New Orleans on the balcony dining table. Flashbacks flooded my mind. His mouth was magic, and I was defenseless against it. When he'd sufficiently replaced the taste of toothpaste in his mouth, he used his height to his advantage, sliding me forward on the countertop, picking me up, and just as he'd done the night before in the dining room, he carried me to the bed. The strength of this man's body was mind-blowing.

He gently laid me down on my back, my ass barely on the bed, and ran his palms from my ankles to my thighs, watching my face as he did it. Like aquamarine jewels sparkling behind long dark eyelashes, his eyes held me captive. He kissed his way up the insides of my legs, and no longer able to handle his stare I let my head fall back, closing my eyes, preparing myself for what I knew was next. Harrison gripped the back of my knee and lifted my leg just enough to enter me, slowly at first. A satisfied moan escaped him and he increased his pace. Listening to him vocally react, audibly hearing how my body made him feel, made it so much hotter for me, and in no time, I climaxed. My hands gripped his ass and pulled him deeper into me, holding him there motionless as I throbbed against him, his release imminent.

He hovered above me with his eyes closed, still inside me. His chest heaving as his body continued to sporadically tense, every muscle rigid as it happened. Locks of curls fell forward, landing against his forehead and he reached for them, raking them back against the top of his head with a twist of his wrist to secure them in place. He smiled breathlessly, his nostrils flared, then opened his eyes and looked down at me.

"I love you," he said, his breathing still heavy.

"I'm pretty partial to you too sweets. You have no idea." I winked at him when I said it. "I could stay here like this with you all day, but shouldn't we be a bit more, I don't know, productive?" I shrugged and laughed at the same time.

"Oh okay, if you insist. Showers, then…on with the day?"

"How about just one shower, together?" I asked as I gazed at him seductively, my fingertips tiptoeing from his abdomen up to his chest. "I want more of you…"

"Oh, fuck yeah." He picked me up and carried me to the shower, eager to make love to me once again.

Harrison had gone unnoticed while we were 'wild swimming' this morning, which was surprising to me. I expected there to be cameras snapping or crowds of people approaching him from all angles. While we were there, my nervous eyes jumped toward the shadows, dissecting the fog, expecting paparazzi to be crouched and ready for their shot, but apparently the locals were used to his presence and left us to swim in peace.

Back at the house we shared a breakfast of toast and eggs, juice and fruit, and Harrison read the daily paper's comics to me. I watched him as he read, enamored with his mannerisms. He laughed wildly with his entire body, exuding a childlike freedom, unable to contain his smile at the corniest of jokes, something that years of stifling myself in my marriage had stripped from me. After breakfast, we showered together again. Wild swimming was a dirty sport, and any excuse to get Harrison naked was fine by me.

We spent the remainder of the morning wandering hand-in-hand through Sir John Soane's Museum, taking in art and architecture, discovering hidden rooms, and stealing kisses whenever we could. The museum was busy and laden with tourists, but once again, much to my surprise, Harrison wasn't approached, and I never noticed anyone with a camera pointed in our direction. Though that may have been a result of Victor and Hank lurking just far enough in the background to take the focus off of Harrison. They could fade into and out of a busy public space without me even realizing, despite their hulking statures.

The blanket of clouds and fog that hung over our morning had vanished by the time we exited the museum, giving way to a cloudless late-summer day.

"You wanna get out of here?" Harrison asked me, seemingly overwhelmed by the crowds. "I just want to be alone with you," he said.

"I thought you'd never ask," I replied.

Back in the quiet comfort of the car, Harrison lowered the partition and let Lawrence know where to pick up the lunch order he'd called in before adding, "We're off to the shore." Lawrence nodded and as the partition returned us to our privacy and the car made its way into the flow of traffic, I snuggled myself into Harrison's arms, breathing him in.

"Thank you for this morning," I said.

"London's incredible, innit?" he asked, his accent slurring his words into something sexier than normal.

I smiled when he said it. "You're something else." I chuckled and the look of love in my eyes gave away just how enamored I truly was with him.

"What did I do?" He laughed, completely unaware, his smile lines appearing around his eyes.

I looked up at him, and crinkling one side of my nose, I mocked him in my thickest British accent, "Innit? Wot? Bloody 'ell!" I exaggerated my expressions to show him I was joking.

Harrison burst into laughter. "I think *you* might be something else, love, not me!"

Settling back into his arms, I asked, "Where are you whisking me off to?"

The car pulled to a stop and through the tinted glass, I watched Lawrence as he entered a small cafe to retrieve our lunch.

"Brighton. It's a bit of a drive, but I figured we can eat on the way and just relax when we get there. It's beautiful, a fun spot. I think you'll love the pier." The edge of his thumb gently rubbed my arm as he spoke.

"You could drag me to hell and back, and as long as we're together, I'm happy," I said, tucking my arm around his waist like a seatbelt.

"Soon enough you're going to travel the world with me, Alice, and I can't wait to scream from the rooftops that you're my girl."

"We've got some significant hurdles to navigate before we get to that place unfortunately, but me too. I've been nervous about photographers. I don't want this to turn into some type of scandal for either of us. You'll be a homewrecker, and who knows what they'll label me. I don't want that public beginning for us."

"Lucky for us, I know most of the paps around here, and if I throw a few quid at them, they're usually pretty trustworthy as far as not publishing, especially if I ask them not to, but I've also never been seen around with anyone I hadn't already introduced to the world. Obviously, if you notice something that makes you nervous, tell me immediately and we'll deal with it. Okay?"

"I will." I nodded, and clung to the way he slurred the word 'obviously' into something closer to ovrishly. *This man and all of his quirks are absolutely adorable.*

"It'll be alright, I promise," he said.

"I love you." I looked into his eyes, my heart ready to burst.

"Well I love you too." he smiled at me so sweetly.

Lawrence returned to the car and handed us our lunch through the partition before setting off again. Over the next two hours, we ate and talked and snuggled all the way to the beach, discussing some of the situations we could potentially find ourselves in with the public on a random night out together, suspicious or dangerous things to look out for in crowds, and how Hank and Victor would always be present in case of an emergency until I get my own security.

As we got closer to the beach, the childlike excitement in Harrison's eyes returned, as if Brighton held some familiar freedom he'd been longing for. He told me one of his favorite memories as a child had been the day his granddad picked him up quite early from school, barely an hour into his day, and drove for hours to get to this beach. Harrison beamed as he recalled his granddad saying, "School will be there tomorrow; let's just have fun today." Harrison had been about ten at the time, so skipping a full day of classes was exciting. They'd spent the day playing frisbee by the ocean, walking the pier and snacking on candy floss and ice cream, and of course laughing as they always did when they were together. It had been a random occurrence but a memory that stuck with Harrison his entire life. Ever since then, Brighton had always been a place he associated with happiness.

When we arrived in Brighton, I noticed the beach seemed different than the ones I was used to. The crunch of the earth under my shoes wasn't soft and silent like at home where the beaches were a fine sand consistency. In northern New England, the beaches are famously hugged by outcroppings of large craggy rocks, fit for climbing on and exploring, the crags dappled with tiny tide pools, and the soft sand perfect for bare feet. But here, the turf was made of fine stones, not typical beach sand. Harrison tried to explain that it was what they called a 'shingle beach' and the ground was actually made from flint cobbles. I could only shrug and smile agreeably, unsure what any of it meant, but content to find a quiet spot to relax.

When Harrison had said we were going to the shore, I expected there would be a long, tall wooden pier and maybe some people fishing from it, with a few snack shacks to poke around in, but this was a destination fit for celebration. The beach space was expansive, there was a massive Ferris wheel lit up in various twinkling shades of neon, and the pier itself was lined with multi-colored blinking lights, shops, eateries, and street performers. The familiar sound of seagulls filled the air and they could be found dotting the ground, searching for tidbits of snacks they hoped had been left behind by beach-goers.

Harrison chose a secluded section of the beach and laid out a large blanket that he brought from the car. The shore itself was nearly empty save for a small family gathering to the far right, quite some distance away. The only discernable figures were a rainbow-striped umbrella protruding from the ground, surrounded by about ten people of various heights, and nearer to us, two parents chasing a toddler in circles around their three beach chairs.

"This place is barren compared to how it usually is," he observed as he sat down and looked around. "In the dead of summer, on a weekend, you can't find the ground, this place is so packed. I'm glad we came today when things are calm."

"I prefer an empty beach, if I'm being honest," I took my place beside Harrison on the blanket. "This reminds me of the beaches at home, except at home we have actual sand." I picked up a handful of earth, letting it fall through my fingers just beyond the edge of the blanket. "Our seagulls look the same, though." I pointed out other similarities in the landscape before offering to show Harrison around my hometown one day, certain he would love it.

He made himself comfortable and went from seated to stretched out on the blanket. He propped himself up on his side to face me, his elbow on the ground and his palm to his temple, he smiled and said, "I'm excited to know everything about you, Alice. Your life's history. Your origin story. I want to see your favorite places and share your memories. I want to be able to see and smell and hear these places and stories when you speak of them."

"You will. All in due time." I smiled back at him as he stared at me. "We have a lifetime ahead of us for all those little things."

"You know, the first time I kissed you Alice, I felt electricity shoot through my entire body. I've never experienced anything like it. It was like the universe was sending me a signal to give myself over to you. To just let my insecurities fall away and live fully in the moment."

I watched him as he spoke, smiling at the way his mouth moved as he talked, the way his eyes lit up when he mentioned our kiss, the nervous habit he had of touching his cheek, even the stubble on his chin and above his lip, patchy as it was, were all things I loved about him.

"I was terrified," I said as I stretched myself out beside him on the blanket. "I thought, *This is it; he's not going to like kissing me. He's going to take me back to the hotel, happy to be rid of me. I'll never hear from him again.*"

"Oh, absolutely not, quite the opposite. I could have laid there in that field and kissed you for the rest of my life. I knew if I didn't keep the day moving forward, we'd never see civilization again!" He laughed.

"I'd be okay with that. Civilization is overrated sometimes," I responded.

"Wanna walk, check out the pier?" Harrison asked.

"In a bit. Let's just enjoy the stillness for a moment." I leaned over and pushed the dark curls that hung near his eyes away from his face and kissed his forehead before rolling onto my back and staring up at the sky. I felt his fingers interlock with mine and we lay there together quietly holding hands, content to watch the clouds pass by.

A short while later, after we'd stripped off our socks and shoes, Harrison rolled up the bottoms of his jeans, I took his hand and we set off toward the ocean. We walked the length of the beach, making our way first to the water, then in the direction of the young family, our bare feet splashing through the incoming waves. The water was cold, much colder than the swimming had been this morning, and my toes quickly began to go numb. I switched sides with Harrison, opting to keep my feet out of the frigid water. We walked hand-in-hand along the water's edge quietly, stopping from time to time to pick up a pretty rock or an abandoned shell that caught our eye, each of us dropping our finds into the safety of Harrison's pockets before moving on to our next discovery.

A brightly colored beach ball rolled past me out of nowhere and into the surf, followed by a small giggling child hot in its pursuit. The young boy stopped at the water's edge, pointing toward his ball, his blond curls dancing as the breeze burst through them. One step further into the sloped shore, Harrison grabbed at the ball as it bobbed past him, attempting to keep it from the deeper water. With the vibrant pink and orange ball now in his grasp, Harrison turned to face the child, intent on returning the toy, just as a large wave splashed up the length of his legs and soaked the back of his jeans. A shriek of surprise burst from him as the cold water hit the back of his thighs, straightening his body against the icy temperature, then he high-tailed it back to the beach.

I expected him to be upset, or at minimum uncomfortable, but all he did was laugh as he ran back toward the child to return the runaway beach ball. I watched his interaction with the boy, playful and funny; his childlike laughter and ease in a potentially uncomfortable situation were a relief to see. He ran past the boy, laughing as he did, letting the child chase him around the beach for a moment before handing him back his beloved beach ball. Small things like this reminded me what a humble, good-natured, and generous man he was, and that fun was paramount to him, no matter what it looked like. The bright side was always the right side for Harrison, and even wet jeans wouldn't sour his day.

When we'd gone as far as the beach would allow, we turned and made our way back in the direction of the pier. The sun behind us was warm against our shoulders as we shuffled through the chilly waves. It struck me as we were walking that our time together was rapidly coming to an end, at least for this trip.

"Harrison?" I asked, my voice subdued.

"Allliiiice?" he responded, trying to make me smile.

"We don't have a ton of time left in this trip, and then I'm going home. I don't know how long it's going to be before I get back here to you. Is there anything you want to do in the next day and a half?" I kept my eyes focused on the beach laid out in front of us.

He chuckled to himself and paused, causing me to look up at him. His hand rubbed at his chin, and I wondered what had crossed his mind that he was struggling to say.

"What made you laugh?" I asked.

"You said you would be going home. I'd hoped you had started to think of being here with me as your home." There was a disappointment in his eyes.

"It's habit, I guess. I'm sorry. You do feel like home to me, Harrison." I remained quiet and waited for him to speak.

"Honestly, I don't want to think about you leaving, Alice. I don't want to think about the nights I'll spend without you, and I don't want to imagine waking up alone again." He paused and took a breath before continuing. "I guess I want to spend our time drinking one another in, sharing a million 'I love you's and touching you for as long as you'll let me. Making promises to one another and creating plans for our future. I want to build memories with you that'll replay in your mind on days that are hard back in New England, memories that will get you back home to me as soon as possible, and I want to take photos so I can look at you even when you aren't with me. I want to be sure that the pillow next to mine smells like you, and that you'll remember what my touch feels like when we're apart."

He stopped walking and turned to face me, still holding my hand.

"Alice, I'm not bullshitting you when I tell you this—I want you to be *my* wife, not his." His voice was urgent with a frustration that almost made me wish I hadn't said anything.

"I didn't mean to upset you," I said, as we resumed walking.

"You didn't upset me, I just—I know what I want, Alice, and I'm anxious for it to be a reality. Sending you back there to misery is weighing on me. I don't want you to go at all. I want you to serve him from here. You don't *have* to go back. I want to send for your things, and have you stay right here in London with me, but I know it's not feasible. I'm selfish, I know…"

"I don't know that I'd call it 'selfish', but you're right; it's not really feasible. There's twenty-two years of stuff to sort through, both literally and emotionally, and it would be cowardly of me not to do it face-to-face. James isn't who he used to be, but that doesn't mean that I should treat him like the enemy. He's a good man; he's just not good for me anymore."

I almost felt bad defending James, but it was the truth. On any given day if he were asked about his marriage, his wife, or his home life, he'd tell you things were fine. The trouble is, he's just so oblivious to my unhappiness. And yes, I was partly to blame for it. I recognized my role in the failure of my marriage. I'd tried several times to tell him, tried to adjust the course of the marriage to allow for an equal distribution of happiness between us, but it had never worked out in my favor. We always fell back into the same patterns and the same habits. I always wound up angry and resentful. And James was so tuned into his own world that he either never cared to notice or was just incapable of understanding how I felt. The days and the months and the years passed by and here we were, stagnant, wallowing in the complacency of it.

"I just hope the process is quick and doesn't completely overwhelm you. Honestly, I wish I could be there with you, to help you through it, but I've got to be in Brazil two days after you leave, and I'll be there filming for at least two months."

"It will be fine; I'm sure of it. And we'll talk or text daily. It's not like you won't hear from me for months and then one day I'll just show up on your doorstep." I was trying to calm his nerves, but I could see he was frustrated.

"If you need out of there at any time, you tell me, and I'll send someone after you. They'll bring you directly to me, wherever I am." He was adamant.

"I will. You know I will."

The rest of the afternoon was spent walking the pier; it was busier than the beach had been, but for a late September Tuesday afternoon, it wasn't terribly crowded. Harrison had purchased and put on a baseball cap and was wearing his sunglasses, so he was fairly well disguised, and I certainly wouldn't draw any attention; I was a nobody around here. We popped in and out of the small shops unnoticed, watched a woman juggling bananas, and listened to music while we took in the sea view. Then on our way back to the car, we stopped for takeaway of fish and chips, which Harrison said was an absolute Brighton must.

As the sun dipped below the horizon, we arrived back at Harrison's house. Dinner had long since been consumed and I was intent to spend the evening as close to him as I could manage. As the hours passed, I was glaringly aware of how short our time together was becoming, and no matter what I did to try to calm myself, my anxiety was taking over.

"Babe?" I asked. "Do you think we could get in the hot tub for a while? I just need to try to relax my mind, and the heat would feel great after today's cold ocean water."

"Sure, what's troubling you, love?" He smoothed my hair away from my face, his thumb brushing my cheekbone.

"All I can hear in my head is the ticking of the clock, and all I can think about is having to leave. It's just getting louder and louder..." I sighed heavily and hung my head, frustrated.

He wrapped his arms around me, and his response told me he could feel how tense my body was.

"It's just a pause; it's not the end. What is it they say? Good things come to those who wait? We'll be alright. C'mon, let's see about that hot tub and relax a bit." With his strong hands on my shoulders, he walked behind me, circling my sore muscles with his thumbs.

I watched him as he stripped down to his underwear and walked toward the hot tub. *No bathing suits? Alright by me*, I thought, and followed suit. Harrison stepped into the steaming water first, turned on the jets, then held my hand as I got in and took a seat across from him. Every part of me that wasn't submerged was instantly covered in goosebumps from the chill in the night air. I sunk my body further into the tub, letting the hot water wash over my shoulders, then leaned my head back against the edge and closed my eyes. *This is perfect*, I thought, *exactly what I needed*. I rolled my head from side to side, stretching my muscles and enjoying the warmth of the water and the pounding of the jets against my lower back. I felt the strength of Harrison's hands on my feet, his thumbs manipulating my muscles, the tension melting away with his touch.

I opened my eyes and found him staring at me, that left dimple of his just daring me not to lean over and kiss it, and shook my head at the sight of him.

"What?" he asked.

"Wot?" I mimicked back to him, but couldn't keep a straight face, and started laughing.

"Keep it up, sista..." He made a playful scowling face at me.

"Or...WOT?" I said again, before throwing my head back again in laughter.

"Or I'll stop rubbing and start tickling!" He tickled my feet with his fingers, then ran them up my legs against my squirming, sending water splashing over the edge of the hot tub.

"Okay, okay, YOU WIN!" I shouted, overcome with laughter. "YOU WIN!"

Harrison grabbed me around the waist with one arm and pulled me through the water to him. His bare skin against me shot a flashback through my mind of the two of us in the bathtub together in D.C. and I smiled.

"Wanna hear a fun story?" I said as I turned and leaned back against his chest, his arms wrapped around my waist.

"Sure, lay it on me." He kissed my neck as I laid my head back against his shoulder.

"Well, it all started when I went for a drive one day, and found you swimming in a stranger's pool," I began. "I thought I'd do the right thing and try to save you from certain prosecution due to your *blatant* need to trespass."

"Oh boy, this sounds like a doozy. Go on."

"You needed to get to New Orleans, and for some reason, you wanted me to drive you there."

"No way, wait! Is this the dream?! YES! Tell me everything!" He was so excited.

I felt his abdominal muscles tense against my back with his outburst, and my hands fell to his thighs as I continued telling him about my dream. I spared no detail, and walked him through every pit stop, every corny joke, all the scenarios that played out between us, and all the characters we met along the way. I even told him of the engagement and the wedding we attended, and how I'd felt when he disappeared and left me alone in a full-blown panic with no other instructions than to 'get to the jet.' He listened keenly and when I was finished, I turned myself around in the hot tub to face him.

With eyebrows raised, he said, "Wow, that was quite the dream. You weren't kidding when you said your dreams were vivid and detailed." Harrison raised both of his arms out of the water and laid them outstretched along the edge of the hot tub, an impressed look on his face.

"No kidding. So, when you approached me that night at the Spaniards Inn, imagine where my mind went. And now you know why I was so affected when we traveled *on a jet* to the Dales, and when we kissed for the first time, made love for the first time, and just…developing this entire relationship with you has been kind of a mind-fuck. Like some parallel life. So many of the things we've said to one another and done together are so similar. It just feels like I know a different you in another dimension, but also this you, in this reality. It's bizarre and incredible all at the same time."

"I can imagine it is quite surreal. Must just mean that we are destined to find one another, to live happily ever after, in every realm of the universe."

I shook my head again; this magnificent specimen of a human sat here smiling at me, not thinking I was crazy even after everything I just told him, and expressing his belief in our being destined for one another. I'd never felt luckier in my entire life.

"I love you, Harrison," I said.

"I love *you,* darling, and I'm telling you now, reality is going to surpass any dream you could *ever* have. Come here." He reached for my hand and pulled me back into him. As he stared into my eyes, he said, "Alice..." He stifled a laugh and tried to regain his composure. "Alice, I need to tell you...It's important that you know..." He paused, a serious look on his face. "You and I have been in this hot tub for far too long. Our skin looks like prunes!" He held up his hands, showing me his wrinkly fingertips. Relieved it wasn't something serious, I shook my head at him again and playfully splashed water his way as he burst into laughter. "Let's get a shower and get in bed, find a movie, and snuggle up."

The rest of the night was spent doing just that. A long hot shower together, then curling up in Harrison's king-sized bed together laughing and enjoying one another's company.

When the morning sun edged its way into Harrison's bedroom, it found us entwined in bedsheets, pillows and blankets scattered on the floor. Harrison, still exhausted from late night talking and lovemaking, was the first to greet the day, and albeit groggy, he threw on a pair of shorts and left me to rest while he went downstairs and made us breakfast. He said French toast and powdered sugar had been tickling his brain since I mentioned it as part of my dream, and he thought it might make me smile to deliver breakfast in bed, even if he didn't have any chocolate cake to go with it.

Curious to see him with Shelby, I snuck to the top of the stairs and watched him without his knowledge. He greeted her as he joined her in the kitchen, and helped her put the dishes away as she emptied the dishwasher, then asked for her help making breakfast. I watched quietly as Harrison did the bulk of the work, and Shelby carved strawberries into the shape of roses to accent the plates, before pouring the juice, and arranging everything neatly on the large tray. When the cooking was finished and the food was plated and ready to go upstairs, Harrison turned to Shelby and thanked her for her help.

"You're always there when I need you," he said as he hugged her.

From the top of the stairs, I cleared my throat. "Good morning." I said, my voice flowing down into the room.

The two of them stepped away from one another and Harrison looked up at me with worried eyes.

"Alice, this is Shelby." he said.

"I see that." I said straight-faced and made my way down the stairs toward them.

"I asked her to help me make you breakfast. I was going to bring it up to you, and four hands are certainly faster than two. See, look what we made for you." He gestured toward the tray.

I knew there was nothing going on and I hadn't walked in on anything inappropriate, it was just a hug but a small part of me was still afraid I could lose him. Harrison didn't strike me as the type I would have to worry about—other women coming onto him, yes, absolutely. But him falling for it, no. I peered over at the tray and then looked at Shelby.

"Looks good. Sorry, Shelby, I didn't mean to be rude." I intentionally wrapped my arms around Harrison and kissed his cheek as I said it.

"No worries Alice, you can rest assured this one's not for me. A good friend, a great boss, sure. Always been a bit of a hugger, but not my cuppa." Shelby waved her hand in front of her as if to say 'no thank you.'

I laughed and thanked her for helping. Shelby left to tidy up the upstairs as Harrison and I shared breakfast, the daily funny papers, and hot coffee out on the patio just as we'd done the morning before.

This morning looked different than yesterday though, because Harrison didn't want to go swimming. He didn't want to venture out and show me the sights. He told me he didn't even want to leave the house. He wanted to curl up on the couch with snacks and blankets, order in dinner later on, and not stop touching me all day long. He said he wanted to tell me he loves me a thousand times, memorize the way he makes my eyes sparkle, commit my beautiful smile to memory, and permanently imprint the smell of my perfume on his brain.

When the paper had been read, the breakfast devoured, and the sweet nothings whispered, we returned to find Shelby in the kitchen again. She handed Harrison a small notepad and asked if there was anything else we wanted at the store. As we wrote down our favorite treats, Shelby took care of our dishes, then headed out to shop for us.

While she was gone, we showered together, and when he told me he needed to make a few quick calls about work for next week, I grabbed my cell phone for the first time in days. No missed calls, no emails that couldn't wait until I got back to the farmhouse, but several unread texts stood out in bold among my notifications.

The first was from Emma.

Just checking in. It's been radio silence and I hope that means you're having fun and not dead somewhere. Let me know.

That was from two days ago. The next one from Emma read:

Friend? You okay? I want all the details.

And the third, sent this morning said, *Alice, I'm beginning to worry. I hope you're okay. Please get in touch.*

I began typing my response, unsure how in the world I would ever explain the last few days.

Hi, sorry for the delayed response, been quite...sidetracked. Having a blast and feeling more alive than I have my entire life, definitely not dead. Can't wait to dish all the details, your head will spin. Love you.

I hit Send and moved down the list to the next one.

The next group of messages were from Nigel.

Checking in, haven't had you on my schedule the last few days, and hadn't heard from you, hope you're having fun!

I responded,

Having a blast, made a connection I could never have imagined and hope you don't mind I gave someone your number to set up a meeting about you becoming a personal driver.

I added a winking face at the end and hit Send, knowing he would send me a response quickly.

There were no messages from James, but I really didn't expect there would be. I began deleting some of my junk emails and was interrupted by Nigel's response.

Who? What? Girl, you better spill it!

I knew he'd be excited, and I could hear his voice in my head as I read his text. I sat for a moment, trying to figure out the best way to explain it because I wasn't sure how much info I should send out into the world before having a heart-to-heart with James. My response was a bit cryptic.

I met Harrison Edwards (!!) he's going to be hiring a full-time personal driver for someone close to him and I gave him your number! He's going to be contacting you to set up a meeting. It's legit, and I expect to hear from you after you two talk!

Emma's response came in next and made me laugh.

Glad to know you're still breathing. But are you breathing heavy—that's the question? LOL Message me when you can, or call, whatever. I'm excited for these deets!

I responded simply with,

So heavy…xo

and left it at that.

Nigel's final text chimed in as my message to Emma was sending.

Oh my God! ALICE IM BUZZING! THANK YOU! I will let you know as soon as I know! xxxxx

I sent back,

xx talk soon

Then put my phone on the nightstand to charge, its battery nearly dead.

I met Harrison in his library just as he was finishing up a call. He had his laptop open and was wearing a pair of glasses I hadn't seen on him before. The man was gorgeous no matter what he had on, that was for sure, but these glasses gave him a Clark Kent vibe that I loved. I sat down and watched him patiently until he hung up the phone.

"I set something up for this evening and I'm not sure if you'll be into it or not. I did it for me, but you can do it too if you want, no pressure," he said.

"What's that?" I asked.

"I've called for my guy, my tattoo guy, to come by around six, just for something quick, but I wanted you to see it while I was getting it done. It won't take long." He smiled and looked back at his laptop, avoiding my inquiring eyes.

"Umm...okay. That's not at all what I thought you'd say, but okay...I don't know if I'll get one. Maybe...I'll think on it." I was apprehensive but wanted to show Harrison I could handle it and go with the flow. I also wanted to share the experience with him.

"No problem. You ready for this movie marathon?" he asked, closing his laptop and securing his glasses in the top drawer of his desk.

"I'm ready whenever you are," I said. "And by the way, those glasses are super hot." I nodded in approval as I said it.

"I'll take your word for it, love. I think they make me look like a dork."

"Not at all. Wear those to bed tonight." I winked at him and used my hand to fan myself.

Harrison took my other hand, chuckling and shaking his head, and together we went to the living room. We curled up in one another's arms under the comfort of the softest blankets I'd ever touched, and spent the next few hours mindlessly enjoying each other's company. We alternated movies, first my choice of a classic romance, then Harrison chose a comedy. It was nice to lie there wrapped up in him, to be the little spoon and just enjoy our time together. There were no deep conversations, no need to explain anything, no feelings of inadequacy. Just love and comfort and happiness.

By afternoon, the sun had disappeared and was replaced by dense gray fog so thick we actually watched it roll in and engulf the house. I gathered up some of the snacks that Shelby had purchased and laid them out on the coffee table while Harrison lit the fireplace.

"The weather in London changes as quickly as it does back in New England," I commented as I dished up microwave popcorn.

"Yeah, it's actually part of why I love living in this city. That, and the change in seasons. I enjoy a good rainy day." He struck a match and held it against the logs in the fireplace.

"I do too. They're good for reflection and well, days like these. Though I can't remember the last time I had a day like this." I bit at the inside of my cheek, a nervous habit that comes out when I say one thing and think another.

319

My mind wasn't on rainy days and movies; it was on its thirtieth revolution around the fact that by this time tomorrow I'd be back to my daily dose of depression. This life-altering experience would be over, and I'd be back in the reality I despised, and worse, preparing to ask for a divorce. I sighed at the thought of it, unsure how I would even approach the situation. *What if James reacted the way he did in my nightmare?*

"Alice?" Harrison's voice broke my spiral.

"I'm sorry babe, I was…somewhere else." My voice depressed.

"I see that. You okay?" he asked.

"Just thinking again about how quickly our time is dwindling and getting anxious about the mess I need to deal with. I just want to stay here under the covers with you and not think about any of it." I pulled the blankets up over my face dramatically.

"Well, stay here with me under the covers then, and let's not think about it until tomorrow. We've got tonight. And we have eternity. There's just a bit of time in between that we'll have to suffer without each other. We both have to find some strength to manage our way through, but we'll be alright. After all, it's just coordinates, we'll be together in spirit. Gotta think positive." He tapped his temple as he said the last bit.

"I know." I pulled the blanket back to my chest, revealing the frustration on my face, my hair a skewed mess.

"I love you." He cocked his head, his eyes full of sincerity, as his hand softly smoothed my wild hair back into place.

I poked out my bottom lip, exaggerating a pout. "I love you too," I said.

We both decided, given the weather, that a scary movie would be the best way to pass the next few hours. A little thrill to keep us on our toes before dinner and this potential tattoo lingering in my future. Harrison snuggled back in behind me on the couch and held me tight as the movie started. His cologne was as comforting as his arms, and as the fire crackled and the fog thickened, I relaxed into him.

Midway through the film, my mind began wandering again. I couldn't concentrate on anything happening in the movie, and to top it all off, I was trying to avoid having a full-blown panic attack in front of Harrison again. The scene I caused as I approached the jet the other day was embarrassing enough. I took a deep breath, and let it out slowly, meant to cleanse my mind, but on exhale my thoughts slipped right into another topic, wondering if I should get a tattoo. Sure, I'd love to have something to remind me of this trip, you know, besides the endless love of a man that made me feel like a complete human being for the first time in my adult life. Maybe something small, something that wouldn't draw a lot of attention, and I could put it somewhere that would only make sense to me. Maybe I'd do it, just to surprise Harrison.

My mind continued to shuffle through random thoughts, but at least tomorrow had been taken off that list. I thought about the farmhouse, my gardens, the sights I had seen on this trip, and what it would be like when Harrison and I could be together indefinitely. I tried to think of the things that made me feel whole, and loved, things that brought me joy, and they all circled back to the man that had his arms wrapped around me. Sure, I'd miss the farmhouse, and the gardens I'd worked so hard on, but I could have gardens here. I'd be back here long before Spring; I could lay in the hellebores I'd always wanted.

I had been happily lost somewhere between awake and unconscious when a nasally snarling snore burst from behind me and brought me back to the present. *So much for a thrilling movie; neither of us are paying attention.* I wasn't sure when Harrison had fallen asleep, or even when I had drifted off, but the movie had ended, and the television screen was black. Harrison quickly settled back into slumber, and I noticed the fog had continued to cover everything it touched, building itself upward now, invading everything within view. It created a premature darkness, both inside and out, and the only light left coming from the fireplace were the muted glowing embers that pulsated red and orange.

I lay there enjoying the silence. The rise and fall of his breathing against my back brought me a calmness, a clarity. I knew what I was going to do. When James was back, I'd see how he behaved. Feel him out. See if our time apart had given him some pause or changed his approach to our marriage. He had two weeks, and then I'd say something to him. I'd simply sit him down, and tell him, "James, I don't want this to be my life anymore. I'm a stagnant human being, depressed, lonesome, and I've been complacent. You may be happy, but I'm not, and I think we should go our separate ways." Yes, that would work. I'd find an attorney in those two weeks, and file for divorce immediately after we have the conversation.

But what if I got there and he was a changed man? What if he told me how much he missed me, how being apart made him realize he could never live without me? What if he started helping around the house and went out of his way to include me in things? What if my being gone awakened some

322

sexual appetite in him that he'd been suppressing?

The thought of James behaving in such a way was laughable. It was such a foreign concept; I couldn't even picture it in my head. I had no idea what something like that would even remotely look like. There was no way he would ever change, and I resigned myself to the idea that my speech wouldn't be in vain, purely because he was incapable of change, or thinking of anyone other than himself and his wants. I couldn't even call them needs. They weren't needs. They were expectations. And I was done with them.

I didn't need the house or the land. His entire life was there, always had been. His job and his friends were there, and he'd worked tirelessly on the property to make it what he wanted. He was comfortable there; he could have it. I had somewhere else to be anyhow and I wouldn't ask for anything other than my personal belongings, and to split our money equally between us. *It should be quick, and relatively painless*, I thought. Though I'd never been through a divorce before, and I had no idea what was quick or what was painless or what to expect at all really. I remember a childless couple in town had been married for over forty years when they filed for divorce last April; by Memorial Day theirs was finalized, and that was fast in my eyes.

Out of the darkness came the sound of someone approaching the front door, but instead of a knock, I heard a key slide into the lock and instinctively I held my breath, terrified. I elbowed Harrison as quickly and as quietly as I could to wake him, but as I nudged at him, all the overhead lights came on, nearly blinding me. Harrison sat up, scowling, confused, and wiped the drool from the corner of his mouth as Shelby made her way down the entry stairs into the living room, a large takeaway bag in each hand.

"Hey sleepy peeps, I've got dinner," she said cheerfully, heading in the direction of the kitchen.

"Thanks for grabbing that. I really appreciate it," Harrison mumbled as he approached her, hugging her the same way he had this morning.

"Yeah yeah, all in a day's work." She shrugged him off of her. "Now get on, so I can dish this up for you."

I was still a bit rattled. I hadn't expected Shelby to be bringing dinner or that she would just use her key and come in without knocking. In hindsight though, I suppose that was normal. The sound of a key in the door shouldn't terrify me; it should have signaled it was someone authorized to have the key to the house. Shelby let herself in every day; why wouldn't she do it now? She was doing it to be helpful, after all, it was just one more thing to get used to.

"You don't have to do all that Shelby; we can plate our own dinner. I don't know what he's dragged you away from just to bring us food, but please don't feel obligated to go to all this trouble." I shot a disapproving look in Harrison's direction.

"Oh, I'm just down the way a bit, no fuss at all. I do this more often than you realize." Shelby grabbed plates from the cupboard.

"Well, I'm thankful for you but really, don't stick around for us. We'll be just fine," I said.

"You sure? Anything else need done before I leave then?" Shelby's accent was thicker than Harrison's and I liked it more each time she spoke.

"Not at all. Go, enjoy your night, but hey, it was so nice to meet you and I hope I'll be back soon, next time without a return flight. Be safe out there."

I cocked my head toward the weather outside the window.

I hugged her and as I did, Shelby whispered in my ear, "You're good for him; I'm glad he found you," then winked at me and made her way back up the stairs before vanishing into the fog.

We ate our dinner together once again at the table, but tonight, there was a heaviness that hung over what little conversation we found. I pushed my food around my plate mindlessly, lost in my thoughts as I played out scenarios in my head. I wondered what might happen when the newness of this relationship wore off, how things would be with Harrison when I was here full-time. *Was I crazy to think this man would be different than the one I'd been married to for two decades?* I reminded myself that he'd already proven himself to be different. I glanced up to find him leaned back in his chair, his hands clasped behind his head, staring at me.

"What?" I asked quietly, nervously feeling heat rise into my cheeks not only from his gaze but at the contours of the solid muscles in his arms.

"What indeed." He smiled his perfect smile, a boyish grin that never got old.

"What's wrong?" I asked before turning away from him, trying to shield the crimson apples of my cheeks, and taking a deep breath.

"Nothing is wrong. Just watching you. Wondering where you were because it didn't seem like you were here."

I shook my head dismissing his concern. "Just have a lot on my mind and trying to sift through it all. Sounds crazy, but I miss you already and I haven't even left yet." I pushed my food across my plate again, certain if I made eye contact with him, I'd end up in tears.

"That doesn't sound crazy at all, darling. Listen, we are going to be fine, don't get down while we still have time together. Let's enjoy it while we can and worry later." His hands reached across the table to comfort me, but a knock at the door interrupted us before I could respond.

"That must be Tate. One second."

Harrison got up and went to the door where he greeted and ushered in a very tall, very thin gentleman that was dressed head to toe in black, carrying a backpack over one shoulder.

"Alice, this is Tate, my tattoo artist. The man responsible for making me look good naked." Harrison patted him on the shoulder. "Tate, this is Alice, my sweetheart."

Tate smiled and said hello to me, then asked where he should set up. Harrison showed him to the living room, then returned to me in the dining room.

"So, think you're gonna get some work done?" he asked excitedly, clearing his plate from the table.

"I think so. Just something small though." I'd decided to put a small 'H.' near my heart, but hadn't shared that yet with Harrison.

"Ladies first," Tate called from the couch.

"Go ahead and I'll finish cleaning up. Surprise me," Harrison said and winked, then kissed me quickly on the cheek.

I went into the living room and explained to Tate that I wanted a small capital H with a period after it, pointed to the spot, and within minutes, he had drawn up the art, laid on the outline and my tattoo was complete. Tate didn't say a word as he worked, just remained focused on the task at hand and I spent that time fixated on Harrison clearing dishes from the table, rinsing them and loading the dishwasher. I was completely entranced with his willingness to do household tasks. Tate worked his magic and it was over so quickly, I barely felt a thing.

"That was so quick! Thank you so much." I looked down and smiled. "This is perfect."

"Alright mate, you're up!" Tate yelled toward Harrison, who was already walking toward us. "No changes since this morning?" he asked.

"Nope, just what we already talked about," Harrison responded as he sat down beside me on the couch.

"Funny, did you two plan this out or something?" Tate looked like he was waiting for the punchline.

We both looked at each other, then at Tate, puzzled.

"Mate, does she know what you're getting?" Tate laughed as he said it.

"What am I missing here?" Harrison asked him and then looked at me, suspicion written all over his face. "What'd you get?" he asked.

I lifted my shirt to reveal the 'H.' displayed prominently against the outside of my left breast, just below my armpit.

Harrison burst out laughing.

"Darling, I love it!" he said. "I've asked for an 'A' in nearly the same spot! I wanted to know I was holding you, safe under my arm and close to my heart at all times." Harrison kissed my forehead. "Great minds, love!" He pulled his shirt over his head, still laughing.

He lifted his left arm and Tate placed the already prepped stencil against his skin. It was larger than mine, but it looked perfect on him.

"Amazing! I love it!" I said when he asked me how it looked.

Fifteen minutes later, the buzzing stopped and the ink had been deposited. Tate was packing up his things and I thanked him again, both for the work he did on me and for making Harrison look good naked, then went upstairs while Harrison showed him out. I took my phone from the nightstand and snapped a quick photo of my new art before sending it to Emma, no message attached. Almost immediately I got a response.

H.?? What is this about? Deets pls.

I sent another photo, this time the one of me and Harrison in front of the falls from our trip to the Dales. Again, no message attached.

I sat there awaiting Emma's response with a smug look on my face. I pictured my friend out on the West Coast, probably at work, trying to figure out what it was exactly she was looking at.

What the actual fuck!? Remind me to go with you on vacation from now on. HOLY SHIT!

I burst out laughing at Emma's response. I knew it would be something like this, and I typed my reply.

Don't show a soul. This is NOT for public consumption. Capeesh? I'll call you when I'm home and settled and fill you in. Hope you enjoy the view as much as I have. xoxo

I hit Send and repositioned my phone on the nightstand as I heard the sound of the front door closing downstairs. Shortly after, Harrison made his way down the hall toward me.

"How you doin'?" he asked as he collapsed down onto the bed beside me.

"I'm okay, better now though." I wrapped my arms around him and kissed his scruffy chin. "I must say, I like the facial hair…for what it's worth," and I brushed my lips across his bristly cheek.

"Glad to hear that, because I have to grow a full beard for this next role. I've never had a beard in my life." He laughed. "They'll have to get a wig for my face."

"That would creep me out I think, gluing a bunch of hair onto my face." I grimaced at the thought of it. "Glad it's you and not me." I patted his chest jokingly, then let my hand rest there.

Wrapped up in one another we lay there in silence. The imaginary sound of a clock in my mind not only grew louder by the second but started echoing with every forward movement. All I could think about were the seconds passing, each one hurling me closer to my flight tomorrow.

"Harrison…"

"Mhmm?"

"Thank you for all that you've done for me, and all you've shown me." I paused, unsure if I should continue.

"Of course, darling, it's truly been my pleasure." His arm squeezed me tighter and his fingers gently swept back and forth over the top part of my arm.

"And for understanding me and loving me for who I am. It feels like my craziest, most insane, farfetched dreams have come true. You've changed my life, Harrison, and how I see myself." I hesitated again, my silence welcoming his response.

"You've always been in there, I'm sure of it. And you just didn't know where to find me. I am an elusive beast after all." He chuckled softly. "It's human nature to rest where you find comfort, but sometimes even the softest bed can turn rigid if you lie in it long enough."

I sighed contentedly. "Thank you then, for feeling like eternal comfort." I nuzzled my face further into his neck.

For nearly an hour we lay there, quietly caressing one another, enjoying the other's touch, until Harrison pulled away and sat up, facing away from me.

"I think we need a fire." he said as he stood and made his way to the fireplace.

"Sure, that would be cozy on a gloomy night like this," I replied.

While Harrison's back was turned to me, stacking logs and arranging the kindling to get the fire started, I took the opportunity to quietly slip out of my clothes, leaving them in a pile on the floor beside the bed. Fully naked, I slid silently under the covers without his knowledge, making sure I pulled the blankets up tight around my neck as I settled in. Still oblivious, Harrison struck a match and held it steady, waiting for the flame to ignite the logs and take over. Soon the fire began to crackle and Harrison stood back, pleased with what he'd created, turned off the lights, then turned to face me.

His exquisite figure was backlit by the growing fire, and he stood there silent, motionless, his dark outline watching me. Doe-eyed, I inched my way up from beneath the covers, the light from the flames illuminating my bare neck, and then my shoulders, and the rise of my cleavage against the sheets. Harrison stood still except to reach behind his neck at the collar of his t-shirt, pulling it over his head and throwing it to the side. The waistband of his boxer briefs peeked from beneath his low-slung jeans, just lower than the deep v-cut muscles that laid above his hips. Every ripple, every bulge of muscle was black against the bright flickering fire behind him.

He walked toward me slowly, pulling at his belt to loosen it, then unfastened his jeans and let them drop to the floor. It wasn't until he crawled across the bed, just inches from me, that his face came into focus. His blue-green eyes cut through the darkness and met mine with an unmatched intensity, his face serious, no dimples in sight. His palms against the bed, his arms like rippled pillars holding him in front of me, his voice was deep but barely a raspy whisper when he next spoke.

"I love your eyes, Alice, for the way they drink me in..." He leaned in and softly kissed my forehead.

"I love your lips, for the way they find me lost and pull me home..." He kissed the tip of my nose and parts of me started to throb.

"I love your fingertips on my body; they keep all the secrets I've ever told..." He brushed his lips over mine and kissed my chin, lingering there as he continued.

"I love your ears; they hear the words I cannot find..." His lips moved against my skin, his breath hot against my throat as he opened his mouth and softly bit my neck, a quick gasp escaping me as he did it.

"I love your creases..." He pulled the blankets back, revealing the rest of me to the firelight. His fingers tickled along the edge of my body, and back up along the underside of my breasts, raising goosebumps out of nowhere. "They guide me when I'm lost." The soft warmth of his tongue on my collarbone caused me to inhale sharply again, and my body tensed against the erotic pressure of his lips.

The logs in the fireplace cracked and popped and the vibrant flickers of light reflected in my eyes as I watched him celebrate my body.

"I love your curves, Alice; they harden...all that once, was soft," He took my hand and placed it firmly against his now rock-hard erection.

"Oh..." I said, pleasantly surprised, and blinked hard as my hand tightened around his girth, hindered only by his cotton underwear. He closed his eyes and inhaled slowly, licking his lips as my hand ran the length of its outline.

"The effect you have on me, Alice, is..." He shook his head as if to signal defeat.

I lifted his chin to face me again, my other hand still firmly where he had placed it.

"Every part of me is yours," I whispered against his parted lips before pulling his body down onto mine and kissing him passionately.

The heat built between us and I reached for the band of his boxer briefs, pushing them gently down over his hips.

"Wait! One second..." he said as he pulled away and ran out of the room.

I lay there confused. *What was he up to now?* I thought, and watched the fire burn while images shuffled through my mind of our last few days together. I'd been reckless with my body and my emotions, and I had zero regrets about it. Given the opportunity to do it all again, I wouldn't change a single thing. Just then, Harrison's voice grew closer as he made his way back to the bedroom.

"I nearly forgot," he said as he stopped in the doorway. Flamboyantly pressing the length of his body against the door frame, turning his face toward the darkness of the hallway.

"Forgot what?" I giggled.

Harrison turned to face me abruptly, then slowly raised his glasses up and onto his perfect face.

I laughed out loud, fully this time.

He seductively slid his back down the doorframe until his butt landed on the backs of his feet, his arms and hands above his head with his fingertips on the door frame, then dropped down to his hands and knees as sexy as he could manage. Trying to look as smoldering as possible, he crawled toward the bed as I shook my head and continued to laugh.

Harrison slid back into bed beside me and with nostrils flared he said, "You said you wanted me to wear these to bed tonight." He sprawled his arms and legs out toward all corners of the bed and said, "Ravage me, darling! Just have your way with me! I'm ready!" laughing the entire time.

"Oh my God, Harrison!" I couldn't stop laughing.

"Drink it in, baby!" he said, then laid his head back into the pillows and gyrated his hips.

I took the opportunity in front of me and stripped what remained of his clothes to the floor. Serious again, I teased my hands across his skin, feeling the strength of his thigh muscles. My mouth explored his body, savoring every inch of him, and bringing him to attention once again.

"Wait. I wanna watch you," he whispered and repositioned himself so his head was at the end of the bed, the glasses securely positioned on his nose.

The flames in front of me now illuminated my face and body as I lowered myself down on top of him again. My hips moving rhythmically, grinding against him, I sat fully erect and gave him the show he wanted, my back arched as my hands grasped at my breasts and snaked themselves down my own body; I watched him intently and smiled as he lost control of himself.

Time and time again over the course of the night we indulged in one another, each of us knowing but never mentioning that it could be months before we would see each other again, before we could touch one another in this way again. Harrison took his time with me, touching, kissing, and complimenting every single part of me that he loved, attempting to lock it all safely into his memory. Trying to put into words how deep his love for me runs, he recited parts of his favorite poetry, tongue-tied against the depth of his emotions.

I was lost somewhere in the undefined space between happy and sad. Consumed by the joy of being with him, and yet also somehow overwhelmed by the thought of having to leave. The last few days with this man had unearthed a version of myself I thought had died with my marriage; a woman who had ceased to exist had been resuscitated, and now, I could never go back to who I was before this. I couldn't control my tears, and as they fell down my cheeks, then down onto my chest, Harrison instinctively kissed them away. His chestnut curls a sweaty scattered mess across his forehead, and his ocean-green eyes feeling like my only comfort in the world, he reassured me he was always just a phone call away. His kisses, a salty testament of his devotion to me, were constant through the night, and my hands barely left his body.

The fireplace had long since gone dark, and the glowing embers lost their fight for life while we lay together in the darkness. Between trysts, we laughed together and shared more secrets, made future plans, and quietly cried with one another until daylight became an eager voyeur at the window.

"What time is your flight?" The rasp in his exhausted voice against his accent killed me.

"Nine." My voice cracked as I held back another round of tears.

I cleared my throat as his hands cradled my face, my tears falling through his fingers.

"It's okay, baby, I'm right here." He wrapped his arms around me, holding me tight, and as his body gently rocked back and forth to comfort me, the tears he'd finally been able to suppress reappeared.

"We're a mess." I got up and went to the bathroom to blow my nose.

Catching sight of myself in the mirror, I was horrified.

"Holy shit, Harrison. You must have struggled to make love to this mess last night." I chuckled to myself, tried to smooth my hair into place, then blew my nose again.

He wrapped his arms around me from behind. "Loving you is never a struggle. And what you look like, darling, doesn't factor into it." He kissed my temple.

"Easy for you to say, you look like you just fell off the cover of GQ," I said to his reflection in the mirror.

"Me? I'm shit." He stepped back and flexed into the mirror, a scowl on his face, nostrils flaring, and his lips pressed together protruding from his face.

"Right, indeed you *are* a mess." I rolled my eyes. "Shower with me?" I asked.

"You never have to ask me twice." He eased up against me quickly, cupped my breasts from behind as he kissed my shoulder repeatedly and walked with me to the shower.

An hour later we'd shared multiple orgasms and Harrison sat on the edge of the bed watching as I packed my suitcase. I could see the exhaustion and sadness in his eyes and knew I probably didn't look much better. I hadn't brought a lot with me, so it was fairly simple to get everything tucked neatly inside my luggage, but my hands felt like concrete blocks as I folded shirts, dragging out the process, imagining that if I never finished packing, the time would never come for me to go to the airport.

I felt like I had lost control of everything. Time was moving at a rapid pace, and it wasn't waiting for me to keep up. It didn't care if I was prepared for what its forward movement brought with it. I felt helpless against it. Harrison and I would only have time to eat a quick breakfast and then it would be time to go. My flight was nonstop, and barring any delays would land me back in Boston around noon. Accounting for potential traffic during lunchtime, I should be in my driveway by 3 p.m. and James was due home around 4. I shook my head at the thought of it. I didn't want to deal with any of this mess and my frustration about it was written all over my face.

Downstairs, there was no Shelby. Harrison had advised her to take the morning to herself so he and I could be alone. He made rye toast and butter for us both, and while he had tea, I opted for juice. I wasn't really hungry despite not having much to eat the night before and continuously burning calories since. With no Shelby, there was no newspaper, and thus no daily comics to lift either of our somber moods. With the toast consumed and the remaining juice washed down the drain, Harrison took my hand in his and said, "Time to go, babe. You all set?"

"Yes, but, no. ...I guess." I sighed heavily then bit nervously at my lip, trying to hold back tears.

Harrison once again wrapped his arms around me and kissed my neck. Moments later when he attempted to step back, I clung to him, refusing to let go.

"Not yet," I whispered, nuzzling my face into his chest; desperate to imprint his scent on my lungs I took a deep breath, and after letting it out, tearfully said, "Please don't forget about me."

"Never. Not for a second could I ever, Alice. You're a part of me now, darling. I'm inclined to tell you you're the one stuck with me, and good luck to you for it. I'm a real pain in the ass, you know? Do you have any idea what you've signed yourself up for?" He was trying to make me smile, and thankfully it was working.

"I'm so grateful for you and all your pain-in-the-ass tendencies. Even the ones that try to brighten my day when I'm being an old miserable hag." I scrunched my nose up at him.

"My God woman! Don't you dare call my future wife an old hag; she'll decimate you!" He stepped back, holding me at arm's length, then winked at me.

My chin trembled as I continued to bite at my lip, still fighting back tears. I hoped like hell what he was saying was true and held his gaze, my tear-filled eyes searching his for the answers I needed before I went back to the U.S.

"C'mon now, let's not leave with tears, darling. Let's leave with excitement to get this next bit over and come back together as soon as we can, okay? Next time 'round is going to be even better than these last few days, because you'll never leave my side again. I'll see to it. Okay? You'll want to enjoy the peace and quiet while you're away because when the press gets ahold of us, it's going to be 'lights, camera, action' going forward. You can trust me on that. I'll text Lawrence, we'll need to get going if we're to make it on time." One more kiss on my forehead, then a long and lingering one on the lips, and he pulled his phone from his pocket to summon Lawrence.

The car ride to the airport was quiet. We lay back against the leather seats, snuggled into one another just as we had on our first day together. I spent those forty minutes breathing in his cologne and brushing my cheek against his ever-growing stubble, rubbing his strong hands with my fingertips, and kissing his jaw. When the SUV pulled to a stop outside my terminal at Heathrow, Lawrence retrieved my bag from the back and Harrison helped me out of the vehicle. Oblivious to everything around us, we stood there for a long while and hugged one another. When we finally stepped out of each other's embrace, Harrison looked into my eyes and then kissed me, slow and sensual, his hands cradling my face. He kissed me in such a way I thought I might collapse right there on the sidewalk, a melted puddle of a person, fully and completely in love with the man in front of me. Neither of us concerned ourselves with who was around, despite how busy it was for a Thursday morning; we just kissed each other like two people in love.

"Alice, I love you. I'm *in* love with you. Don't take too long to come back to me, okay? I need you with me to be complete." He struggled to find a half-smile with tears in his eyes, the faint indentation of his dimples triggering me.

"I love you, babe. I love you *so* much. I'll be back as soon as I can, I promise." I pushed myself up on my tiptoes and kissed each of his dimples. My fingers woven into the back of his hair slid forward across his jaw and tenderly touched each dimple, lodging the feeling of them into my permanent memory. I closed my eyes as I said, "I love you," and kissed him again full on the mouth, then took my suitcase by the handle and walked into the airport, certain that if I turned around to take one last look at him, I'd assuredly run back into his arms.

7.

Heathrow was busier than I anticipated, busy enough to keep me focused on the task at hand instead of collapsing in a heap of messy tears. I managed to check in and get to my gate without too much trouble, and it was only a short wait before we began boarding. Soon I was firmly planted in the seat I would occupy for the next eight hours. My mind was a tornado of images of the last few days, scrolling through my brain like a highlight reel. The smile that reflected in the window as I stared out at the tarmac soon faded into glossy reflections of the tears on my cheeks as they caught the London sun. Feeling helpless, I slid the shade down on my window, pulled the neck of my sweater up above my nose to smell him again, and tucked my bag under my arm securely, wishing it was Harrison I was holding onto. I closed my eyes and allowed the sleep that had eluded me to creep in.

I remembered nothing of my flight, only that the person next to me had jostled me awake when the plane had come to a stop in Boston. Thankful

I'd gotten some rest, it wasn't without its drawbacks. My neck was sore from being propped against the wall of the plane and my head now radiated with pain in my temples and behind my eyes. *The drive home is going to be a long, miserable trip*, I thought as I made my way to the baggage claim area. My suitcase was one of the first to appear, so I quickly snatched it from the belt and headed for the car.

The rancid smell of hot garbage had subsided due to the rain that was falling in Boston and I immediately began to wonder if the weather had made its way far enough north for James to be home earlier than planned. I put my suitcase in the trunk of the car and settled into the driver's seat for the long trip home. Seatbelt securely fastened, I fished for my wedding band in my purse. Finally finding it, I reluctantly slid it back into place on my left hand and stretched my fingers against the confining metal. It felt like the chokehold had been returned to my throat. I sighed and pulled my phone from my tote bag, turned it on, and plugged it into the car charger.

Multiple notifications appeared. Two texts from Harrison. The first one read:

I miss you. Let me know when you land safely. I love you xx

The second one said:

I'm in my bed, and you're not here. Doesn't feel right without you in my arms. I miss you xx

I responded to the second one:

In Boston, in the car headed North. Should be about 3 hrs drive. I'll text you when I arrive. I wish I was there with you more than you know. I love you so much more than you realize. xxxx

Moving down the list, my next message was from Emma.

Call me on the ride home. Fill me in!

I thought to myself, *I'll call after I get some food in me.* The last message was from James. It read, as I suspected:

Headed home.

That was it, no I love you or I can't wait to see you. No emotion. It was sent less than thirty minutes ago. Surely, he'd arrive at the house before me. I sighed, set my phone down without responding to him, and turned the key in the ignition.

"Let's find our way out of this shit show," I said aloud to no one.

After maneuvering out of the maze that is Boston Logan International Airport, I hit a drive-through for a quick lunch and then spent the next two hours explaining every detail of my trip to Emma. I started by detailing the dream I'd had about Harrison, just to fill her in on the backstory so some of the details of my trip would make more sense. It felt good to purge everything to someone who wouldn't criticize my actions or put me down for my choices or behavior. Emma was the kind of friend that was simply happy for my happiness, and would fight her friends' battles with them, no matter how they found themselves in the predicament. I could have told Emma I murdered someone, and she was the kind of friend who would just assume they deserved it. The kind of friend everyone needed, and most people rarely, if ever, find. She was a source of unrelenting support, and I loved her endlessly for it.

We talked about what I planned to do when I got back to the house, and what I planned to say to James. Emma even offered to make the trip across the country to be there for me if I needed someone. I expressed my appreciation, but I knew this was something I was going to have to navigate alone, even though Emma's support from afar would be an absolute necessity. We discussed my options for the future, how I'd met Nigel and suggested him as my potential driver for when I return to London, and when I told Emma she'd be the first on my list if I ever needed an assistant, she squealed so loudly at the idea, I was sure it blew one of my car speakers.

When we ended our call, I was glad I'd had the distraction for the majority of my drive. The weather was still overcast and the wind had picked up a bit since leaving Boston, but the rain had ended. It would feel good to spend the last hour of my drive marinating in the silence, gathering my thoughts, trying to map out my plan, but mostly just preparing myself for whatever scene I was going to walk into. It didn't make it any less terrifying though, and it didn't alleviate the fact that I knew I was going to break my husband's heart.

But wait a minute, I thought, *the man has never done a load of laundry in the time we've been together. He's never washed a floor or made dinner. He's never balanced the checkbook or done anything, at all, to help alleviate my daily workload or to make me feel like I was all that mattered in the world to him. Hell, he hasn't touched me in months. He's had twenty years to turn things around and has blatantly opted not to.*

That was all the fuel I needed to ignite the flames of my irritation. I'd left the house spotless, so now, if James was home before me, I couldn't wait to see what I'd walk in and find.

An hour later, I turned into my driveway and climbed the gravel road to the farmhouse. The landscape surrounding me was still damp from the day's rain, and I was anxious to get out of the car. I'd traveled enough for one day. As expected, James' truck was in the driveway, but he was nowhere to be seen. I took my suitcase from the trunk and brought it, along with the rest of my belongings, to the house. An empty cooler sat on the porch, along with a fishing pole and a tackle box.

As I stepped into the mudroom, I saw his dirty boots had been left in the middle of the floor. If I wasn't so used to finding them there, I likely would have tripped over them. His empty duffle bag was slung into the chair, and upon further inspection, his muddy clothes had been dropped on the bathroom floor and forgotten about, gritty sand and chunks of mud scattered all around them. A wet towel was tossed over the shower rod and a sopping wet washcloth laid on the shower floor. He'd obviously come in, taken a shower, and just left his shit where it fell. I felt the heat growing in my ears and wondered where the rest of his clothes were.

"Hello?" I asked.

No response. I glanced around and found no one before I proceeded further.

In the kitchen, the counters on either side of the sink were littered with dirty plastic containers, a thermos, and a coffee mug, and on the table was a pile of mail six inches tall.

"Hello?" I asked again a little louder, and again got no response.

I carried my bag and my suitcase upstairs and set them in my closet. I'd sort through them later. Clearly, I had other things to deal with. In the corner of the bedroom I found the rest of his dirty clothes, piled into and overflowing the hamper, covering a two-foot radius around it. I nodded silently to myself, clenching my teeth, annoyed.

"Of course. Welcome fucking home." I said out loud before yelling, "HELLO?" for the last time.

Still no response.

I sighed and snatched the clothes off the floor, jammed his filthy, dusty clothes into the hamper, and carried it to the washing machine. Once the first load of clothes was started, I went to the sink and began rinsing the dishes that were piled on the counter, arranging them neatly in the dishwasher as the anger grew in my chest. *This man can do whatever he wants, with no regard for me. There's shit everywhere, and where the hell is he? Who the fuck knows,* I thought, as I became increasingly careless with the dishes.

"Hey." His voice came out of nowhere.

I didn't look up or react, just continued with the dishes as I responded "Hey. I didn't hear you come—"

"What's for dinner?" he interrupted.

Infuriated, I dropped what I was doing and spun around to face him.

"Are you fucking kidding me?" I asked enraged, my ears throbbing.

"Well, I haven't had a decent meal in a week. I'm starving." He approached me, arms outreached, smiling as if he were going to hug me.

"Nope." I put my hands up in protest, dirty dishwater dripping down my arms.

"What do you mean 'nope'? Nope what? I can't hug my wife? I was joking around." A confused look washed over his face.

"You were *not* joking, and for the first time in ages we've spent time apart, with basically no contact and the first thing you have the nerve to say to me is 'what's for dinner?'? While I'm up to my ass in your dirty laundry that's strewn all over the house, along with the mud and dirt that's scattered everywhere, and I'm washing the dishes that you've piled up on the counter for me?!" I shook my head and turned back to the sink.

"Sorry. What do you want me to do?" he asked, sounding like my attitude was an annoyance to him.

I spun around again, even more mad than I was a moment ago.

"What needs to be done, James! Why do I need to give you direction? You can't see the floors are covered in mud? You couldn't deal with these dishes? You couldn't put your laundry in the washer? You can't make yourself something to eat? Why does it all fall on me? The house was spotless when you walked into it. You made this mess, then left it for me to deal with. And now you want me to cook you dinner. You don't see how that might piss someone off?" I stood there glaring at him.

"I can see the time away didn't do you much good," he said smugly and headed for the door.

"Hold it! Sit down. Let's chat." The way I barked at him must have made him nervous because he spun around and looked at me, eyes narrowed.

"Have a seat," I repeated, and he begrudgingly pulled out a chair and sat at the kitchen table.

"This conversation really isn't something I anticipated having as soon as I walked in the door, or one that I wanted to have while angry, but here we are..." I wiped the water from my hands and sat down at the table, the pile of mail stacked in front of me.

"What, Alice?" he said, annoyed.

"Are you happy, James? Truly? Can you say this is the life you want?" I gave him a matter-of-fact look. "Because *this* is *not* how I want to spend the rest of *my* life."

"What the fuck does that mean?" The anger in his voice made me reluctant to continue, but this was my chance to say my piece. He apparently didn't need two weeks to show me how he was going to act, and I wasn't going to waste this opportunity.

"It means I'm not happy. I haven't been happy in years, with any aspect of our marriage. Emotional, physical, it's all hollow. I cook, I clean, I do all the things I can for you, I try to make you happy, and keep you content and I feel completely ignored, overlooked, and honestly, taken advantage of. You go to work, you come home, you eat, and then you're asleep. You aren't going out of your way to lighten my load or make me feel special. We don't do anything fun together anymore. You don't do or say anything to make me feel like you're even remotely attracted to me. And I've just gone about my business through the warning signs, and just let it happen. I'm not blaming you; I'm blaming us both."

"Well, I—" he tried to interrupt me, but I wasn't having it.

"I'm not done yet, James. I need to say this. I need to get this out of my heart. It's killing me and we need to talk about where it's going wrong. I feel like a stagnant person. I'm depressed most of the time, and the loneliness I feel in this marriage is affecting my self-worth. I've lost myself completely, and by trying to be everything *you* need, I've become nothing for myself. Being away for a week showed me just how little I factor myself into my daily life. I wasn't a roommate, or a maid, or a cook for a whole week. I got to explore architecture and take photos and I was finally feeling good in my skin. I truly enjoyed myself. I was actually happy. And when I realized it, it felt foreign. I couldn't even recognize it at first. I was just—"

"So, what? You want to go to counseling or therapy or whatever it's called?" His face sullen, he nervously moved the pile of mail so it was sitting in front of him now, trying to keep his hands busy, embarrassed by his apparent failure.

"I don't know that therapy is the answer," I said.

"I never set out to make you feel like...*this*. I guess over the years things just got comfortable. You know, you automatically just do all this stuff and I don't even think about it, Alice. You've just always been there, and gotten it done. I'm sorry. I'm sorry you never said anything to me, and I'm sorry you feel this way." He was mindlessly thumbing through the stack of mail while simultaneously avoiding eye contact and trying to pin the blame on me.

"Apologies are never gonna fix this," I said. "Words just aren't going to get it done anymore. You're sorry *I* didn't say anything and you're sorry *I* feel this way, but I haven't heard you say you're sorry for *your* contribution to the way I feel, or the behavior *you* displayed that made me feel like this."

His face softened, knowing I wasn't budging from my decision, now he was going to try to make me feel bad for him. Unfortunately for him, I'd seen him do this before.

"You're all I've ever known, Alice, and I've never been a fan of change. You must know that about me by now and I won't pretend I've been doing all I can; I haven't. Just," he sighed, "Don't leave me." He hung his head. "I can't do any of this without you. I don't want to."

"I feel like I've spent twenty years giving second chances to a man that had no idea he'd even dropped the ball. I wait to see change, hoping that you recognize my unhappiness, hoping you'll make some major turnaround without us having to go through some blowout argument, but it never happens. You're always just, back at it again, doing what pleases you, going about life in your own world, and it feels like I don't factor into any of it, at all. And you don't open up to me, you haven't since, well, since we lost—"

"I know, Alice. Can we not talk about that? I just—" He put his hand up in protest.

"Not talking about it is exactly what landed us here, James. And I try to read you, but I can't. I say to myself, 'he's still grieving, let him process,' but it's been decades, James. I lost a baby, *and* my husband in that whole process. Did that ever occur to you? I lost you both that day, and I'm not a mind reader, it's hard to know what you're thinking when you won't talk to me. I can't help you if you don't share your thoughts with me, and you never seemed aware that I too, needed help."

James sat there in silence, then leaned forward and laid his forehead against the cold kitchen table, his arms dramatically outstretched, shoving mail in all directions.

"I fucked it all up, Alice." He took a deep breath and let it out slowly.

"I don't think I'd say all that, James," my expression blank. I couldn't see his face, but the manipulation had begun and I recognized it instantly in his body language.

"I did. I ruined your life." He sulked, and after a moment, he sniffed quickly through his nose, trying to appear as if he were crying, but I wasn't buying the bullshit he was selling, not anymore.

Out of the corner of my eye, I noticed something familiar on one of the magazines on the table. I picked it up bewildered and immediately recognized the scene that graced the cover. The headline read, *'Harrison Edwards caught canoodling on his private jet with a mystery woman!'* The zoom on the photo was so amplified it became a blur of colors and fuzzy outlines, but it was most definitely me and Harrison on the tarmac, ready to board the jet for the Dales at the exact moment I'd buried my face in his chest and he'd embraced me to dissipate my anxiety.

Shocked at the realization, I piled the other pieces of mail on top to hide the image. It wasn't so obvious that James would recognize me if he saw it, and the angle of the photo didn't show my face, only the back of my head. Nonetheless, my heart rate skyrocketed, partially from the surprise of seeing myself on the cover of a globally distributed magazine, but also from the rush of seeing Harrison again.

"You didn't ruin my life, James, because quite frankly, my life isn't over yet," I said matter-of-factly and smiled while he couldn't see me.

His head shot up from the table and he looked at me in disbelief. "I can't believe that you're so calm about this." His face was dry, not a tear in sight, but I wasn't surprised.

"Well, you have to understand, I've felt this way for more than half of our marriage. This isn't new to me. And I'm sorry, by the way, that it's so shocking to you, but that further proves my point that you aren't tuned in to me or how I feel at all. In my head, I resent you. In my head, the little voice is saying *Alice, he's never going to be any different. It's been years that you've suffered in silence while he plays pretend like this is normal.* Well, James, this isn't normal, and I think maybe you should get some help for your emotions and figure out why you can't seem to show them to me or express them out loud. I think you should do some grief processing therapy or something along those lines. I'm sorry that all those years ago my body failed us, and brought so much heartache into our lives, but in the years since, you failed me too, and I just can't overlook it, or myself, anymore. I had a lot of time to think while I was away, and I think it would be best if we just—"

James interrupted me, "No. Alice, don't finish that thought, please. Please. I don't want that." He was terrified, and I could see it all over his face.

"And I don't want *this*, anymore," I said with a look of resolve on my face.

James stood up from the table slowly; the backs of his knees pushed the chair away from the table, making a loud grinding sound against the floor. The muscles in his jaw clenched and his hands balled tightly into fists. I sat there quietly watching him, waiting for his next move. When he said nothing, then turned and walked toward the door, I quietly breathed a sigh of relief. The visions of the nightmare I'd had felt very real while I watched

352

him walk away, and I thought to myself, *I'm glad this is almost over, I've had enough from you.*

He stopped at the door, out of my direct line of vision, and said calmly, "Alice, I do love you. I don't wanna throw our marriage away, but it seems you've made up your mind. Is there anything, anything at all, I can do to change it?"

Part of me felt bad; I didn't want to hurt him. I didn't want to make him feel the way I'd felt for so many years, but I had to be honest with myself, and with him.

"No," was all I said.

I listened as he drew in a deep breath and sighed heavily out through his nose. Then out of nowhere, he slammed his fist through the wall. Fragments of sheetrock fell to the floor as I sat still in my chair, my heart pounding in my chest. I remained seated, silent, wondering if he'd circle back and approach me with the same rage. The rage I'd seen firsthand in my nightmare. But he didn't. He left, slamming the door so violently the glass shattered out of it, forcing a shocked gasp out of me as thousands of tiny glass shards fell to the floor, tinkling and scattering themselves through the hallway.

Alone again, I was safe. I'd made it through the initial hard part of the conversation, but now there was an even bigger mess to clean up than there had been to begin with. I didn't want to think about that right now. I wanted to connect with something that would soothe the ache in my soul, so I pulled the magazine out from under the pile of mail and flipped to the article. It made my heart happy to see Harrison again with his arms wrapped around me, no matter how fuzzy the image was. In my mind, I could still feel the way his muscles pushed back against me as he embraced me, and when I closed my eyes, I could still smell the warmth of his cologne, taste his kiss on my lips. I lost myself in my thoughts, letting the happiness I felt in London flood my mind and bring me back to center. A full, deep breath and a long exhale later, I returned my focus to the article.

It was incredibly brief, and thankfully they only had the cover photo and another blurry shot from behind as we were climbing the stairs to the jet. My face wasn't in either of them, which I was relieved about. There was minor speculation about who I could be, where we were going, and how long the relationship could have been going on. Nothing concrete, just enough to bait people into the 'developing' story, as the magazine had phrased it. *Gossip rags*, I thought, then grabbed my phone, snapped a few photos of the magazine, tucked it back into the pile of mail, and sent a text to Harrison.

Good news bad news, babe. Which one you want first? I sent it and waited at the table for his response.

Home safe, I hope? Good news first. I hope you're missing me by now, I'm a mess without you. xx

I'm home, safe, and definitely missing you. Good news is, I've already told him I'm leaving. I hit Send, and again waited.

That was quick. You didn't waste any time. Are you okay? I'm glad the initial shock is over. What's the bad news?

Well, I came home to these photos in a magazine that was sitting on my kitchen table. He put his fist through the wall and broke the glass out of the door when I told him I was leaving. I didn't get into anything about you, just how I've been feeling for so long, but I'm okay. Everything's fine. I attached the photos and hit Send again.

Doors are replaceable. YOU aren't. I'm going to worry about you every second until you're back here with me. As for the photos, I can't stop them, it's already happened. Just the beginning, this is normal really, I'm surprised this is all they got. The good thing is, they can't see who you are and you aren't wearing anything that directly points to it being you. So, not terribly scandalous. Soon enough your every move will be scrutinized. Did you unpack yet?

I love you. I haven't unpacked, but I need to and to pick up this mess then head to bed. I'm exhausted. We'll talk tomorrow. I love you so much. xxxx

I slipped something into your bag. I hope it makes you smile. I love you, beautiful. Talk tomorrow xxxx

I got up from the table, slipped my phone into my pocket, and finished putting the dishes in the dishwasher. When I approached the door, I realized that he'd slammed it so hard it had pulled through the frame to the other side. I righted it as best I could, then tacked up a few pieces of cardboard to try to keep the cold New England air from coming in overnight. I swept the majority of the glass and debris from the floor before pulling out the vacuum to get the finer pieces. Once again, I was left to pick up his mess.

Mentally and now physically exhausted after a full day of travel, then arguing and cleaning, I went upstairs to gather some clean pajamas and my still packed shower items. Inside my closet, I opened my suitcase and pulled out a bag of dirty laundry, tossing it to the side. Harrison said he'd sent me home with something unexpected, but after emptying the bulk of my suitcase onto the floor, I didn't find anything unusual. I sat there frustrated, wanting to wash the weight and grime of the day off of me and get some rest, hanging on to a glimmer of optimism that tomorrow would at least put me one day closer to seeing Harrison again.

I grabbed at the top of my suitcase, intent on slamming it shut, and noticed something dark barely poking out of the typically unused upper compartment. I slid my hand in slowly, unsure of what I'd find, but felt the softness of cotton against my fingertips. When I realized Harrison had tucked one of his t-shirts into my suitcase, I pulled at it aggressively, drawing it up to my face. His dark blue, rolled-up bandana fell out of the shirt along with one of the seashells we picked up in Brighton as I held the shirt against my nose, inhaling the scent of him as deeply as I could until my deep breaths made me feel lightheaded. I couldn't hold back tears any longer. The flood gates of my entire heart burst open, and I sat on the floor of my closet and openly wept.

I mourned the loss of myself and the time I'd lost to a twenty-year marriage, and the loss of the man who I had held out hope would right the sinking ship. I let free the fear that had filled me when his fist hit the wall, the sadness I felt for the work we'd done on the farmhouse that he'd destroyed in a moment of rage. I cried for the newfound love in my life, the fact that I'd had to leave him, the way I missed his touch, and how he made me feel when we were together. I cried out all my heartache while clutching the only comfort I had until I simply couldn't cry anymore. Eyes swollen, I tucked his shirt, the seashell and his bandana safely back into my suitcase, wiped the mess from my face against my hands, and went downstairs to wash it all away.

When I crawled into bed that night, James still hadn't come back inside. I never even thought to look in the driveway for his truck. Maybe he was out in the garage. Maybe he'd left the property. I didn't really know, and I was too exhausted to care. As soon as my head hit the pillow, I was asleep.

There were no dreams, no nightmares, no interruptions to my sleep that night, and when I woke the next morning my head was ringing, pulsating from the crying I'd done the night before. My eyes felt like glazed balloons ready to pop inside my head. I never heard or felt James come to bed, and never felt him get up and go to work, but his side of the bed had clearly been slept in. He'd chosen to lie beside me, not on the couch or in the spare bedroom, but I was certain there had been no goodbye kiss, and no 'I love you'. Twenty-two years of habit had ended, and a part of me couldn't help but feel sad about it.

I lay there with my hand extended to his side of the bed, letting it rest against the empty space where his body had been. I wondered if this was going to become normal, us avoiding each other, moving in secrecy. I didn't hate James. I couldn't, and I knew he didn't deliberately do this to me. It wasn't malicious, and I didn't want us to behave hatefully or stop speaking. Hell, we'd spent decades loving one another. I couldn't just turn that off, right? I held onto the hope that we could at least remain friends and that this split could be amicable. I shook my head, knowing I was probably crazy to think he'd let that happen. I was both mentally and physically worn out. I rolled over onto my side, facing away from James' side of the bed, and snuggled into my pillow. I didn't want to think about it anymore. I lay there with my eyes closed and made a mental list of the things I needed to accomplish today. The same old shit as usual, but at the top of that list was contacting an attorney and following their direction on how best to proceed with the rest of my life.

I got up and did what needed doing despite the pounding in my head. I made the call and set up an appointment for that afternoon with a local attorney, then called Harrison. The relief I felt just from hearing his voice on the other end of the line was immeasurable. We didn't talk long. I explained everything that had happened since I got home, thanked him for sending his t-shirt home with me, and detailed how it had helped me fall apart just as I'd needed to last night.

"Don't let it break your heart, love," he'd said. "You know who you are. Embrace her, remember her as I do, happy, carefree, and bring her back to me."

His words of reassurance put my heart at ease, and with a renewed strength, I was reminded once again why I loved this man. He was young, and he hadn't been through any of this before, but he understood that I needed to process all of these emotions in order to come out the other side a complete person, ready to fully love again. The fact that he recognized it and was open to supporting me while I figured out how to navigate it, and that he was willing to love me through it, spoke to his character. Harrison filled me in on the newest details of Brazil and his filming schedule. He'd be leaving Sunday for at least two months, but would update me when he knew the shooting times. We traded heartfelt 'I love you's and hung up, then I spent the rest of my day catching up on laundry and the housework that James had once again created for me until my appointment time.

The afternoon, and my appointment, moved along swiftly. I gained some much-needed clarity and direction from the attorney I met with and was happy with my choice of lawyer. I very plainly laid out my expectations of giving James the house to live in or sell, and that I had no interest in any of the proceeds if he chose to sell it. I only wanted to be sure that we split the current savings and residual investment finances, and that I was able to keep anything personal that I brought into the marriage. I would pay my own legal fees, and James would be responsible for his. From my perspective, it was very cut and dry. I wasn't interested in taking anything from him other than my physical being and my personal belongings. He could have the rest to do with as he pleased. My attorney assured me I wasn't asking for anything more than I deserved, quite the opposite actually, and this case should be settled quickly based on my desires, and James would be served within seven to fourteen days. I wrote my lawyer a check, shook her hand, and headed back to the house.

James once again was nowhere to be found when I arrived home, but that didn't stop me from making dinner for us both as usual. After all, some habits were harder to break than others. I ate my dinner alone, something I've always hated to do, but have grown accustomed to, then made him a plate and wrapped up the leftovers. When everything was cleaned up and put away, I settled onto the couch to watch a movie, assuming James would come rolling in just about any time, but as the television droned on in the background, I once again found myself drifting into daydreams.

This time I was walking along the sidewalk on my way to the Spaniards Inn, just as I had done less than a week ago. Only this time, James was there with me. He was walking a few steps ahead of me, and I struggled to keep up with his long strides. Once we were seated inside the pub, James took it upon himself to order lunch for us both. As he did, Harrison walked past our table; slowing to lock eyes and smile at me, he moved as if caught in slow-motion, but never stopped. He behaved as if I were a stranger, as if we'd never met before, but I knew him. I remembered him, he felt familiar, like I'd known him in another lifetime. I wanted desperately to reach out to him, to remind him who I was, what we meant to one another, but because James would lose his mind in a fit of jealousy, I only smiled back longingly, my eyes calling out to him with all the words I couldn't say, desperate for him to turn around and come back. Wishing he'd take me by the hand and whisk me away with him. But he never did. He just continued on through the dining room and out to the garden, and no matter how badly I wanted him to reappear, or to run after him and wrap my arms around him, I knew I had no choice but to stay right there at the table, sitting with James.

The sound of a pickup truck in the driveway brought me back to reality, and I sat there thinking that if James had gone to London with me, that scenario is exactly what would have happened. Fate would not have intervened, and I would be no closer to real happiness than I was a month ago. I'd be drowning in loneliness, eclipsed in his shadow, just as I'd always been.

"Hey," he said as he sat down in his chair in front of me, a forlorn look on his face.

"Hi. I made you some dinner," I responded.

"Thanks. I'll heat it up in a minute. I wanted to say a few things to you, Alice. Is that okay?" He was sincere in his delivery, seemingly no longer angry.

"Of course. What's on your mind?" I asked, thinking to myself, *He wants to talk? This is new.*

"I want to genuinely apologize to you. Alice, I'm deeply, regretfully sorry that I made you feel insignificant in our marriage. Or overlooked or undervalued. I don't have any excuse for it. I didn't even realize I was doing it until it couldn't be undone. You've always been the most beautiful woman in the room, Alice. You've had my entire heart for as long as I've known you, and I'm sorry I didn't make you feel that way every day we were together. I'm sorry I kept it to myself. I should've done better by you."

In my mind, I thought, *Okay, we've cycled through denial, anger, and now we're into bargaining.*

"Last night when you said I became a hollow man after...you know...you're right, I did. I became so afraid to show love for fear of losing it. And I didn't show you affection for the fear of us creating another life and potentially having to relive the entire nightmare over again. All I ever wanted was to share a family with you, and I never knew that loss would affect me the way it did. I shut down and closed myself off. I should have talked to you about the vasectomy. I regret the way that played out, and I became content with just you as my family. Us together was all I needed, and instead of telling you all this, and sharing my thoughts, I just lived inside my own head. It's the biggest regret of my life."

I didn't respond, just nodded to show understanding, and let him continue.

"I'm begging you, Alice, give me another shot at making you happy. Let me try to fix this, to show you I can change, that we can come out the other side of this. Don't walk out on me, please. I need you more than you'll ever know." He reached for my hand as he dropped down to his knees in front of me, desperation in his eyes. "Please, Alice. I love you."

"James, you know I love you. I've always loved you. And actually, I do know how much you need me. I feel it every day when I pick up your clothes, and your dishes, and the things you leave laying around. I feel it when I clean up after you and do your laundry, and when I make sure your bills are paid and your appointments are made, and that you have lunch for the next day. How much you need me has never been in question. I worry about what life will look like for you when I'm not doing all these things for you anymore. I'm not angry with you; I want you to know that. I know the way things have been wasn't a conscious decision you made. You didn't set out to make me feel like an overlooked roommate, and you didn't mean for me to feel lonesome. Last night, yes. I was definitely angry last night because I just flew from another country and drove three hours and you couldn't even ask me about my trip. You just wanted to know what I was cooking you for dinner after you'd strewn mud all through the house and left it there for me to deal with. Last night I was pissed. But today I've done a lot of thinking, processing, and I've let it all go. I'm done carrying the weight of anger."

"I'm sorry for that," he interrupted, hanging his head in front of me.

"Well, I'm going to be honest with you, James. I spoke with a lawyer today."

"Alice, no." He snatched his hands from mine as he recoiled, his words desperate as tears welled in his eyes.

"I need you to know that I don't want anything from you. I don't need the house; I don't want money. It's not my intention to hurt you. I would never want to do that, but I need to do this for myself, James. It's time." My words were calm and heartfelt.

He collapsed on the floor, repeating over and over how sorry he was, that he could change and to please rethink this. Despite how terrible he was making me feel, I knew in my heart that this was what was best for me. I couldn't waste any more time worrying about how *he* felt. He'd had years to recognize and rectify his behavior and had done nothing. But I understood how he felt. Hell, I'd spent plenty of time in tears over the last two decades, desperate for his attention, but that was over now. I was out of tears, and my future was waiting for me.

"James, I don't want this to be messy and angry. I want us to be okay with each other, and it might sound farfetched, but maybe try to be supportive of one another. I'm not asking you to leave, but I'll go if you want me to. If you can't be around me, I understand. Like I said, I don't want the house. It's yours. Live here or sell it, whatever you want or need to do."

He looked up at me on the couch, "Where will you be if I stay here?" he said.

"Eventually, I'm going to go back to London, I think. I felt at ease there and the people were welcoming."

"Alice, my God, you're leaving the country?!" The color drained from his face as he waited for me to answer him.

"Yes, James. I hope in time you'll understand that I've felt like a caged bird neglected for years, and that maybe I deserve to spread my wings a bit. I hope one day you'll be happy for me, proud of me even. Like I said, we don't have to hate each other."

"I don't hate you, Alice, I never could. I love you too much. I'm so sorry it's come to this." He laid his head in my lap and cried while I sat there, patting his back.

Eventually his sobs subsided, and I got up to warm his dinner for him in the microwave. We sat beside one another on the couch that night for the first time in years and watched TV, both of us lost in our own thoughts, neither of us saying much. And when it was time for bed, we climbed the stairs together, crawled into our respective sides of the bed we'd shared for years, and while James fell asleep, just as if nothing at all was any different than any other day, I sent an 'I love you' text to Harrison.

It was the middle of the night for him, but his response was swift.

Well, I love you, darling. How was your day? Not much here, readying myself for Brazil, missing you terribly. My body is still knackered from all the love we made but I can't find rest. I'm just spinning out over here, waiting for you, wishing you were beside me again.

I responded:

Making progress. Spoke with counsel about what's to come, told James I filed and that I'd be returning to London at some point. He's understandably upset, but I think he's processing it fairly well. I haven't mentioned you, and I think it's better not to. I don't want to kick him while he's down. Knackered, eh? I wish I was there. If I could fly to you I would. My body aches for you. Try to rest and we'll chat tomorrow. I love you xoxo

I laid my phone on the bedside table and was asleep almost instantly.

The next morning was the start of the weekend, and I had gone out early to work in my flower gardens. The cold New England air in my lungs was invigorating and I hummed to myself as I picked and pruned, deadheaded and weeded while the world woke up around me. I paused when I felt eyes on me, only to look up and find a doe and this year's fawn had stopped at the edge of the field to watch me as I worked. I smiled at them and softly said 'good morning' before returning to the task at hand. I sure was going to miss this landscape. I had spent ages trying to get these gardens laid in, and watching them find maturity had been one of my greatest joys. The farmhouse really was a slice of heaven, and it would be hard to leave, but all that awaited me was a far better reward than what I was leaving behind.

I spent the majority of the day in my gardens until my back hurt so badly I couldn't continue. My afternoon was spent on the couch curled up with the heating pad, exhausted. I was certain I was coming down with something. *Probably picked up some illness on the flight home*, I thought as my head once again began to pulsate. I drifted in and out of sleep until James greeted me at dinnertime with a bowl of warm chicken noodle soup. He waited for me to sit up, then handed it to me, "I brought this for you. You don't seem like you feel very good."

Groggy from my nap, I steadied the bowl against the blankets on my lap.

"Thank you so much, that's thoughtful."

I certainly didn't want to lead him on, but it was a generous gesture, and one I wasn't used to from James. Twenty-two years and he'd never fixed me a meal.

"I'm not sure I can manage this though; the nausea is terrible. It just kind of came out of nowhere."

James sat down beside me as I attempted to drink some of the hot broth.

"Did you have any lunch today?" he asked.

"No, I was just out in the garden and figured I'd eat later. Now, I don't really have an appetite." I shrugged and leaned forward to take another small sip of the liquid and didn't stop him when he started rubbing my back.

"How's that?" he asked as his palm slowly circled my shoulders and upper back.

"It's nice, thank you. You don't have to do all that though." My eyes closed midway through my sentence, and I began to sway with the rhythm of his hands, careful not to upset my soup bowl.

I remembered then what it felt like to be touched by my husband. He had always been soft with me, cherishing each moment, despite how infrequently it had happened.

ALICE! Stop it. One nice gesture doesn't fix twenty years of neglect.

I opened my eyes and took another sip of the warm broth before I relaxed back against the couch. His hands had no choice but to find their way back to his own personal space.

Despondent, he hung his head. "I didn't mean to overstep. I'm sorry."

"It's fine. I'm just exhausted," I said, warming my hands against the bowl in my lap. "Maybe a hot shower and a good night's sleep will get me back on track for tomorrow, but first, I'm gonna try to at least finish this broth.

Thank you again; I really do appreciate it."

James sat with me until I got up to shower, tending to me as much as I would allow, and when I was finally able to get the rest of my dinner down, he took the bowl and rinsed it in the sink, before placing it in the dishwasher. I wasn't sure if I was delusional, or if he was really stepping up to help me. Mystified, I thanked him once again and headed for the bathroom.

The warm steam of the shower welcomed me, and I laid my forehead against the cool tiles of the shower wall; bracing myself with my forearms, I let the heat of the water pound into my shoulders and down the length of my back. My mind wandered back to the first time I'd indulged in Harrison's shower with him. My heart ached to be back there with him. Maybe once James was served, I would just go. What was stopping me? He knew the end was coming. Why did I need to stick around for it? I made a mental note to ask my lawyer about it Monday, then promptly threw up right where I stood. I swished several mouthfuls of hot water, spitting it down the drain, then rinsed the shower down. *Where in the world did this illness come from?* I felt like I'd been hit by a truck. I washed up and noticed a tenderness to my breasts that wasn't typical. I was due anytime for my period, although they had been a bit sporadic the last few months. *Menopause*, I thought. *Bring it on, I'm ready any time to be done with periods.*

I rinsed myself off, turned off the faucet, then stepped out into the bathroom. James had brought me clean pajamas at some point, but I didn't remember when. Dry and dressed, I sluggishly made my way to bed. James had brought up the heating pad from the couch and laid it out on my side of the bed, and a glass of ginger ale sat on my nightstand. He'd even set a pail beside the bed in case I was suddenly sick again. *Who was this man?* I thought. *Oh right, he's the guy from twenty-two years ago. Haven't seen him in a while.* Even the plague hadn't slowed my snark. Maybe this was a sign I wasn't in fact dying. I crawled into bed, pulled the blankets up around my neck, said goodnight, and fell asleep almost immediately.

The urge to vomit woke me suddenly the next morning and I hung myself off the edge of the bed, my arms braced against the upper edge of the bucket below me. Dry heaves. I had nothing left in my stomach to throw up after last night's shower. James was already gone, thankfully. I hated to be sick in front of anyone. I still felt like complete hell and my head was throbbing. When the dry heaving stopped, I rolled back into bed and lay there hoping that whoever had passed this illness to me was somewhere equally as sick. It had to have been someone on the plane, right? *They deserved it*, I thought. *Jerks.* Then it dawned on me, *Was Harrison also sick?*

Realizing I hadn't talked to him at all yesterday, I reached for my phone and found multiple texts from him.

Just checking in love, haven't heard from you and miss you xx

The second one read:

Alice, love are you alright? Usually you write me back quickly. I'm worried xx

The last one was a bit more pointed.

Alice, call me. I need to hear your voice. Straight away, please. I love you xx

I hit Send on his contact and moments later heard his voice on the other end of the line.

"Darling, are you alright?" he sounded anxious and I instantly felt bad.

"I'm okay. Really not feeling well at all. Are you sick too or am I the only one lucky enough to feel like a wrung-out dish rag?"

"I'm fine. No illness here at all. What are you feeling? What are your symptoms?" His voice sounded panicked.

"I've been vomiting, exhausted, achy, pounding headache, just generally fatigued, I guess. It's terrible. I spent the day working in my gardens yesterday and by mid-afternoon, my back was killing me, so I came in and laid down, and then the nausea started. I must have gotten this while I was on the plane. Ugh, I'm miserable."

"Oh, darling, I'm so sorry you're going through this. That sounds brutal."

His accent was adorable when he said 'brutal' and I wanted to laugh but I didn't have the strength.

"I love you, and your perfect face and the way you love me and I just miss your accent and I miss everything about you," I whined. "Thank you for making me smile. I needed to hear your voice, and it's definitely made me feel a bit better. I'm planning to ask my lawyer tomorrow about just doing all this electronically, so maybe we can be together sooner. What are your thoughts?" I asked.

"That would be perfect, Alice! Let me know as soon as you have an answer, so I can set up a jet. I can't wait to see you again!" I admired his enthusiasm; I just didn't have the energy to reciprocate it.

"I just wanna be with you. Whenever, wherever, however I can be. I'm not going to travel feeling like this, that's for sure, but I'll talk to my attorney and let you know."

"Well, get some rest, feel better, and as soon as you do, come home to me, baby. I need you with me. I miss you."

"I miss you too, babe. I'll let you know soon. I'm gonna go. I'm not feeling too good. I love you so much."

"I love you too, darling."

I hit the End button on my phone and once again hung myself over the edge of the bed, hugging the bucket as the dry heaves returned.

"Make it stopppp..." I said, but no one was there to hear me.

Over the next few days, my symptoms waxed and waned. I kept ginger ale on hand, and saltines nearby at all times, which my mother always said were helpful during the flu. I slept with a pail beside the bed for when the symptoms came on suddenly, but aside from that, life proved to be quite amicable between me and my soon-to-be-ex-husband. We were able to navigate daily life fairly easily under the same roof, as not much had changed from before. I still did the cooking and cleaning when I wasn't exhausted or vomiting, and James was more willing to help around the house due to my being under the weather. There was obviously no sex or affection to think about, and with it off the table altogether, things went quite smoothly. Now we were actual roommates, not just posing as such.

I left a voicemail Monday for my attorney but by Thursday still hadn't received a call back, so when I wasn't doing work for Arlo, I'd kept busy by sorting through all our stuff in storage. I separated and organized and then packed the things I hoped to take to London with me. Half of my things would go into a storage unit here, and some would be coming with me. Over time it would all end up with me, but for now, I didn't need to bring everything across the pond. I'd stacked what I deemed James' boxes on the opposite side of the room to keep everything divided appropriately, and at the end of the week, I realized just how little I would actually be leaving with. This impending move seemed to be turning out easier than I'd anticipated.

Harrison and I shared a few calls and texts over the last few days but with his traveling and getting settled in Brazil coupled with the mountains of belongings I was pouring over; our chats were brief and scattered. The sound of his voice grounded me when the chaos of my mind became too much and he reminded me what I had to look forward to once all this work was done.

By the following Sunday afternoon, I had sorted through and repacked our entire history together as a couple and was once again exhausted. I'd noticed myself taking more frequent breaks and spending more time on the couch all week, but assumed it was a combination of residual jetlag and whatever was left of this flu I had. *Was this illness just holding on, or was this something more? Should I be worried? James wasn't sick. Harrison wasn't sick, just me.* Then out of nowhere, it occurred to me. I was three days late for my period. I was never late. Early if anything, but never late.

Maybe this wasn't an illness at all. I thought back, reliving all the ways I'd been reckless with my body in London. I'd had unprotected sex with Harrison more times than I could count, and hadn't thought twice about it. James' vasectomy had conditioned me not to worry about birth control, but now, the consequences of my actions could be very, very real.

Jesus Christ, I thought to myself as the panic began to set in.

The breast tenderness, the vomiting, the fatigue, the back pain and cramping; they weren't period indicators because it had never shown up. *How could I be so stupid to think this was the beginning of menopause? How the hell am I too young for menopause and too old to have a child and somehow in this stupid predicament? Fuck!*

I was shaking by the time I drove myself to the next town over, afraid I might run into someone I know if I went to my local drugstore. I timidly approached a clerk and asked for help choosing the test that was best suited for the earliest detection, then used cash to purchase it. Here I was, a forty-year-old woman, feeling like some young girl, terrified my parents might find the evidence. Knowing I couldn't dispose of this in my home garbage for fear that James would see it, I took the test inside the store's public bathroom. I was such a mess of nerves I could barely pee, and shaking so bad I was sure I'd miss the stick altogether, but somehow, I managed to get it done.

Now, to wait. Three minutes until a digital diagnosis would seal my fate. I leaned my head against the wall of the bathroom stall, closed my eyes, and tried to regulate my breathing telling myself, *In through the nose, out through the mouth Alice. It's pre-menopause. Control yourself. In through the nose, out through the mouth.*

I checked my phone. Two more minutes. My thoughts began to spiral.

What would Harrison think of me? How could this happen? Would he think I did this on purpose? Would he want to keep it? This isn't THAT, Alice, it's the start of menopause. Don't be stupid. In through the nose, out through the mouth, Alice. He wants a family, he said so. Jesus Christ he's one year younger than James was when we got pregnant twenty years ago. UGH! Stop it Alice. He told me he wants forever with me. It will be okay. He'll be happy. He won't push me away. Right?

My heart rate was rising.

I'll go to Brazil. He'll take care of me. Everything will be fine. Won't it? But what if I was too old for this? Wouldn't I be high-risk at my age? No, women my age do this all the time these days. Don't they? Did I want to be a new mother this late in life? This was not how I pictured this going at all. Jesus how much longer?!

I checked my phone again. Thirty seconds. That was all that stood between me and the rest of my life. I closed my eyes again and took a deep breath. The only thing running through my head now was Harrison's face and flashbacks of all the love we'd made. Another deep breath, then I opened my eyes and reached for the test that was sitting on the back of the toilet. I had never been more anxious in my entire life as I sat there, eyes closed, holding the test in my now trembling hand, too scared to look at the results.

In through the nose, out through the mouth one last time Alice, you got this.

When I opened my eyes, the word 'Pregnant' was staring back at me. It took me a moment to realize what I was looking at as I blinked repeatedly, scowling down at the indicator in my hand, certain I wasn't reading it correctly. I shook it violently, thinking it might change the outcome. Nope, the word 'Pregnant' was still taunting me in bold letters on the indicator. I stared in disbelief at the tiny word that just changed the rest of my life. Suddenly all those thoughts that had swirled in my head were gone, and I was left dumbfounded and disoriented, my mind a complete blank.

I sat there, unsure what to do next, until the sound of someone pounding on the bathroom door and yelling, "Hello? Almost done in there?" startled me out of my black hole of terror and back to reality.

I yelled back, "Sorry, just a moment!" as I gathered up my things, making sure to snap a clear photo of the test before discarding it along with its packaging into the trash, then quickly washed my hands and vacated the bathroom.

I drove back home in silence, but the sound of my thoughts was deafening.

When should I tell him? How should I tell him? We'll be okay. It will all be alright, right? That's what he always says. And, he loves me. He said so. My God, I'm too old for this. Aren't I? Maybe I should call Emma. Emma would know what to do. No, it's not fair to share with her before telling Harrison.

I needed to figure this out on my own. Maybe I could wait a few days and take another test. *Is a false positive even a thing?* This was all happening so fast. There is no way that James could find out about this; he would be devastated.

Like a wave crashing down on me, I felt a surge of heat come over my body and my mouth began to water. I knew I was going to be sick. Frantic, I pulled over to the side of the highway and ran around the back of the car to shield myself from the onlookers in traffic, retching until I had no more left to purge. The sooner I told Harrison, the sooner I could calm my nerves about all of this. The fear of his reaction was killing me.

I managed to get myself back home and cleaned up before James got home and I struggled to cook dinner without feeling sick to my stomach. The nausea and nerves kept me from eating, and the tornado of thoughts in my head prevented me from engaging in any kind of decent conversation. I'd used the television to fill the silence most of the evening and hadn't noticed when James kept solemnly glancing in my direction.

"You've been quiet tonight," he said while I sat on the couch in a daze.

I looked at him blankly for a moment before I responded. "Sorry. My mind is...scattered." I shook my head.

"I wanted you to know that I was served the papers today, Alice."

There was a sadness in his eyes, as if he'd thought maybe I wouldn't actually go through with it.

"I hope you know I'm not mad, and I won't make this difficult, but I'll also never be the same again without you. You've been my best friend for...ever. I don't know how to do life without you."

Overwhelmed, I started to cry. My emotions were all over the place and I could no longer control them.

"James, I'm so sorry. I never wanted to hurt you." Tears streamed down my cheeks.

"I know. I know you didn't. I wish it had turned out different for us." Now

James was crying with me. "You are the love of my life, the highlight of my every day, and I thank you for everything you've sacrificed to keep me happy all these years. I wish I could give you the time back, and we could start again. I'd do so many things differently, Alice."

I wiped my wet face against the shoulder of my t-shirt, then covered my face with my hands, unable to stop myself from sobbing.

"James, I think I'm going to head back to London sooner than planned. I love you; I want what's best for you, but I don't think I can stay here much longer. It's just making it harder for us both."

"I understand," he whispered, and pulled me up from the couch, hugging me tightly. "I'll miss you every day for the rest of my life, but I want you to be happy, Alice, whatever that may look like. Chase your dreams, and know that no matter where you are, I love you."

My knees nearly dropped out from under me when he told me to chase my dreams. There was no way he knew that in my subconscious I'd run off on a road trip with a handsome stranger and fallen in love. No way he knew that dream had ultimately sent me to London and that's where it had come true.

James fell asleep quickly that night, just as he had for years, and once he started snoring I took a deep breath and grabbed my phone.

Hi babe. I miss you. Hope you had a good day. Been busy sorting and packing, but finally done. He got served already and says he won't make it difficult. Haven't heard from my attorney, but I'd really like to make a plan to get to you soon. Hope filming is going smooth. I love you. xxxx

I hit Send and waited for his response.

Moments later his message came through.

I'm ready when you are, just say the word! Filming is good. I got an offer to direct my first film today! I'm so excited. Big things are in the works! Get some rest, it's late. We'll make a plan tomorrow. I love you so much xxxx

I let out an exhausted sigh, set my phone on the nightstand to charge, and rolled over, but sleep didn't come. I tossed and turned for hours trying to map out a plan, trying to find comfort when my comfort was all the way in another country. There was no way I could sleep; I was way too stressed about telling Harrison he was going to be a father. Tomorrow morning, as soon as James was gone to work and I was alone again, I would tell him.

The night dragged on for what seemed like days, and I watched the sun rise from the same spot I'd been in all night. I was still awake when James' alarm went off, I wished him a good day as he went downstairs to get ready for work, and then listened, waiting anxiously for him to leave.

When I finally heard the door close behind him, I sat up in bed and reached for my phone. My hands shook as I reluctantly dialed Harrison's number, my soul desperate to hear the soothing sound of his voice and to let myself melt into his accent, but completely terrified of his reaction.

"Hey, you," he said when he picked up the call. I could hear his smile as he said it. He was obviously happy to hear from me.

"Harrison..." My voice waivered as I struggled to speak; his name slipped past my lips as barely a whisper as I mustered the courage to share the news. "I…" I cleared my throat, trying to steady my voice and buy myself a bit more time. "I have something I need to tell you."

"Alice, love, are you okay?" His concern was met with silence. He paused a moment before repeating himself. "Alice? Hello? Are you there? Are you alright?" This time his words were more urgent.

"I love you," I said clearly, my eyes welling with tears.

"Well, I love you too darling. What's wrong? Talk to me." The more he spoke the more nervous I became to say it out loud.

"Harrison…I'm having your baby…"

Acknowledgements

Thanks go to my husband, who has been an endless fountain of encouragement, who paid me no mind when I lay awake that January night at 2 a.m. typing the first four pages of this novel into my phone simply because I couldn't get the words to stop running through my head, and when everything else fell to the wayside because I was entranced in what I called 'research and development'. My muse has become a fixture in our household over the last few years, and I appreciate that you welcomed my affinity for him without judgment. Your acceptance of the me that I became through this process is priceless. Thank you for allowing me the space to grow and expand, and for believing in me when even I didn't believe in myself. It's made all the difference.

To Oscar, who has always been my daily sounding board, the best secret keeper and has always loved me without judgment. You listened to all my ideas and gave me the best constructive criticism as well as endless snuggles. You're the best there ever was, and will ever be. I love you the absolute most.

To H., for bringing sunshine to my life. You found your way into my subconscious and fueled me to delve deeper into my imagination, helping me reach my true potential. Without you, this dream (literally and figuratively) would never have found its way to fruition, and this book would never have seen the light of day. You have illuminated every facet of my life in ways I can never describe, sparked true joy, and helped me feel comfortable with who I am becoming. Thank you for being the transcendent, glittering phenom of a person that you are. You're pure magic and I adore you.

To my mother, I'm not sure what you ate during pregnancy to create this imagination of mine, but I thank you endlessly for it. You've always been my biggest champion, and I wouldn't be here without your selfless, unwavering love and support. I hope I've made you proud beyond all expectation. I love you so much more than you will ever truly understand.

To my Gram, and to my Dad, I did it! I know you're together somewhere, both of you smiling from ear to ear at this accomplishment of mine, proud of me for seeing it through. I miss you both more than I can put into words; I hope you dance and laugh and check in on me from time to time until I see you both again. xoxo.

To my editors and my graphic designer, I love each of you more than you know. You were there for me at the drop of a hat, providing guidance and insight when my messages of confusion, frustration and desperation would chime in at all hours of the day and night. I can say with confidence that none of this would be possible without the talents that each of you possess. Thank you for your loyalty, love, understanding and for your dedication to me and this project.

To my family and friends, your love and support mean the world to me. While this novel may not be the content you were expecting from me, I hope you enjoy it just the same. I love you all.

To my inner circle/my Harries, y'all are wild and I love each and every one of you. This novel was a labor of love, and the support that I found in each of you is incredible. I've never known such camaraderie. We are spread to all corners of this earth but find comfort in one another and delight in a shared love, a singular 'destination' if you will. You each have touched my life and changed it for the better in your own enchanting ways, and I can only hope that I have given you the same gift.

To everyone that contributed, listened, advised, or otherwise put up with me during this process, I thank you. For taking the time to hear me and understand, for your belief in me and my capabilities, and for your unending support.

Thank you, thank you, thank you!

Potential Triggers:

Please be advised, this book may contain other triggers for you that are not listed here.
These are the most blatant.

Abandonment

Abortion/Miscarriage

Alcohol Use/Abuse

Anxiety

Betrayal

Cheating/Adulterous Behaviors

Criticism

Death/Dying

Depression

Divorce

Explicit Language/Swearing

Gaslighting

Grief

Incurable Disease

Loneliness

Loss

Menopause/Menstruation

Pregnancy

Rejection

Sexual encounters

Slurs

Teenage Pregnancy

Violence

Vomiting

Please, always put your mental and emotional health first.

About the Author

Nakia Cramer is an American author born and raised on the coast of Maine. With a love of literature instilled in her at a young age by her grandmother, Maxine, Nakia always knew she wanted to become a writer. *She Lives in Daydreams* is her debut novel.

When she's not writing, Nakia enjoys sharing time with her husband, David, and her dog, Oscar. She also enjoys photography, kayaking and spending time in nature observing the wildlife that surrounds her Maine lakefront home, as well as traveling to the Gulf Coast.

Follow along with Nakia on social media for updates!
On Facebook at AuthorNakiaC and
On Instagram, Twitter and TikTok at AuthorNakia

Printed in Great Britain
by Amazon

36186700R00220